WHAT SHE WANTS TONIGHT

A Holder County Novel

JILLIAN NEAL

Photography by
REGINA WAMBA

Edited by
HAPPILY EDITING ANNS

Written by Jillian Neal

Published by Realm Press

ISBN: 978-1-940174-59-4

First Edition

First Printing – December 2020

To all the girls who long to be seen for who they are, instead of being viewed through the lens of expectation that tries to turn them into the person everyone else wants them to be

CONTENTS

An ice pick of dread plunged deep into Jack Denton's mind when he saw the area code of the incoming call. The fogged glass door to his office in the Holder County Courthouse announced that he was the man. The fact that he was the youngest district attorney of one of the wealthiest counties in the state of Oklahoma meant absolutely nothing to his parents. Public service was not something they would ever value.

His mother knew he wasn't likely to answer a call from her direct line, so now she was being sneaky. Rolling his eyes at her scheming, he went on with his sentence. "Hello, Mother."

She puffed out a quick breath of what was likely surprise that he knew precisely who was phoning him that afternoon. "Jackson," she drawled in her thick Kentucky accent. "Your secretary said you weren't taking any calls this afternoon. He wouldn't listen when I tried to explain whom I was and that you were to answer calls from me."

Jack ground his teeth. "Mitch is a legal assistant who works for all of the county prosecutors. He is not my secretary."

"What time will you be arriving this weekend?" In classic Beverly Denton style, she ignored anything that she did not want to be true.

Jack went silent for a sluggish heartbeat. He rubbed his head. Perhaps that might help the dread not reach vital portions of his brain.

"Why are you under the impression that I'll be attending Tiffany's wedding?" He'd done his best to scrub all notes of Kentucky from his voice, but that didn't mean he couldn't be just as direct as his mother. That particular skill was how he got answers in the courtroom.

"The Fitzgeralds have been dear friends of our family for generations. You know this. I'll have Beckett pick you up Saturday morning early. What's the closest air field to that little town you insist on living in? You'll need a date. I'll need to know her initials for the napkins today. We're already putting Elise in a bind with only a week until the wedding."

Jack stared at the leather inlaid desk before him and regretted purchasing the antique behemoth just to prove something to his father. The leather might prevent him from being able to beat his head against it hard enough to achieve unconsciousness. Blacking out from this particular conversation was the only way he was going to be able to endure it. His mother never listened to any voice other than her own anyway, so consciousness wasn't a requirement on his part. "I highly doubt Elise Fitzgerald is waiting on pins and needles for the initials of my plus one, Mother."

"I've taken the liberty to have the embroidery done for Alexandra Tempton since I assumed you don't actually have a plus one. You and Alex always seemed like a good pairing."

A geyser of bile erupted from Jack's gut to his throat. Alex Tempton was a vile human being who frequently ordered her parents' housekeeping staff to clean up after her toy poodles after she allowed the dogs to grind their shit into the rugs. If what his brother said was true, she'd also ordered her father to buy and then shut down a local dress shop because they hadn't had her size in stock on a dress she found appealing.

"I have a plus one." The lie, born of sheer desperation and repulse, spilled rapidly from his lips.

"Oh, really?" His mother sounded irritated, which was the way he preferred her to be. "Anyone we know?"

"God, no."

"Then what initials shall I have Elise put on the napkins and gifts?"

Jack hated this. He hated that every conversation with his parents somehow evolved into a script of lies coming from a place inside himself he didn't recognize. Why did he still care what they thought of him? The singular truth of it all was that he hated them, hated all that they stood for, and hated the way they existed in the world, and yet, for some unfathomable reason, he wanted to be the one that saved them from themselves.

At that moment, the universe tossed him a lifeline by way of a quick knock on his door—a knock audible enough that his mother heard it as well. "I have to take this. I'll get back to you." He ended the call, set the phone on the desk, and let his head fall into his hands. "Come in," he called loud enough for whomever needed to hear him, since he'd effectively created a mouth-muffler with his hands.

The quick click of his savior's heels announced Meridian Holder's entrance. He lifted his head and, for what had to be the hundredth time in the last four years, tried to determine if she was an angel of heaven or of hell.

Reading people was his superpower. It made him a damn good attorney. Discovering the deepest, darkest secrets people tried to keep hidden served him very well in the courtroom and in the bedroom.

And yet, he'd met his enigma in his assistant district attorney. He was never able to tell what Meridian was thinking, what drove her, what she really wanted out of life. Part hometown cowgirl, part cutthroat attorney. Part angel, part demon. Mercurial on the best of days and never to be crossed without paying a heavy penalty.

Her long auburn hair was done up in one of those twists that served to have a similar effect on his gut. His eyes trailed down the long feminine column of her neck. His throat went dry, but in an effort to never be like his own father, he studiously skipped over the small swells of her breasts, accentuated perfectly in the silk button-down shirt she was wearing. Instead his eyes landed on the brown leather skirt that skimmed an inch or two above her knees.

Right after he'd been elected as DA, he'd gone in her office to get some paperwork and had glimpsed a few stunningly sinful boudoir photos that were only slightly covered by some files. He certainly wasn't intended to see them. He imagined they were for some lucky bastard deserving of a hellcat like Meridian. Or perhaps for herself, but they certainly were not for him. However, those photos had driven him to distraction. He'd burn for the things he'd imagined based on those very photos. If his hand could talk, her father would likely have shot him twice, once to get the job done and once for good measure.

It took an inappropriate amount of time for his eyes to travel back to hers. Not that they weren't equally as resplendent as the rest of her. He came from a long line of Kentucky whiskey barons, and Meridian Holder's eyes were the precise shade of a priceless reserve, single-barrel, rare and untouched. The woman herself was every bit as off-limits and every bit as intoxicating.

Concern furrowed her brow. "Bad day, I take it?"

"Day. Life. Whatever. Did you need me?" He hated himself even more for wishing she did, but Meridian was not the kind of woman who needed anything from anyone. She was every bit as lethal as she was beautiful. He was thankful they were always on the same team for the most part.

"What happened? Is this about the eminent domain case on Hackberry because I can talk to the Moores if you need me to."

"No, but thank you for the offer. I think once they saw the check they were willing to forfeit the minimal distance needed for the new bridge."

Meridian helped herself to one of the chairs in front of his desk. Of course she did. The woman saw no need to ask permission for most anything. If she wanted it, she went out and got it. From where Jack was sitting, there was nothing sexier than that. "It's my"—he gestured to his phone—"family issues. I'm supposed to go back home for a family friend's wedding. I'm not particularly looking forward to it."

"Why not?"

Jack had graduated top of his class at Duke. He'd worked for his father for eighteen months, following in the family name and business like he'd been bred to do, until he'd discovered far more than he could ever forgive. He was one hell of a lawyer, and he sure as fuck knew when he was being put on the stand, but for some reason the desire to verbalize a small portion of the insanity that was his family to a sympathetic ear was too tempting to be denied. "I hate my family, hate everything they stand for, and among a lengthy list of other reasons why I don't want to attend this blessed event, the bride is my former fiancée."

Meridian's lush lips puckered into a low whistle. "Damn."

"More like damned." He stupidly, recklessly felt the need to go on, to reassure the woman seated across from him who likely required no reassurances at all. "I was never in love with her. I don't even like her. We were betrothed for all intents and purposes. Her father is a business associate of my dad's."

"If you don't want to go, why are you going?" said the woman who would never even be able to fathom what went into his role in his family.

"I haven't seen my brothers in over a year. Plus, there are things there I...need to check on. There are people who count on me."

Meridian's eyes narrowed a half notch. "So, you need a date."

Jack prided himself on never being surprised. The speed at which she'd put the few pieces of the puzzle together irritated him. God, did he sound as desperate as he felt? "What makes you think that?"

She gave him a quiet chuckle, one that caused the twist in his stomach to tighten with approval. "No one wants to go to the wedding of their former fiancée alone, and you are married to your desk which is tough to travel with and makes an even worse dance partner."

"Funny. So, in answer to your original question, yes, I'm having a bad day. What did you need?"

He immediately recognized the shrewdness that Meridian was known for as she cocked her head delicately to the side. "I'll make you a deal."

Every single thing about this woman was dangerous. Her family owned the largest cattle ranch in all of Oklahoma and had not only founded the county of which he'd been elected DA, but they also made certain every citizen of the county was cared for to the best of their ability. Jack had the utmost of respect for all members of the extensive family, Meridian included, but crossing the Holders would result in him being removed from office and from town, no questions asked.

Making a *deal* of any kind could result in disastrous consequences. Not certain if he was suicidal or just masochistic all of a sudden, his eyebrows lifted. "What kind of deal?" He told himself he was only entertaining her, making certain that she knew she was indispensable to both him and the county, which she was. Her work was second only to his.

An indescribably sexy smirk formed on her features. "I," she stated pointedly, "will happily attend this lovely family wedding with you, but in return..."

Jack knew there would be a *but*. The woman was never afraid to ask for what she wanted. That was yet another thing Jack found incredibly sexy. "What?" he demanded. Not that he had any intention of taking her up on her offer. It would be akin to asking her to climb Mt. Everest in those six-inch heels of hers.

"I get to represent my family in the Marsden mustang case. Me and only me."

CHAPTER TWO

Jack leveled her with a look that he was certain he'd shown her before. She always refused to save herself. Come hell or high water, she'd been determined to run against him for DA two years ago and had lost miserably. Not that she didn't deserve his position, not that she was even the inferior lawyer, maybe, but the citizens of Holder County were often concerned that the Holder family shouldn't own too much land or hold too many county seats. They seemed to believe the adage that absolute power corrupted absolutely. It wasn't something Jack disagreed with. After all, he had lived the absolute corruption of owning the world.

"No," he stated. "It's been fine for you to represent individual members of your family when the need arose, but this is a case against Holder Land and Cattle, the company which you work for and profit from. It's a frivolous lawsuit, and you'd only hang it up in court, costing the county more money. It's open and shut. Your family is obviously taking outstanding care of the mustangs for the state despite his ridiculous claims. Marsden is the very reason the state has laws about frivolous lawsuits. The case isn't going to go anywhere. I need you on cases that we have an obligation to devote our time and efforts to."

"That's the deal. Take it or leave it." She spun on those fuck-me heels and sashayed toward his office door. Her delectable ass, plump and ripe, was framed in that skirt like a priceless piece of artwork. It made promises he sure as hell wished she'd keep.

And damn he was weak. And stuck. And needy. And...desperate. "I can't ask you to do that. My family is impossible. They're genuinely awful people. I can't ask you to run that gauntlet. I won't let you."

She spun back around with a look of bemusement painted across her face. "Are you seriously suggesting that I might not be tough enough to handle your blue-blood family out in Whiskeyville, Kentucky, District Attorney Denton? I do know a thing or two about large families with money."

She didn't know. She had no fucking clue. Her family was good, and kind, and cared about other people and their plight. Besides, the Holder money was pennies compared to the Denton dynasty. But she'd challenged him and also left him no other option but to agree with her. He'd never call her weak, but she had no idea what she was volunteering to do.

His eyes fell to his desk for what she'd just trapped him into. "I would never suggest that you're weak, Meridian. I imagine there isn't much you can't handle." Shame crawled up his spine. He didn't want her to have to endure the Dentons, but if she was going to keep insisting, he also knew he'd eventually give in. God, he really was an asshole just like his old man.

"Good. I'm glad we've firmly established that fact. I'll be just fine. I'll even do some reading on the Denton Distilleries legacy just to make certain I'm prepared."

"I really wish you wouldn't."

"I'll take the file on Marsden's claim now."

No. He would not let her fall on a sword for him. He was better than that. She wasn't going to be deterred. She never was. So, perhaps he could scare her off. "What's your middle name?"

"Why do you need my middle name?"

"The napkins and glassware for the wedding will be engraved with everyone's monograms, of course. Oh, and I'm sure my mother will have you sets of towels and robes made prior to our arrival." There.

Take that, Miss Holder. That was a mere microcosm of just how out of touch with reality his family was.

Her mouth fell open, but she shut it back quickly though she couldn't quite hide the shock from her eyes. "Oh, well, okay then. Skye is my middle name. So, MSH."

"MHS actually," he corrected. "Your last name is by far the most important, and what better way to display that than with monograms on every flat surface." He narrowed his eyes.

"Right. I guess I've never really had anything monogrammed. Does that mean I'm supposed to bring the towels and robe back with me?"

So, he was getting through then. He shrugged. "That depends entirely on whether or not my mother likes you, and she'll never really say one way or the other so your guess is as good as mine."

Meridian smiled like the cat that had cornered the canary. "Since I don't really care if your mama likes me or not, I'll just take them anyway." She seemed aware he was trying to scare her off. Dammit.

"She'll have my father send you a bill for them." He raised the ante.

"I assume since I am doing you a huge favor that things like robes and towels will be covered by you."

Girl was good, and she knew it.

Jack wasn't taking the bait. "She's sending one of the Lears to pick us up Saturday morning."

She appeared unaffected everywhere except those all-telling whiskey eyes that widened for a split second. "You...don't sound like you appreciate that."

"I think Lear jets are clichéd, pompous, and in this case, ridiculously unnecessary."

"Then I guess I'm glad I'm going as your date and not your mother's."

"The wedding and all of the events leading up to it will be black tie. We'll be there for a week. You'd need three or four designer gowns minimum. Gloves, hats, the works."

"I'm not wearing gloves, but I'll send you a bill for the rest."

Jack's jaw clenched so tightly his molars staged a protest. "You know, for once in your life, you could just back down for your own good."

She threw her head back in laughter. When she was finished, she flipped through the files on his desk. "We've been working together for years. Surely you know me better than that. I've got what I came for. I'll be packed and ready Saturday morning. I just need to make sure I'm caught up on work for next week since I'm going on this impromptu vacation."

"Vacation?" Now it was his turn to laugh. "We'd have a better time if we visited Satan's summer home."

"We'll save that for our next trip." She winked at him and whisked out of his office.

CHAPTER THREE

Meridian rushed back to her office lest she break out in a victory dance in the middle of the paralegal corridor. Jack was almost always pressed, polished, and put together. Seeing him so ruffled delighted her.

It was terribly unfortunate that he was so freaking good-looking. Her reproductive organs loved the idea that maybe someday she could be the one that thoroughly undid him.

But that was not why she'd made her offer. Bill Marsden had been a thorn in Holder Ranch's side since he'd purchased the small parcel of land that ran the southwest border of the ranch. He'd already made a claim and a fuss over water rights a couple of years ago that had gone nowhere. Last Christmas he'd bitched to Meridian's Uncle Barrett that the snow runoff was killing his grass. One time a few of the Holder's cows had pushed down one of the fences and ended up on his property. He'd taken that to the sheriff who'd laughed him out of the station. If you decide to buy land next to a cattle ranch, you're going to end up with cows on your land at some point. Getting the Holders fined for something seemed to be Marsden's life goal. This claim that the mustangs housed on the ranch weren't being properly cared for was just another lie that Marsden was hoping to profit from somehow.

Only this time, he'd gone for the jugular. He'd filed the suit against Holder Land and Cattle instead of grievances against the Holder family, hoping to access even more money, Meridian was certain.

She refused to let the likes of Marsden come after her family or after the mustangs they housed out on Holder Ranch. She'd burn him at the stake and make certain that every other surrounding ranch knew no one messed with the Holders and walked away unscathed.

Meridian was just a little girl when Holder Ranch had become one of a few dozen ranches in Oklahoma that had agreed to take on and house some of the overpopulation of mustangs in the area. The mustangs had been destroying crops and making life difficult for Midwesterners due to their wild nature and the vast overpopulation. The Bureau of Land Management had teamed up with state officials to gather them up and get them to ranches that had land to care for them. The mustangs were one of Meridian's favorite parts of the ranch. She loved the horses and that she got to help feed and care for them. The program had run beautifully for decades. Her family traded land they would use for raising cattle to house the mustangs instead, and they were paid by the state to care for the horses.

But now, the state government had decided that the cost was too high, and they wanted to destroy the horses instead. Meridian couldn't stand the fact that this ridiculous lawsuit claiming that her family wasn't taking proper care of the horses might bolster their arguments against keeping the mustang program going.

And there was so much more to this case than Jack would ever understand. If the Holders brushed off one lawsuit, there would be others. There would be an endless line of people eager to take advantage, eager to prove that the state shouldn't waste money on the wild horse and burro program. She had to make certain Marsden was charged with the legal fees and a hefty pain-in-her-ass tax to keep anyone else from getting any bright ideas about taking on her family or the horses. The Holders took excellent care of every animal that lived on their ranch. They prided themselves on it. They even checked the turtles that lived in their ponds to make sure they were okay.

There was only one issue with the timing of this lawsuit. None of the Holders knew how they'd ended up with four pregnant mares in their last delivery of horses but they had. Now they had to figure out if it was the fault of one of their studs, or if the mares had been pregnant when they arrived on the ranch. The state always made certain that mustang mares and mustang studs were sent to separate ranches, so those were the only two choices—they were pregnant when they arrived, or the Holders were in trouble. They needed to figure that out before the Bureau of Land Management sent out a state inspector to check up on the Holders, to make certain they were caring for the horses. Because of this ridiculous case that Marsden had dreamed up, the state inspectors wanted to come sooner than later.

Having four unreported pregnant mares could potentially strengthen Marsden's false claim that they weren't taking adequate care of the horses, even though they checked them daily. If the foals were the fault of a Holder stud, Holder Ranch could end up buried in extensive fees that might force them to have to sell off land to pay the fines. It seemed impossible that one of their studs could've gotten to the far pastures where they housed the mustangs, but it was still something she had to consider. She needed to state inspectors to stay away until they knew what they were dealing with and had secured the funds to pay the fines if that was going to be required.

What did Jack know about horses anyway? He was a trust-fund baby born with a silver spoon firmly planted up his ass. Looks aside, he wasn't going to stand in her way. As always, she ordered herself not to focus on the fact that he was a damn good lawyer and an awfully good guy. He was also brilliant and always fought for the underdog. Dammit. She needed to stop admiring him like this. They were coworkers. That was it.

Even if she wouldn't mind finding out a little bit more about Jack Denton. In her experience, most men ruined their good looks by speaking. That wasn't the case with Jack, but that didn't mean that after meeting his family and his former fiancée she couldn't come up with something to end this ridiculous crush she'd had on him for years.

According to him, she was going to have to acquire a few more outfits for their upcoming travels if she was going to play her part. She glanced at the planner on her desk and then at the stack of file folders all representing cases she was working on. She'd needed a vacation for years, but necessity did not create opportunity very often.

Quickly assessing the calendar, she decided what she could delegate, what she could put off indefinitely, and what she'd have to work on in Kentucky. While she was figuring, she called her cousin Harper. She'd always been the sister Meridian didn't have, since she'd been stuck with three stupid brothers instead.

"Hey, you never call me from work." Harper sounded flattered, and Meridian felt bad for how little she got to hang out with her family. "Are you okay?"

"I'm good. I think. I might've done something a little bit stupid, but I'm pretty sure I didn't."

Harper chuckled. "I'm pretty sure I'm going to need more info on this stupid thing you may or may not have done."

It wasn't until she'd said the words out loud that Meridian began to really consider what she'd volunteered to do. Oh well, she was already in for way more than a penny. "I volunteered to go to Kentucky with Jack for some kind of family wedding, or an almost family wedding. I don't know. Whatever you call the wedding where his former fiancée gets married to someone else."

Harper was silent for far too long.

"Say something," Meridian demanded.

Instead of speaking, the phone filled with Harper's hysterical laughter. Life had been tough on her cousin ever since her husband had passed five years earlier, so Meridian loved to make her laugh. However, this time she did not appreciate it. "Stop laughing."

Harper audibly choked back more laughter. "I'm mostly laughing at whichever part of your brain thought this was not stupid."

Meridian made a face at the phone. "Okay, you know what, I'll just have to save our mustangs by myself without your help. I was going to see if you wanted to come to Tulsa with me tonight, because I need dresses that make Jack drool, but I'll go alone."

"You are so not going alone. This is the most fun I've had in years. I'll see if Chase can watch the boys. But what does this have to do with the mustangs?"

Meridian quickly explained that if she couldn't delay the Marsden case that the state would be required to send a representative out to the ranch before the foals were born. That tamed Harper's humor. "Okay, okay, I'm sorry I said it was stupid. I mean, really, it's so benevolent of you. You're a real saint. Volunteering to go all the way to Kentucky to pretend to be the, what, the girlfriend of your boss? Who is also the guy you've been drooling over ever since he came to work with you. Mother Teresa would be proud."

Meridian refused to speak. Childish? Yes. Did she regret it? No.

"You're telling me to fuck off in your head, aren't you?" Harper knew her too well.

"Several times."

That got her another round of laughter. "Oh, and this has to be illegal."

"It is not illegal. We are just...colleagues doing each other a favor."

"I think what you mean is that you're just going to be colleagues doing each other. The last two words were unnecessary," Harper goaded.

"Now I'm flipping you off in my head."

"Mm hmm, because you know I'm right."

"You are not right. This is me doing something for him, so that I get to make certain that Daddy and Uncle Barrett don't get into trouble over those foals, and we aren't swimming in fines from the state. And so I can make sure that Marsden doesn't give anyone else any bright ideas about our land and our horses."

"All right, fine, what time shall I be ready? I'll pick you up at the courthouse so we can have more time to shop."

"I think I can get out of here by four, but we're going to have to work quickly. I can't leave early any other night before our trip."

"How fancy are we talking for these dresses?" Harper inquired.

"Old Kentucky money fancy. Gloves and, hell, I don't know, maybe even corsets and bonnets."

"And you think we're gonna find that in Tulsa?"

"Do you have any other places in mind?"

"No, but you are aware that in Blue Blood, Kentucky, an Oklahoma cowgirl is gonna stick out like a goat on a cattle ranch, right?"

"Who cares? I don't need these people to like me. I just need Jack to assign me that case and walk away."

"That might be what you think you need, but I'd bet my portion of this big ass ranch we live on that isn't gonna be all you get."

CHAPTER FOUR

Like everything regarding his family, having a potential date to this ridiculous wedding was a double-edged sword. He'd pay more than the obscene amounts of money his father had hidden away in dynasty trust funds just to witness his mother attempt to hold court with Meridian Holder. The Denton prized Regency clawfoot dining room suite wouldn't survive the carnage Meridian would inevitably leave in her wake, and that wasn't even a quarter of what his family deserved.

To be able to watch her inevitable amusement at the half-wit debutante-wannabes that circled around him like he was injured prey every time he was home would be worth the entire Denton estate.

And yet, there was no way he could really allow her to come with him. He couldn't do that to her. Mixing his old life with the one he'd fought to find and keep just wasn't something he could allow himself. It would never work. It would be like two planets trying to share a single moon. The inevitable nuclear collision would create something that would eat them all alive.

And yet...

He still hadn't marched himself into her office to explain why she could not come with him. It wasn't that he didn't have the balls to tell

Meridian Holder no, unlike most men. His balls were a part of the problem however.

He'd worked so hard to become a *reformed* manwhore. But, dammit, his old ways still sang for him on occasion. Maybe...just maybe, he could show Meridian all of the best parts of Kentucky, the façade of the estate that so beautifully covered the malignant business practices that kept his family on Forbes lists and running in elite social circles. Perhaps if he played all of his cards right, managed to keep his temper in check when dealing with his parents, he could be the guy that got to see the way she looked in those photographs she'd failed to hide.

For a solid week after seeing them, he'd convinced himself that she'd left them in a conspicuous location on purpose. Meridian was too calculated, too precise, to have made a mistake like that, but that was a pipe dream of delusion.

Scraping the last few drops of resolve he'd managed to locate in his weary frame, he made it outside of his office door and headed toward hers. One foot in front of the other. He would not subject her to his family. If he ever wanted a chance with her, taking her to Louisville was sure as hell not the way to go about getting it. Besides, Meridian was too real, too genuine to be wooed by something as stupid as Derby horses, luxury whiskey, and posh parties.

He brought his fist to her door, a duplicate of his facing the opposite direction, and hesitated. *You are a weak motherfucker just like your old man.* That thought did it. His fist connected.

He knocked again when she didn't answer after a full minute. Still nothing. His heart pounded out a ridiculously stupid staccato beat as he told himself that he was allowed to open her office door. He was her boss, after all.

He leaned his head in, trying and failing to be nonchalant, but found the office empty. His determination and self-loathing had blinded him to the fact that the office was dark. She'd gone home early but had forgotten to lock up.

Shock and bitter disappointment fought for dominance over relief that he didn't have to tell her she couldn't go with him. Meridian was every bit as much a workaholic as he was. They were almost always the last two left in the courthouse. He'd bitten entire holes in his tongue to keep from asking if she'd like to accompany him to Rusty's, the local honky-tonk, after work several nights a week. On the rare occasions that they had a business dinner, it was always with clients or legal staff.

He'd even invent excuses to work on cases with her. It was ridiculous. He'd never had to work for female attention before, but something about her made him willing to do whatever it took, no matter how incredibly stupid it was, to be close to her.

He considered heading to Rusty's to see if he could find her. Then he remembered that it was highly unlikely that she would be there, but he sure as hell would find either one of her brothers or one of her many, many male cousins. He'd learned a few things about cattle ranchers in his time in Oklahoma reinventing himself. One thing he knew for certain was that cowboys had a very low tolerance for men they considered unworthy making plays for their sisters or cousins. And he would never be anything but unworthy of her.

Saving him from his own thoughts instead of his mother this time, his phone buzzed in his pocket. Meridian's name splashed across the screen, and he almost dropped the damn thing on the marble floor in an effort to answer.

"I'm standing in your office. I...didn't know you were leaving early."

"Shopping." She sighed. "So, listen, Harper thinks I need more guidance on what I need clothing-wise for our trip to Kentucky."

Jack's stomach sucker punched his sternum. "Uh...right. About that..."

"Are you going to let me have the mustang case?"

That would go against every promise he'd run on, every ethic he clung to in his job, and she knew it. "I can't let you have it even if you do come with me. I won't let you hang this up in court and ruin your reputation for something you know isn't going to fly."

"You just let me worry about my reputation, okay? Friends do favors for friends all the time. This is just a favor and then you are giving me that case."

"This is substantially more than a favor. I wouldn't wish this on my worst enemy much less you."

She railroaded through his lack of substantial argument. Of course she did. "Now, you said black tie for the wedding itself, but what else am I dressing for? I like to be prepared for anything."

———

———

———

To her shock, Jack actually knew quite a bit about the dress code for this week-long wedding thing. She imagined if some woman had called one of her brothers with the questions she'd asked, they all would've made some jackass comment about not caring what the female in question wore as long as she was naked when they got home.

But Jack would never do that. He was classy and sophisticated. Two qualities one was not likely to find in cowboys. They had their purposes of course. One or two of her cousins could even almost outride her, but Meridian had precious little use for cattlemen.

"You are not talking me out of this," she informed him yet again as he continued to feebly try to convince her not to come. "I'll see you at work tomorrow." She ended the call and rattled off the lengthy clothing list she'd need to her cousin.

She also considered her options in Tulsa. Glamorous Gowns and Something Blue Bridal Shop were not likely going to cut it. His family sounded woefully pretentious, and she prided herself on always blowing expectations out of the water. She needed designer clothes. She had to do this right. The only problem was that she did not have the credit limit for a week's worth of designer clothes.

Harper was still eyeing her from the driver's seat. It unnerved Meridian not to be the one driving, so she wished her cousin would hurry up and get them to the mall. "Why do you keep staring at me?" she finally demanded.

"I was trying to think if I've ever seen you so unnerved."

"I am not unnerved. What do I have to be unnerved about? Why is this a big deal?"

Harper rolled her eyes. "Well, Cleopatra, if you'll pull your skinny ass out of the river of de-Nile, I think I have a better idea than the mall for what it sounds like you need."

"I'm listening."

"Do you trust me?"

"That is such a leading question. Do I trust you not to drive us into that telephone pole? Yes. Do I trust you to help take care of my cattle while I'm gone? Also yes. Do I trust your opinions on me and Jack and this trip? Not in ten million years."

"Fine. But just so that I can thoroughly enjoy this when it blows up in your face, do you trust me on finding you clothes because I really do have a brilliant idea?"

"Okay, I trust you on clothes as well."

Fifteen minutes later, they were pulling into the small parking lot of a high-end thrift store that Meridian didn't even know existed. "Okay, you are brilliant," she conceded.

Harper beamed at her. "I know I am. Does this mean that you'll listen to me about you and Jack?"

"Let's not push it."

As Meridian began trying things on, Harper continued to push her point. "Explain to me again why, if you're just doing a friend a favor—a week-long, across-the-country favor, mind you—you need clothes to make Jack drool? That doesn't sound very friendly to me."

Grinding her teeth at that, Meridian pretended to be studying a loosened button on the custom-made-for-someone-else Dior jacket. Harper cleared her throat when Meridian didn't answer. Glaring at her cousin, Meridian pretended to be unaffected. "Men...enjoy drooling. That's proven. They're like dogs."

Harper's laughter filled the small store. "Oh, I so cannot wait to throw that comment back in your face. I think I'll save it for my maid of honor speech."

"Never getting married. Will never need a maid of honor. I'd sooner give up my career than ever walk down an aisle to meet a man-dog. Now, what do you think of this jacket with these jeans and these boots?"

Harper's smirk was louder than her laughter. "Jack's gonna need a spittoon."

CHAPTER FIVE

After successfully scoring suitcases full of designer clothes for just a few hundred dollars, Meridian informed her cousin that she needed ice cream. Specifically, she needed the kind of ice cream which was acquired at Woodland Hills Mall, which would also gain her access to lingerie shops.

Once they'd acquired two large cups of Black Forest and Oreo, Meridian had to figure out a way to lose her cousin long enough for her to slip into Victoria's Secret to acquire some new undergarments. Not that anyone would know what she was wearing underneath her new used clothes, but she told herself she would be even more confident if *she* knew her bra and panties matched. Plus, a few new nighties would be required. She had to look the part all the time, right? What if there was some kind of fire or something in the middle of the night and she had to run out of her bedroom? She couldn't very well show up in the front yard in a torn Oklahoma State T-shirt and a pair of frayed flannel pants. That would ruin the entire effect.

"So,"—Harper licked the ice cream from her spoon and let her eyes close as she savored—"where exactly will you and Jack be sleeping? Since you're engaged and all."

"We haven't even discussed the specific status of our fake relationship, but we are definitely not pretending to be engaged. Plus, his family is old money proper. I'm imagining the Queen of England crossed with Vatican Nuns levels of propriety. I'm sure I'll have my own room, so you can get that thought right out of your head. Nothing improper will be going on."

"You look mighty disappointed in that." Her cousin continued to prove just how well she knew Meridian. "You know, Ryan and I used to have all sorts of fun sneaking around his grandmother's house when we visited there. Disapproval can be an aphrodisiac."

Meridian never knew what to say when Harper talked about Ryan. It had been years since his death, and it killed Meridian that he wasn't here every day adoring Harper the way he always had. The visible pain in Harper's eyes that she tried to hide when she spoke of him wounded Meridian.

She hated seeing her cousin hurt. She hated seeing anyone hurt, especially if there was nothing she could do to ease the pain. It was the thing that drove her to be an attorney. Removing the source of the pain from society only solved half of the problem. The victims were never the only ones hurting. It was why she and Jack had worked tirelessly to try to bring prison reform to Oklahoma. Hurt people hurt other people, and she'd fight for both sides until her last breath.

Unless someone came after her family and then all bets were off. Marsden and his ridiculous case were driven by the latest clickbait news headlines about Oklahoma not being able to afford to keep the mustangs on ranch land. She'd just as soon roast Marsden on a spit as look at him.

Doubling down on her determination to handle the case entirely on her own, she glanced around at the nearby stores. They only had a half hour until the mall closed, and she needed to move quickly.

"Didn't you want to get Josh some new Pokes stuff for his birthday?" She gestured to the nearby sporting goods store.

Harper's left eyebrow lifted as she studied Meridian. "Josh's birthday isn't for three months, and why are you trying to get rid of me?"

"I just thought while we were here." She shrugged off the question.

"Uh huh, Mer, I have two kids. I know sneaking when I see it. I can sense it. Sniff it out a mile away. Spill it."

Meridian rolled her eyes. "I just need to pick up some new panties."

The only positive thing resulting from the truth here was that every note of pain over memories of Ryan dissolved as Harper laughed again. "And you think that I'm not going to help you pick out the things that Jack Denton will absolutely *never* be seeing you in," she mocked.

"Just a work friend and this is just a favor," Meridian insisted yet again.

"Get up. We only have a half hour and we have a lot to do." Harper yanked Meridian out of her seat. "And it's called friends with benefits"—she emphasized the last three words—"not friends with favors. Who knew you were so bad at this?"

"If you don't shut up, I will bring Josh and Noah every piece of candy I can find in this mall and in every single gas station between here and the ranch, and I will give it all to them at bedtime tomorrow night."

Harper chuckled. "You're evil."

Meridian gave her a broad beaming grin complete with the fluttering of her eyelashes. "But I'm very sweet about it."

————

————

Friday morning, Jack found himself walking into Meridian's office without even the pretense of knocking. He had less than twenty-four hours to forbid her from coming with him to Kentucky. The only problem was that forbidding Meridian to do anything at all would only result in her doing the thing you didn't want her to do faster and with less regard for things like her own personal safety and judgment.

She held up a finger when he entered and then pointed to her cell phone at her ear. "I am so looking forward to meeting you, Mrs. Denton," drawled from her. All of the blood rushing through Jack's body froze at once. "Jack has told me so much about all of you." The roar of panic in his ears was too loud for him to fully understand what she was saying. "Really? He hasn't mentioned me at all, huh? Well, you know what they say, once you start to fall in love it happens fast."

Jack only made out the words *fall* and *fast*. His mind supplied him imagery of a deadly explosion at the end of the rapid fall. Blinking seemed the only bodily function he was capable of, so he did that several times hoping to jump-start the rest of himself.

It worked, at least partially. He was able to mouth the words, "Why in god's name are you talking to my mother?!"

Meridian wore her cat-with-the-canary-in-her-iron-sights grin. "She called me," she mouthed back with a complementary shrug. Oh fuck, this was bad. Very, very, very bad. There was no telling what his mother was up to, but it was definitely something villainous. Holder was not a surname that existed on the approved list of mates for the Denton boys. That was the very reason Jack had to refuse to take Meridian with him. He could not allow her to endure the scathing burns his mother would wield via backhanded compliments and outright impudence.

He stood rooted to the marble flooring until she ended the call. "What the hell did she want and what did you say?" he demanded.

Meridian's eyes narrowed, and Jack knew he'd gone several steps too far. "Who pissed in your Cheerios this morning?"

"My mother is capable of many things, none of them good."

"She seemed perfectly nice, but far more importantly, I do not need to be *protected*," she spat the word like rattler venom from her lips, "and it's really starting to piss me off that you can't just let me help you out. Your family cannot possibly be as bad as you say they are. They raised you, didn't they?"

Aware that there was a slight compliment woven into that, Jack tried to figure out which point to counter first. "My family is worse than I'm describing them. Far, far worse. I should never have told them you were even potentially coming. I gave them your name. That was too much. I've already not protected you."

She rose from behind her desk and took seven very deliberate steps to stand before him. Those heels of hers brought her lips dangerously close to his. Her scent, some erotic combination of cheap perfume, wildflowers, and saddle leather, teased at his nostrils. For years he'd told himself that must be how all cowgirls smelled, but it wasn't. It was distinctly Meridian. His nostrils flared either in awareness that the fight-or-flight portion of his brain should be engaging now and wasn't, or in desperation to bring more of her scent to his lungs. He wanted to drown in it. To put himself out of his own misery by losing it all in her.

The tip of her tongue gently caressed her bottom lip. "Hear me say this, Jack,"—his name struck from her lips like a hammer connecting with a nail—"I just informed your mother that we were falling in love, so we're doing this. I do not need to be protected. I'm a big girl. I can take care of myself."

He shook his head. "You don't know what you're saying. You don't know them. I protect the people I care about. It's who I am. It's why I do what I do. It's why I left Kentucky."

"Then care about me less," she countered.

"That isn't possible." For the first time in four years he saw something he'd never seen before—Meridian Holder didn't have a comeback.

CHAPTER SIX

Still dizzy from being so close to Meridian in all of her stubborn, sexy glory, when Jack finally made his way back to his own office, he found someone waiting on him inside.

Maddox Holder, one of Meridian's older brothers and the one closest to her in age, stared him down. Every curse word Jack's grandfather had taught him formed rapidly on his tongue, but he bit them back. "Maddox," he managed. "How are you today?"

The guy was an Army Ranger by trade, frequently worked with some secret specialized government protection agency, and was referred to by all who knew him as Maddog, given his wild stunts and temper. Jack generally regarded him as a pin-less grenade. Since Maddox had never come to Jack's office before, he could only assume Maddog was there to let Jack know what he thought of Meridian going to Kentucky.

Clearly, Jack needed to seek some kind of psychological testing because, again, that fight-or-flight instinct wasn't kicking in. It seemed to be defunct.

Maddox stared him down. "I'm all right, I guess. You, on the other hand, are either goddamn fearless or dumber than you look."

Keeping him talking might delay the fists flying so Jack considered his words. "I'm most definitely not fearless, so I guess I'll have to go with the second choice. I assure you that any interaction I have with your sister will be with the utmost amount of respect and"—he scrambled for more words that might reassure Maddox—"dutiful, gentlemanly, all of that."

Confusion clouded Maddox's whiskey-colored eyes, not nearly as light and pristine as his sister's, but the resemblance was still there. "Wait. Do you think I'm here to scare you offa her?"

Stupidly, Jack's brain supplied, "I'm not really *on* her. No, wait. Uh, isn't that why you're here? To protect your sister from me?"

Maddox laughed. "Meridian sure as fuck don't need me or anyone else to protect her. Jaysus, it was us that needed to be protected from her when we were kids. I'm here to protect you, to figure out what the hell you're thinking taking her out to Kentucky to meet your folks. She's gotta be after something and seems to me you're playing right into her hand."

"What on earth would her meeting my family get her?" *Other than misery*. He left those words off in the interest of keeping Maddox on point.

"She's probably still pissed you beat her out for the DA position. Girl does not like to lose. What if she's digging up dirt on you or something to use the next time your seat's up?"

Jack knew that wasn't even a remote possibility though there would certainly be enough dirt to dig in on his family's estate. "Come on now, your sister hates to lose, but she always, always plays fair. She would never cheat to win. She wouldn't consider it a real victory if she had to run a smear campaign to get elected."

Maddox shook his head and gave Jack a consolatory pat on the shoulder. "And there it is. You've got the hots for her. I was worried that was the real reason you were going along with this. Just be careful, man—ain't nobody nowhere who will ever tame my baby sister."

"I would never want to tame her," finally spilled from Jack's lips, but Maddox was on the elevator by the time the thought had moved from the firm implantation in his mind to his mouth. Since he was alone, he allowed the thoughts to continue their growth. *God, why would anyone ever want to tame her? She runs hot and wild always. What man in his right mind would try to put out her fire?* She burned hotter than fireball whiskey, and the truth of the matter was that he wanted to spend a week getting drunk on her. Letting her burn away the scars from his time in the Denton Dynasty.

He wanted to be the object of her attention if only for a week. He wanted to keep up the ruse of their romantic relationship if that might mean that he got to have his hands on her in some small way occasionally. Despite the desperate levels of selfishness and the guilt he would never outlive, he wanted to take a small piece of heaven with him to hell.

It wasn't until later that afternoon as he wrote up the eminent domain contract—something he'd done so many times in his career he could do it asleep—that his own words came back to haunt him. *She always, always plays fair.*

He took his hands off of his keyboard and sat back in his chair to stare out at the town square he'd grown to love. Meridian always did things by the book, so why was she so hell-bent on representing her family in the Marsden case? He understood her dedication to protecting her family. My god, he more than anyone else understood that, but she was going to end up hanging the case up in court on technicalities. She'd already drawn up a continuance on the trial without so much as asking him. Why did she want to delay it? What the hell was she up to?

Maybe Maddox was right. Jack refused to believe that she was after information about him, but she was after something. He needed to find out what going with him to Kentucky really had to do with the mustang case.

———

Jack's decision to take himself out to Holder Ranch that evening was three-fold. But all three of his reasons for being there would have the same result—protecting Meridian, even if he was protecting her from herself.

Deciding that he'd claim ignorance if he got caught, he turned in the wrong entrance to the ranch. Meridian lived two entrances down from where his truck was currently cruising. That was fine. He wasn't there to see her yet. He needed to see the mustangs. His family had bred and trained Derby horses for generations. The Denton horses had come home with the roses sixteen times and had gone on to win the Triple Crown five times. He might not have known much about wild breeds or ranch horses, but he knew enough to be able to tell if there was something going on that Meridian was trying to keep under wraps. At least, he hoped he did.

Driving slowly along the expansive field the Holders kept the thousands of mustangs housed in, he didn't see anything out of the ordinary. A few of the mares headed his way, but they all appeared perfectly healthy and happy with their circumstances.

The Holders were the very best of cattle ranchers. They had generations, buckles, land, respect, profits, and knowledge to their credit. They would never do anything malicious to a horse. He had no real idea what he was even looking for, but he certainly wasn't seeing anything that Meridian would try to hide.

Giving it up as a stupid idea anyway, he turned in the grass and headed toward the portion of the ranch run by Gentry Holder and his children—which included his beautiful, brilliant, stubborn only daughter—to enact the next two sides of his plan. He would either successfully scare her off or prepare her. Either way, at least he was doing all he could to protect her whether she wanted to be protected or not.

CHAPTER SEVEN

Meridian shook her head at Harper. "No one will find out. Everyone at the office will just assume that Jack and I decided to go on vacation the same week, not in the same place," she informed her cousin while methodically folding the Dior jacket to add it to the suitcases her great aunt had given her when she graduated from high school. She didn't ever travel, so new luggage was not an item she would spend money on.

Harper's jaw cocked to the side as she stared at Meridian like she'd sprouted a third boob from her face or something. "My god, when it comes to Jack Denton you are dumber than dirt under a cow patty. This is Holder County and you are a Holder. Literally everyone will find out. The Sanderson's baby that's not due until January probably already knows." She shook her head. "Look, I want you to have what Ryan and I had back in the day, and I think Jack might be the only guy you could ever fall for, but I'm worried about this. Everyone is going to say that you're trying to sleep your way into his job. You know they will. I don't want you to have to live through that."

"I give exactly no shits what people in this town think of me. You know that."

"I know you like to say that, but it's a bold-faced lie. You care because they didn't vote for you."

"That will change next time."

"Will it?"

"By next year when his seat is up again, yes, it will. People have shockingly short attention spans and even shorter memories."

"Maybe, but they seem to remember every single mistake our family ever made and several we didn't."

"Then just don't tell anyone where I am."

"Right. That'll work."

A knock on the front door shook the ladies out of their debate. "Who is that?" Meridian wondered aloud as she made her way out of the bedroom. Everyone who lived on the ranch generally just let themselves into her house, a habit she couldn't seem to break them of, and since she lived twelve miles from the gates no one else made the effort.

Harper scooted around her and peeked out the dining room window. "It's Jack," she whispered.

"He's probably here to make one last effort to keep me from going. Clearly, he needs to be schooled in cowgirl."

Harper giggled. "He clearly needs to be schooled in your own special brand of stubborn. I know a lot of cowgirls, and none of them hold a candle to you."

Meridian pulled open the door instead of responding to her cousin. "Hey. What are you doing out here?"

Jack held up two fancy suitcases. "I brought you luggage, and my father's pilot would be suspicious if we didn't arrive at the airstrip together tomorrow. I assume you don't want to have to get up at five in the morning to meet me somewhere, so I thought maybe I'd stay here tonight." He sounded precisely like he did in court when he was nailing the final points home to the jury.

Meridian tried to hide her amusement. Did he seriously think he was going to scare her out of this?

"Come on in." She opened the front door wide and stepped back to both allow him entrance and to reveal her favorite cousin.

"Hey, Jack." Harper waved.

"Oh," he cleared his throat like that would help. "Ms. Reeves, I didn't know you were here."

"Yeah, I walked over. My house isn't that far from here, and Ryan's brother, Chase, took the boys to soccer practice for me so I had a night off."

Jack nodded, but he'd clearly rehearsed whatever it was he planned to say based on the premise that Meridian would be alone. Oh, this was too good. "I get up at four thirty to run my feed trucks before I come into the office, but if you want to stay, you're welcome to the couch." Meridian gestured to the leather behemoth that sat in her living room as Jack trailed after her into the house.

"Oh, uh, I had no idea you got up so early."

"Yeah, well, part-time cowgirl, full-time attorney, remember?"

"Of course."

"I have my own luggage. You didn't have to bring me any."

Whatever she'd just said rushed confidence back into his gaze. "My mother is very particular as I've tried repeatedly to tell you. I suspect she phoned you this morning because she already suspects that we're lying about our relationship."

"Would that be so terrible? I'm really just going so you don't have to show up at your ex-fiancée's wedding alone, right?"

Harper cringed. "I'm gonna head on home. Chase will be back with the boys soon. Have fun, you two." She scooted out the front door.

The tense set of Jack's shoulders eased when she left. "When it comes to my family, I refuse to leave any hole open for them to manipulate either of us because they will. If you're determined to play my girlfriend, then that's what we're going to do. That means I need to know a great deal more about you, and you need to know more about me. It means when we're in their presence we're behaving as a couple would."

Refusing to call his bluff, she shrugged as if that was no big deal at all, while desperately wishing that her reproductive organs would stop their victory parade, complete with fireworks, that was going on deep in her nether regions. "Fine. Have a seat. You want a beer?"

"Sure." A note of defeat tugged at his tone, which delighted her.

She grabbed two bottles and handed one off as she joined him on the couch. "I do have a question before we start making certain we could win the Newlywed Game."

Jack took both bottles from her hand instead of just one and proceeded to open hers for her. Meridian decided to allow the gesture instead of reminding him that she could do everything by herself and for herself. "Ask me," he encouraged.

"If you hate your family so much, why go back? Why do you need to show up at this wedding at all?"

"That's two questions for the record, and I suspect you'll figure that out pretty quickly, after we arrive on the estate."

"But you won't tell me now?"

"No. Now, tell me about your childhood. Tell me anything someone you'd been dating for a while would know."

"I've never dated anyone long-term so I have no idea what they might know about me."

"Well, that makes two of us."

"What do you mean by that? You were engaged."

"I was not engaged. I was all but betrothed. My mother went on with the announcement in the papers without so much as asking what I wanted for my life. That's how the Dentons work."

"Interesting. So, you weren't in a relationship with Tiffany?"

He shrugged. "Other than being thrust together at required events our entire lives, no."

A quick smirk formed on Meridian's features. "So, you fucked her, you just didn't want to marry her."

To her shock, Jack gave her a responding smirk. "As much as I regret that decision, it wouldn't even make it to the top twenty list of things I wish I'd never done. But to the reason I'm here, just like when we go to trial, I'd rather know too much than not enough. Let's start with your earliest memories and go from there."

Meridian didn't care for this particular line of questioning or the way he'd taken over the conversation. She couldn't argue with the reasoning behind it, but it galled her nonetheless.

A deluge of wonderful childhood memories flooded her mind. They were intertwined with a few bad ones by way of brats she had to attend school with, until she landed on her first real memory. "I was around three and trying to feed my horse an apple while hugging her at the same time. She bit my hand. I was scared my daddy would be upset with her so I never told anyone, but I learned my lesson on trying to do too much around animals at once. How about you? What's your earliest memory?"

"Uh..." Jack took a long drag of the beer. "I was around the same age as you and was in my nursery helping my nanny—the one I liked, not the one I didn't—pick up toys." Meridian trained her face to show no surprise even though having multiple nannies did shock her. "My father came in, lifted me up in the air, and spun me around, which wasn't normal for him. I think I only recall this because it was such a bizarre reaction from him, but he was thrilled that one of our horses had won the roses. My parents had just gotten home from Churchill Downs."

Terror and shock washed down Meridian's chest along with the beer she'd just sipped. "Your family raises Derby horses?" gasped from her bile-soaked throat. "Do you ride?" She needed him not to know anything about horses at all. The mares were very obviously pregnant. If he knew horses, he would know they were expecting. She reminded herself that Jack still wouldn't know what was or was not on the reports from the Bureau when the horses arrived. With a deep breath, she settled again.

"I know how to ride, but don't do it often," he assured her.

Turning the tables on her opposition was her classic move, so she went with what she knew. She wasn't going to be the only one trying to stand on unsteady ground. "I did some research on your family. I didn't read anything about thoroughbreds."

To her relief, panic stormed in Jack's dark eyes. He managed a hesitant nod. "The horses are certainly not what my family is best known for. Not likely something Wikipedia would denote."

Setting her beer on the coffee table, she leaned closer to him, wanting to crowd his mind by crowding his space. "I dug a little deeper than Wikipedia. The Denton Distilleries Dynasty, quite the alliteration." She gestured to a stack of papers on her coffee table that she'd printed off about the Dentons, most of which she hadn't even gone through yet, not that she'd ever admit that to him.

The words seemed to physically wound him. Meridian instinctively backed off. It was the first time in her life she'd ever done so. She couldn't comprehend her own actions. "Don't look so put out. I didn't find anything too terrible. If you don't read between the lines, they don't seem as bad as you describe them."

He averted her intense gaze. Staring steadfastly at her tile floors, he took an audible breath. "The whole damn story is written between the lines, and my parents' only concern is making certain that they own that real estate."

CHAPTER EIGHT

Of course, she'd researched. That didn't surprise Jack at all. Meridian was nothing if not thoroughly prepared. He knew being surprised was not something she enjoyed. That was part of what had driven him to the ranch that evening. He'd hoped that telling her about his family's Derby horses would build a foundation for her to confide in him about whatever it was she was worried about with the mustang case.

He just had to show her that she could trust him with whatever was going on because something obviously was. There had to be a reason she was willing to put her neck on the line for Marsden's lawyers' axe.

"I read that you have a brother," she informed him. That was a throat punch she didn't even know she was throwing.

"I have three brothers—same as you."

Frustration tensed in her eyes. She'd missed something and that obviously bothered her. How had she never figured out, over the past several years, that they were far more similar than they were different? He didn't like to be surprised, and he didn't like not knowing when he was traversing a minefield.

"Oh," came out in a quick breathy syllable. "Are they...?" She cringed.

"No," Jack sought to assure her, to wipe even the potential sadness from her. "They're both very much alive. They just...only exist in that space between the lines that we were just discussing."

"Interesting."

Of the many tools in a lawyer's arsenal, the one that most often got results was the truth. "I've spent the entire week trying to talk you out of coming with me, as much as I selfishly want you there. What's it going to take? If you want the Marsden case, you can have it, but I want to help you with it. I want to present it in court. I don't want you risking anything for your family. When you've represented them in court before, it was them against a foe. This foe is against this ranch. Marsden will muddy the waters to make them seem deep. I'm worried you're going to get in over your head."

A softness he rarely saw eased the angles of her face. "You want me to come with you to Kentucky?"

"I could count on one hand the number of people in my family that I can stand to even be in the same room with. Every event leading up to this wedding will be a hellish abyss of pompous privilege. I have to go because there are people there who count on me, and I refuse to let them down. A situation has come up that I need to deal with now. But,"—he rubbed his hands together in an effort to keep himself from brushing the few escaped hairs from her high ponytail off of her temple—"having someone who can keep me grounded, remind me that there's a whole world outside of that malignancy, and just having a friend there who's strong enough to yank me out of the tides is highly appealing. That doesn't mean that I want to expose you to everything we'll be forced to endure while we're there."

Meridian scooted closer to him on the couch. Unlike the last time she'd done that, which had been an intimidation technique, this time it was because he needed her closeness and she sensed that. "If you want me to come with you, then I'm coming. We're not all that different, you know?" she whispered.

He chanced another hit of those eyes and the fervency they held. So, she did know how similar they were. "How do you figure that?" He wanted to hear her say it.

"We're both willing to go through hell for people that depend on us. I will fight for my family until my very last breath. I suspect you'd do the same for whomever it is that you're going back to take care of, so, let me help you."

"Does that mean you'll let me help you with Marsden?"

"I don't need any help." The words went into his ears like daggers and then sliced through his chest.

"I disagree."

"How about this—let's get through Kentucky and then we'll see," she negotiated. That was a much bigger deal that most men would recognize. Meridian did not negotiate. He tried to take solace in her offer.

Sitting back on the couch lest he coax her face closer to his, he tried to order his scrambled mind. "What's your favorite drink? You will be asked that several times."

"A whiskey sour."

"Isn't that apropos."

After a quick grin, she went on, "I suppose when someone in your family asks me, I should tell them I prefer them made with Denton Select."

Jack chuckled at that. "Do me a favor and tell them you only like Jefferson's. My brothers and I get a kick out of watching that vein in our father's head throb on occasion."

"How about you? What's your preferred Denton Brew?"

"Come on now, you know me better than that. I only drink Maker's Mark."

She beamed at him. "To piss your daddy off?"

"Naturally." He lifted his beer bottle to her in tribute. When he'd downed the last sip, he tried to come up with some reason to keep her talking. "Is there anything a boyfriend would know about you that I should know before we get on that plane tomorrow?"

Her signature smirk turned deliciously wicked. "There's a lot a boyfriend would know about me, but none of it's likely to come up over the dinner table."

His cock leapt to attention like she'd just sent up the Bat Signal and he was suiting up. "That doesn't mean I don't want to know." Inappropriate? Hell yeah. But nothing about this was normal. Emily Post had not written anything like this in any of her books.

She shook her head at him. "How many of the women I'm going to meet this week have you had in your bed?"

"That's not likely to come up over dinner either."

"You'd be surprised what women will discuss."

"Clearly I've been hanging out on the wrong side of the ballroom then."

"I've never even been in a ballroom."

"Well, as you say, saddle up. You'll be in so many of them this week you'll likely hate them almost as much as I do." He made his way into the kitchen to toss their empty beer bottles.

"Hey, Jack." She followed him into the kitchen.

He tried and failed in an effort to stop wishing he could hear his name hang on her lips in the breathy groans he drew from her with his hands, with his tongue, with his cock. "Yeah?" He choked on the word and on his own need.

"I need people at work not to know where I am this week if we can help it. I...don't want people to get the wrong idea about us."

He studied her eyes, the set of her jaw, the slight movement of her neck with her harsh swallow. "There is no county bylaw about us seeing each other romantically. You know that."

"I do know that. It's just," she shrugged, "as much as I hate to admit it, people do like to talk about my family."

Good. At least now she was thinking somewhat sensibly. Surely it would only be a few quick steps away from that admission to the obvious conclusion that she was giving Marsden the opportunity to skewer the Holder name in court. "Fine. I think Mitch is the only person in the office who knows we're traveling together. Hopefully, he'll be discreet."

"Thanks for understanding."

"I understand reputation more than you'd ever know. I should go." He said the words, but his feet made no effort to follow through.

"I thought you were staying here." The direct challenge turned her impish grin on with the flip of a switch.

"I was just trying to scare you into not coming."

"I don't scare easily."

"I already knew that. I'll pick you up at six. Please do use the luggage if you don't mind. Let's not leave Beverly much to gossip about. It'll really piss her off."

CHAPTER NINE

The next morning, long before the sun warmed Holder Ranch, Meridian buried her face in Kagan's neck. Her horse turned her head to hug her back, soothing Meridian's restless soul.

"There's my girl." Her mother's voice added a warm blanket of calm to Kagan's hug. Meridian lifted her head.

"Hey, Mama. You're up early."

"I wanted to see you before you go off on your trip with Jack. I made you some coffee." She handed over a Coleman coffee thermos.

"Thanks. Yours is the best." She quickly helped herself to some of the restoring warmth. "I don't know anything about ballrooms or blue bloods or bourbon or anything," erupted from her mind and spilled out of her mouth. "I shouldn't have demanded to go on this trip. I don't like not knowing things."

Leigh Holder grinned at her daughter. "Yeah, we figured that out when you were about two and got mad at your daddy because Maddox knew how to tie his shoes and you didn't."

Meridian rolled her eyes at her mother's laughter. Leigh gave Kagan a few loving strokes as well. "I don't know much about any of that stuff either, baby doll, but I do know one thing. If they put a bowl down in front of you that's full of lemon slices and water, it's not lemon soup—

it's a finger bowl. I made that mistake on a date at the country club one time and that's how I ended up married to your daddy instead of somebody with a trust fund." She winked, and Meridian joined her mother's laughter.

But a minute later, Meridian was gnawing her own lip, a habit she'd thought she'd broken. "What's a finger bowl?"

"It's to clean your hands. Ridiculous thing when we have soap and sinks, if you ask me, but fancy people tend to enjoy ridiculous things that make other people feel inferior. But you listen to me, do not let these people make you feel less than. You are Meridian Holder, Gentry and Leigh Holder's little girl, a damn good lawyer and an even better cowgirl. A good sister, a good cousin, a good person, and that, honey, is all that really matters in this world. We're all gonna end up in the same sized box. If they want theirs to be lined in gold then more power to 'em. You have a heart of gold, and I think that's way more important."

"Thanks, Mama." She threw her arms around her mother. That hug soothed her even more than Kagan's had.

"You might want to shower before Jack comes to pick you up. Them fancy people might not like it if you smell like a horse barn."

"I don't really care what they think," she insisted.

"I know that, but you care what Jack thinks and kinda wouldn't mind his family liking you."

"How did you know I care what Jack thinks?"

Leigh grinned at her. "If you like knowing things, you should become a mama. We know everything. Like I also know that this trip is to save those foals and this ranch from the heavy hand of the state, but it's also because you want to spend a week with Mr. Denton. Honey, why don't you just admit you like him? I suspect he feels the same."

"Because then everyone will talk. When I finally become DA, they'll somehow equate it to me sleeping with him."

"What if you didn't try to take his job?"

Meridian huffed, mostly at her own stubbornness. "I don't like not being best either."

Her mother shook her head. "You not being DA doesn't make him better than you. We're so quick to assign rank and importance to things that aren't. Someday you're gonna figure out that being happy is worth a whole lot more than any title anywhere. But you have to be brave enough to let things go."

"I'm not that brave." Meridian had no trouble admitting that.

"Not yet. But you will be when the time is right. I know that too."

———

———

Dread sawed through Jack's gut as his truck tires ground down the gravel to Meridian's home. Everything about this was wrong, and yet he drove on.

He *would* protect her. The vow cemented itself in his mind and in his heart, and that was the anchor he needed to go on with this. The motor choked on the gravel dust when he finally hit the brakes at her porch. The Holders saw no need for things like driveways when gravel and grass worked just fine. It was yet another thing Jack loved about Oklahoma. There was no pretense. There was only what you could hold on to at the end of the day.

As the fog of gravel settled, she appeared there like an angel stepping from the clouds. She was struggling to get the Mont Blanc bags out her front door while carrying a thermos of coffee, her purse, and her keys. Jack sprinted from the truck to her side to assist. "May I?" He had no intention of taking no for an answer but gave her the courtesy of asking.

"I've got..."

"Uh huh, I can tell." He lifted both suitcases and left her to the saddle leather purse, keys, and coffee. Trying not to grimace, he noted his first mistake. That handbag would be the topic of discussion behind her back. Without access to the Denton accounts, he could no longer afford to procure Birkins or Louis Vuittons, so there wasn't much he could do about it. He knew she'd never consent to going without a purse.

"What?" she sniped as soon as they were in the truck.

"Nothing."

"Don't lie. Something worried you."

"It's your handbag."

She clutched the large purse to her chest. "What's wrong with it? I love it. I had it made from the leather on the saddle I learned to ride on."

And it looked as such. "See, this is precisely what I've been trying to tell you about my family. There is nothing wrong with your bag. It's perfect because you enjoy it. It's real. It means something to you. The lack of brand name on it means my mother will pick it apart. I don't want to give her any ammunition."

Meridian spared him an eye roll as she downed another sip of her coffee. "I really do not care what your mother thinks of me unless it makes this trip harder on you."

Jack let that repeated declaration baptize over him. "The entire state of Kentucky cares what my mother thinks. Maybe I'm unaccustomed to being around someone who doesn't."

"You've been out here a while. I guarantee you nobody in Oklahoma gives a pile of manure what your mama thinks."

Jack laughed both at her phrasing and at the absurdity of the statement. "Trust me, cowgirl, if my mother waved her wand of power and changed our Midwestern Territory Director for the Oklahoma market and that in turn raised the price or availability of Denton liquors here, people would care. If that in turn, affected the price of our liquors at Rusty's, right here in Holder County, even you might care."

Meridian's eyes narrowed. "*Our* Midwestern Territory Director? *Our* liquors? Here I was thinking you were the Holder County District Attorney, no longer a whiskey baron."

"Old habits I guess. Forgive my slip, but you get my point."

"Your mother likes to feel important."

"Very much."

"And my handbag will make her feel not important?"

"It's more that it will give her a place to start tearing you down."

Jack couldn't quite keep his eyes on the road as Meridian yanked an old woven makeup bag from the purse, popped down the passenger side mirror, and proceeded to put on her favorite brutal red lipstick.

He'd spent years imagining that very color all over his cock. "Bring it on," she challenged after her warpaint was perfectly in place.

"Do me a favor and don't say that to her."

He parked at the small airstrip in the unincorporated portion of the county between Holder City and Odell. Trying to discreetly study Meridian, he was certain she'd never flown on a private jet, much less the Denton private jet. He slung his bag over his shoulder and carried the suitcases he'd loaned her.

"Mr. Denton, sir." Beckett grinned as he reached for the luggage. "I'm sorry to have to tell you that we'll be flying against a headwind from a storm cell so the flight will be a little longer than normal."

"You work for my father, Beck, not me. You don't need to call me sir, and the weather isn't your fault. I'm not in any hurry so no need to apologize. This is Meridian Holder, my girlfriend." He knew it was a problem when men took great comfort in their lies, and yet the one he'd just told felt entirely too good to ignore, too good to not to continue telling it. He was his father's son after all.

CHAPTER TEN

Meridian spent the majority of her energy trying to pretend that flying on a private jet was no big deal. She'd never even flown first class anywhere before so this was all extremely bizarre. Plush leather couch-like things were in the place where regular people seats should be. There was a kitchen, a large screen TV mounted on the wall between the seats and the pilot, a small bedroom, and a fully stocked bar.

The flight attendant, Muriel, came by again and asked if she'd like something else to drink. "I'm fine. Thank you though." She'd done that every fifteen minutes for the last hour and a half. If Meridian accepted anymore Dr. Pepper, she was going to float the rest of the way to Louisville. When Muriel returned to the small kitchen area of the plane, Meridian finally leaned into Jack who'd had his arm propped behind her shoulders for the majority of the flight and asked, "Why does she keep doing that?"

Jack tried to smother a grin. "She wants to make sure you're comfortable."

"The refrigerator is right there. If I was thirsty, I could just get something myself, or if she really loves her job that much I could wave my hand or something. I don't like being waited on."

"She's also my mother's favorite spy, which I'm beyond certain is why instead of working in the house today, she's pretending she knows how to be a flight attendant." To her absolute shock, he brushed a kiss on her cheek. Okay, then. Apparently their fake relationship started right now. She was not prepared for that. How dare he do that before she was ready? And...how come she liked it so much? "You're going to need to stop looking like you'd prefer to murder me when I kiss you if we're going to pretend to be crazy about each other," whispered across her ear.

She shivered from the breathy caress. "I just...wasn't expecting it." To prove that she was going to hold up her end of the bargain, she nonchalantly laid her hand on his thigh, closer to the heat behind his zipper than he would ever have expected—she refused to be the only one caught off guard—and eased her head onto his shoulder. "Better?"

"Much." He choked on the word, deeply pleasing her.

"You're going to need to not sound like I'm gagging you when I touch your leg if we're going to pretend to be crazy about each other," she quoted back.

He cradled her close, and the lines of reality blurred. "I feel certain that I am not the first man to ever choke on lust from you, cowgirl."

She liked that response far more than she really should.

"We'll be landing soon." He changed the subject which she supposed she was okay with although his last comment still hung in the lack of air between them.

"Where do private jets land at airports? I should probably act like I've done this before," she whispered.

"We won't land at the airport. We'll land on the Denton Airstrip on our property."

Hole-e-fuck. Well alrighty then. "Will all of your family be there when we arrive?" It would be much easier if she could meet them a little at a time to get her bearings.

"I doubt it. There's something like seventy-five various family members with interest in the company at this point. Surely they won't all be there until the wedding. My father will put off having to see me until he can't escape anymore. My mother will pounce like a starved jackal as soon as your boots are on Denton land."

"You speak so kindly of her," Meridian teased.

"I am being kind. Reserve judgment until you've dealt with her."

True to his word, she heard the landing gear engage as lush green hills blurred by the windows. The closest sensation she'd had to the experience of being dropped into an entirely unknown world were those awful dreams where she felt like she was falling with no one to catch her. "This must be what it's like for Maddox when he parachutes into enemy territory," she commented.

"Brilliant girl. I'm glad you're finally listening to me." Jack planted a kiss in her hair this time, and Meridian told herself that she did a much better job of behaving as if that was totally normal, even though nothing about it felt normal at all.

It felt right. It felt dangerously stupid and deliciously good all at once. It felt like coming in from a storm of ice and snow and sinking slowly into a hot bath that dissolved all of the pretenses she made up in her head and the frostbite that nipped at her soul.

She lifted her head and was certain her eyes displayed the panic fizzing in her chest. "Kiss me," she ordered.

"What?" He didn't look opposed, just surprised.

"Kiss me for real. On the mouth. I'm apparently about to have to convince half the state of Kentucky that we're in love, and I'm not going to fail. I've never failed at anything except becoming DA, and I don't intend to make a habit of it. Kiss me until it doesn't feel weird anymore," she whispered frantically. "Do it now."

———

———

———

Jack didn't have to be ordered twice. "Look at me." He cradled her delicate features in the palm of his hands. "Thank you for doing this for me. I swear to you I will not let them tear you apart the way they've done everything else that meant anything to me."

He leaned in, giving her a half heartbeat to pull away, and when she didn't, he brushed his lips tenderly against hers. A quick shaky exhale from her fueled the blaze of need roaring in his groin. He turned his head, threaded his fingers through the fire of her hair, and devoured a soft, sweet little moan.

The kiss ignited. She opened for him. Their tongues tangled in the middle and fought for dominance. He fed her a desperate groan, forcing her to forfeit as he drew her tongue into his mouth and sucked.

Unable to think, unable to do anything but take, he devoured her. His left hand gripped her ass and squeezed—god, he'd fantasized about that ass so many times his dick was tired of his hand. Her legs parted every bit as easily as her lips had. Damn.

He drank in her obvious need, her hunger that matched his own, and steeped himself in the flavors of her. Apparently, his hands weren't the only ones that were inquisitive. She slipped her palm up his thigh and gently traced along the stiff steel length of him.

"Fuck," slipped from his mouth when she turned again and allowed them breath.

"Jack," met his curse in the middle. The words tied themselves in the knots that kept them inextricably bound to the kiss.

She stirred every primitive instinct he possessed, the ones he'd tried so hard to rid himself of. Her lips were already kiss-swollen, but he wanted them bruised.

Contentment—that had been his goal when he'd run away from this place they were descending upon. He refused to be like his family. No one should try to own the world. He only wanted a small piece he could call his own. He wanted to serve the public that his family robbed from.

But now—this, her—he'd never be content. He'd always need more, a willing junkie for her lips, for her body, for her mind, for her.

Letting the greed drive him, he slipped his hand from her delectable ass to the cream of her thighs. The skirt she was wearing was loose, thank god.

A shuddered gasp of breath signaled her realization that he planned to take everything she offered, and he'd beg for whatever she withheld. The hem of the skirt slipped quickly over the back of his hand as he explored.

The deep clearing of a male's throat nearby took several seconds longer than it should've to make Jack stop his quest to discover just how wet he'd made her, his new personal goal.

She jerked back, but their eyes remained locked in an embrace all their own as they chased their breath. Shock, need, confusion, and chaos reflected from her all-telling gaze, an emotional mirror to his own, he was certain.

"We're sorry to interrupt," Beckett eased cautiously, likely concerned he was going to be fired for the intrusion. Despite the greed now eating at his soul, Jack was determined never to do anything his father would've done.

Blinking in an effort to break the emotional connection between them proved woefully ineffective. A deep breath only served to bring more of the intoxicating scent of her arousal to his lungs.

Finally, she was able to turn to face Muriel and Beckett, forcing Jack to do the same. "It's fine," he lied outright. It was not fine. It was blasphemy. It was, indeed, a fireable offense. "We got..."

"Carried away," Meridian concluded for him.

"Your mother is waiting for you both in the house." Muriel's announcement dripped with scolding disdain. That statement told Jack everything he needed to know about his mother's hopes for Meridian. She'd likely chewed his father's and the entire staff's ears to shreds informing them that this was all fake. Certainly, Jackson would never fall for someone outside of her jurisdiction, outside of Bourbon Country. He could all but hear her shrill disdain. The woman had her head shoved so far up her own ass she failed to see that rebellion fed her son. It drove him. For most of his life, it had been his singular goal.

The fact that he knew reckless rebellion so intimately meant that he recognized the flare of it in Meridian's eyes as she picked up on Muriel's condescension, and nothing ever burned as hot and wild as whiskey.

CHAPTER ELEVEN

The fog rolling in off of the river only furthered the sense that Meridian had arrived in some kind of parallel universe. The confusion and passion from the kiss stirred violently into a Molotov cocktail in her belly. My god, where had he learned to kiss like that? Part of her wanted to meet the woman and thank her, but she needed to remember that kisses like that were a part of this bizarre, fake reality they were weaving. They weren't really hers to own or be thankful for.

She'd imagined kissing Jack Denton a thousand times in the last few years. He'd never seemed remotely interested, which only further pissed her off. Perhaps it was the enveloping fog that made it more difficult to remember what it was she'd been so angry about.

Her determination to become the DA might've been all-consuming, but determination doesn't necessarily equal results. Jack took her shaky hand as they stepped down onto the perfectly manicured lawn. Her head turned methodically one way and then the other, but she could never have seen it all from their current location. Only a wrought iron fence with a rather colossal D every ten feet was really discernible.

"Are you okay?" Jack's husky whisper reached her ears like a lifeline being hurled toward her at sea as she went under for the last time.

"Not really." Her words were barely audible, almost eaten by the fog.

"Me or all of this?" The desperate concern that pierced his words centered in her heart.

She considered the question and only had the power to be honest. "Both."

His powerful arm—my god, how had she never noticed how substantial he was—wrapped around her and pulled her close. His warmth soothed her. The flutter of her heart found a rhythm and her mind settled some. "I'll get you home any time you want to go. Just say the word."

Going home before the wedding would be akin to giving up, and that was not something she would ever allow herself. He guided her through the fog. The farther they walked away from the river the clearer the grounds became. Checking her surroundings with more assurance now, she noted that Muriel and Beckett were still back at the plane. "The kiss," she whispered.

"Yeah, I know," he assured her with a tender grin she wasn't certain she'd ever seen him display before. "We'll talk about that as soon as we're out of earshot of the spies. Oh, and welcome to River Chase Estate."

Meridian scanned the periphery again and saw no one. Her brow furrowed.

Jack nodded his head toward some kind of garden shed cottage that looked absolutely nothing like the serviceable work sheds on Holder Ranch and more like something she'd seen on Downton Abbey. It was surrounded by lavender bushes, hostas, and a few dozen other bushes and flowers that Meridian didn't even know the names of. The entire estate seemed to have cobblestone paths that led in multiple directions.

She narrowed her eyes and saw someone move behind the shed. A gardener pruning the already perfectly pruned landscaping. She nodded her understanding and felt stupid for not noticing the gardener before.

Tucking closer to Jack served two purposes. It made her feel safe, and it was precisely what she would do if they were really in love and coming to meet his family, right? She told herself not to overthink it.

The quiet sound of an electric motor drove up behind them. Meridian spun on her boot heel half expecting to be attacked, but Jack grinned. "I wondered when you'd show up." The man driving the golf cart exited and chuckled as he approached. Jack whispered, "One," in Meridian's ear. He held up his index finger only furthering her confusion. Seeing that she wasn't getting it, he quickly explained, "I can count on one hand..."

The people in his family he actually likes, she recalled. Apparently this guy wasn't like the pilot and the gardener and Muriel.

"Meridian, this is my cousin, Sloan," he introduced. "Sloan, my girlfriend, Meridian Holder." The way the word girlfriend rolled off of Jack's tongue with such ease sped her heart yet again.

Sloan shook his sandy-blond head as he took Meridian's right hand and brought it to his lips. She yanked it back. Who the hell did these people think they were? Jack ran a reassuring hand up and down her back.

"It's a pleasure to meet you, Miss Holder." He steadfastly ignored what she supposed was her own rudeness. "Man, Aunt Bev has been on a tirade about you two. I figured you were bullshitting all of us. I kept thinking that first, you'd never fall in love, and then that if you somehow did you'd sure as hell never bring her here. Guess I was wrong on both accounts."

Meridian was going to need to sit down. The almost-violently green grass kept swapping places with the grey skies. The stone statues and wrought iron fencing and buildings and every other physical structure suspended in odd animation somewhere in between. In love? They looked like they were in love? Maybe Sloan had a penchant for sipping a little of the Denton brew early in the morning.

He eased a monogrammed, silk handkerchief from his jacket pocket and handed it to Jack. "Got a little something there you might want to get off before you go in the house." He motioned for Jack to wipe the collar of his shirt.

Meridian blinked several additional times in an effort to make the ground and the sky stay in their correct locations, while also noting what Sloan was referring to. It took her four full blinks to see her vivid red lipstick on Jack's collar and lip-shaped smears on his neck.

She didn't even recall kissing his neck. Now, she wanted to do it again so she could remember it.

"Thanks," Jack huffed as he scrubbed the lipstick from the collar only somewhat successfully. It went from red to pink at the very least.

Determined to pay much better attention and to not let Jack's physical presence, or his lips, or his voice, or his warmth, catch her off guard anymore, she noticed when Sloan delicately let what appeared to be a leather checkbook slip from the arm of his custom fit suit coat right into Jack's palm. He quickly placed it in the internal pocket of his own jacket. *What the hell?*

When her brow furrowed, Jack turned and brushed another kiss at her temple before he whispered, "I'll explain later."

"Might want to, uh,"—Sloan gestured to his own lips—"do your mouth too."

An embarrassed chuckle sounded from Jack as he cleaned himself up. Self-conscious now, Meridian whipped a compact from her purse and removed the out-of-place lipstick from around her own lips.

Sloan couldn't seem to wipe the stupid grin from his own features, however. "Hey, we going to Watershed while you're here?"

"Of course," Jack assured him. "The sooner the better. Meridian's going to hate it here as much as we do, so blowing off some steam will be necessary."

What the fucking hell were they talking about? She hated nothing more than not understanding things. Never in her life had she been anywhere that her family's reputation didn't precede her. Even at Northwestern, people knew her. Blades of discomfort and confusion raked under her skin, inciting her blood. She resisted the urge to stomp her booted feet and demand to understand what was happening.

With a deep breath of dewy Kentucky air, she managed to quell that particular sensation but just barely. Even the air here didn't make sense to her. She'd couldn't recall the last time she'd been anywhere that the scent of hay and manure didn't perfume her lungs. Her teeth clenched with enough force to make her jaw ache. The fact that she wanted to race to the gates and shake them until someone, anyone, released her from this bizarre insecurity only made her angrier.

The riptide of fury constantly threatened to yank her under. She needed Sloan "the suit" Denton to leave so she could demand that Jack explain everything to her right now. Patience had never been her virtue, and he was playing with fire. She suspected he knew that. Intimidation was not something she would ever handle well. She was the one who intimidated people in the courtroom. Once again, the sensation that everything she'd ever known had been turned upside down upset her.

Jack gave her a reassuring squeeze that did nothing but piss her off even more and then he gave Sloan a nod. "I'll call Drew and Finn once we escape introductions and get something planned."

"Just let me know when." Sloan gave them a wave and headed back to his golf cart.

The tight clench of Meridian's lips unhinged. "Do you all just ride around on golf carts? I thought you had horses." Why that was what came out of her mouth right then she had no idea, but it was as good a question as any.

Jack's smirk did nothing to soothe her rapidly disintegrating mood. "I'll take you out to see the horses in a little while. Maybe that will improve your mood. This is an estate not a ranch. The horses are only for the jockeys to ride, and I suspect that Sloan was coming off of the Denton golf course, saw the plane land, and needed to get to us before we got inside, hence the cart."

"To give you the..."

Panic flared in Jack's eyes and then suddenly, his lips were on hers again, consuming the rest of her question.

Feeling much more herself this time, Meridian jerked away from him. "Who the fuck do you think you are?" seethed from her.

Jack ran his hand over his mouth again. "Your boyfriend, remember?" He spoke through his teeth. "Now hush and let's go inside. I told you not to come," were his last hissed words before he took her hand and half dragged her toward a three-story monolithic home.

CHAPTER TWELVE

An American and a Kentucky flag few across the wide front steps of the wraparound porch. Meridian's temper cooled just enough for her to manage another deep breath. "I'm never going to get used to not smelling Oklahoma," she commented to herself.

Jack spun on the porch and tucked them between two sets of windows. "I'm sorry," he sounded like he meant it. "I know you hate not knowing things. I just can't explain everything right now, but I swear I won't keep anything from you. You just have to play by my rules."

Meridian gave him a slight nod. "I don't like that any more than I like not knowing things," she admitted.

He winked at her and she really, really wished that something as stupid as a wink would not melt the icy chill she'd been planning on giving him, but it did. Stupid, traitorous reproductive organs. "I know that too." He grinned. "It might be good for you. You ever think of that?"

"You ever had someone knee you in the balls on this front porch?"

That got her a deep, husky laugh that only further stirred her attraction. "Yes. Twice actually. Now, are you ready?"

"No."

"Yeah, well, me either, but here goes." They made it to the lead-paned front door just before it opened.

"Welcome home, Mr. Denton." A maid, who was about Meridian's mother's age, dressed in the full-on black and white uniform deal, beamed at him. "We're all so pleased to see you."

"It's nice to see you too, Rosalind. I'd like you to meet my girlfriend, Meridian Holder." He gently placed a hand on the small of her back and guided her inside the largest home she'd ever even seen, much less stepped inside of.

Rosalind curtsied. She actually, really, legitimately curtsied, and Meridian almost vomited. She extended her hand, took Rosalind's, and lifted her back up so they were eye level. "Please never do that again," she pleaded. "That is completely unnecessary. I'm just...me."

Jack grinned at Rosalind. "Remind you of anyone else you know?" Again, he was speaking cryptically.

Rosalind nodded and gave both of them kind grins. "Oh, I see why you like her, for sure, Mr. Denton. Sounds like you two were made for each other, but don't you let your mother know I said as much."

"Never," Jack assured her. "And Mr. Denton is my father, remember? I'm just Jack."

"Your mama doesn't like that either."

"Even better."

While they bantered, Meridian took stock of the interior of the house. It much reflected the outside. The walls of the massive entryway were wallpapered in the blue and white equivalent of old money. Every room she could see off of the grand hall looked like Laura Ashley and Southern Living had a baby who'd vomited all over the house. Large oval-framed paintings, taller than she was, hung high above her head. She recognized a very young Jack in one of them and could only assume that the other was one of his brothers. Despite his insistence that he had three brothers, there were only two paintings.

Still, it was as oddly impressive as it was intimidating. And there it was again. The feeling of intimidation was like swallowing bile by the gallons. She hated it. There was another person dressed similarly to Rosalind dusting a nearby room that held a grand piano and was lined with old bookcases.

"Is that Maggie?" Jack gestured toward the woman as he asked Rosalind the question. "Sloan mentioned her to me."

Rosalind nodded. "She's been here a few months. She has the cutest little girl. Maggie was going to the university, but the baby needed some medical treatments so she took a year off to work." Rosalind's voice dropped so low Meridian almost missed the last sentence.

Jack matched her whispered tone, "Is my mother going anywhere today?"

"She has a meeting at the university," Rosalind stated. Meridian still had no clue what was going on.

"When she leaves, send Maggie up to see me if you get a chance," Jack instructed.

The air in the hall electrified with tension as the low click of heels echoed closer. Jack's Adam's apple bobbed with a hard swallow, and Meridian straightened her back so she more closely matched both Maggie's and Rosalind's stances.

Meridian had done enough research on the Dentons to know precisely who was approaching when Mrs. Beverly Denton entered the hall. She gave her son and Meridian a visual appraisal that said she thought they were vastly overpriced.

"I see your new venture hasn't managed to correct your habitual tardiness, Jackson." Beverly angled her cheek to her son to be kissed.

Jack left her hanging there, and Meridian coughed over her giggle. Fury sizzled in Mrs. Denton's eyes as her head jerked away.

After clearing his throat, Jack pulled Meridian tighter to him as if he could physically block her from the stench of his mother's pretentiousness. "This is my girlfriend, Meridian Holder." He lowered his tone to a lethal level. "Be nice."

"It's lovely to finally meet you, Mrs. Denton." Meridian extended her hand which Beverly begrudgingly accepted.

"Yes. I'm sure. Jackson, I've arranged for a few friends to come by for dinner and drinks this evening. The wedding festivities begin tomorrow, but the Beaumonts and the Parkers wanted to see you prior so I indulged them on your behalf. The Fitzgeralds are making time for you tonight as well. I'm sure you don't mind."

"Dinner is fine," Jack begrudged. "But tomorrow night, Meridian and I are going into town to see Finn."

Meridian grinned like she was excited to go hang with Finn, whomever he turned out to be.

His mother continued speaking as if Jack had said nothing at all. "The ladies' bridal tea we're hosting is Wednesday morning. I've kindly added Ms. Holder to the guest list." She gave Meridian another once-over. "I do hope she has something appropriate to wear."

Jack made no effort to hide his eye roll as Meridian narrowed hers. "I'm so thrilled Tiffany has moved on. I can't imagine ever having to get over Jack. He's everything I ever could've dreamed of in a fiancé." She made certain her syrup-sweet drawl contained pure venom. *Take that, bitch.*

Jack's eyes goggled. His mother huffed and puffed like the big, bad wolf. "Fiancé?!"

After a few uncomfortable nods, he recovered. "Yes, we were going to tell you at dinner. I planned to ask for Gran's ring while we were here. We're both thrilled, so it's difficult to keep it secret, of course."

Okay, so clearly Meridian's effort to royally piss off his mama had more consequences than she'd originally estimated. Oh well. In for a penny, in for a pound.

Beverly Denton was the visual interpretation of appalled—eyes the size of silver platters and mouth hanging open for every fly in Kentucky to vacation inside. Meridian couldn't quite contain her grin. If she'd set fire to their stupid golf course using their own bourbon, it likely would've gone over better. At some point Beverly would learn not to mess with Meridian.

Feeling much better about everything, she plastered what she hoped was a kind smile and gazed at Jack like he placed the moon and stars in the sky for her. After he'd gotten over his shock, he actually seemed pleased his mother was so thrown.

"I'll just take Meridian up to our room," he informed everyone within earshot.

"Rosalind will carry up your bags," Beverly spoke robotically.

Jack guided Meridian toward one side of the double spiral staircase.

"I don't need anyone to carry my bags, Mother. Never have. Never will."

Almost as if to prove his capability to his mother, he managed all three bags in one hand and kept the other arm around Meridian as they made their way up the staircase and down a hallway that contained, she counted, twelve doors before he stopped.

CHAPTER THIRTEEN

Rushing them inside his childhood room, Jack sealed the door shut, set down his jacket and luggage, and checked both closets and the adjoining bathroom before he rounded on Meridian. "Fiancé?"

"Sorry." She wrinkled her nose adorably, and to his shock, his irritation melted. How could one woman be so lethal one moment and cute the next? "I was trying to piss her off. It's fun. I get why you try to do it so much."

Rubbing his temples, he supposed he had to agree. She was standing in the middle of his room slowly turning to take it all in. "Who is that?" She pointed to the painting of his great-grandfather hung in pride of place on the center wall opposite the bed.

Trying to remember how very odd everything about this world would be to her, he sank down on the bed. "Uh, that is my great-grandfather Barnsley Denton the third."

She mouthed the word, "Wow," as she continued to turn. "Wait." She halted. "We're both staying in here? Together?"

Jack threw his arms out to her. "Well, we're apparently engaged. Surely you don't mind sleeping with your fiancé."

She crossed the plush carpeting and settled in one of the velvet barrel chairs by the windows. "I'm sorry," she offered again. He knew

Meridian was not one to apologize often so he took it to heart. "I'm clearly way out of my league here, and I hate that. I had no idea this would be so fucking difficult. I'm better in the courtroom than I am in ballrooms, I guess."

He knew he probably shouldn't appreciate her recognition of the magnitude of their situation, but he did. "It's fine, just so long as you're aware that you've now taken this to a level I'm not sure either of us were prepared to handle. We're going to have to be quick on our feet. Can you handle that?"

"Can you tell me what the hell has happened since that plane took off in Oklahoma? What was that kiss? Why did Sloan give you that checkbook? And who is Finn? Oh, and where is the watershed? Why does everyone here spy for your mom? She seems awful. And was she seriously pissed off that we were late when it was her pilot that got us here? Does she often get mad at God over the weather? Does she find that a productive use of her time?"

Jack stood and paced the length of his room. "If I answer all of those questions truthfully, will you give me the same courtesy?"

She considered that for a moment and nodded. "Of course."

Now he had her right where he wanted her. He really was the better lawyer even if he'd never point that out directly. "Have you ever thought about kissing me?"

Oh, she did not like that question. She visibly recoiled as if that wasn't answer enough. "I believe the offer was that I would be honest with you *after* you answered truthfully," she countered.

Jack redacted his thought on who was the better lawyer. "As if that wasn't answer enough." He grinned just to watch her roll those beautiful eyes.

"Fine. Yes. I've thought about kissing you...a lot. Now, back to my questions."

An awareness arced between them. The verbalization of their mutual attraction seemed to cement them further than that kiss or the announcement that they were engaged. He greeted her honesty with his own. "I've thought about kissing you every single day since we met four years ago. I've imagined it...fantasized about it so many times I got carried away. I apologize if I took advantage."

Her eyes revealed a hunger as they rose to meet his. Jack discreetly turned, hoping she wouldn't notice the effect she had on him. "You didn't take advantage." Her very admittance was laced with both need and self-betrayal. "What else have you thought about us doing?" Her gaze darted around the room running from his now. "What do you do when you think about me?"

The space between them took on a pulse he'd never felt before, certainly not in this room, not in this house, never at River Chase. He answered her question with one of his own. "What would you say if I preferred to show you the answer to that question instead of telling you?"

She stood and made three quick steps to stand before him. "What if I prefer to be told before you show me?"

He noted that she didn't say she wouldn't let him show her. Perhaps this trip home would be the best in memory. "Then we'd have to come up with some kind of compromise, wouldn't we?"

Her delicate tongue that had filled his mouth so deliciously on the plane tasted her bottom lip. "Answer my questions and then we'll discuss a potential compromise."

His entire body tensed with parched thirst. Her words did nothing to break the spell she had him so thoroughly captivated by. Getting involved with her would probably lose him every single thing he'd earned and fought for since he'd left Kentucky, but at that moment he just didn't care. Jack edged closer to her, magnetically drawn to those eyes, to those tender curves, to her lips. "You are incredibly dangerous, Meridian."

"I know." Her grin was half-coy, half-evil. She took one more step toward him, so close now that their breaths mingled and danced. "You're not the only one with something to lose," she reminded him. "If anyone in Holder County found out about us, I would never become DA."

His grin matched hers. "You say that like I'll ever lose the seat."

Her lips were already swollen from their first kiss. The whiskey gold of her eyes was now hidden behind the pure, black need. She traced her hand down his chest igniting a blaze like flint on steel. "I always get what I want eventually," she informed him.

Jack's shallow breaths weren't deep enough for him to catch her scent, and it drove him mad. His large, capable hands wrapped around her back and erased any distance between them. Her sweet little hips bucked so readily against his stiff cock. Her body begged even if her mind was being stubborn. She tried unsuccessfully to quell a needy moan. She didn't want to reveal her hand, but it was much too late for that. "What is it that you want right now, cowgirl?" he growled low and hungry.

She shuddered against him as if admitting what they both already knew physically tore something from her. "You."

"If the lady always gets what she wants...." He captured her lips with his own, feasting on her flavors yet again. God, he would never get enough. This time was even better than the last. There was more room to move, more space for him to own her. Gripping her ass again, he ground the heated apex of her thighs against his cock. Even between layers of frustrating clothing, her gasps and almost begrudging sighs satisfied him in a way nothing else ever had.

As he pressed himself harder against her, making certain he tempted just the right spot with every pass, he informed her of how this would work. If he was going to gamble on his entire life, then he wanted all of her, every single secret, every dark, delicious desire he knew existed right there under her skin. "I'll make you beg," he informed her with a cocky smirk that came so easily to all of the Denton boys. "Make you plead for me to soothe the very places I make you ache."

She lifted her head from his shoulder, a smirk of her own forming on her bee-stung lips. "I do not beg for anything. Ever."

"If that's a challenge, Miss Holder, I accept."

CHAPTER FOURTEEN

Meridian was shockingly wet—so wet, in fact, she was concerned that if he kept talking she was going to be standing in a puddle of her own desperation. What the hell was he doing to her? Primal, sophisticated, complicated, and forbidden, everything Jack was to her, served only to make her crave him more.

He spun his tongue at her collarbone and traced his lips up her jaw. A needy shiver quaked through her. She tried to be angry at her double-crossing body, but everything he did felt too damn good for her to be able to complain and complicate this.

His whiskey-smooth voice strummed from her ear to her chest to forbidden places beyond. "All of those cowboys you play with just don't do it for you, do they, honey? They don't understand people like us who are never satisfied. They don't know how hard and filthy you need to be fucked, do they?" He punctuated the last two words with a slow, almost violent grind of his hips that stripped away all of her stubborn resolve.

"No," whimpered from her. To keep herself from saying more than that, she gripped his hair and pressed his mouth back to hers. His hand twisted under her skirt, shoving it upwards before he traced over the black satin of her panties. An embarrassing, carnal moan tore from her lungs.

"You're soaked. Soaking wet for me. Your body already knows how to beg. Let's see if your mouth can't learn."

She locked her jaw shut in adamant refusal, while her body continued to try and lure his hand to her pussy. Desperate whimpers escaped the prison of her lips. Chuckling, he continued to torture her with a refusal of his own. He did nothing but tease and trace her satin-trapped clit. Her entire body vibrated with every stroke of his fingers like she was an instrument only he knew how to play.

And yet, he refused her any kind of satisfaction. "God, you really are a dick." She'd intended that to sound far more irritated than it had, but it had come out in a breathy, yearning mewl.

That got her a deep, throaty laugh that somehow only made her weaker. "Oh honey, look around you. I know precisely what I am. What I didn't know is that you like it." Driving home his intended goal, he eased her panties to the side and teased and tended the wet and raw folds of her but refused to enter her where she needed his fingers. One stroke and she would come. That's all it would take. She just needed to be full of him. *Please, please* almost slipped from her lips. Almost.

The knock on the door was so faint Meridian wasn't entirely certain she'd heard it until Jack eased his hand away, righted her panties, and slid her skirt back down her legs. Her heart stuttered out of rhythm, and the entire room spun. A silent echo of shock filled the air around her and nothing at all made sense, a sensation she was getting tired of feeling, until he wrapped his arms around her, steadying her.

Her own actions continued to surprise her as she nuzzled her head on his substantial shoulders and let him cradle her tenderly. "I've got you," he soothed softly against her ear. "That wasn't how I'd planned on that ending."

She tried to laugh and nod but only ended up sighing into his neck and cuddling herself closer. She clung to him like an anchor in the storm.

The next knock was more audible. "Just a minute," Jack barked.

"Oh, I'm sorry, sir," trembled from whomever was outside his room.

They both lifted their heads at the same moment. Jack cringed. "Are you okay?" he whispered.

"I'm fine," Meridian assured him, though she wasn't sure she'd ever told a lie quite that big before.

Smoothing her hair and trying to not look like she was on the verge of bowing before Jack to beg for mercy, she returned to the velvet chair near the window. Another round of heat bloomed across her cheeks as Great Grandpa Barnsley's eyes seemed to shame her from the frame on the wall.

Jack buttoned his top two buttons and fixed his rumpled hair in the mirror all while heading toward the door. He yanked it open to reveal a cowering Maggie. Apologies erupted from her. "I'm so sorry, Mr. Denton, sir. I didn't mean to bother you."

"You're not a bother to anyone. Come on in." Jack did not lie quite as convincingly as Meridian had.

"Your mother left to go to a board meeting at the university so..."

"You were worried this was your only chance to talk to me," Jack concluded for her.

"Yes, sir." She turned and did the curtsy thing to Meridian just like Rosalind had.

"Okay, you people have got to stop that." Meridian shook her head. "Sit down. Take a load off." She gestured to the seat beside hers. "I'm not the queen."

Jack's grin and wink at her continued to have a spellbinding effect on her internal organs, and she was going to have to figure out how to make that nonsense stop right along with all of the curtsying.

Maggie sat on the edge of the chair like she wasn't allowed to take up any more space than that. The next time Meridian encountered Beverly she was tempted to knock her upside the head with a bottle of Denton Reserve.

Maggie fidgeted with the apron of her uniform. "I don't really know how to go about this. Rosalind said to talk to you about Abbey, but I'm not sure what you want to know."

Jack settled on the corner of his bed and gave her a kind smile. "Abbey is your little girl, right?"

Retrieving a phone from the pocket of her uniform, she showed Jack and Meridian a picture of an adorable plump-cheeked, blue-eyed baby girl drooling all over a teething ring. An IV line was taped to her inner arm. "This is her." Maggie stared adoringly down at the phone. "She was six months old last week. A few weeks after she was born, she went into sepsis from a kidney infection. Uh," her voice trembled along with her hands. Meridian reached out and held Maggie's right hand in her own. "It's my fault. I was so tired, and I must not have noticed that she wasn't quite herself that night before I put her in the crib."

Meridian shook her head. "Please don't blame yourself. It isn't your fault."

Maggie managed a nod. "She coded and we almost lost her twice, but they saved her. She had to have one kidney removed, and she still has to have IV antibiotics at home. My boyfriend has gotten really good at giving them to her though. He's amazing. But she got another infection and now she's back in the hospital. It's just that the bills are a lot and there will be more surgeries.

"If her other kidney should have any trouble, then I'm going to donate a portion of mine, but I can't afford to take any time off work. My parents started one of those GoFundMe things, but we don't really know that many people. My boyfriend lost his job as a graphic designer because he took off so much time when she was in and out of the hospital. We're in bad shape. He got another job last week as a contractor for an online sales company but no benefits for six months. I don't know what to do. He's trying to work from the hospital and take care of her while she's there. Your father said I could work tonight at the dinner party for a few extra hours, but that won't go far."

Jack rolled his eyes. "How incredibly generous of him," he huffed. "Listen, I'm sorry that was all he offered to do. Sorry, but not surprised." He moved to their luggage and removed the suit jacket he'd thrown on top. Retrieving the checkbook Sloan had given him, he leaned over the cherry wood desk in his room and wrote out a check. "Here."

"Mr. Denton, thank you, but I...you're going to get into trouble."

"Good." He tore the check from the book. "Listen, you take this to the bank. There's not enough in this account for me to cover the hospital bills, I'm sure, but this will help. Get some groceries, get Abbey some new toys, take your boyfriend some dinner, and pay a few bills. You two just worry about Abbey. I'll talk to Sloan tomorrow, get some funds moved around, and see if we can't take care of the rest. You're not working tonight. If my mother has something to say about it, she can take it up with me."

Tears raced from Maggie's eyes. She shook her head in disbelief. Meridian tried to breathe around the conflicting emotions of anger at Jack's parents and awe at him that gathered in her throat. She continued to try to soothe Maggie by holding her hand and offering her tender, reassuring smiles.

"I can't thank you enough for this, but I don't mind working tonight. I want to try to earn some of it. I don't want your parents to be angry with you."

"My parents have been angry with me for years. It has nothing to do with you. Your little girl needs you right now. My mother will throw more dinner parties, and you can pick up extra shifts when Abbey isn't in the hospital."

"Chad and I will figure out some way to make this up to you both," Maggie vowed as she tucked the check safely in her bra.

Meridian stood to join the two of them at the desk. "You two can make it up to him by Abbey being healthy and home from the hospital." She knew she had no right to make that statement, but she also knew it's precisely what Jack wanted.

He nodded. "Couldn't have said it better myself."

Maggie gave them both a teary smile. "I wish the world were full of more people like you two. You're so lucky that you found each other. "

CHAPTER FIFTEEN

"Wow." Meridian breathed the word as she stared at him. Her impressed smile made Jack want to earn a thousand more, every day if he could.

"My parents are so caught up in their ridiculous world, they have no idea what it's like to live in this country with next to nothing. They don't understand how expensive it is to be poor."

"Yeah, but it's not just them. We're the richest country in the world. People shouldn't have to bankrupt themselves because their babies get sick."

Jack had to give her that.

Her brow did that thing where it furrowed and made her lips purse. Jack found it all to be completely intoxicating. He loved watching her think. "Did you know about Maggie before we arrived? Is she why you had to come this week?"

Part of him wished he could delay the answering of her questions, but he knew he had to school her before his mother's asinine dinner party. "I didn't know the specifics, but Sloan mentioned that we needed to step in." He settled in the chair Maggie had occupied and gestured for Meridian to sit in the one beside him. From that vantage point by the window, he could see when his mother's Land Rover came through the east gates.

"I take it Sloan doesn't have signing privileges on that checking account," she assumed correctly.

"Sloan is my father's younger brother's oldest son. He is the head of accounting for Denton Distilleries. As per usual with accountants, he can't spend any of the money he's in charge of monitoring. That's where I come in."

"How long have you been doing things like that? How have your parents not noticed the missing money? It's more than obvious they disapprove of you, so why is your name still on the accounts?"

As each question compounded on his shoulders, Jack sank lower in the chair. The velvet was as hot and itchy as it had been in his youth. The desire to run from the house, through the gates, and as far away from River Chase as he could get coursed through him yet again.

He drew a deep settling breath. "Sloan makes certain that money gets moved around often enough that no one notices. You have to understand the sheer number of accounts, the constant mergers, petty cash in the tens of thousands, the legacy estate accounts that the family shields both here and offshore. My father knows corn mash, rye, and barrels. He knows how to make whomever he's speaking to feel like the most important person in the room, but the money isn't something he pays a great deal of attention to unless things get out of hand.

"He trusts Sloan to make certain that my mother always has more than enough to supply her whims and that he has enough to run the estate and get a new Rolls each year. As long as all of that occurs, the rest is, quite literally, gravy. I'm still on the accounts because my father's highest hope is that I'll realize the insanity of leaving and return like the prodigal son. I would sooner hurl myself down a coal mine elevator shaft."

Intensity rolled off of her in waves as she considered every aspect. He'd watched her work long enough to know the way her brain maneuvered through information. "How very Robin Hood of you both," she finally summed. "You are aware they could have you arrested for this."

A half grin lifted the edge of Jack's lips. "Are you trying to protect me, Miss Holder?"

She narrowed those eyes again. "Maybe."

Standing to pace once again, he tried to think of some way to explain the complicated, intricate world of whiskey baron money. "They would never press charges against me because it's all one big ship, so to speak. In order for them to have me or Sloan arrested, they would have to submit financials to the courts. All of those legacy accounts, the shell game they're able to play with every brand label, and the tax-shielded money that far exceeds what's legal would be made public."

Meridian's eyes lit with understanding. "If one of you goes down, the entire ship goes with you."

"Precisely."

"Damn."

"Or damned perhaps. I'll just take this opportunity to remind you that I tried to get you not to come."

"Are you trying to protect me, Mr. Denton?"

"Definitely."

"Well, stop. I want to help you. Are there other people here that you need to give a bonus to? There have to be."

"I try to give a little something to all of the staff while I'm here, and I'm related to the other people who need my help."

Fascination sparked in those all-telling eyes. "Finn?"

Jack gave a slow nod. "And Drew."

"Who are they exactly?" Her tone edged back toward prosecutor.

"My brother and my half brother."

"Why does your mother not want you to see them?"

"I told you, they exist in the space between the lines." He didn't relish the abhorrent pain woven so tightly in with their stories. He couldn't stand to think of what they'd been through.

"Drew is my father's bastard child by one of the staff members. He was born when I was around ten, but I didn't know of his existence until I'd come back to work for the company. His mother was traded off to one of the other well-known bourbon families, and he got nothing because to my parents he doesn't really exist. It's extremely convenient to ignore that which you don't want to be."

"And Finn?"

"The Watershed Bar is a predominantly gay bar downtown where we all meet when I'm home to blow off steam and remind Finn that not everyone in this family is as bigoted as my parents and my older brother are."

She was on those heels in a split second. "They sent him away because he's gay?! Are you serious?"

"Finn and I are only eighteen months apart. We were thick as thieves our entire childhood. I'd gone to work representing Denton Distilleries just like I'd been bred to do my whole life. When Finn came out to me and Greer, I wasn't surprised. Sloan and his younger sister, Lila, and I took him out to Watershed to prove we wanted him to be happy. That's all that mattered to us. I thought nothing of it. It never occurred to me that my parents didn't already know. Greer went with us, but he was...oddly quiet, maybe. I still don't know what he thinks, but Finn says he doesn't approve so I believe him."

Fury sizzled in Meridian's eyes. "I guess it really is extremely convenient to ignore that which you don't want to be."

"My parents and their ilk make a habit of it. They spent the next six months essentially erasing Finn from the family, from the accounts, from everything. He was finishing up at the University of Louisville where both of my parents sit on the board. They sent him to get his master's degree at Concordia in Portland. When he returned, they explained that they felt he needed to work outside of the family business. They stopped speaking of him at all after that. Can you imagine being erased from your family?"

"No." She shook her head in part to give credence to her truth, Jack assumed, but it also appeared to be in abject disbelief.

"It was all done so efficiently, no matter what I tried to do to stop it. I'd ended the sham of a relationship with Tiff a few weeks before, but Finn was the final straw for me. I had a showdown with my parents and I left. Now, we both try to confound my parents whenever we can. Finn became a marketing manager and graphic designer for Churchill Downs. My parents have no choice but to deal with him on occasion if their horses compete. We make a great deal of profit supplying whiskey for events there. It's too large of an account for my parents to be able to erase it from existence. Finn is excellent at his job, but sticking it to my parents is too much fun to resist. Sloan and Lila and I try to help out the staff the rest of the time."

"I guess you two are still thick as thieves." She beamed up at him. "I'm so sorry for all of this. I had no idea."

"Any other questions before I go see the kitchen staff? I need to get down there before my mother gets back, and I need to call Sloan to explain about Maggie."

Meridian considered for a breath. "Just one. Why did you say that I'm dangerous? It seems to me you're more than willing to take on danger at your own personal expense. I don't feel like much of a threat as much as I love to think of myself that way."

Chuckling at her wishes, he was surprised she'd asked that particular question. "Meridian"—he bought himself a little more time —"when I left here I walked away from all of the money, every connection, everything I'd ever known. I walked out of those gates. Finn picked me up and put me up in his apartment, but I had to get out of here. Everyone in Kentucky knows my parents and the power they wield. No one was stupid enough to choose me over them. I phoned an old friend from school to see if he knew of any available jobs for a lawyer. His father is Senator McCoy. His dad arranged for me to get an interview to work for Holder County. I didn't have a job for months before that. I couldn't continue to live off of my brother after all my parents had put him through. I took a Greyhound to Tulsa and slept in the bus station. I hitchhiked the rest of the way."

"I'm so sorry," she spoke in barely a breath.

"I'm not looking for sympathy. I'm telling you that I know how delicate the thread is that holds my entire life together. You are the most dangerous creature in existence for me."

"I don't understand what I have to do with any of that."

Of course she didn't. Privilege didn't work that way. It was so integral to the core of whomever we all become that stepping away from it is akin to pulling flesh from bone. Those who had it didn't recognize it because it's next to impossible to live more than one life. "You come from a very long line of men and women who make good, honest choices. But your last name is the very same as the county that employs me to also make good, honest decisions. If your Uncle Barrett decided he didn't approve of me, I would never even have a part-time job in town much less hold public office. Your father and your uncles don't have to have titles because the power they hold and the respect they deserve is etched in every square inch of that town square. It's all over the entire county. Every street, every school, every public building, every cattle truck that barrels through town—they all serve to remind the rest of us that you were there first, that the entire county was built up around your family, that the decisions ultimately lie not with the courthouse but with Holder Ranch. And you...are their princess."

Incredulity formed quickly on her features. "I am not a princess."

"Aren't you though? No other name strikes fear in the heart of anyone in that county more than yours. You can't honestly sit there and believe that if we tried to have some kind of relationship and I somehow fuck it up that I wouldn't be the one they'd run out of town on a rail to save the queen. I don't have another friend with a father who's a senator. I took my one chance to escape this hell. I won't get another."

She shook her head. "You're wrong, but why do you think you'd be the one to fuck up our relationship?"

Jack was surrounded by decor that cost more than most people made in a year and a home and estate that were worth millions upon millions of dollars, but nothing would ever cost more than the truth. "Because I come from a very long line of men who make terrible, dishonest decisions. It is very likely the only thing I know. And yet, I am..." he considered his words carefully. His soul wasn't for sale.

"You are what?" she repeated.

"More attracted to you than anyone I have ever encountered."

Her response looked like it cost every bit as much as his. "That attraction goes both ways."

"So, what do we do?"

She shrugged, and then her famous cat-and-canary grin formed on her features. "We are a long way from Holder County, and I did announce to your mother that we are engaged. No one back home will have any idea what goes on here, right?"

"Our worlds are certainly very far apart." His entire body tightened as he leaned closer to her. He prayed she was about to say what he thought was coming.

"You never know—after a week, you might never want to see me again."

"I highly doubt that, princess."

"No harm in finding out."

"I was really hoping you'd say that." Intent on picking up where they'd left off, he took her hand and yanked her back into his arms.

"I thought we needed to go see how the kitchen staff is getting on?" Her reminder sounded like pure torture.

"In just a minute," he negotiated with his lips against hers. He wasn't a man who doubted his own abilities. After a few seconds, he wagered that he could make her perfectly willing to delay checking on the kitchen staff.

Yet another knock interrupted. An audible huff tensed her chest against his. "There are entirely too many people in this house."

"Agreed." Jack once again tried to make it appear that he did not have a raging hard-on before opening his bedroom door.

Rosalind smiled at them. "I was just checking to see if you need anything steamed before dinner this evening."

Jack more than sympathized with the abject disappointment painted on Meridian's face as she laid her suitcase on his bed and unzipped it. "I guess wrinkles aren't allowed here either." She shook out four dresses that Jack had never seen her wear. "As soon as he tells me what to wear tonight, I can steam it if you just tell me where. You don't need to do my laundry for me."

"I don't mind," Rosalind insisted. "I like looking at fancy people's clothes."

"But I'm not fancy," Meridian insisted. "I bought that secondhand. I can't afford Chanel in real life."

"My princess prefers to identify herself as a cowgirl," Jack explained.

"Oh." Rosalind gave them her broad beaming grin, the one that made Jack willing to go check on the rest of the staff to see if he couldn't lighten their load financially while he was in town. "You should take her down to the stables. Your brother just bought two new ponies."

"I'll do that soon," he promised.

Meridian held up four dresses, two on each hand. "Which one?"

Since she had asked, he decided he wouldn't mind selecting what he would get to see her in for the evening and what he planned to take off of her as soon as this fucking dinner party was over.

CHAPTER SIXTEEN

Jack handed the green silk Chanel dress off to Rosalind. Meridian hated the idea of someone waiting on her but wasn't certain how to stop it from happening. When Rosalind whisked from the room, Meridian asked, "So, is this going to be more of an Emily Gilmore kind of dinner party or a Blair Waldorf one?"

She found herself noting the way Jack's dark hair still looked mussed from her fingers and the way his slight beard sharpened the angular edges of his face.

"What would the difference be?" he asked.

Meridian considered. "Overtly pretentious and controlling versus back-stabby and drama-inducing."

"C. All of the above."

"Fun."

"I told you..."

Meridian placed her index finger over his mouth. "Do not say that you told me not to come, or I'll renegotiate the terms of our one-week deal."

He brushed a kiss on the tip of her finger. "I don't believe any terms were ever finalized. Perhaps we should go over that."

Refusing to show any weakness, Meridian rearranged her features to those of a hardened lawyer. "State your terms, Counselor."

When she'd first met Jack, she'd wrongly assumed that he was all ego and bravado. Through the years, she'd learned that he was neither of those things. Jack Denton was certainty. Self-assuredness practically oozed from his pores. She went back and forth between admiration and annoyance of it. But right then she allowed herself to acknowledge how incredibly sexy that certainty was when it belonged to her, even if it was only for a week.

When Jack didn't respond, she crossed her arms over her chest. "I'm waiting."

"My terms?" When his smirk morphed from certainty to ego, she offered him a complimentary eye roll. "Sorry. I'm just in shock."

Her arms and her mind unfolded. "Why?"

"I've just never known you to really listen to any opinion other than your own. I was surprised you asked me to state mine, I guess."

"That is not true. I'm just generally right, so I've never seen much need in hearing anyone else's."

He shook his head at her, but it was the adoring grin on his face that caused her heart to falter and her ovaries to start that stupid cheerleader routine again. "Well, since you did ask, my terms are fairly simple," he informed her as he proceeded to hang the rest of the clothing from both of their suitcases in a closet the approximate size of Rhode Island. "My family's estate, my room, my bed...my rules."

The breath of air held stagnant in her lungs disintegrated. God, why did that sound so utterly appealing? It was preposterous. It was not something she'd agree to in this lifetime or the next. She clasped her hands to keep him from seeing her tremble. "If that's...all you've brought to the table, then I'm afraid I'll have to walk away."

———

———

———

Jack knew he'd taken a gamble, but he also knew Meridian had no idea she'd played right into his hand. How could he have been so stupid? All these years, he'd considered her an enigma, but she wasn't at all. His fear of ever trying to figure her out had blocked him.

Removing the now empty suitcases, he gestured for her to sit on the bed beside him. Always cautious and determined to win, she considered his invitation but finally relented and settled on the mattress.

"You know we're not actually negotiating a contract or someone's plea bargain here, right?" His eyebrows lifted with the question.

He got a single nod in response.

"So, perhaps we could actually just discuss what the hell we've gotten ourselves into minus all of the lawyer-speak."

At least that earned him a grin. "Fine. What have we gotten ourselves into?"

"Better question," he corrected, "what are you so afraid of?"

"I'm not afraid of anything." The response was far too automatic to have ever been the truth.

"I answered all of your questions. I thought you were going to be honest with me as well."

"I am being honest. I'm not afraid of you. I just don't like being told what to do."

More lies. She might not like it outside of his bed, but she would never have responded the way she did when they were kissing if she wasn't hungry for more. "How long have you been solely responsible for your own orgasms, honey?"

Her eyes goggled as a huff escaped her. "That's a little personal, isn't it?"

"More personal than what we're planning to do as soon as I can coax you back up here after this ridiculous dinner? Or hell, this house has something like seventy rooms and closets, I'm not picky."

"No, you're horny," she goaded.

"Guilty as charged. But come on, surely you don't think me Neanderthal enough to ever try to persuade you to do something you don't want to do, so what harm is there in letting me take you places you've never gone before? Or is *that* what you're afraid of?"

One breath, two. Their eyes were locked in a battle of raw wills, and he refused to look away. Finally, she glanced at the wall just behind his head. "Fine. Maybe it is."

Jack held out his hand to her. She begrudgingly placed her knotted fist in his open hand. Gently, he eased her fingers open, one by one, and laced them with his own. "Trust me," he whispered. "I won't let you down."

She erupted off of the bed. "Are there going to be like seventeen forks I'm not going to know what to do with at this dinner? Do you have whiskey with meals here? Or is that like an after-dinner or before dinner thing? Or both? It's probably both. Why did you pick that dress? Why does your mother automatically hate me? Is it because of Tiffany?"

"Meridian,"—he kept his tone even and calming and waited on her to draw breath—"what did I just tell you?"

"To trust you." She sounded as if he'd suggested she pole dance in the middle of the table for the evening's entertainment.

"And?" he prompted.

"That you won't let me down."

"I didn't just mean in bed, cowgirl. If anything throws you, ask me. I won't leave your side. You seemed to enjoy driving my mother to distraction, so by all means use any fork you like."

"She really is puckered at both ends."

"To say the least." Laughing at her assessment, Jack wondered how this dinner was going to go.

One thing the Denton sons had been taught from a very early age was never to let anyone see you looking concerned. Never let anyone know your feathers were ruffled. The consequences could be dire. Stocks could fall, suppliers could back out of deals, price per barrel could lower in a foreign market, all because someone in the Denton family didn't appear absolutely certain that the sun and moon set on Denton corn mash and rye. So, though he was concerned with what might happen that evening, he would never have let on.

There were very few things that Jack trusted implicitly. He didn't even trust himself. He was the product of Palmer and Beverly Denton after all. But the vow he'd just made he knew he would keep. He would never let her down.

He was going to have to prove himself to her if he was going to get her to let him help with the Marsden case and if he was going to be able to keep her begging for more of him. One mattered far more than the other.

"So, why did you pick that dress?" she asked again. "I want to learn all of these ridiculous rules you have to live by. Apparently, I have to go to some bridal tea for your ex-fiancée and you won't be there then. Plus, can I just say that it's very weird that your family is throwing some kind of tea for her. Shouldn't they have taken your side?"

"They would never have taken my side, and I will be at the tea. I also have a female cousin, Lila, I mentioned before. You'll meet her tomorrow night. She'll be there, and you can trust her."

"You're going to come to a ladies' bridal tea?"

"I'm not going to leave you alone with my mother. I can drink tea. I'll even practice the pinky thing just to make Beverly happy. I won't let you down. I'm going to keep saying that until I get it through your stubborn head. But to answer your question about the dress—I chose it because you look stunning in green and because I want to take it off of you tonight."

Panic lit the flecks of gold in her eyes. "That was a stupid thing to do. What if I'm underdressed or overdressed or wrongly dressed?" She was officially coming undone. If it hadn't had anything to do with him, Jack would've thoroughly enjoyed this. He'd never seen Meridian so ruffled.

Standing and guiding her into his arms, if for no other reason than to feel her tuck her head on his shoulder, he soothed, "You will be perfect in that dress, and when I get you far enough away from whomever my mother has coming over tonight, you will be perfect undressed as well."

He'd been bred and raised on the finest whiskeys in the world. His palate was still well-trained enough to be able to discern the difference between a 93.7 proof small batch reserve and a 122 semi-limited. With a single sip, he could tell you not only the family who owned the distillery of the brew but also the year and season of the mash. So, he certainly knew that Meridian Holder's essence would be the most delectable thing he'd ever have on his tongue.

CHAPTER SEVENTEEN

Meridian stepped into the deliciously soft silk dress and stared at her reflection in the mirror. When she'd boarded the private plane that morning, she could never have even fathomed that she'd end up right where she was standing.

She'd been attracted to Jack for years, but she'd always let her irritation that he seemed to have the adoration of the county that her family founded keep her from doing much about it. She'd tried to tempt him to say something to her, to admit he found her equally as attractive, with the photos she'd had one of her cousins-in-law take for her. She also knew that ploy was not only undeniably childish, but it was downright mean. Unable to fully nail down her motivation, she'd buried the photos in a file cabinet and had forgotten about them until today.

Now she had to go out there and convince a bunch of trust fund princesses and bourbon tycoons that she was madly in love with the Dentons' middle son. There was no sure footing on which she could stand. Her only choice was to cling to Jack to keep herself upright, and nothing about that felt particularly sure either.

The only way out was through. Holding the spaghetti straps of the dress to her shoulders, she slipped into the bedroom. "Can you zip me up?" She hated how her voice shook but loved the responding tremor that worked through Jack as he drank her in. Lust shimmered in his eyes. The dress was totally worth it. "Jack?" she urged when he didn't respond.

"Possibly," he finally responded.

Grinning at that, she stepped to him. "I'm glad you like it."

"Like doesn't even begin to cover it." He let his fingertips trail down the bare skin of her back en route to the zipper sitting at the top of her equally bare ass. The dress was too thin for her to wear undergarments. A low growl sounded in her ear. "How the hell do you expect me to get through this dinner knowing that this flimsy scrap of designer silk is all that keeps me from your body?"

"Think of it as foreplay," she teased, enjoying herself now.

"Four years of foreplay, cowgirl. Every time I've ever imagined anything involving your zipper at the office it was moving the other direction." He slowly slid the thin zipper to the top of the dress.

"I didn't know you were attracted to me," she confessed.

"As that would've been wildly inappropriate given our current positions."

She spun to look at him. "After seeing the way you interact with your family, wildly inappropriate seems to be your preference."

"I'll go along with that"—he drew a deep breath—"but as I pointed out earlier, you are lethally dangerous to my career, and self-preservation is hardwired into us all."

"You've been dealing with whiskey barons too long. My uncles are entirely too fair and kind to get rid of you just because we dated and then stopped."

"Are you suggesting that you might like to extend our one-week deal after we return home?"

"No, I'm just pointing out that I have much more to lose than you ever would. The residents of Holder County revere you."

"And why do you think that is, Miss *Holder?*" He placed heavy emphasis on her last name to make his point.

Fine. Maybe he had her there. She supposed it was possible that the town adored him because her family thought so highly of him. "My family knows I'm out here with you. Mama was fine with it. Daddy was grumpy about it, but he's always grumpy about me and anyone with a dick being around each other. All dads are like that."

"The assumption that all fathers care about their kids as much as your father dotes on and cares for you only further proves my point."

"Which is what?"

"That seeing something from a perspective other than our own is exceptionally difficult and often exceptionally uncomfortable." He offered her his arm. "Shall we?"

The intercom wired in from the front gates had buzzed a few times. People were obviously arriving. Whether she was ready or not, it was show time. "Let's get this over with."

"I promise to reward you mightily after this is over."

"I'm holding you to that."

"You can hold me to anything you'd like, cowgirl." He secured her hand in the crook of his arm. The feel of his bicep and the heat of him settled her enough to allow him to guide her back out into the long hallway.

———

———

———

Meridian looked like a seductive green flame as Jack guided her toward the entrance hall. He resisted the urge to construct some kind of cage for her out of his body to keep her from even potentially being emotionally harmed that evening. But for a woman who hated the idea of being protected, he suspected that would go over about as well as trying to convince his father to pay off all of Maggie's daughter's hospital bills anonymously.

Well trained in spying on the inhabitants of River Chase, he slowed their approach when he saw his father's office door open just a crack and heard his mother's frantic whisper. He and Meridian shared an intrigued glance. She used her head to gesture to a nearby nook that probably served some logical purpose at some time, but now only held a massive Lalique vase and floral arrangement.

Listening intently, he heard his mother hiss, "That ring is for Greer. Jackson knows that. I'm telling you there's something odd about this entire situation. He's proposing to her. How did that happen? I refuse to believe this isn't fake just to anger us."

His father sounded bored as always. "To be fair, he rarely calls. Neither of us have spoken to him in months. I suppose it could be true, definitely not as planned though. This complicates everything."

"I've spoken to him. I called his office twice this week."

"To insist that he come to Tiffany's wedding. Maybe she's in trouble. Jack's overblown sense of morality has always made him irrational and reckless."

Meridian's mouth dropped open, and Jack ground his teeth, angry at himself for feeling shocked at anything they said at this point. When would he learn to let nothing that went on at River Chase surprise him?

"I couldn't get anything out of Jackson's secretary," his mother huffed.

Meridian turned her confused glare on Jack. "Mitch," he mouthed but then waved off further question. He'd assure her that he never told his mother that their legal assistant was his secretary after they'd finished eavesdropping on this current conversation.

"I should probably phone her father and apologize for the situation. Maybe create some goodwill. We could arrange to make it all go away. She could take care of that while she's here."

Meridian's fingernails dug deep into Jack's forearm. Damn, that hurt. "He cannot call my father and say that!" For words that held no volume, they were plenty threatening.

"He won't," Jack assured her as he pulled her claws from his arm.

"You just make certain that ring stays in this family and that girl does not," Beverly demanded.

"Jack is still a part of this family." His father didn't sound particularly thrilled by that.

"Perhaps I should've been clearer. You make certain that ring stays with someone who has our family's best interests at heart."

Jack yanked Meridian into a nearby guest room and listened to his parents head toward their party.

"Jack!" she seethed. "Do you have any idea what my father would do if he thought I was pregnant?!"

"Weren't you just the one trying to assure me that your father was level-headed, kind, and calm?"

"Do not throw my words back in my face, Denton. Your parents are insane."

"I am well aware. I'll talk to him after the party, but he's not going to call, not tonight anyway. He'll be too busy trying to impress Katherine Setton."

"Who the hell is Katherine Setton?"

"His mistress."

That took her a few seconds to recover from. "Your father's mistress is coming to a dinner party hosted by your mother?" Shock dripped from each word.

"Of course, but Rich Kline will likely also be in attendance."

She continued to blink at him as if that would make any of the nuances of the evening palatable. "Let me guess," she started.

"My mother is his mistress," he concluded for her.

"The moral fiber of your family—"

"Would leave one freezing on a cold Kentucky night. I'm aware of that as well."

"Also, it's incredibly sexist that there isn't a commonplace word for the man involved in an affair. Mistress is used to describe the woman as if she somehow belongs to the man, but the guy in the relationship just gets away without a title."

"Shall we call Rich her man-stress?"

"Yes. We shall." Oddly, this seemed to soothe a little of her fire.

"Fine. They are both involved in extramarital affairs to secure business acquisitions. That's what I'm trying to tell you. Money is the driving force behind everything they do. He only said what he said to appease my mother. He wouldn't place a call to your father because it wouldn't gain him a dime."

"My parents wouldn't be upset if I was pregnant," she vowed. "They'd be upset that they didn't hear about it from me."

Jack gave her a solemn nod. "I know. Believe me, your family is everything I wish mine would aspire to be, but they never will. I have to play the cards I've been dealt." The image of Meridian pregnant should not have elicited such a primal response from him. He called himself an asshole for good measure. But the internal scolding did nothing to erase the idea from his head—or both of his heads if he were being honest. Did she want to have children? Was that something he even had the right to ask her? Likely not. He was only pretending to be engaged to her and hopefully giving her a week of pleasure. The situation was fraught with confusion and potential pitfalls. He was going to have to watch himself while watching out for her.

CHAPTER EIGHTEEN

Meridian took more comfort in Jack's solid arm around her waist as they stepped into the front hall than she probably should have, but she was exhausted from constantly second-guessing her own feelings and motives. She liked being with him, being beside him, being *his* if only for a little while.

When they got back home, she could throw herself back into both of her jobs and get rid of anything that wasn't going to be reciprocated. She even allowed herself to admire his assuredness as he kept her tucked safely to his side while lifting two cocktails from the tray one of the kitchen staff held.

"Jackson," a man around Jack's father's age gave them a kind grin. "Look at you. How long has it been?" Jack released Meridian only long enough to exchange a handshake.

"Mr. Beaumont, how are you, sir? This is my fiancée, Meridian Holder."

Meridian smiled politely and accepted an inquisitive nod from the man.

"Holder? Holder? Do I know that name? Where are you from, dear?"

"My family owns a cattle ranch in Oklahoma."

Beaumont's entire expression changed. He eyed Jack with some expression Meridian couldn't quite name. Confusion, maybe? Or was that disappointment? "I see. Well, I know your father misses you up here. Can't be a family business without the family, now can it?"

Jack's jaw visibly clenched before he took a quick sip of the cocktail. "There are plenty of Dentons around. I'm not needed, and we're very happy in Oklahoma. I always tell people not to knock it until you've seen a sunrise."

"Oh, well, of course." Beaumont gestured to Meridian. "Cowgirl has to stay on the ranch, right?"

Jack made no effort to hide his obvious annoyance. "Even if Meridian wasn't a part of my life—not something I ever want to have to think about—I'd never leave Oklahoma. It's my home."

For some unfathomable reason, hope expanded like a balloon in Meridian's chest. She couldn't help but grin. Oklahoma might not have wealthy whiskey families rolling in liquid money and a bourbon district, but it had wide open spaces where you could exist without judgment.

Beaumont gave Jack a consolatory pat on his shoulder. "Ah, never say never, son. Blue blood runs deep."

A few other people came up to greet them, and by the fourth conversation of a similar nature, Jack's mouth was drawn in a hard line and restlessness brewed heavy in his eyes. "Want to go get some fresh air?" She gestured to a set of French doors that led to the side of the wraparound porch from what appeared to be the library.

"That won't be far enough away to breathe, but it's a start." They slipped out while Rosalind was opening the front door for more guests.

Meridian guided them to the end of the porch as far away as she could get them from any onlookers.

Jack squeezed his eyes shut before downing the rest of the cocktail. "They're delusional," finally grumbled from him. "They've had me cast as a role in their head since I was born. Any time I've ever done something that didn't match the person they decided I should be, it's obviously just because I'm confused or being led astray." He offered her an apologetic glance as the sun sank low behind the fancy garden sheds. "It couldn't possibly be them. They never even fathomed that maybe

I'm the one that woke up and figured out that this world they keep is nothing more than a house of cards all built on lies. If one card slips, it all falls."

"I'm sorry." Meridian stood steadfastly beside him. "I kind of know what that's like. It kills me that they do this to you."

Jack shook his head. "I appreciate the sentiment, but no you don't. Your family is happy for you to be *you*."

"Sometimes. But I'm a woman. Every single person that I meet immediately places expectations on me. You should try being female in a law school that was predominantly male. Even half of the residents of Holder County have me fitting in a role in their head. They do it to all of my family. Some of them haven't had a conversation with me since I was six, but they're certain they know what I'm all about."

Jack gave her a thoughtful nod. "I guess you do understand." One of the things she found most intoxicating about him was that he listened to her. Really listened to understand not just to make a rebuttal. "Do you have any advice for me then, cowgirl?"

She gave him a mischievous grin. "My personal favorite is to do something shockingly rebellious. I used to do it more than I do now. I was always trying to get people to see me, the real me, by forcing a conversation where I could prove my intelligence and my worth. But... that doesn't always work. I did finally figure out that saying fuck 'em all and doing what makes you happy is the best form of rebellion."

———

———

———

Jack eased the cocktail flute from her hand and set it on the wide porch rail. He wanted—no, he needed—something to replace the Denton whiskey on his tongue. The only thing strong enough to erase the bourbon in his blood was standing before him concerned. She was trying to make him feel better. She'd never known him as Palmer Denton's second son or Barnsley's grandson. He wasn't a whiskey baron prince to her. The knowledge that he was all of those things meant nothing to her at all. He was just him.

"Do what makes me happy, huh?" He caged her between his body and the white brick of the estate house.

Her lips parted as she stared up at him expectantly. Her breaths sped, creating a delicious friction between her breasts and his shirt. His hands grasped her hips and pressed her closer still, close enough to let his cock bathe in the seductive heat gathering between her thighs. A quick gasp escaped her lips. He took it all for himself, capturing it and plundering her mouth.

Meridian's hands wound under his jacket and clawed at his back as an electrical current of need arced between them. Her hips bucked, and the stuttered moan said his cock had hit just the right spot. He allowed her breath and trailed needy bites down her neck. Her instructions to fuck 'em all echoed in his head as he clasped one hand over her right breast. "There is only one person I want to fuck, honey, and it sure as hell isn't anyone inside that house." Her nipple was a tight bead against his palm. The thin silk between them a terrible protector of her obvious arousal. Determination that he would not only protect her desires but also surrender to them surged through his veins.

He stole her next moan as well, letting it feed the starving beast housed in his soul. The beast always fought for what it knew was right, for his brother, for justice, for truth…for her.

It had never before been sated. But a hint of satisfaction filled him every single time she was in his arms. On her next slow grind against him, he clasped his hand on her ass and squeezed. A low, hungry growl worked up from his groin and filled her mouth. Continued proof that she was bare under the dress went to war with his desperation to claim and protect her. It robbed him of any other option than to give in to the reckless desire to mark her as his own and keep her from the vultures that tore at his skin every single time he was home.

He longed to put her back on that ridiculous plane, take her back to Holder Ranch, and live in bed with her exchanging sexual favors for sustenance. God, he wanted to hear her beg for him and only him.

"Jack," slipped from her lips as his hands gripped harder and he began to punish her neck with his lips.

His half-moaned name had him surging against her body again. His cock was so hard he'd ache for hours even after he was finally spent. "That's right, baby. Say it. Tell them all who makes you so wet you drip." He wanted to rent a motherfucking billboard to let the world know he owned every shivered quake, every needy moan, every single clench of her climaxes.

"There," hung on a breath as she rocked against him. "Right there. God...Jack...mmm."

"That's it. Take it from me, honey. Ruin this fucking dress with what I draw from you. I'll clean you up with my tongue." Her breath quivered on a frantic groan. "I should put you on your knees, fuck those beautiful lips until they're so swollen no one doubts what I did to you." A storm of need lit in her eyes at his threat.

He sank his mouth back to hers with greed. Their tongues tangled for dominance that he took or perhaps that she let him have. It didn't matter. The only thing he needed was to be inside of her.

A rather loud clearing of another male throat took several seconds too long for Jack to really hear. It was subverted by the need that currently dominated his mind. Thankfully Meridian was more aware than Jack at the moment, it seemed. Her head jerked back from his and her right leg slipped down his left so she could regain her footing. A lightning bolt of panic crackled through her gaze.

That was all he needed for the protector housed deep in his soul to banish the beast for the moment. Jack turned and physically blocked her from their interlopers with his body. He spoke before he really took in the situation, not something he typically did. "What the hell do you want?"

His father and older brother, Greer, had juxtaposed expressions. His father blinked rapidly as if to make what he'd just seen come into better focus or perhaps to erase it altogether, but a goading grin formed rapidly on his brother's features.

Greer ran his hand over his mouth as if that might wipe away the delight. "Uh,"—he cleared his throat again—"Mom's looking for you and so is Tiffany."

Jack could not think of two women he wanted to see less. "Patience is something both of them could stand to learn."

Meridian stepped around Jack and extended her hand. "I don't believe we've met. I'm Meridian Holder." Her hair was tangled from his grip, and the dress was wrinkled. She strategically kept one arm placed awkwardly across her chest in a failed attempt to erase the arousal from her nipples. Her lips bore marks of his aggression as well, and Jack wished he could find an ounce of shame, but he couldn't.

His father narrowed his eyes at Jack as he accepted Meridian's hand. "My son seems to have forgotten all sense of propriety, but might I remind both of you whose land you are currently standing on."

Meridian's smile faded into annoyance, like a sunset that turns to a vicious storm. "How could we forget?" She gestured to the Denton Distillery logo landscaped in hedges and flowers on the nearby grounds.

Standing up to his father wasn't something many were willing to do. If Jack wasn't extraordinarily careful, he was going to end up falling for her.

"Your mother put a great deal of effort into this event to welcome you home, Jackson. Don't leave your guests waiting."

"We'll join you momentarily," Jack decreed.

This did nothing to appease his father, which Jack saw as a bonus.

Placing his hand on his father's shoulder, Greer guided them back toward the house. "Let's just give them a minute."

CHAPTER NINETEEN

Scalded with irritation and still a little dizzy from having Jack's attention ripped from her palms, Meridian tried to smooth the silk dress and her hair.

"I'm sorry." Jack's fingertips traced along her bare shoulders as he expertly coaxed her into his arms. "Are you all right?"

"Do you think your affections are so intoxicating I can't make a quick recovery, Denton?" She tried to tease but missed the mark.

He gave her an obligatory chuckle anyway. "I can hope, can't I?"

"I suppose we were being rude."

"I hate asking you to play by a rulebook they've created in their minds."

Meridian lifted her head. "I'd say it's a fairly safe bet that Emily Post frowns on what we were doing in the middle of a dinner party. It's not just your parents."

"I like it better when you're not defending them."

Pleased at that, she gestured her head back toward the party. "Let's get this over with."

Jack secured her hand on his arm and guided her inside. A swarm of servants with trays of drinks were still moving between the many rooms of the downstairs that contained guests. However, the guests themselves had all stopped chitchatting. Their words were vacuumed from the air as they tried to discreetly observe Meridian and Jack.

Several people made their way toward them. Fake smiles and disdain-filled eyes swam before her. She tightened her hold on Jack who gently patted the hand he had in the crook of his arm.

"Jackson…" A blonde, dressed impeccably in some kind of designer dress Meridian was certain she'd never heard of, beelined ahead of the approaching partygoers. "Now, you just have to introduce me." She attacked Jack, landing both of her hands on his face so she could plaster his cheek with pink lipstick. "We are all just dying to hear all about…what did you say your name was, honey?"

"I didn't," Meridian sniped, "but I'm Meridian Holder."

Jack was busy scrubbing his cheek with his fingertips. His jaw cocked to the side. "Tiffany, congratulations to both you and Brenton. I'm sure you'll make each other very happy."

Meridian was fairly certain she was the only one aware that he'd just insulted the two of them.

Tiffany's diamond-drop earrings bobbed with the force of her nod. "Brent's just a doll, really. Honestly, Meridian, I do not know how you put up with Jackson. Doesn't he drive you crazy?"

Meridian exchanged a quick glance with Jack. "He does drive me crazy in all of the best ways." *Check.*

Jack played his role perfectly as a cocky smirk formed on his features. He painted a tender kiss on Meridian's cheek. "That's my job, isn't it, sweetheart?" *Checkmate.*

An unmistakable flare of jealousy burned away the false charm Tiffany had obviously worked to maintain in her gaze. She glanced around the room, and in a few quick moves dragged a man, dressed similarly to Jack, back to their forced conversation. "Meridian, this is Brenton Cox, my fiancé."

Brenton gave a hesitant nod to them both. "Jack, how are you?"

"I'm great." Jack extended his hand. "Congrats on the upcoming nuptials."

"Yeah." Brenton didn't sound too confident in the plans for his life. "You too."

It was astonishing to Meridian just how quickly news of their impromptu engagement had spread through the crowd. Jack's mother was quite the gossip.

"I wish you the best of luck." Jack continued to hammer the nail into the coffin, something Meridian rather liked.

"Yeah. I might need it. Hey, you're okay with me and Tiff,"—he paused and gestured to the fuming woman at his side, regarding her like a detonated bomb—"right? No bad blood or whatever?"

Jack laughed at him outright. "None at all, my good man. None at all." He wrapped his arm around Meridian's shoulders and pulled her close. "I wish you only happiness, and I mean that sincerely. I hope you two are as happy as we are."

"Yeah, me too." Brenton didn't sound like he believed that would be the case. Meridian actually felt sorry for them.

When Tiff guided him back to the flock of females in the corner and began whispering heatedly, Meridian laid her head on Jack's shoulder. "So, what's the arrangement there?"

Speaking so only she had any hopes of hearing him, he explained, "Tiffany's parents are Marcus Fitzgerald and Elise Whitney. Their pairing is legendary among the baron families of Bourbon Country. When they married decades ago, their families joined forces. They are now the owners of the lion share of Fitzgerald Whitney, which is one of the largest beverage wholesalers in the US. Brent's family owns an entire network of boutique consulting firms that serve families like mine and Tiff's. They handle high-end PR, advise on investments, tax shields, vacation homes, gardeners, everything. The marriage would mean that the Fitzgerald Whitney family has access to that network for free."

Meridian nodded. "But that isn't nearly as valuable as a marriage merger between a Denton son and the country's largest beverage wholesaler's family. No wonder your parents were so pissed you called off the wedding."

"Since love beyond the love of money is a foreign concept to my parents, it's not really that surprising. Thank you again for putting up with this. It means a lot to me."

Meridian let those words trickle from her ears to her heart, soothing the pricks of intimidation. "You definitely owe me."

He winked at her. "I am but your faithful servant, darling. I'd be remiss if I didn't remind you that I happen to excel in sexual favors."

"I'll keep that in mind."

Two little girls with hair bows larger than their faces zipped by them, heading toward the front porch. They had crayons and coloring books clutched in their hands. Meridian just caught the cover of one of the books as they passed. "Are those seriously...?"

"Denton family coloring books?" Jack filled in for her. "Yep. They started those after my departure. They told themselves that me leaving must've been a result of not properly indoctrinating me in the ways of the bourbon dynasties."

"Wow."

"Welcome to my world."

"I'm really sorry." Meridian turned to stare at him. She wanted him to understand that she genuinely was devastated for him.

"Me too." His attention was diverted almost immediately by two men who were apparently in the middle of some kind of joke when they arrived.

"Jackson, settle a bet between us." His goading tone made Meridian instantly hate him. "About how many cow-tippers would you say you prosecute a week out in wherever the hell you're living now?" They both guffawed as if that was the most hilarious thing anyone had ever said.

Meridian opened her mouth to make a comeback—something along the lines of subtracting the number of women they'd slept with from their IQ resulting in a negative number—but Jack shook his head ever so slightly.

"It really is the ideal job. I spend more time on the golf course than I ever got to working for Denton Distilleries," he informed them.

Oddly, that worked. Their laughter ended abruptly. Meridian was impressed with how Jack handled them. There wasn't a golf course within sixty miles of Holder County, but he'd lied with ease.

One of the men let a low whistle slide between his perfect teeth. "Damn. Maybe we should look into cattle towns. I can't seem to get out of the office here."

"If you'll excuse us." Jack guided Meridian away from Moe and Curly.

"That was impressive," she whispered.

"Nothing more appealing to the obnoxiously wealthy than making money while you do absolutely nothing to contribute to the world."

"I feel like I'm in some very bizarre episode of *The Twilight Zone*."

"It's not likely to get better until after dessert. The men will adjourn downstairs to the billiard room, and the ladies will flock after my mother for drinks in the lounge. Then we can escape both."

"Now, I think I might've somehow fallen into a game of Clue. Should I keep my eyes on all the candlesticks?"

Jack gave her a grin that melted a little of the disdain forming rapidly in her stomach. "In this house, you're far more likely to be killed from the dagger in your back than the candlestick in the drawing room, Miss Scarlet."

Beverly Denton whisked into the room bearing the largest of the fake smiles Meridian had yet witnessed. "Appetizers are being served in the dining room. Everyone find your seat." She made her announcement with a practiced sense of ease, but her eyes betrayed her. Had Meridian not been such an excellent reader of people, she might not have noticed that Jack's mother looked frightened.

CHAPTER TWENTY

The air was thick with cocktail-laced tension as Jack guided Meridian into the dining room. He tried to imagine what it must look like to her. When her extensive family gathered to dine together, they pulled out folding tables and chairs and ate burgers and steak in her mother's backyard. He had no idea what Meridian would do if she compared the honest, eclectic appeal of her ranch to the pretentiousness of his mother's dining room complete with not one but two Queen Anne butterfly extended tables that each sat twenty-four. Jack certainly wouldn't blame her for demanding to go home.

He also hadn't quite figured out his mother's game this evening, and that concerned him more than anything. Was this ridiculous party meant to show him everything he was missing by flouting their money, what he could have if he'd just keep his mouth shut and look the other way on all their wrongdoings? Or was this meant to intimidate him with their prestige and power, as if he'd forgotten it all? Was he to play the role of potential prodigal son, or was he the fatted calf?

His mother had certainly pulled out every stop. The best linens, the silver platters and chafing dishes, and his great-grandmother's Wedgewood graced the tables. He ground his teeth.

His father directed them to take seats near his parents and brother.

His parents' closest friends, J.D. and Ellen Hirsch, took the seats opposite Jack and Meridian. So, he was the fatted calf apparently.

As trays of pickled shrimp cups, mushroom crostini, and bourbon-bacon-wrapped dates with chèvre were passed around, his mother turned her coveted attention on Meridian, meaning everyone at the table looked her way as well. "Meridian, I don't feel like we know anything about you at all, and now you and Jack are getting married. Do you two intend to hold the ceremony here at River Chase or perhaps at the club? That would be most ideal."

Refusing to show even a flicker of doubt, Jack shook his head. "No," they both answered simultaneously.

Meridian grinned at him just the way young lovers would. "We're getting married on my family's ranch. I've always wanted to get married there."

Beverly nodded. "I see. And where did you say you went to school, dear? Jack's never mentioned it."

"I did my undergraduate work at Case Western and got my law degree from Northwestern."

Jack gently placed his arm over the back of Meridian's chair. "She's being modest. She graduated top of her class and received the Global Legal Profession Award for significant contributions to the field of law. Northwestern had no idea what they had on their hands when she arrived and blew every other student out of Lake Michigan."

A subtle note of shock glimmered in Meridian's eyes as she gave him a tender smile—one she'd never given him before, one that held vulnerability at its depths, one he wanted to earn a thousand more of before they went home. Did she really not think he paid attention to the degrees and awards hung behind her desk, to the depths of her intelligence and professionalism? Did she think he somehow missed every perfectly executed case along with every soft sway of her hips and tight purse of her lips?

Jack's father tried to pretend he wasn't impressed. "Well, I'm certain all of those accolades must be beneficial to your family's cows in some way." Before Meridian could skewer him on a cocktail pick, he turned to J.D. "Had any luck with the barrel tagging at your new outfit?"

J.D. wiped the remnant bacon grease from his mouth and grimaced. "We're getting pushback from the older employees. They don't understand the RFID tags any more than they understand that I lose hundreds of dollars in taxes on every missing gallon in a lost barrel."

Jack's father gave a bereaved nod. "We're having similar issues. My employees don't seem to understand that we have six and a half million barrels aged, and I need to know where they are at all times."

"If they like being paid, you do, anyway." J.D. lifted a glass of bourbon punch to Palmer.

Beverly shook her head. "Dear, I'm certain Meridian isn't interested in hearing about our stock issues." The sharp edges of her pointed smile were enough to make Meridian bleed. Jack instinctively pulled her closer. "Just the woes of running a business, of course."

Meridian squared her shoulders against Jack, and he eased back. The woman didn't need his protection no matter how badly he wanted to provide it. She leaned in for the kill. "I can sympathize." She went so far as to pat his mother on the hand. "You should try keeping up with stock that moves of its own accord, not to mention that barrels don't frequently get lost or killed by storms, snakes, and coyotes. As for taxes,"—she took a slight sip of her punch as if she were thoroughly enjoying the conversation—"cattle ranchers pay full sales tax on equipment, feed, medicines, and then pay land tax on every acre. Of course, we are aware that without paying taxes we wouldn't have roads to drive cattle trucks on, fire stations that help with spring burns, schools, police, hospitals—since cattle ranching is a dangerous job—and every other foundation of civilized society. So, I do know a thing or two about running a profitable business that benefits us and the community, Mrs. Denton."

Jack's heart gave a thunderous applause. "I forgot to mention that her undergrad is in business with a specialty in supply chain management. Isn't that right, sweetheart?"

"Well, you know, I wanted to help the family cows," she sneered at his father.

J.D.'s booming laughter filled their end of the dining room. "You should hire her, Palmer. Surely that would get the boy back to Kentucky." He gestured to Jack like he was one of the Wedgewood salad plates—an item to be loaned out as they saw fit. Jack made no effort to hide his eye roll. Perhaps movement would remind all of them that he was a real, live boy who'd cut his own marionette strings.

"Perhaps I should," Palmer spoke between his clenched teeth, and Jack couldn't remember ever having so much fun at River Chase.

"I appreciate the offer"—Meridian seemed to be having almost as much fun as Jack—"but Jack and I both love working together for Holder County."

Jack nodded. "I've never had a job I found more fulfilling, and I'm not just saying that because I get to work with her every day, although that is priceless to me."

J.D. was still chuckling. "Oh, come on, son, everyone can be bought for something. Name your price for you and Meridian coming to work for Denton Distilleries."

Palmer huffed and puffed like the wolf in children's nightmares. "You mind your own whiskey, J.D. It's always been easier for you to spend my money than your own."

J.D.'s eyes sparkled with what appeared to be greed. "I just want to hear the kid's price."

Jack's eyes fell to Meridian. He just needed a hit of her lethal intelligence and her brutal beauty before he turned back to the ugliness of the conversation at hand. "We aren't for sale, Mr. Hirsch."

Ellen came to her husband's rescue. "Bev, how are we with the donations for the art auction? I've narrowed down two of the"—she waved a perfectly manicured hand as if to shoo away a fly—"art auctioneer sites. Although one is entirely too eager if you ask me. I plan to bring it up briefly at the ladies' tea later in the week."

Jack's mother pulled on her best admonishment expression. "I wouldn't do that. We don't want to take away from Tiffany's gathering."

"I suppose you're right. We are running out of time. That was my concern."

"The auction will go off without our having to take away from the bride-to-be. She's been through so much already." She shot a pointed look at Jack. "What is the charity this year?"

"The Getton Gallery, same as last year. It's for their new wing. You know the one they built a few years ago was somewhat unsightly, an oversight by the director apparently."

Bev gave a knowing nod. "Yes, well, I heard the director spent rather a lot of time in Paris last year, so perhaps it would be more prudent for her to stay in Louisville and do her job."

"I heard the same."

Ah, how the wealthy loved their pet charities. A way to appear benevolent to the onlookers while doing nothing but lining their own pockets on the back end. Jack was certain Denton would be paid mightily for supplying the whiskey for the event where the new and unneeded gallery wing was revealed.

As the appetizer courses were whisked away by the staff and bowls of the chef's famous—at least in Kentucky—Greek egg and lemon soup were placed before everyone, Jack's mood improved slightly. It was one of his favorite dishes, but he doubted his parents even knew that.

Meridian was seated close enough to him that he felt her stiffen beside him. Trying not to call any more attention than was already being directed at her, he leaned and brushed a kiss on her cheek which was the perfect cover for his question. "What's wrong?"

She turned to him with a loving smile he refused to put much stock in—she was a decent actress after all—and spoke between her teeth, "Do I eat this or put my hands in it?" Confusion and irritation fought for dominance in her eyes. One always begat the other.

Since there were still several dinner guests rather interested in the two of them, Jack matched her grin. "I love you, too, sweetheart," he stated audibly. That did absolutely nothing to quell the panic in her eyes, but it definitely made it appear that she'd whispered her affections to him and he was responding. He looked down at the soup as if he'd just noticed it was there. "Oh, this is the egg and lemon soup I was telling you about on the flight this morning. I'm so glad you'll get to try it. I'm no good at making it, or I would've fixed it for you before." He downed a hearty bite. "Give it a try," he urged.

She managed a nod and did reach toward her silverware, but she didn't quite get to the spoon. It took quite a bit to shock Meridian. He'd seen her prosecuting cases that would have baffled most. Occasionally, the most shocking things would come out of someone on the stand, and she handled them all like she had ice water running through her veins. But his vow had her wide-eyed and staring at him like he'd just announced his intention to set the table on fire for fun.

He gripped her thigh and gave a gentle nudge trying to wake her out of her stupor. That worked somewhat. She did at least start to eat.

"This is really good soup," she even admitted a few minutes later. "I bet Mama could teach us to make it. She can make everything."

"I'm on board for a Leigh Holder cooking class anytime." Jack meant that sincerely. He loved being around her family anytime they would have him.

His mother's eyes narrowed, and somehow her nose rose even higher in the air. Of all the things that should've irritated her, he wouldn't have thought him learning to prepare soup would be one of them.

The dinner misery and gossip droned on for another two hours. Meridian was constantly fidgeting and smoothing her dress until Jack was concerned she was going to rub the silk thin. As much of a possessive asshole as it made him, the thought of her thighs suddenly being visible to anyone but him had him tipping the glass of iced sweet tea harder than was advisable. He needed the slap of ice to cool him off.

CHAPTER TWENTY-ONE

Certain she was overthinking every single thing, Meridian continued to let Jack telling her that he loved her *too* pummel her mind. There was such confidence in the way he'd said it. Like he said it all the time without any doubt. Not without *thought* but without question. As if he did not only love her, but he knew she felt the same way about him. It was actually genius. No one suspected that she'd been about to dunk her fingers in the soup.

And god, it was really good soup. Ugh. This night, this stupid estate, his insane family...it was all too much. All she really wanted was to climb into her favorite sweatpants and curl up with a new season of *The Great British Baking Show* now. Since that was absolutely not going to be happening, she resigned herself to whatever else was heading her way.

The gentle tense of his bicep as Jack cut a bite of the bourbon pecan pie heightened her awareness of him. The fork slipping between his lips, the flex of his ridiculously perfect jaw, the tender smile he gave her just before wiping his mouth on the linen napkin were all some kind of bizarre pie porno or something. So, maybe sweatpants and British television weren't *all* she wanted. "Are you okay?" he whispered discreetly from behind the napkin.

No. Nope. Definitely not. "Yeah, I'm just a little tired," she lied.

He immediately set down his fork. "We can go."

Clearly, he was also losing his mind because they were still trapped at a table with his parents and half of the population of Louisville. "Not yet," she admonished.

Concern tensed in his dark brown eyes. He gave her a hesitant nod. "Just say the word and we'll go upstairs."

It was actually kind of sweet that he was so willing to whisk her away, but she was a little tired of all the gawking and whispers. If they left, all of these people wouldn't bother to whisper anymore. They'd just say whatever it was they were thinking outright. She might not really care what they thought, but she wasn't going to make being bitchy easier for them.

The heated suspicion that she was being stared at crawled up her back. Meridian turned to try to catch someone in the act. Instead, she was the first witness to Tiffany's frantic head shake and her shoving back from the table. "What?!" gasped from her as she turned to face the woman who had to be her mother. "How could you?" Taking to her designer heels, she whisked away. As the room fell silent, the click of her heels announced her speeding up as she moved through the entry hall. The slam of the oak front door shook the rest of the house.

The quake seemed to shake Brenton into action. "Tiff?" He raced after her.

Everyone sat in stunned silence. All eyes turned toward Tiffany's family. Her mother waved it off like it was no big thing. "Just wedding nerves," she assured.

Meridian's eyes met Jack's. "That wasn't nerves," he whispered.

"Do you think he's cheating on her?" It was the only thing Meridian could think of that might've elicited that reaction.

"I doubt that, but I certainly don't know."

Before Meridian could contemplate further, his mother grasped his hand. "I think you should go check on her."

Jack's face contorted into irritated confusion. "Why? It has nothing to do with me."

"I think it might," Beverly insisted.

Meridian recognized Jack preparing to go into full legal battle, with irrefutable evidence, as to why he had nothing to do with whatever was up with Tiffany. But he didn't get the chance. Brent returned and headed directly toward Jack. He shot a nervous glance around the room before leaning between Jack and Meridian. "Tiff wants to know if she can talk to you."

———

———

———

Jack's mind scrambled. None of his past experiences had given him any training in how to handle his ex-fiancée requesting to talk with him a few days before her wedding to another man.

Offering Meridian a nervous glance, he tossed his napkin down in his plate. "Do you mind coming outside with me?"

"Not at all." Meridian folded her napkin, stood, and took Jack's hand. He couldn't help but make comparisons. Going to talk to an ex would've had Tiffany threatening to tell her father about Jack's behavior. Meridian did not seem intimidated at all.

He reminded himself that of course she wouldn't be. They weren't a real couple. Nothing about this was a reality. If only he didn't long for it to be his reality more with each passing moment, he would've been able to handle Tiffany with a lot more ease.

Following after Brent, he guided Meridian out of the dining room. Every single eye in the room trailed their footsteps. When they were out of earshot, he caught up to Brenton. "What is this about? I haven't spoken to Tiffany in years."

Brent stopped short and turned around. "My sister let it slip that the Fitzgeralds are divorcing. Tiff's completely freaking out."

Meridian's cringe echoed Jack's internal one. That was why a marriage to Brent was so important. They needed access to a legendary PR spin to avoid their stocks bottoming out. A tug of empathy pulled on Jack's heartstrings. He felt sorry for both of them. The children of the barons were nothing more than game pieces moved at will of the markets and the whims of their parents.

Tiffany had always been the ideal pawn. She always did whatever her parents wanted without question. That was part of what Jack came to despise about her. She had no thoughts of her own. Until that moment, someone running out on a dinner party would've been all she gossiped about for weeks on end. Until it was her. Until it was your own world shattering around you. Until every grain of sand slipped through your fingers. Until every string unraveled. Then running was the only choice. He'd been there. He knew.

He still wasn't certain what her parents ending their marriage had to do with him, but he supposed he was about to find out. They were heading toward the ivy-walled center of the award-winning Denton garden. Following Brenton under the lavender trellis, Jack tried to draw a deep breath. Tiffany had a well-known and well-proven temper.

Instead of righteous indignation, he was met with a woman shaking with tears. Her hands trembled. Brent rushed toward her, but she waved him off.

Turning her tear-stained eyes on Jack, she drew a shaky breath. "Why did you...call off our wedding?" Her voice fractured on what he suspected was the truth he was certain she was not prepared to hear.

It would only crush her further, so he flipped through the largest reasons—*I didn't love you. I refused to be a pawn for my parents anymore. I can barely stand to be around you*—and scrubbed his hand through his hair instead. "We...would've been a disaster together." There. That was another truth.

She gave him a shuddered nod. "Okay. Then, why did you propose?" Another round of tears threatened her eyes.

Jack looked helplessly at Meridian. He didn't know what to say. Surely Tiffany did not really want the real answer to that. Meridian squeezed his hand. "She deserves to know the truth. Her whole world was built on lies," she whispered.

Tugging at his tie, he went on with it. "It, uh, was what I was"—he cringed—"instructed to do."

To his shock, a hint of relief dried a few of her tears. She turned on Brenton. "What about you? Why did you propose?"

Brent bought himself a few seconds by clearing his throat. "I think you're beautiful, and smart and sweet."

Tiffany managed to roll her swollen eyes. "At least he told the truth." She threw a manicured hand toward Jack. With that, she whisked from the walled garden.

"But I am telling the truth," Brent called after her.

They all followed her out. She took off at a run. Jack knew better than to chase her. His family had chased him, and it had only made him run farther faster.

"What do I do now?" Brent demanded.

Meridian answered before Jack could think of any advice. "Let her go. I'm sorry. I get that you really might be in love with her, but she has the right to figure this all out on her own."

"Do you really love her?" Jack asked. "Or did your family jump at the chance to have a tie to Fitzgerald Whitney Distributions?"

The weight of the truth hung Brenton's head for a few breaths, but he snapped it back up to stare Jack down. "Both. It's both."

"Then give her some time. Maybe you two can find something good to hold onto in all of this."

"I don't even have a ride," Brent whined.

Meridian and Jack both rolled their eyes. Jack slapped him on the shoulder. "Can't help you there. I was flown here." He grabbed Meridian's hand as she started back toward the house. "Come with me," he begged.

She spun back. "Where are we going?"

"Anywhere but back inside there."

And there it was—that genuine, dazzling grin that accompanied her nod. "Sure."

Brent backtracked to them. "Can I say something before you two go?"

"Sure," Jack agreed.

"You need to get her out of here."

Jack had been expecting a threat to stay away from Tiffany, something he would've gladly complied with, but he was dumbfounded with Brent's demand.

Meridian edged closer. "Why do you say that?"

Shaking his head and gesturing to the vast lawns and buildings around them, he said, "I don't know. Maybe it's this place. I mean, look at what they did to your brother. And to you," he added suddenly. "I used to be so jealous of you, especially after your engagement to Tiffany Fitzgerald was announced. It made me furious that you never seemed like you cared about her. I would've treated her better."

"I know you would've," Jack assured him.

Brent's head lifted. "But now that I see the way you look at her,"—he nodded to Meridian—"I get it."

"You get what?" Meridian urged.

"The way you're supposed to look at the woman you love. I don't know if even I look at Tiff the same way you look at her. So, maybe you should just get her out of here now. Maybe it's River Chase. Maybe...it's all of our parents. I don't know."

Still processing every word Brent had said, Jack prompted, "What don't you know?"

"Don't let them ruin what you have. They seem to ruin everything good. Everyone's furious that she's here anyway. I don't see how you two are going to be able to get away unscathed."

CHAPTER TWENTY-TWO

Meridian refused to outwardly display any of the three-tailed tornado of emotions that whipped through her. Her hand was still clasped safely in Jack's as he walked her farther and farther away from the estate house. He said nothing, so she remained silent as well.

Moonlight filtered through the maple tree branches casting an otherworldly glow on the path as they walked. She had no idea where they were going, and nothing frightened her more than the fact that she was willing to follow him anywhere without question.

She barely recognized this version of herself, and yet she walked on. Jack halted abruptly. "Do you want me to carry you?"

"What?" Of all the things she expected him to say, that was not one of them.

"We're only halfway there, and you're in heels."

"Is it grass for the rest of the way?"

Jack nodded, and Meridian promptly kicked off her heels, gathered them in her hands, and forced a slight grin. "I'll be fine."

"I won't let them hurt you," spilled from his lips in a fervent vow.

"I'm not scared of them." As far as she was able to discern her own thoughts, that was true.

"You should be." They walked on another few paces. "Brent was right."

Now they were getting somewhere. "About which part?"

Jack's jaw flexed visibly. For the first time in her life, Meridian waited patiently for an answer. Finally, he stared directly at the ground and informed the grass that, "I'm putting you at risk having you here."

Meridian reached and grasped his chin. She lifted his gaze back to hers. "Don't lie to me."

"That's rich," he countered.

"What the hell is that supposed to mean?"

"Why did you draw up a continuance on the Marsden case? What are hiding from me? What's going on with the mustangs that has you making—pardon me for saying this—incredibly stupid decisions that could impact your entire family's way of life? Why did you insist on coming here with me?"

Fury ricocheted through Meridian's mind. Dammit. "How dare you?" She tried to sound threatening, but he'd hit much too close to her worst nightmares.

"Spare me the courtroom diva routine. You want me to tell you the truth, fine, but I'd appreciate the same from you. Every single thing Brent said is true. There, I said it. I've never cared about anyone the way I care about you. And...that scares me."

Shock staggered through Meridian, making her physically sway. Words spilled thoughtlessly from her mouth. She had no option to halt their progress. "Four of the mustangs are pregnant and that wasn't on the record sent to us when they arrived from the state." She gnawed the inside of her mouth for a split second but that did nothing to stop the confessions. "Best-case scenario for my family is that they weren't registered as being pregnant, that someone in the state made a mistake, but that's the worst case for the horses because when that happens the state might take the foals before they're really ready. The state legislature wants to end the mustang program and kill the horses because of the cost. Worst case for us, one of our studs got into their pasture, and then we're really, really screwed because that is never supposed to happen. We could lose a tremendous amount in fines. We could lose the horses altogether. I need to keep the inspectors off of the ranch until the babies are born and we figure out what happened. That's why I filed the continuance."

Jack reached for her hand again, but she pulled away.

"I'm not finished. I told myself I wanted to come with you so that I wouldn't feel badly when I took the case from you. I told myself that this made everything fair, but I was lying."

Jack gave her a solemn nod. "Then why did you really want to come here with me?"

Momentarily certain she was having an out-of-body experience, she went on with the final truth. "I wanted to spend the week with you." Her eyes squeezed shut as if she couldn't be in the physical presence of her own vulnerability. "I wanted to know why you make me question every single thing I've ever believed, everything I've worked so hard for...everything I've ever wanted."

She was so dedicated to the act of keeping her eyes shut that Jack was able to sweep her off of her feet and into his arms. Her eyes sprung open. "What are you doing?"

"Carrying you."

"Put me down!"

"No."

"Jack. What the hell?"

"Every question you just asked I also have. Let's go figure out the answers together. Then we'll figure out what to do about the horses. I will not let your family lose anything at all. I will never let anything or anyone hurt you."

"I don't need your..." he cut the word *help* from her lips with his own. The kiss was the perfect combination of demanding authority and soft bourbon-warmed lips moving in time with hers. She opened her mouth readily, allowing him in. Her skin pulsed and her pussy begged for the strokes of his tongue against her. Her nipples gave throbbing demands for his attention. His low groan vibrated her soul. She wanted to feel every one of those sounds he made.

Drugged from his all-consuming kiss and the feeling that she was being whisked away from every problem they were leaving in their wake, Meridian let herself enjoy this. She tucked her head against his chest. Maybe having someone to rely on outside of her family wouldn't be so terrible, but he wasn't the only one that was scared of what they were doing.

Caught up in this world that was all Jack, where he stood between her and every other thing, she wasn't certain what was happening until he stood her on the grass before a stone front porch of a small cottage. She pulled her heels back on and looked around. They'd traveled so far on Denton property that she could no longer see either the immaculate gardens or the estate house.

"Where are we?" She spun on the porch trying to get her bearings.

With the same assuredness that Meridian was growing addicted to, Jack turned the doorknob. "This is one of the guesthouses. The stables are over there. I was going to take you to see the horses, but I'm just not that patient."

Her heart jolted and then broke out in wild applause at all of the delicious things that could be accomplished in an empty guesthouse. Jack turned the knob slightly to the right, pressed down with his full weight, then jerked it back left. Much to Meridian's relief, it sprang open.

He gave her one of those incredibly cocky smirks and gestured inside. "Shall we?"

Matching his smirk with one of her own, she took his hand and feigned confusion. "Shall we what?" She raced inside the home.

Jack kicked the door shut, pulled her back to him, and spun to pin her between the door and his body. "As it turns out, I didn't get to finish my dessert."

"Poor baby," she teased.

"I'll be fine," he assured her. "I'm about to make a feast out of you."

"That a promise?"

"I'm going to have to fill that smart mouth with my cock and see if I can't get you to hush long enough to hear me out."

A low grunt met her hungry whimper as he filled her mouth with his tongue and his bourbon-laced heat. She'd never wanted to get drunk on anything so much in her entire life. She pulled his tongue fully into her mouth and gave gentle sucks.

When he finally allowed her breath, she cooed, "I assure you if I was giving you a blow job, you sure as hell wouldn't be doing anything but begging me for more."

"That a promise?" His capable hands worked the silk of the dress up her legs. He bunched it in his fists just above the mound of her pussy. A desperate shudder worked through him, drawing another moan from her. "So fucking beautiful. My god," he growled.

His palm skimmed over the swollen, tender skin, making her quake. His fingertips continued to trail up her tightly clenched stomach, teasing her with the silk as he worked, making her feel like she was a gift he was slowly revealing, savoring, reveling in. A priceless piece of art behind a velvet curtain. Slowly, his hands climbed to her breasts until he lowered the zipper just enough to lift the dress over her head and toss it on the floor. She was the reward of a magician's final, stunning act, left in nothing but her strappy black heels.

Uninhibited carnality ignited in his eyes. "Let's see you make good on that promise, cowgirl." He had his belt undone and the slide on his slacks open in record time. "You're going to have to take me deep, honey, and suck nice and hard to scramble my mind enough that I can't talk law."

Distantly aware that he'd just tapped into her inherent competitive nature to get himself a blow job, Meridian should've called him on it, and yet once again she just didn't care. She wanted his length in her mouth, wanted to make him melt under the persuasion of her tongue. And if she searched in that distant, recessed space of her mind, she knew she'd find that what she wanted was to give him this.

With quick, adept fingers, she worked through the buttons on his shirt, parting it over the chiseled planes of his chest. Desperate to feel the hot burn of his skin against her palms, she let herself explore. His eyes closed and his mouth clenched tight.

"You're not the only one with office fantasies, you know?" The words lit from her lips in a breathy mewl that spoke of her desperate need far more than the words themselves had allowed.

"Show me, honey. Show me what you'd do if I had you on your knees at my desk. Put your hands on me. I promise I'll reward you. I'll fuck you so hard you won't ride a horse for a week."

A harsh gasp wrenched from Meridian's lungs as the world around them continued to spin. Nothing was familiar here. She was standing in the entryway of a home she'd never been in and hadn't even seen the rest of.

When you stand in an unknown landscape, a foreigner in a foreign land, the only knowns are the truths you carried with you. The truth was she'd wanted Jack Denton since she'd first met him, and she just wasn't strong enough to deny him anything at all.

Teasing her thumb back and forth along the silk band of his boxers, she stared him down and licked her lips. His fists clenched on either side of her head. "We're calling Mitch and having the continuance withdrawn," ground from his mouth in raw challenge.

"No, we're not." She dipped her fingers beneath the elastic and circled his head, drawing a strangled curse from him. Now they were getting somewhere. His erection was every bit as long and thick as it had felt grinding against her, and yet it was somehow twice as hard as she'd imagined.

Another round of need pooled between her legs. She had no idea how long she'd be able to go before she did beg him to fill her so full nothing else mattered.

CHAPTER TWENTY-THREE

Jack's thighs tensed as he arched up with a groan, forcing more of his cock into her hands. He was so fucking gratified to finally have her touching him he swore he almost would've settled for a hand job just to be with her like this.

But he was incapable of not feeling the selfish desperation he always felt around her. Still, he had to keep it together long enough to get her to listen. Her refusal to admit that she might need to look at things from another perspective had her making grave mistakes. He wouldn't let that happen ever again.

Forcing more words from his already addled mind, he used the breath trapped in his lungs to elaborate. "The inspectors need to come now, and you need to tell them that you received four unregistered pregnant mares."

She tightened her hand around him and gave him a gentle tug. A frantic shudder shot through him as a tidal wave of hot cum sought her touch. She spun her tongue against his collar bone before she rasped, "And what happens if the foals look like one of our studs? They'll notice that next year when they come to inspect."

Jack had engaged in this bet knowing he would lose happily. He just hadn't quite guessed how quickly his loss would come or how fucking much it would feel like a win. She kissed her way down his midsection as she sank slowly to her knees. He ground his teeth and forced out one more point before he gave himself over to the persuasion of her lush mouth. "When they're born, issue an apology to the state and immediately return the money for the foals."

Staring up at him through her dark eyelashes, she slowly spun her tongue around his head and then she sat back, leaving a cool breath over the wet lash. "This is why whiskey barons should never be cattle ranchers," she informed him. Before he could even contemplate a response, she was cleaning the pearlescent drop of precum from him and he was thrusting at her lips, shamefully desperate for more of her mouth.

Keeping himself upright with one hand against the door, he laced the other in her hair. Taking control with her was yet another gamble, but this one he was certain he would win. As he cinched his fist tighter, her moans spoke volumes. "That's it, honey. Let me hear you. How else will I know for certain that what you want is for me to take control? Now, suck me."

Her hands slid up to the waistband of his trousers and boxers. She yanked them lower. His cock swelled to the point of abject pain. She dug her nails into his ass and finally, mercifully let her tongue dance up and down the thick bulging veins begging for her mouth.

"Suck," hissed from him as he gave up focusing on anything but how good she looked naked on her knees and how intoxicating the velvet heat of her mouth was going to be.

She complied now, giving up any pretense of not liking to be told what to do. She slowly let him breach her lips as she began to bathe and suck in rhythm. Her right hand fastened to his base and moved in accordance with her pulling mouth. And Jack was done for.

All hopes of the point he'd needed to make were gone. She was too good, too skilled, that mouth far too lethal for him to have a shred of hope. He just didn't care anymore.

Without giving himself explicit permission, his hips made a hesitant thrust, and she swallowed around him like a pro. The pressure built with every expert pull of her mouth and her hand until his head fell back in ecstasy.

But in that moment, as he took his eyes off of her, a thousand uncomfortable realizations hit him all at once. How many times had this happened to him on his family's land? How many women had he touched here, not like an exploration but like a transaction? And dammit, how many times had he sworn to himself that he would never be that man again?

He took a step back and gently released her hair. Confusion fought for outrage in her eyes.

"It can't be like this," he whispered as he leaned low and lifted her off of the ground again. "Not like this," he reiterated, more for himself than her.

"What are you talking about?"

"I need you to hear me out, and then I need to take care of you, not the other way around." Frustration overtook the other emotions evident on her features. "Don't worry, baby. I still know exactly what you want, what you like, and how hard you need to be fucked. I'm just not going to come down your throat before I've filled your pussy full of me. I need to see you come undone for me before I allow myself that pleasure. That's all I'm negotiating for here."

When her rushed breaths eased a moment later, she rolled her eyes and grinned. "I guess Miss Scarlet should get to come first." Always a step quicker than him, it took Jack a split second to recall their conversation before dinner about Clue.

"Precisely. But I don't want to be Colonel Mustard. It's easily the most useless of condiments."

"You get to be Mr. Boddy," she informed him with another quick kiss on his neck as he whisked them back to the master bedroom.

"Because you like my body or because you're going to do me in? I'm fine with either answer, honestly."

A delighted laugh spilled from her. "Guess you'll have to wait and see."

Using his shoulder to hit the light in the master bedroom, far more quaint and simple than anything in the estate house, he managed her with one arm and threw back the down cover before he laid her out on the pure white sheets.

His patience was immediately rewarded by the stunning visual display of sensual helplessness, of her needy and wet, staring back at him as he stood over her.

His mouth went dry, and his palms itched to touch her again, to satisfy the longing in her eyes and the hollow ache he knew she felt between her legs. With a sensuous smirk, she sat back up. "As long as we're negotiating could we do the 'me hearing you out' part later?"

He cradled her face in his hands, unable to keep from touching her flushed skin. "Like I could ever really tell you no."

She liked that; he could tell. "Good. I hate being told no."

"So I've noticed."

"Take your clothes off, Mr. Boddy."

"Anything you want, Miss Scarlet."

Thankful for the early morning hours he normally spent jogging around the Holder County square—once a man runs it's difficult to determine when it's safe to stop—he stepped out of his brown leather derbies, a relic from his former life. He made quick work of tossing his shirt and slacks to the floor. But he paused before climbing over her, giving his ego a second or maybe three to appreciate the whiskey fire ignited in her eyes as it licked at his skin.

Before he could tease her about her obvious approval, her hand snaked up his chest and then teased back down to his cock. His eyes closed as her fingers explored.

"I want to hear more about your inappropriate workplace fantasies, District Attorney," she cooed.

Unable to keep the truth from her, his soul as naked as his body, he grunted. "That leather skirt you wear all the time..." A moan choked back the next words. She backed off with her hand. To prevent that trick from happening again, he wrapped his fist around hers. "I shove it up over your fucking gorgeous ass, lean you over my desk, and fuck you until you're too weak to stand. Too weak to do anything but let me hold you until you're begging me to do it again. Every single person who comes in that courthouse can hear what I'm doing to you. They know who you belong to, know who you beg for."

A breathy moan preceded her wiggling in the bed, trying to create her own friction, trying to do his job for him, to rob him of the pleasure. He refused to allow that. "Does that make you wetter, baby?

Make you ache?" He tipped her chin up until she had nowhere to look but deep into his eyes. "I'm a selfish lover. I need you to understand that. I tried to tell you. I try to fight it, but it's in me. It's who I am. I want it all. Every time you're wet and needy, you come to me. I make it better. Me and only me."

"Fuck, Jack," came out in a desperate mewl. "What are you doing to me?" She was sitting on her knees now and grinding against her own heels.

"Giving you what you want. There's nothing wrong with begging when you know I'm the only one selfish enough to satisfy you because that is the only thing I want. Lie back, honey, let me taste what I do to you."

CHAPTER TWENTY-FOUR

The few seconds it took Meridian to untangle her legs and lie back on the cool sheets were more than her patience was willing to give. She was soaked. Her nipples were drawn to stiff, aching peaks. Her hips swayed involuntarily, and she just couldn't bring herself to care.

"Now," whimpered from her mouth.

A low, conquering growl groaned from him. He gripped her ankles and brushed teasing kisses on her inner thighs. Instead of him heading right where she so desperately needed his attention, he ascended her body, spinning his tongue between her hip bones, teasing at her navel, licking the underswells of her breasts. Making circular worship patterns around her nipples before he finally sucked one and then the other.

"Perfect mouthful," he complimented.

Her restless hips attempted to lure him back to the lips of her pussy.

"You're going to have to be still," he informed her with enough bravado that she immediately challenged him.

"And if I don't?"

The darkness that he fought and she craved shadowed his eyes again. "Be careful, sweetheart." His throaty warning only made her press him harder.

"You don't scare me."

"I should." He brushed kisses at the corners of her thighs and pussy. His eyes closed in what appeared to be pure ecstasy as he spun his tongue there and inhaled deep like she was a bottle of priceless reserve somehow made specifically for him.

"Why?" She clawed at the sheets under her, desperate for his affections just a little lower.

"I'm not a nice guy. I'll punish you." He spoke that particular warning at the top of her slit as he feathered more kisses there. "And you'll like it."

Her heart pounded out a beat she didn't even recognize as her own. Her hips moved in rhythm both because she'd been told not to move and because remaining still was beyond her ability.

In response, she was punished. He dipped two fingers in her deep and fast. He was only partially wrong. She didn't just like it, she loved it. She craved it. "Yes," she urged.

Proving his prowess, he continued to fuck her hard and filthy with his hand while lazily brushing kisses around her clit. No other man had ever seemed to understand the juxtaposing sides of Meridian. That she wanted to be owned while simultaneously being cared for. His tongue teased at her clit now, never making direct contact. Clit-adjacent attention had always, always been her undoing, and this was the first time a man had gifted her with her most coveted of desires. All others saw the bundle of nerves as a means to an end. Press button, activate orgasm, then get to the part they wanted. Only Jack seemed to understand that the reward was there hidden in plain sight, and he was willing to work for it.

She soaked his chin as almost inhuman mewls of thanks poured from her mouth.

He lifted his head and met her eyes as she stared down at him. "Do you want to come on my mouth, princess?"

Losing all sense of herself in the pounding thrum of his fingers, she did something she'd sworn she would never do. "Please, please," groaned from her, loud and desperate.

"That's it. Let me hear you beg."

He returned his mouth to her clit and increased the pressure of his tongue but still held back from making direct contact. She bucked in his face. He pounded his fingers harder and faster.

The sensations overwhelmed her. Her hands abandoned the anchor of the sheets. She needed something stronger, something steadier, something more certain to cling to. Her fingers threaded through his hair, and her thighs tightened against his chin.

Her breaths disintegrated into frantic gasps, like porcelain thrown against stone. The pressure he built forced sobbed pleas from her. The world turned to a dizzying fray where nothing made sense, nothing but the way he played her like an instrument only he understood.

"Jack," shuddered from her.

"Let it come for me, baby. I've got you." With that, he fastened his suckling lips to her clit, and she fell apart in a riptide of ecstasy on his tongue.

CHAPTER TWENTY-FIVE

With every drop of Meridian that he devoured, Jack swore she was some kind of heavenly tonic that healed the wounds stabbed brutally through his soul. She tasted like heaven spiced with a dose of hell. She was a blend far grander than any single-barrel would ever produce. She was perfection.

She seemed to come back to earth in small degrees. That was fine by him. Quickly locating his discarded trousers and fishing the condom from his wallet, he tossed it on the bed and climbed beside her. She curled up in his arms and let him revel in her and in what they'd just shared. "That was incredible," he whispered into her mussed hair, now a wild auburn mane splayed over the white sheets.

"Yeah," she lifted her head, "it was." Shock whispered through the words. "How did you know..." Her head lowered again.

Cradling her face again, he brought it back up. "How did I know what?"

Determination tensed in her features for a split second. "That I would like that?"

"You have dominated my attention since the moment we met. I have been so fascinated by you I'm surprised I've accomplished anything at all. I've paid attention to your every reaction. Having you in my arms only heightened my awareness. Every moan, every breath, every quiver of your beautiful body, I pay attention. I always will." Sinking his lips back to hers, he took more. He wanted her to taste herself on his lips, to taste how good they were together.

If he was going to ultimately end up losing everything he'd worked so hard for, he wanted to own her pleasure. It was the only reward worthy of the sacrifice. Needy for her vulnerability, he climbed over her and settled the weight of his erection against the tender wet curls of her mound.

More responsive than any woman he'd ever been with, she bucked against him. A quick shiver shot through her body as he cradled her closer still. "Tell me what you want," he urged as he slid his cock back and forth against the wet heat. His body was primed and desperate to take her deep and hard, but nothing worth having came easily. When she opened those intoxicating eyes to stare at him, he faltered. Tender vulnerability was awash in the whiskey. It wasn't something Meridian let anyone see, and yet she was showing him. "Anything you want, just tell me."

"Hold me down," gasped from the tight trap of her lips, "and fuck me."

"You read my mind," he informed her on a low growl. Making quick work of the condom, he wove their fingers together, pressed the backs of her hands into the mattress, and let her feel his weight over her.

Slowly, relishing every centimeter of the heavenly velvet of her, he pressed himself inside. With every deliberate, rhythmic thrust, he sought to get deeper. Everything he'd ever understood about the way his world worked spun away from his mind. The only thing that mattered was more of her.

Her delectable little body drew tighter with each pass. It was a licentious paradise, the most divine torture. He groaned out her name like he'd just learned the secret prayer that would save him from the sins born into him, the ones he had no chance of outrunning.

She was the answer to his every supplication, the home he'd longed for but had never found. Near constant moans of pure need spilled from her lips.

"Look at me," he whispered. Her eyes blinked open. "So fucking beautiful,"—he pressed in to his hilt and watched as his body teased at her clit with his grind—"I want more. I want you to be mine."

"I am," she vowed reverently.

That wasn't exactly what he'd wanted to say. He wanted to tell her that he'd loved her for years. He wanted to sigh it into her skin, to stitch an impenetrable barrier around her heart that he would guard with his life. He did have just enough sense left in him to know that professing love in the middle of sex was likely to be taken wrong, and everything about this was too good to besmirch.

He was certain he would eventually do something to mess this up, but he refused to let it be that night.

Clasping both of her hands in one of his, he took his other palm and pressed it just above where his cock was spreading her wide. "Yes," mewled from her. "Oh, mmm, I'm gonna...mmm."

Her warning was tangled with unintelligible moans. Sexiest, most satisfying thing he'd ever heard. His pulse hammered out an SOS. Hot cum blazed to the place where they were joined tight. Not yet. Not fucking yet. He clenched his jaw as if that would hold back the need to drill himself so deep into her she'd never be rid of him.

"Not until you beg me for it," he informed her. He backed off with his palm, and she bucked harder searching for it again.

"Please," she whimpered restlessly. "Please, I need you."

Those three words shredded through him. They took him down to the very fibers of who he was and discarded every piece that had been surreptitiously implanted in him by his family. She was the only thing that mattered, and he would rebuild himself, replace the brokenness, to hold her. If he had to, he would rebuild his entire life again for her.

"I've got you," he assured her as he gave himself over to the divine agony. Her body rhythmically milked his cock. Her shoulders dug back into the mattress as she reached for more of his length. He pounded harder and pressed against her with his hand.

She broke loose on a tensed groan of his name, and he followed her down the spiral of bliss from which he was beyond certain they would never be able to return unchanged.

He collapsed against her as hot spurts of cum filled the condom and blurred his vision. In the haze, he imagined what a life devoted to her might look like and how he could go about getting it.

———

———

———

Emotion clogged Meridian's throat as she floated back down to reality —to Jack's arms specifically—slowly. She hated to cry and refused to give in to the bizarre tears that threatened her eyes now. What was wrong with her? She'd just had life-altering sex with a man she'd lusted after for years. Beyond satisfied was the only allowable emotion after something like that.

She was just with it enough to realize that the answer was in the question. Cuddling closer into his arms and burying her face in the warmth of his chest, she tried to hide away from the knowledge of which parts of her life had been altered.

"I'll be right back," he whispered in her hair.

She didn't want him to leave. It frightened her, and she'd prided herself since she was a little girl on never being afraid. Anger was a far more useful emotion than fear, and it was often her preference, but she could locate no fury in her body. There was only longing for him to return.

He flipped off the lights as soon as he'd disposed of the condom and cleaned up. Climbing back beside her, he folded her into his arms as she took stock of her body. She was limp and sated. She was both anxious and exhausted.

"Are you okay, sweetheart?" Concern thrummed in the whiskey smoke of his voice, still deep and rugged from their passion.

"I don't think so." The fear prevented her from lying. She needed to both acquire and provide the truth in order to assuage the overwhelming anxiety threatening to eat her alive.

"Me either," he spoke the words that allowed her to draw a full breath. "Want to talk about why we're not okay?"

She tried to swallow around the lump of confusion so she could speak. It only worked semi-successfully. "Everything is different. I...don't know what to do with that."

"Not everything, right?" he soothed. "I've been wildly attracted to you for years. Nothing about that has changed other than I'm even more attracted now. You won't know what to do with me. I'll be relentless."

His cocky apology made her grin despite her fear. "Then why are you not okay?"

"You are still extremely dangerous to the life I've built, and yet I have no desire to end this in a week, or...longer even."

She stroked her hand over the light smattering of hair on his chest. His honesty emboldened her own. "I have never given up on my goals for anyone. I've never even changed them. I never had to, which I know is ridiculously spoiled of me, but it's true. Nothing ever mattered more to me than being the best at what I do. And now..."

He lifted his head to stare down at her. The moonlight shimmered in his eyes. "I don't want you to change for me or anyone else. I'd never want you to give up on your goals. If you want to be DA...I'll try to figure out a way to make that happen."

Meridian slid to her side and propped up on her elbow. "That's what I'm saying. I don't know if I want that to happen, and...that scares me. But if we kept seeing each other back home I can't ever be DA. Not with the way our county works. They'd prefer to elect road-kill than a woman they think slept her way into getting you to not run against me."

He sank his lips to her forehead in a lingering kiss. "We don't have to figure anything out tonight, but I won't let you give up anything for our relationship. I don't deserve that."

Weary of hearing that from him, she went on with the truth. "You know you're a really good guy. I still haven't figured out why you think otherwise."

CHAPTER TWENTY-SIX

Jack considered her question and chanced turning the tables. "You get frustrated and angry at yourself when you don't know things or understand them fully. You hold yourself accountable for the things you're certain you should know even though there's no reason for you to know them. You rely so much on yourself that sometimes you miss the help that's right in front of you. We all do that to some degree. Maybe that's why I'm convinced that I don't deserve you. I've always thought that if I could've just figured out, or somehow sensed, the backroom dealings and hidden money that flows my parents' way that I could've saved them from themselves. If I'd just seen what was coming for Finn, I could've saved him too."

It was so unlike Meridian not to argue, Jack was shocked when she gave him a solemn nod. "I just don't ever want to be wrong. What if me being wrong costs someone something?"

Jack hugged her closer. "Welcome to my whole world. Me being wrong cost people everything. That's why I'm certain I'm not a good guy, but I'd be lying if I didn't say it thrills me that you think I am."

She lifted her head and gave him a sweet grin. "Maybe we should both be nicer to ourselves and to each other."

"I need to make a confession before you decide you should be nicer to me." Guilt had ridden him hard most of the day, and after what they'd just shared, he had to tell her.

Skepticism furrowed her brow. That was a look he was far more accustomed to than her solemn nods and sweet grins. "What did you do that you think is so bad?"

He went on with what might be the end of this fledgling relationship despite his best efforts to keep it going. "It was a while ago, back when we were working on the Graham case. He was being arraigned that afternoon, and we were both going to court to make certain that Judge Winton refused to set bail below the maximum. You were already downstairs, and I realized I'd left two of the written testimonies from his victims in the folder in your office, from when we were reviewing them the night before. I went back to get them off your desk before joining you." With every word he spoke, the cringe on her face deepened, and her already enflamed cheeks went from apple to overly ripe raspberry. Curious at her reaction, he went on, determined to get this out. She had every right to know what kind of guy he was. "I saw..."

"The pictures of me," she concluded for him.

He went on. "I should've told you then, and more than that, I shouldn't have indulged my baser nature and looked at them. I really am very sorry."

She wrinkled her nose and squeezed her eyes shut. "So, that's your proof that you're a jerk?"

Completely baffled at her reactions, his mind scrambled. "I'm sure there's more I could come up with."

That actually made her laugh. "Oh god, Jack, I'm the one that should be apologizing."

"Why?"

"Because I had those pictures taken to try to get your attention. I did them for you. I'll admit I forgot they were on my desk that day, but you're not the jerk. I am. I should never have had them done. I don't even know why I did. I told myself it was to get back at you for beating me in the election, but that wasn't really it."

The alleviation of guilt he'd carried for so long was dizzying even if it didn't make sense. "If you did them for me, why didn't you show them to me?"

Her eye roll was welcomed at this point. There was his spitfire. He was starting to miss her. "How do you propose I should've gone about that? Marched into your office and handed them over? 'Here, Jack, I can't stop thinking about what it'd be like to sleep with you, and I'm more attracted to you than I've ever been to anyone, so I thought I'd have these done and see what you thought. Also, I'm pissed you won the election and wanted to torture you a little, which I know makes me an epic bitch.'" She shook her head. "I'm nuts but I'm not quite *that* nuts."

"None of that makes you a bitch," he vowed readily.

"Yeah, right. If it doesn't make me that, then it definitely doesn't make you a jerk."

"When we get back home, can I see them? I was too ashamed to look at them the way I wanted to."

Her flush reddened yet again, and he loved that she was a fair-skinned redhead just for that effect. "You just saw everything and then some. You don't need the pictures now."

"I still want them. I've thought about them every single day since I first saw them. I've jacked off to thoughts of them more times than I can count. There's another confession for you."

She looked extremely pleased at that particular confession, so it was more than worth it in his book. "You make me do incredibly stupid things. Things I would never in a million years do unless it's to get your attention. There, that's my confession."

"You already know that me even being with you is stupid, so maybe we could be really unintelligent together and chance this."

"Yeah, maybe we could. Now that you can just have me come to your office and take my clothes off, you won't have to snoop in my office anymore," she goaded.

"Now that I've vowed my sword to you and the house of Holder,"—he gestured to his crotch just to hear her laugh again—"maybe if this doesn't go well, you'll still put in a good word for me with your family."

"My family would not banish you from our kingdom. Just promise not to break my heart."

"Never." He brushed a wayward strand of hair behind her ear. "And maybe you'll let me help you with the Marsden case."

She hesitated for a beat but then seemed to want to try out this new, yet somewhat undefined relationship. "Okay, why do you think we should report the pregnant mares?"

This was decidedly not sexy afterglow talk, but it was possibly even more important. "I'm worried your family is being set up."

"What?! Why do you think that?"

"The timeline worries me. It didn't occur to me until you were talking earlier, but it sounds like Marsden filed his claim right after the last herd was delivered to Holder Ranch. I was a little distracted by your mouth being on my dick, so I didn't mention it then."

"That's no excuse," she harassed.

He chuckled. "Am I supposed to be sorry that I find you so utterly distracting?"

"You don't need to apologize for that, but no one knew we were getting more horses that day. Marsden couldn't possibly have known that."

"The people delivering them had to know. I did some research after the case came through. Marsden has a brother who works for the Texas Bureau of Land Management. It's not a big leap to assume they concocted some kind of plan together with his brother's knowledge of shipments in the Midwest. I didn't think much of it until you said something about the pregnancies, but maybe they're banking on you not figuring out they were pregnant or on not reporting it. Your family has paid their way out of legal cases that weren't worth fighting before. I'm betting they're hoping to be on the receiving end of that this time."

"I was stupid for not figuring out about his brother. What if Marsden set our stud loose when we weren't near the stables? Oh my god. I was really, really stupid."

"Stop. Not knowing something isn't worthy of apology. On the surface, it looks like Marsden's just after a payout from your family, but I'm worried this goes much deeper. Did you file the continuance before we left?"

"No. Mitch was going to do it for me Monday. How did you know to look up his family?"

"Old habit." Jack ran his hand up and down her back trying to soothe her. "You don't come from the family I come from and not need to know whom everyone is related to and what their relations could either gain or cost you."

"What happens if the foals are ours though? We could lose the horses. They could bury us in fines."

"I do still have a favor or two left with Senator McCoy, but I don't want to have to use it unless I have to. I'll call Mitch in the morning and tell him to go to the office and shred that continuance form before it accidentally gets filed. You call your dad and the Bureau of Land Management to report the pregnancies. We'll take it one problem at a time. If the mustangs aren't a result of your stud, there's nothing to worry about."

"Yeah, I know." She sounded like that possibility was somewhere between slim and none.

"Hey,"—he pulled her closer—"I will never let anything happen to Holder Ranch. I promise you."

"You're a pretty good district attorney, you know that?"

"She says begrudgingly," he teased.

"Seriously, thank you for being so great...at everything." Her harsh swallow tensed against his chest.

"Well, I don't pledge my sword to just anyone."

"You better not." She nuzzled him again, and he was completely addicted to that continued high of her needing him, of him being her hero even if he came from a long line of villains. "Can we stay here tonight? Is that allowed out here in Bourbon Country?"

Grinning at that, he planted his next kiss on top of her head. "We could, but there's a significant problem with your plan."

"And that is?" He watched the golden flecks in her eyes dance in the moonlight as she lifted her head.

"I only had that one condom with me. The rest are back at the estate house."

"I see, and you think we might need another one before morning?"

"No, honey. I think we might need another dozen before morning."

She fell back against the sheets and pulled them around her. "That is a problem because I like it here and I don't like it there, but condoms are definitely worth it."

Jack leaned back against the headboard and gathered her closer to him. "I agree with your assessment, but there is another problem too."

"What's that?"

"It's more difficult for me to distribute checks from out here, and I feel bad asking Rosalind to have to clean two houses."

"Oh." Devastation struck her all-telling eyes. "I wasn't thinking. I thought we'd clean up after ourselves. Now I feel bad even suggesting it."

"Again, there is nothing wrong with not knowing something you had no reason to know."

CHAPTER TWENTY-SEVEN

They tiptoed back into his parents' home like young lovers who didn't make curfew. Jack, with his shirt still hanging open, and Meridian, still barefoot and flushed both from their love-making and the walk back in the cool night air. There was no mistaking what they'd been doing in their time away. As if that wasn't enough, Jack was loaded down with their sheets since they both felt badly asking the maids to have to do extra laundry and had determined that there must be some way they could wash them and sneak them back down to the guesthouse.

He loved sneaking around with her in any capacity. He loved the mischievous glint in her eyes when she was helping him cause a little worthy trouble.

Unfortunately, when they stepped into the dark, quiet kitchen, long after the party had disbanded, harsh lights cast them in shadows immediately. They were caught. Jack had to remind himself that he was not seventeen and had done nothing wrong despite the enraged look on his father's face. Jack hated that some part of him still cared what his father thought at all.

Tapping in to that anger, he narrowed his eyes. "Problem?"

His father spoke through clenched teeth. "Where have you been?"

Chuckling, Jack shared a quick conspiratorial wink with Meridian.

"We needed some fresh air," he informed his father who was not a stupid man and could most certainly tell where they'd been. The question was preposterous.

"I think what you *need* is to remember that you are guests in my home and this"—he gestured to the bundle of sheets pressed against Jack's bare chest—"is completely inappropriate. You left a party thrown in your honor that your mother has worked on for over a week."

"My mother doesn't work on anything at all. She orders everyone in this house to do her bidding for her, you included. I never asked for a party. I never asked for any of this. I was ordered home to attend Tiffany's wedding. It was, by the way, Tiff that called us outside if you'll recall."

"And you did nothing to help that situation either."

"How do you know what I did or didn't do? Why do you care, for that matter? This wedding has no bearing on your bottom line." That was the only thing his father really cared about.

"No, it doesn't. You already ruined that when you decided not to marry her yourself."

"And there it is. You should've just started with the truth. It will get you further faster." Without giving the motion much thought, he wrapped his available arm around Meridian. He was no longer certain if he was telling the truth or not, and he didn't care. "I decided to marry someone I'm in love with, someone who makes me a better person and a better lawyer. Someone I want to spend the rest of my life with. Successful marriages aren't born of business wagers and back-room deals."

Meridian stared up at him. The mischievous look in her eyes had transformed to awe. His heart pounded out a frantic ovation.

"This is not who we raised you to be." His father had the audacity to gesture to Meridian with a sneer. Jack dropped the sheets on the tile floor and was in his father's face before he could blink.

"Don't you dare," he seethed. "Don't you fucking dare drag her down into your malignant world to try to make her seem like the broken one. Who I was then and who I needed to be in order to live with myself are two very different men."

"And I love both of them." Meridian's calm cool voice doused the blaze igniting between the two men. Jack was certain that wasn't really true. She was helping his case or maybe even getting back at him for the way he'd handled her soup question at dinner. But god, it sounded good. It soothed still-festering wounds deep in his soul. It sounded far too much like his every fantasy come to life, and he was much too weak to tell himself not to believe her words.

His father took two hesitant steps back. "This isn't a prison," he huffed. "If you don't want to be here, leave."

Meridian edged closer, like a lioness circling her prey or perhaps protecting her mate. "Isn't it though?" she stated. "Do you know the best way to keep a prisoner from escaping, Mr. Denton?" His father refused her a response. Jack's blood continued to boil. "You just have to make certain they never realize they've been imprisoned."

Jack dealt the final blow. "One of the first things you ever taught me about business was that if someone wastes ten minutes of my time, eight of them were my fault. That applies here. We're going to bed. If you want us out tomorrow, say the word."

Because he knew his father so well, Jack knew his words weren't even a gamble. Palmer Denton would never demand that his middle son leave. Jack knew too much, held too many aces in his hand. This was the rope bridge of tension where they continued to duel, and it would be that way until his father's last breath. Jack had no way out of his only life, no matter how much he longed to strike a match over an open, aged barrel and walk away.

———

———

———

Meridian appreciated Jack's hand, gripped in her own, as they made their way to his bedroom. She wasn't certain why she'd said what she said, other than Jack needed her help and she couldn't have stopped herself if she tried. Besides, if they were really engaged, then she would love both the man he'd been and the one he'd become. That's how love worked, at least in her world. But her worry over her pattern of continuing to do incredibly stupid things because of Jack bubbled nervously in her stomach.

They finally stepped into his room and he secured the door. Her breaths came a little easier then. "Can I ask you something?"

"Of course," he soothed as he stripped out of the shirt he was really only half wearing. Momentarily distracted by him again, she closed her eyes so she could speak.

"In your parents' eyes, what would have been appropriate tonight after Tiffany called you outside?"

The jangle of his belt broke her resolve, and her eyes flashed open. She wasn't a saint, after all. His smirk said he liked that she was distracted by him, but he went on with his answer. "Their first preference would've been for me and Tiffany to have come back in and announced that we'd decided you and Brent no longer exist and that we have fallen into mad, passionate love and the two of us were going to wed this Saturday. If I'd impregnated her on the way inside, all the better."

Meridian's eyes goggled as she fought a flare of jealousy. She reminded herself that she did not care what his parents thought. "What would their second preference have been since that seems beyond comprehendible thought."

"I'm glad you are aware that it's preposterous. Every single time I come here, by the time I leave, I feel like the insane one." He shook his head. "Their second choice would've been for the four of us to have come back in and assured everyone that it was just a quick case of nerves before the wedding and everything was going to go off as planned."

"Do you think that will happen? Do you think Tiff and Brent will figure it out before Saturday?"

Jack gave her a sexy half grin. "I don't know either of them well enough to even make a prediction. You, on the other hand, I know exactly what you're about to do."

Rather liking his flirting, she matched his expression. "What am I about to do?"

"Ask me to unzip that dress."

She certainly couldn't deny that he was right, but that didn't mean she was going to let him know that. "That sounds more like what you want to do next."

"Couldn't we have a mutual goal? We do work well together." He traced his fingertips across her collarbone. The move managed to steal the air from her lungs. When his fingers arrived at her shoulder, he turned her around and painted kisses along the bare skin of her neck. Chill bumps charged down her arms. "Are you cold, sweetheart?"

"A little."

"The house is a hundred years old. No matter how many times the HVAC system is replaced, it's still cold at night, but I have a solution to that problem." The quick whisk of the zipper left her back open to the cool air. His warm hands were instantly on her shoulder blades and stroking downward in a delicious juxtaposition.

"What is your solution?" She already knew, but she was having far too much fun to have stopped the game.

"We strip down to nothing. I take you to bed. Tuck you under all of the covers and keep you nice and warm with my body heat."

When Meridian turned, the spaghetti straps of the dress, already loosened from the number of times it had been taken off and put on that evening, tumbled down her arms revealing her breasts. Her nipples were a deep flushed pink both from the temperature and her arousal.

A hungry groan echoed from Jack and took up residence directly between Meridian's thighs. "You are cold, baby." He clasped his hands over her breasts tenderly. "Come to bed with me. You are the only thing in my entire world that makes any sense at all."

"Does that scare you the way it scares me?" Her question held no volume, only breaths of curiosity.

"Yes. And no. And everything in between." He tugged the dress down and lifted her back into his arms. Before he turned off the bedside lamp, he stared at her with a question not only pinned in his eyes but also on his lips. She started to ask him what it was he wanted to know but thought better of it.

He seemed to decide the same.

CHAPTER TWENTY-EIGHT

After an incredibly awkward breakfast with Jack's parents, where fewer than ten words were shared between the four of them, Meridian finally escaped back to Jack's room to call her father.

It rang several times, but he didn't answer. Checking the time on her phone, she knew he was on horseback gathering cattle. She called her Uncle Barrett instead, on the off chance that he was back in the office.

"Hey sweetpea, you all right out there in Kentucky?" His low cowboy drawl softened all of the places in her heart that threatened to harden due to her current surroundings.

She grinned. "I'm all right, but I need to talk to you. I think I might've made a huge mistake."

She could almost see the concern that she knew would tense in her uncle's eyes. "I can be on the next flight out from Tulsa, or I can get one of my boys to show me how to send you a plane ticket to your phone. How far are you from the airport?"

Truthfully, she had no idea since she'd been deposited directly into this bizarre world. "I don't need to come home. That isn't it." She took inventory of her mind and body to make certain she wasn't lying to

Barrett, since the man could see through a lie like a torn window screen. "I'm good actually. Really good."

Her uncle's smooth chuckle soothed even more of her nerves. "Well, all right then. What is it you think you might've made a mistake about? Not Jack, I take it."

"No. Not Jack. He's pretty great actually."

"I've been saying that for a while, but you hadn't ever been too keen on listening."

"Yeah, I know. I'm too stubborn for my own good. Believe me, I get it." Refocusing, she pressed on with her mistake, although discussing Jack was far more appealing. "I think we need to report the pregnant mares as soon as possible."

She heard the old desk chair roll on the worn hardwoods in Barrett's office. "I hate to do that. I'm worried sick one of our studs got loose. I don't want to lie to the Bureau."

"I know, but Jack thinks we might've been set up, and I have to agree."

"Explain that."

She went over the potential connection between the Marsden case and the mare delivery. The weight of running not only a ranch the size of the Holders' but of also caring for an entire community echoed in her uncle's sigh. "If you and Jack agree that this is what we need to do, I'm more than willing. But I have to tell you if those foals end up being ours, I'm taking responsibility for that. I won't take money from the state for horses that they don't owe us for keeping."

The reassurance that her family's moral compass always pointed due north had her sinking to the bed in relief. "I know. We can deal with that if it comes, but right now we need to get a management inspector out to confirm the pregnancies before Marsden takes us to court."

"All right, I think I'll give Scotty Strenton a call." The comfort of that statement bothered Meridian the same way the realization that she was now sitting on a freshly made bed, that neither she nor Jack had made, bothered her. She wondered how many steps there were between being able to call in favors with the head of the Bureau of

Land Management and strategically trying to arrange your children's lives in accordance with your earnings.

"Okay, let me know what he says," she stated robotically. "Love you."

"Love you too, sweetpea. You let me know if you need anything at all. If you and Jack decide maybe you like each other enough to make this permanent, my brother's gonna have my hide. He's holding out on you falling for a cowboy."

Meridian rolled her eyes. "Like I'm not surrounded by enough of those. I don't need to bring more of them into my life."

"We're not all that bad now, are we?" Barrett teased.

"I guess not. You're pretty great."

"I like to think so." He chuckled. "I'll let you know what Scotty says. You have fun out there, and tell Jack we said hello."

"I will. Bye."

Fighting the desire to rumple the sheets and remake the bed herself, Meridian reminded herself that there was nothing wrong with her family knowing people in high places that had direct impact on cattle ranching in Oklahoma. They were sixth-generation ranchers of the largest ranch in Oklahoma. How would they not know people in power?

Her attention snagged as the door opened and Jack entered. Panic etched his features. "Are you certain you locked your office door before we left Friday night?"

"Of course." The alarm on Jack's face did nothing to soothe her own. "Why?"

"I was going to ask Mitch to go in and shred the continuance, but he was already going into the office when I called him. When he got there, he found your office door open."

Meridian tried to remain calm. "The lock sticks sometimes. Maybe it didn't catch or something. Did he go in there? Had anything been moved?"

"He went in and assured me that everything looked normal. I wasn't sure where you had those pictures, so I didn't want him digging too deeply anywhere."

Meridian's face flamed. "Oh god. I forgot those were in there. Who would've...?"

Jack joined her on the bed. "We don't know that anyone did anything wrong. I found a tomcat in my office one morning a few months ago. The door was locked, but it hadn't closed all the way so he was able to push it open. The courthouse isn't exactly the most secure."

She tried to triage her panic. Worst case, someone had gone through her office and potentially found the boudoir photographs meant for Jack. Best case, it was nothing. "Maybe I could get Callie to go up there and make sure the photos are still in my filing cabinet. She took the pictures for me, so she's seen them already."

Jack considered that. "Do you have a spare set of keys to your files somewhere that she can get to?"

She shook her head. The only two keys were on the ring in her purse and in Jack's pocket. "No, and Mitch would've been able to tell if it had been opened. It's a legal file cabinet. You don't just break into those and leave them unmarked."

Rubbing his morning stubble, Jack nodded. "That's true. It's probably nothing."

She finally gave voice to the dread gnawing her biscuit-laden stomach. "You don't think Marsden would...?"

"I don't know," he soothed. "I doubt it. Other than the case file on the mustangs, is there anything in your office he doesn't already have access to in his copy of the suit? Is there anything that would help him with his case that he would suspect is in your office?"

"No. It's an open and shut case, like you said. The only thing that might help him win is in the bellies of those mares."

"Are you okay?" Jack finally asked.

"Logically, there isn't anything to worry about, but it is weird."

"Would it make you feel better to get Callie to go up there and see if she can get into the cabinet without the keys?"

"Maybe, but she's covered up in babies and calves and...my cousin generally."

He grinned at that. "Tell me how I can help. I can book us a flight back home if that would make you feel better. I do need to see my brothers before we go, and I need to check in with a few more staff members, but that's all I'm really here to do."

Meridian refused to take away any of the good things that Jack had come to Kentucky to do just because her office door was open. It was far more likely that in her distraction of thinking of spending the week here with him, she hadn't fully closed the door. "No." She shook her head. "It's fine. Nothing had even been moved. There isn't anything in there other than those photos that I wouldn't let people see. I'm beyond certain they are locked safely in my cabinet. There's nothing to worry about."

"I had Mitch make sure he shut the door and then try to get back in. He couldn't."

That eased a little of her nerves. "I'm sure it's nothing."

"If you change your mind, just say the word."

"Has anyone heard anything about the wedding? Is it still going to happen?"

"According to my brother, nothing has been called off yet, so I assume so. Now, if you're sure you want to stay, I thought maybe we could go play tourist for the day. I don't want you to judge all of Kentucky based on River Chase."

Pleased with his plan, she grinned. "That sounds fun." Anything that got them out of that house suited her just fine. "What am I supposed to wear for playing tourist?"

His eyebrow lifted in intrigue. "Are you asking me what I want to see you in or what's appropriate for our activities?"

"Yes." She laughed.

He considered for a moment. "There's no dress code for today, but I love to see you in a pair of Wranglers and your boots."

"That works well for you because that's my favorite thing to wear."

"I'm a lucky man."

CHAPTER TWENTY-NINE

Jack wanted nothing more than to spend the day impressing Meridian. He longed for her laughter and those smiles she gave only him. He wanted to drown in them. He'd wanted to ask her since he'd gotten her back to the bedroom the night before if there was any chance she really meant what she'd so adamantly declared to his father.

Could she really love who he was now? Asking her to love who he was then was out of the question. He wouldn't want her to accept who he'd been. He only wanted to know if he had any chance at all, but he'd chickened out.

It would've been too crushing to watch her try to gently let him down, because of course she was not in love with him. He wasn't *that* lucky.

Keeping his arm around her as he guided her the opposite direction on the estate from the guesthouse, he tried to think of anything else to say besides *I know you don't love me yet, but I'm hoping maybe someday I could change that.*

"You're awfully quiet," she finally called him on it.

"Just thinking about us."

"Want to let me in on that conversation in your head then? It's making you look a little constipated."

Laughing at her honesty, he shook his head at her. "Mighty feisty this morning, cowgirl."

"Yeah, well, I can't seem to be around your parents without letting my rebellious side overrun my good sense."

And there was his answer. She was just trying to infuriate his father. That was something he more than understood. Palmer Denton had the same effect on Jack. "Here I was unaware your rebellious side wasn't always running the show." He winked at her and earned one of the first grins of the day as she elbowed him in the side.

Trying to disguise the ache in his chest, he typed the key code into the barn that had been converted into a sixteen-car garage. Dust floated in the air dancing in front of the few windows.

As soon as their eyes had adjusted to the light, she spun around between an R8 and his brother's newly acquired Flying Spur. "Who the hell needs this many cars?" gasped from her.

"No one," Jack assured her, "but we do need to pick one for our day."

She wrinkled her nose. "Do the Dentons have any that aren't douche-mobiles?"

Loving that the Audis and Bentleys did nothing to impress her, he laced his fingers through hers and guided her to the back bay. "I had a feeling you wouldn't want to have anything to do with the sports cars."

He lifted the cover off of his own personal favorite. Her mouth fell open, much to his delight, as he revealed the perfectly restored '71 blue and white Chevy Cheyenne pickup. "An appropriate carriage for my princess." He opened the passenger-side door and bowed for her to enter.

"Holy fuck," finally came out in broken syllables, making him laugh. "You seriously own a restored Cheyenne?!"

Jack considered that question. "The estate owns it. I just happen to know where the keys are." Again, he gestured to the door he'd opened for her. "Shall we?"

"Do you seriously think I'm not driving this?"

Humored at her preparing to dig in those boot heels, he shook his head at her. "I get to drive today, but I'll let you drive it back here tonight after the bar."

"No."

"Meridian."

"Jack, it's a Cheyenne, and you clearly already get to drive it whenever. I want a turn."

"You'll get a turn, but you don't even know how to get out of the gates, nor do you know how to get to all the places we're going. Come on."

"You can just tell me where to turn."

"I'm telling you to turn and get your cute little ass in the passenger seat." He wanted to see what she'd make of that.

"I do not like being told what to do." She threw that lie back in his face.

"By anyone but me," he informed her. She narrowed her eyes. "Would you like me to prove my case right here, honey? I'm more than willing."

He knew she was wavering when her shoulders eased. "You promise I can drive it tonight?"

Rather enjoying teasing her, he held up one hand. "I, Jackson Hearst Denton, do solemnly swear that I will support the Constitutions of the United States and the amendments therein, and of this state—"

She rolled her eyes at his recitation of the attorney's oath and made her way over to him. He continued on, "That I will honestly demean myself in the practice of law—"

"Would you shut up?" she goaded.

"I'm not finished," he informed her. "That I will discharge my duties to my clients to the best of my ability; and that I will conduct myself with integrity and civility in dealing and communicating with the court and all parties."

She climbed in the truck. "You really are a dick sometimes."

"So help me God," he concluded before they were both cracking up.

"I get to drive tonight," she reminded him through a broad grin.

He lifted his hand just to listen to the melody of her laughter again. "Do not...!" She grabbed his hand and yanked him closer. He leaned in and took her lips in a decadent kiss. She placed his hand on her breast and he was done for. A yearning growl spilled from his mouth to hers as she opened so readily for his tongue. His dick immediately suggested several changes to his planned schedule, mainly that he get her out of those Wranglers and himself deep inside of her.

Her shallow breath escaped the tight trap of their lips. He moved his lips to her neck and caught her nipple between his thumb and index finger. Her moan made him throb. "Needy, honey?"

Her eyes blinked open. "How is it I can't seem to get enough of you?"

"I plan to use that to my advantage."

"How so?"

"I can't reveal all of my cards to you, now can I?"

"You could." She smirked as he lifted his head.

"I could, but I won't. Now, should we go play tourist, or would you prefer to go make use of another one of the bedrooms in the guesthouse?"

"Can I have both?"

"You can have whatever you want, princess."

Eventually they made their way back to the garage, but Jack was only semi-sated despite having just been deep inside of her. She wasn't the only one who wasn't sure they'd ever get enough. Now he just had to convince her they were a match made in heaven, even if they were currently standing much closer to hell.

They started at his favorite coffee shop over in Lexington. While she studied the chalkboard menu hung behind the registers, he studied her. "Caramel really is everything," she informed him thoughtfully.

"I have to disagree."

She pulled her gaze away from the menu. "You don't like caramel? Were you dropped on your head as a child?"

"I'm too hardheaded for that to have done any real damage, and I do like caramel. It just doesn't taste as good as you do," he whispered near her ear. A quick shiver shot through her making his banter more than worth it. "Therefore, it cannot be everything."

"You are very naughty," she informed him.

"I should probably be punished."

She cocked her jaw to the side. "And how would you like to be punished?"

The barista at the counter cleared her throat rather loudly, shattering the heated air surrounding them. They both spun to face her. Jack had no idea how long it had been since the people standing in line in front of them had ordered. He grimaced.

"Uh…" Meridian's cheeks turned the same shade of auburn as her hair. "I want a water and also The Student." She pointed to the caramel coffee confection on the board.

"No problem," the woman nodded and then turned to Jack.

Still in the mood to flirt, he shot a lusty look at Meridian and announced that he'd have The Principal to go with her Student.

While Meridian was laughing, the barista hit a few buttons on the register. "For here or to go, Mr. Denton?" Shit. Of course she knew him. Every blessed person in town knew him. Yet another reason he'd run far and fast from Kentucky.

He swallowed down the heady dose of discomfort and prayed nothing he'd just said would embarrass Meridian. "Here." The woman handed over the cup of water before they left the counter. Guiding Meridian to a table near the back windows, he tried to shake off the feeling that everyone in the shop was staring at them. "I'm sorry about that. I have no idea who she is," he offered in an almost silent whisper.

Meridian waved it off like it was no big deal that their flirting overtly about a yet-to-be-explored kink had been intruded on. "You do remember who I am, right? I can't go anywhere in Oklahoma without everyone knowing me, my mama, my daddy, all of my uncles, my great-granddaddy, hell, even the ranch dogs we buried two generations ago. I'm used to it. It's kind of nice that it wasn't me, honestly. At least she didn't want to let you know what she thinks you ought to have done with the profits from the distilleries a hundred years ago."

Intrigued at that, he said, "People try to tell you what they think you should do with the profits from the ranch?"

She nodded as she pulled the wrapper off of a straw and flattened it between her fingers. "Everyone has opinions about everything we do. You get used to it, but that doesn't make it any less annoying."

Not certain where the idea had come from, Jack caught one end of the wrapper and eased it from her fingers. He never considered himself particularly romantic or creative, but he went on with his idea. Taking her left hand in his, he threaded the wrapper around her ring finger and twisted the paper down until he'd effectively created her a paper engagement ring complete with a large wad paper diamond. "We're supposed to be engaged, right?" He winked at her.

She stared at the ring like he'd really put a massive diamond on her finger. "So fancy." She giggled.

"It's the best I could do," he offered with a laugh.

"I love it!"

But could she ever see herself loving him? That was the question he really wanted the answer to. The barista set their drinks down in front of them and smiled at the paper ring.

Still beaming, Meridian held up her hand. "Stunning, isn't it?"

"Girl," the woman laughed, "he's loaded. You need to ask for more than that."

"Nah." Meridian shook her head. "I think this is perfect. Money can't buy happiness, right?"

"You keep telling yourself that." The barista made her way back to the counter.

CHAPTER THIRTY

Still wearing her paper ring, that she secretly really did love, Meridian climbed back in the truck. "Are we going to do one of those tours of the bourbon trail? Do I get to wax seal a bottle or something?" Her laughter was cut short by Jack's visible cringe.

"If you really want to go, we can."

"Oh my god, do people rush you there? Do they want you to sign their bottles of Denton Family Reserve or something?"

He rolled his eyes. "It's not quite that bad."

"So...it's *almost* that bad?" She tried to imagine what that would be like.

"It's more that if we go down there, word will immediately get back to my parents and they'll get ideas that I do not want them to have."

"Ideas like what?"

"That I have any interest in rejoining the company." He eyed her cautiously before continuing, "All eyes would be on you, and you didn't seem to like that at dinner last night."

"Why would all eyes be on me? You're the bourbon baron."

He lifted his eyebrows but said nothing. That was enough of a clue though.

"Because I'm engaged to the baron." She lifted her left hand. "Of course."

"Please never call me a bourbon baron again. I...hate that."

"Oh, I'm sorry."

"It's just...not what I want my legacy to be."

Supremely interested in that, she edged closer to him in the truck. "What do you want your legacy to be?"

He turned down a tree-lined road dripping with fall colors. "That I reshuffled the deck I was given, maybe."

"This is beautiful," Meridian complimented the scenery before she went on with her interrogation. "But explain what you just said."

He held out his free hand, and she quickly laced their fingers together. "Don't mess up my ring," she instructed.

"I promise." He considered for another few moments. "I didn't grow up the way you did, but for a long time I thought I had. Every single person I thought was supposed to be a role model for me had fallen from grace before I was even born. They just did a hell of a job keeping that from me. But when I found out that the cards I'd been given were from a marked deck, I hope people remember that I demanded a new deck. I reshuffled the cards. I walked away, and I'd do it again a thousand times over."

Amazed at his fortitude, she squeezed his hand. "That's impressive as hell. I hope you know that. Everything about you is impressive." That fact was getting harder and harder to deny. "And I don't think you should hate to be called a bourbon baron. You didn't ask to be born into your family or for them to do the things they've done. You know not every Holder was the pinnacle of morality. Some of my ancestors were kind of terrible."

"Maybe, but the current generations put an end to that. Mine chose to make things worse. What we had wasn't enough. We wanted more. That's the thing with greed. There will never be enough money, or enough brands, or enough of anything to ever make them step back and say, *we have enough, now let's do something for someone else.*"

"Okay, but you did walk away from all of that, and I think you should give yourself more credit."

He gave her that sexy smirk that did dangerous, stupid things to her. "I'm glad you're impressed. Now, would my cowgirl rather head over to Keeneland and lose some money on some thoroughbreds or go shopping for some ridiculously clichéd Kentucky souvenirs?"

She pretended to consider. "You know, I have always aspired to being one of those old ladies that has a spoon from every state. I don't have Kentucky yet. Oh, and one of those tiny Derby hats with the feather fascinator things that I can hang from the rearview of my truck."

Jack's chuckle was yet another thing that did those stupid, dangerous things to her heart. "I can get you a shot glass from River Chase to go with your spoon collection."

"Wow. A free shot glass and a paper ring. I'm really being spoiled here."

"I know how to woo my lady," he teased.

"Clearly. I want to go to the track, but I've never ever gambled on anything so I'm sure I'll be bad at it."

His brow furrowed like he found that odd. "Never?"

"Nope. I only like sure things. I don't like to lose, remember?"

"Of course. But I would be more than happy to give you a little guidance. You know good horses. I know good jockeys. We make a damn good team. Maybe we'll win."

"Are we going to drink mint juleps while we're there?"

"Naturally. To do otherwise would be completely uncouth."

"Well, I wouldn't want to be uncouth."

"Not until we get back to my bed anyway." Jack winked at her.

Meridian couldn't recall the last time she'd spent an entire day laughing. Everything about being with Jack made her happy, and that was probably the stupidest most dangerous thing of all.

He sent her another flirtatious grin. "You know the way you really win at Keeneland is to bet on the long shot."

"Is that so?"

"It is. Between the two of us we can analyze breeds, jockeys, trainers, and we can calculate speed, but a long shot that wins—nothing beats that."

"Sounds a little dangerous. Why not bet on the sure win?"

"Life never has sure wins, honey. That's why everyone likes a long shot."

———

Jack escorted her into The Watershed Bar twenty minutes late that evening. When she'd invited him into the shower with her, he'd had no hope of turning her down. They were still laughing and teasing about his fifty-dollar win on a horse named Boots and Heels.

He'd left the winnings in the paper cup of a man near the track who was down on his luck. After that, they'd split up for a half hour while Jack went to buy the man cold weather gear and Meridian purchased him three hot plates from the local diner. They'd ended their afternoon letting the man use Jack's phone to call his son who'd been searching for him.

To say they were high on life would've been a significant under-statement. Jack couldn't recall ever enjoying a day more. A tinge of nerves twisted in his gut as he led her into the bar, but he couldn't quite determine why.

Meridian's bottom lip slipped through her teeth as they stepped inside. She was nervous too, then. Jack pulled her closer in a side hug. "They'll love you," he reassured.

"I hope so."

For all of her adamance that she never cared what anyone thought of her, he was touched that she wanted people who meant the world to him to like her.

Watershed was the perfect upscale bar, an eclectic mix of subdued class and neon lights that somehow all seemed to work together. Aged barrel casks turned tables mixed with corrugated sheet metal fixtures. The walls were created of ancient stacked stone and bedecked with vintage sepia photos of couples in love in all its many forms. The upstairs portion was much quieter than the honky-tonk bars back in Oklahoma but every bit as comfortable. The dance floor was on the opposite side, down a wide staircase that led to a whole other world—more neon and less subdued, more carnal dungeon and less intimate gathering area. Two pool tables were situated in another corner near two old guys throwing darts.

The owner/bartender, Margie, had been a fixture at Watershed since its inception in the late eighties. She grinned at Jack and Meridian as they entered. "They've been waiting on you."

She pointed to the large booth in the back under the custom stained glass chandelier that sported vintage Denton bottles of bourbon. Every major bourbon family had their old bottles in design somewhere in the bar. Whether or not that was an honor or a "fuck you" to the family was entirely up to the patrons.

Jack guided Meridian back to their established table. Finn was shaking his head and laughing. "I was a little worried you were late because you were digging a Dad-shaped hole somewhere at River Chase." He stood and hugged Jack. "How are you, bro?"

"I'm good. Great, actually. Finn, this is my...uh, fiancée, Meridian Holder." He paused, not wanting to lie to his favorite brother. Directing Meridian to the table at large, he went on with introductions. "Honey, these are my brothers Finn and Drew. You already met Sloan, and this is Sloan's younger sister, Lila."

Finn laughed. "The Bourbon Bastards." He gestured around the table.

"Some of us a little more literally than the others," Drew harassed.

Meridian beamed while Jack prayed his half brother's dark humor wasn't indicative of a deeper problem. "I'm so glad to finally meet all of you," she gushed.

"Sit." Finn forcefully scooted Lila over to make room for Jack and Meridian. "It's nice to finally meet you as well. Jack never shuts up about you." Confusion furrowed Meridian's brow. Jack wondered what Finn was referring to as he continued, "He failed to let me know he was engaged, but I guess I should've figured that out on my own."

"Well, it's...kind of a new development," Meridian offered feebly.

"I guess I bring you up more than I was aware," Jack whispered near her ear. How many times had he discussed Meridian in the last few years? Clearly enough for Finn to have expected them to get together at some point.

She turned to face him while he was still leaning close, and the invitation to take advantage of the close proximity of her lips wasn't something Jack could deny himself. He did try to keep this kiss somewhat chaste, but the Bastards all laughed and shook their heads anyway.

A warm flush crept to Meridian's cheeks. Jack's dick stirred in his jeans. "I'm sorry," he offered the table. "I'll try to keep my hands to myself."

Lila rolled her eyes. "It's not your hands, duff-ball, it's your lips. And what do we care? Isn't part of the reason we're here because you should be able to kiss whoever the hell you want? I will say, though, Aunt Bev is fit to be tied over you two. Good for you, Jack."

Finn chuckled as he eyed the bar. "Mom was holding out hope for you and Tiff, man. She may never get over the money you're losing her, and you're obviously doing it on purpose."

His mockery of their mother sounded just like her. This time it was Jack who rolled his eyes. "I'm sure she'll just transfer her shallow hopes to Greer. Maybe he'll come through for her."

Finn's face morphed to shock before he responded. "Uh, I'm not so sure about that. He just walked in."

A contagion of heads turning to stare at Greer whipped around the table. Jack recognized the determined discomfort his brother was trying to conceal behind a tense smile. Finn offered Greer a slight wave. Relief flooded Greer's features as he headed their way. "May I?" He cleared his throat like he wasn't entirely certain they would let him enter the Bastards' domain. Jack wasn't entirely sure they should.

"Sure." Once again, Finn scooted Lila closer to Sloan and made room for Greer. The question on everyone's minds—why was he here?—hung in the whiskey-soaked air.

"I...just...thought I'd come see where you all sneak off to every time Jack comes home."

Finn slapped him on the shoulder. "Welcome. Haven't seen you in a while." The hurt over that truth pierced Finn's words.

"Yeah, I know. I'm sorry. I need to get over to your place more often. It's difficult when I'm the one they keep the closest watch over."

Jack hadn't ever really considered what his departure, followed so closely after Finn's, might've done to Greer. "Do they know where you are?" Jack wondered.

"They're having dinner at Bellemenson with the Fitzgeralds to discuss the implications of their divorce, according to Frank."

Frank was Jack's parents' personal secretary.

"Interesting." Jack waved a waiter over. "What can I get you, honey?" He'd steadfastly kept an eye on Meridian as she took in all of the information coming to light at the table.

Offering a polite smile to the waiter, she shrugged. "A whiskey sour."

The waiter gestured to Greer. "With Denton Reserve, I assume?"

Meridian shook her head. "No. With Maker's Mark, if you don't mind."

Greer gave a weary headshake while the rest of the table chuckled.

"I'll have the same," Jack added.

Greer chimed in, "Make it a round for the table. All Maker's Mark."

CHAPTER THIRTY-ONE

Meridian wondered if she was the only one who'd noticed how extremely uncomfortable Sloan had become at Greer's appearance. This family had more secrets than whiskey barrels. Searching the recesses of her mind, she discovered that she wanted two things primarily—to help Jack hide the ones that needed to remain hidden, and to go home.

She and Jack hadn't officially decided to throw all caution to the wind and keep dating back in Holder County, though. She knew he was waiting on her to okay that, because it was her, after all, that would be giving up ever becoming the DA as soon as they were outed, not that she ever had much of a chance even if they never dated. Was it really too much to ask to have a killer career and magical love story? Then again, did she already have that? If only she could make sense of how he so thoroughly undid her that she was willing to give up lifelong dreams, this would be much easier.

Sloan scooted abruptly out of the booth. "I just need to make a quick phone call."

Lila frowned. "No business tonight. You know the rules."

"This isn't business." His words were clipped. The hardened edges seemed to irritate his little sister. Meridian offered her an understanding smile. Brothers were massive pains in the ass most of the time.

Lila took another quick sip of her drink. "I wish I knew what he was up to."

"You probably really don't," Meridian assured her.

She grinned. "You're probably right. Do you have brothers?"

"Several of them."

"I'll buy your next drink." Lila laughed.

They all slid quick glances to Sloan standing at the entrance door with his phone pressed to his ear. His jaw was clamped tight, and his eyes betrayed his panic.

Whomever he was trying to get on the phone didn't seem to be answering. He shoved the door open to step outside but was met by a woman coming inside. They collided in the middle.

Everyone at the table gave up pretending not to notice and watched the show from their seats. The extremely attractive woman smiled and embraced him, but Sloan looked morose. They clearly knew each other, but Meridian had no idea if Sloan was pleased with that.

After a long-drawn minute, he finally embraced her tenderly.

"What the hell is going on?" Meridian asked Jack between her teeth.

"I have no idea."

It appeared that Sloan was whispering something in the woman's ear. She lifted her head from his chest, and all of her earlier pleasure bled from her features as she glanced at the table.

Both Sloan and the woman seemed frozen in that time and space. Jack stood and took Meridian's hand. They hightailed it to them.

Jack offered the woman a polite smile. "Are you two okay?"

"Jack," the woman returned his grin. "It's...nice to see you again." She didn't seem too certain of that.

Meridian noted Jack's stiffening in concern. He didn't know who she was. "I'm Meridian Holder. It's nice to meet you...?" She offered her hand.

"I had no idea Greer was going to show up here," Sloan cut off the introductions.

"None of us did," Jack assured him.

"I'm Sophia Willamon," the woman offered Meridian.

Jack gasped, "Sophie?"

She grinned at him again, this time a little more genuinely. "We haven't seen each other in a few decades. If I hadn't known you were coming tonight, I wouldn't have been able to pick you out of a lineup, so no apologies."

Instead of that putting Jack at ease, it seemed to elicit more panic. "And you two are...? Together?"

"For about a year now," Sloan spoke like he was being strangled. "I'd planned to tell you all tonight. Obviously."

Meridian tried to keep her temper at bay over not having any idea what was going on. She proved more successful than she had the day before, so she was proud of that. "I take it you two dating isn't something Greer should know about."

"Sophie's father is Marcus Willamon," Jack explained, "River Chase's master gardener."

Sophie added, "Three time award winner of the Build Magazine Gardening Award, merit award recipient of American Private Gardens Award, and featured in Southern Living seven times."

Meridian appreciated that she was proud of her father's incredible work, but she wasn't sure how that was going to help them out of this situation. Unless Marcus could whip up a hedge row that Sloan and Sophie could use to escape behind or knew how to grow and brew something to make Greer forget that he'd seen her, gardening wasn't going to solve their problem.

Sophie seemed to realize this too. "What do you want to do?" she asked Sloan.

"How bad would it be for your parents to know about this?" Meridian asked Jack.

"It's not just his parents, or his aunt and uncle," Sophie merged the conversations. "My father will be furious."

Sloan was Denton's head accountant. He was in charge of her father's paycheck. It was definitely more complicated than dating your boss's daughter. This had much further reaching implications. Sloan was who made sure that Jack was able to come in and give bonuses out to the staff. If his parents found out about Sophie.... As Meridian began to consider all of the implications of their relationship, she, too, descended into a spiral of panic.

"We have to get you out of here," she urged. "We'll pretend that you two just happened to walk into each other and recognized each other."

"Or you could just ask me to keep my mouth shut," Greer's voice sounded from behind them.

They all spun. Sloan stepped in front of all of them. "I hate to ask you to keep it a secret. We hate that it has to be a secret, but for now it does."

Greer shrugged. "It'd be nice to finally be included in a secret from the part of the family I actually like. Come sit down with us, Sophie. Even though no one ever bothered to ask me, I do know where my loyalties lie, and it's not with my parents."

As they all headed back to the large booth, Jack spoke quietly, "Hey, Greer."

Greer slowed his pace and joined Jack and Meridian. "Yeah?"

"I'm sorry we never made you feel a part of things. We never quite know where you stand," Jack explained.

"I forgive you. I just hope Finn will eventually forgive me. It caught me off guard when he came out. I was an ass. I didn't understand it, so I decided I didn't like it. I know why you did what you did."

"Did it really catch you off guard?" Jack inquired.

"You two were a lot closer growing up. You're a lot younger than me. I was away at college during his high school years."

"Yeah, I guess I never considered that either."

"I guess we all have regrets," Greer concurred.

The tension abated at the table somewhat. They all dispersed to either the pool tables or to head to the bar for food and more drinks.

Meridian and Jack watched Finn chat up a guy seated at the bar. Meridian couldn't help but chuckle to herself.

"What's so funny?" Jack put his arm around her.

"I just noticed that the guy Finn is talking to was downing that bottle of beer like he was trying to make it come."

"I wouldn't want to deny him that." Jack joined her laughter.

"No, you only deny yourself that."

"Would you like me to stop denying myself that, honey?"

"I'd like you to do a lot of things."

"I'm listening."

She gripped his thigh under the table. Heat spilled from the zipper line of his designer jeans. "Sometimes it's fun to be a little rough, a little bit naughty." The whiskey she'd consumed robbed her of some of her practiced inhibition.

"I couldn't agree more." Jack whispered kisses on her cheek. "Grab me," he ordered. Meridian's heart fluttered in her chest. Using the table for cover, she obeyed, palming her hand over the distinct bulge in his jeans. A needy groan sounded in her ear. "Good girl," his tone dripped with hunger. "Did you wear this dress because you know how hard it makes me?" She was wearing one of her favorite short dresses that she often wore to work.

"Maybe." She definitely knew but wasn't quite ready to reveal all of her cards just yet either.

"Then things are going to get very, very naughty, honey. I hope you're ready."

She smirked at him, certain that the fire ignited in his eyes matched the heat in her own. "Try me," she challenged.

Electricity sizzled between them. They stared each other down, all of the questions they still didn't quite have answers to penned in their eyes. "How long do we need to stay here?" That particular question ached with her need.

His eyes closed in an extended blink. "I can't leave them here with Greer," he choked. "As badly as I'd like to."

That brought Meridian up short. Despite her desperation to keep doing more of what she was doing, she pulled her hand away from his fierce erection. "Do you think he's lying about keeping Sophie and Sloan's relationship a secret?"

Jack swallowed hard. He downed another sip of whiskey as if that might cool the burn between them. "I don't know," he sighed out the answer. "My brother is a peacemaker at his core, and while that might be a positive attribute in some cases...." He shook his head.

"If you don't stand for something..." Meridian offered.

"You'll fall by the might of the Denton strong-arm."

"Damn."

Jack grinned at that. "Damned, remember? Everything the Bastards have worked so hard to put together could be destroyed by him running his mouth. I can't have him thinking he can play both ends against the middle here. There is no peace that can come from him trying to please us and my parents."

Meridian glanced over at Greer who was awkwardly trying to play pool with Drew. "He seemed sincere. How did he know where we were?"

"I'm sure my mother mentioned that I was coming to see Finn tonight. Greer came here with us right after Finn came out to us. He made some...unappreciated comments that night and then went radio silent about it all. I brushed it off as shock at the time, but he never apologized, never really reversed course. I hope he does have guilt over that. But trusting him would be incredibly stupid on my part, and I'm only supposed to be making bad decisions when it comes to you." He winked at her.

Before Meridian could comment on that, Drew appeared at the table. He lifted his highball and turned around to give Greer a distinctly fake grin. Spinning back, he begged Jack, "Please, for the love of god, come play pool with us and make this slightly less awkward."

"Sure." Jack nodded as he lifted his eyebrows to Meridian. "We'll be right there."

"Thank you." Drew begrudgingly headed back to the table.

"How well do they know each other?" Meridian asked.

"He surfaced right before Finn came out. He's only six months younger than Finn, and his mother petitioned my father for tuition money when Drew wanted to go to college. So, they don't know each other well. Do you mind if we join them for a game?"

"You go ahead," Meridian offered.

Jack chuckled and shook his head at her. "Do you not play well, cowgirl?"

"I've only played once, and I mean, you grew up with a billiard room in your house, so you obviously have an unfair advantage."

"Look at me," he demanded. Meridian's eyes found his again. "You know, you could ask me for my help."

He had her there, she supposed. "I'm not good at that either," she admitted.

"Two things you could improve at once, then."

Glancing at his brothers waiting on them expectantly, she gave in. "All right, fine—Jack, would you teach me how to not suck at pool?"

"It would be my distinct pleasure." He stood and offered her his hand.

CHAPTER THIRTY-TWO

Still hard up and aching from her affections to his crotch, Jack tried to focus on the task before him. The truth of it was that pool was a sexy game if you knew how to play. If he played with even half of his skill set, he could appease Drew, try to figure out what the hell Greer was up to, and indulge a little of the wildfire sparking in Meridian's eyes.

He, of all people, knew Meridian was as multifaceted as ten other women combined. She was a hundred-sided die, and one had to know how to roll to determine which side of her she chose to reveal. He'd been hopelessly devoted to the study of her for years. He knew how to roll the dice and win.

Instinctively, he sized up the table, his familial opponents, and then watched Meridian approach the cue stand and reach for the first one she saw. Jack rushed to her and shook his head. "We're playing teams," he informed his brothers. "Go ahead and rack them up." Then he spoke so only she could hear him. "Not that one."

"Why not?"

"It has no tip, for one thing. Just try trusting me on this, would you?"

"All right, fine," she goaded.

He grabbed the only cue remaining that had a decent tip. It

appeared to be slightly warped to the left, but he could compensate for that. He was certain Greer and Drew had selected the straighter cues.

Chalking the tip, he dragged it between two fingers to remove the excess dust. Meridian stared at him. "Wow." She shook her head. "I have no idea why that's so sexy, but couldn't I just watch you play?"

Pleased with her request, he shook his head. "It'll be much sexier if we play as one. Trust me, remember?"

"Okay, fine." She shrugged. "Teach me."

Greer slid the rack back and forth on the table and then lifted it like he'd done in the thousands of games they'd played together growing up.

"Your break," he offered Jack.

Jack chuckled at that as he led Meridian to the opposite side of the table. "Do you seriously think I can't play as well with her?" He knew why his brother had offered to let him break.

"I think this might be the only chance I ever have of beating you," Greer harassed.

"See." Meridian looked wounded. "Just let me watch you."

"He's full of shit," Jack stated loud enough for Greer to hear him. "Trust me." He'd say it until she finally took the action without prompting. "Pool is geometry and nothing more," he explained as he lined up the cue ball. "Three-fourths of the game is lining up the shot."

"I wasn't that great at geometry either," she huffed.

"Then we'll make up for it with chemistry." Jack stood directly behind her and leaned her low over the table. The quick change of her breath only served to make him harder. She pressed back against him. "I love having your ass up against me," he whispered as he aligned the cue with the ball using her fingers as his slide. "We're shooting low on the ball to spin it back so we can pocket the balls that break to this side of the table first."

She wiggled her hips ever so slightly, playing a game all her own. He growled low in her ear. "If you keep that up, I'll find somewhere in this bar to fuck you, honey." She repeated the motion in a friction-induced challenge directly to his groin. "Be still for just one minute, but after I win this game you can do that all you like while I drill into you from behind."

A quick catch of her breath and a stilling of her body preceded him breaking the balls in a perfect split.

They joined Drew as Greer lined up his first shot. "If you want to escape this game, there's a young lady at the bar who seems interested in you," Jack informed his youngest brother.

Drew glanced that way discreetly. "Yeah, I saw her. I somehow bet she wouldn't let me teach her to play pool like that." He gestured to where Jack had bent Meridian over the table.

Jack laughed. "Maybe try buying her a drink first."

"Does she look familiar to you?" Drew asked.

Jack hadn't paid that much attention to the blonde. She'd been in direct lineup of his shot, and he'd noticed that she was overtly staring at Drew. Trying to be more discreet now, he studied her more closely.

His blood ran ice cold, and the boner he'd been certain he wouldn't rid himself of until he unloaded deep in Meridian wilted. "That's Farrah Fitzgerald," he spat. "What the hell is she doing out here?" Watershed held so much appeal because Bourbon Country steadfastly ignored its existence.

"Who?" Meridian and Drew asked simultaneously.

"Tiffany's little sister," Jack spoke low and kept his back to Farrah.

Meridian pretended to be sizing up the position of the balls on the table, but Jack saw her study Farrah. She returned to his side. "She looks like she got stood up."

"How can you tell?"

"She keeps glancing from Drew to the door. She's obviously interested in him, but hasn't made a move yet. Plus, she looks pissed."

Drew rolled his eyes. "She's probably slumming it down here to piss her parents off or something."

Jack flipped back through a few memories of Farrah. She was several years younger than Tiffany. He hadn't interacted with her much growing up. In fact, he only remembered seeing her twice, but he did recall her being defiant on numerous occasions to gain her parents' attention, which Tiffany tended to dominate. Her outlandish stunts had led to her parents shipping her off to boarding school for most of her life. Drew was likely correct. She was probably here to infuriate her father.

"She's coming over," Meridian alerted them.

"It's your shot," Greer urged impatiently.

"Right." Jack wasn't certain how to proceed.

He slowly guided Meridian to an easy corner pocket shot while trying to eavesdrop.

"You look so familiar," Farrah cooed flirtatiously to Drew. "Have we met before?"

"I'd remember meeting you," Drew informed her. "Do you come here often?" The clichés became that way for a reason.

"No, I've never been here before. I was supposed to meet my sister here, but she hasn't shown." Jack and Meridian shared a quick uncomfortable glance. Just how many people knew where they were? "What's your name?" Farrah inquired.

"Drew." He provided no last name. Smart kid.

"I'm Farrah." She grinned at him as Jack once again lined up the shot and leaned Meridian low over the table. As long as he lined up the shots correctly, he could play blindfolded, so there was no real need for him to pay much attention to the game. "Do you want to get a drink or something?" She gestured back to the bar.

"Don't let us hold you up," Greer encouraged him.

Farrah's head jerked to the side as Jack sank the three in the side pocket and knocked the five to the center. "Aren't you the Denton brothers?"

"Guilty as charged," Jack allowed. "How are you, Farrah? It's been a few years."

"Jack, oh my gosh. You're...uh...older."

Meridian choked back laughter as Jack nodded. "Yeah, I guess I am."

Farrah cringed. "Well, we all are. I didn't mean it like that. You look great. Really, really great."

Meridian's eyes narrowed. "Jealous, honey?" Jack got her back for laughing a moment earlier.

"What brings you out here tonight?" Drew picked up where he'd left off.

"Like I said, I was supposed to meet Tiffany and Brent here. I have no idea why they wanted to come all the way out here. Were they supposed to play pool with you guys or something?" she asked Greer. "Couldn't you do this at our house?"

Greer shook his head. "No. Not to my knowledge." He turned to Jack. "Did you know Tiff was coming?" Something in his brother's question irked Jack.

"I had no idea," he assured everyone.

"Weird," Farrah shrugged. "I'll call her later. So, do you want to get that drink?"

"Why not?" Drew returned his cue to the cabinet and followed her to the bar.

"Guess it's just us." Greer shrugged.

"What the hell is going on?" Jack demanded.

Looking surprised at the question, Greer gestured to the table. "I'm planning to sink the four in the side."

"Not with the game. How is it that you and Tiffany and Brenton were all planning to be here tonight? That's entirely too much coincidence."

Greer bristled. "What? Do you think we were planning an intervention for you or something?"

"Were you?"

"No," he scoffed. "I want to start coming here to see Finn with you. I told you that. I had no idea Tiff was supposed to be here. How would I know that?"

Jack made mental note of Drew leaning closer to Farrah, of Sloan and Sophie climbing the stairs up from the dance floor, of Finn giving his impish grin to the man with the beer bottle, and to Lila sitting quietly back at their booth watching them all. "You knew Mom and Dad were going out to the Fitzgeralds' tonight."

"I asked Frank to be sure they weren't going to be around. I swear to you, I didn't know about Tiffany. Do you really think Finn and Drew would be in on some kind of meeting where we try to talk you into coming back to Kentucky? They love you. They hate me."

That punctured a little of the fury that filled Jack. "They don't hate you."

"Maybe they should."

"Why?"

"Because I'm the holdout, right? I'm the brother that goes along with what Dad wants. I'm the one who won't stand up to him."

"And why is that?" Jack cornered his brother.

Greer folded his hands on top of his cue. "I don't know."

Meridian touched Jack's tensed shoulders. "I imagine it can be difficult to know who you are outside of the world your family has built. It would take a really strong person to rebuild their life in a different way all over again."

Greer gestured to Jack. "You've always been stronger than me. It bothers me when they're angry. It bothers me that my family is split. I want to be a part of both, but if you don't want me here, I'll leave."

Jack considered his offer. "I don't want you to leave, but I do want your loyalty. In fact, I'm going to demand it."

Greer held up his hand. "I will never discuss what I've seen here tonight with anyone but the people who are here. What do you call yourselves? The douchebags or something?" He tried for a joke and significantly missed the mark.

"The Bastards," Jack corrected. "For very obvious reasons."

CHAPTER THIRTY-THREE

They were down to the last three balls on the table. Greer and Jack had gone shot for shot, until Greer had missed one that had bounced back and forth in front of the pocket. Jack had nailed his next shot, and Meridian was as impressed as she was turned on. The way Jack had confronted his brother immediately placed him on a pedestal in her mind. Jesus, if she wasn't careful she was going to fall head over boots and there'd be no turning back.

Before Greer could attempt to sink two balls with one shot, Lila made her way over to them. "Looks like your former teammate is busy with Farrah Fitzgerald," she commented.

They all directed their attention to Farrah and Drew. They were slowly edging closer to one another and sharing a flight of whiskey shots. Greer shrugged. "I'm glad he's enjoying himself."

"Let me take this last shot," Lila pressed him.

He stared at her like she was crazy. "Not a chance."

"Come on. We both know you tend to choke under pressure."

"I do not."

Jack drew Meridian to his chest while they waited. She wrapped her arms around him, and in the midst of all the crazy this night had provided she found peace. He whispered in her ear, "Lila is not wrong."

Meridian didn't really care who won this game. She wanted to be alone with Jack anywhere else.

"Come on, Greer," Lila continued.

"Fine, but if you miss, I never want to hear anything else about me buckling under pressure from either of you."

Meridian felt Jack nod against her head. Lila must have also agreed. Meridian begrudgingly turned and, to her shock, watched Lila's perfect trick shot. She hit the cue ball off the side. It shot toward the side pocket, knocked in the ball there, and somehow ricocheted to sink the other ball as well.

"I don't miss," Lila informed her cousins.

Jack laughed. "I never said you did."

"Rematch," Greer urged. "I'll let you beat me this time."

"I can beat you anytime you don't have Lila's help, but not tonight." Jack wrapped his arm around Meridian. "We can play at River Chase. I want to dance with my fiancée."

"You can buy me a drink to toast our win," Lila offered Greer.

"Fine," Greer grumbled.

As Meridian let Jack guide her toward the staircase, she wondered, "Do you think Farrah knows who Drew is?"

"I doubt she did before she came over, but she might now. I'm not sure how open he is about his parentage."

"I get that."

"Me too."

"Are you as good at dancing as you are at pool?" The idea of being pressed against him swaying to the music was highly appealing, although not quite as intriguing as his threat to find somewhere to fuck her in this bar.

"No." Jack laughed as he pulled her even closer. "But at least if I'm against you, the effect you have on me will be somewhat concealed."

Thrilled with that confession, Meridian laid her head on his shoulder and pretended to be confused. "What effect is that?"

Jack's hand slipped farther down her back and gripped her ass. "You don't just make me hard, honey. You keep me hard. You make me ache."

"I could take care of that for you," she whispered.

"You're going to, but first you're going to dance for me."

At the bottom of the staircase, they slipped into drowning darkness. They blinked in an effort to adjust to the lack of light. Heavy percussive beats shook the floor that was flooded with red and blue neon lights that concealed far more than they revealed. It was like stepping into an entirely different world, all black iron beams and strobe lights.

That feeling of being submerged in something altogether unfamiliar was something she was oddly growing accustomed to here in Kentucky. But this time was different. Jack's arm was slung protectively around her, and somehow nothing about their new setting felt disconcerting.

His arms were a strong, steady foundation, almost like...home.

Two guys were cutting up the center of the dance floor, but around them couples were pressed together dancing close. The bar down here was positioned near the long back wall, and unlike upstairs, people had to shout their orders for the bartenders to be able to hear.

Jack led her to the dance floor. They blended into one of the external amoeba-like crowds. The song bled to one with a slower, heavier beat and breathy lyrics—sex through speakers.

The wildfire blazed fiercely in Jack's backlit gaze. It burned away Meridian's weak excuses that she'd clung to with him. Her fear that she'd never be DA if she fell for him lost its voice, and yet her hands shook from all she'd held back. Every sacrifice she'd watched him make for his family transformed something in her. She never wanted him to sacrifice for her. The knowledge that he would was enough.

He was right there, poised against her, staring at her like he wanted to devour her, and she wanted nothing more than to be devoured. She swayed against him, letting the music move through her. He moved in rhythm with her body.

His capable hands gripped her hips as she thrust against him to the beat. With her arms up, her tits swayed in his face. Not seeming to mind that they were in a crowded room, he managed to lean and spin his tongue at the hollow above her collarbone.

Her moan blended in with the music, but she knew he'd heard it when his eyes closed in desperate agony. The secret moment in a room with hundreds of other people surged heated desire through her veins.

Jack's fingers threaded through her hair as he brought her lips to his own. Whiskey heat and need blended on their tongues as they got drunk off each other. Meridian wasn't certain how he kept them swaying other than the fact that the beat of the music matched their animalistic hunger.

Keeping one hand in her hair, he brushed her thigh with the other, teasing at the hem of her dress, pushing it higher. She groaned urgently, a plea for him to follow through with his threat.

She'd suspected that Jack had a voyeur streak about him with his office-sex confession that everyone would hear them and then again when he demanded that she say his name when they were out on his parents' porch. She had no idea how much she would like the idea of people watching what only he could make her do. It was heady and forbidden. It tapped into the well of wild housed so deep in her soul. The cowgirl in her needed to ride wild. He somehow held the keys to every locked door of her—her heart, her laughter, her mind, her sin.

"Dance for me, cowgirl," he demanded.

Stepping back slightly, he watched no one but her. The intensity of his focus heated her skin. It burned through her, scorching every inhibition she'd ever even pretended to hold dear.

Never before in her entire life had she been so completely in control of who she was, what she wanted. Him. There were a thousand lies about them spinning around Kentucky, but this was a single truth —she wanted him in every possible way she could have a relationship with him. No one had ever made her feel so sexy, so seen.

She didn't have to live up to the expectations of every cattle rancher, every voter, every Holder. No, she only had to dance for him. Every role anyone had ever cast her in fell away. Here, she was herself giving this to him, and no one else would ever matter.

She let the music pour through her as she began to move just for him. She dragged her hands up her own thighs, lifting the dress ever so slightly. She imagined his hands on her body and moved to the strum of his fingers. She lost all those things she'd never really wanted to be and became fully herself.

Her eyes blinked open to find his gaze, dark and almost angry with yearning. He returned to her side in two quick steps. "You're attracting quite the audience, and I do not share." She'd never heard him sound so possessive. Why was that so utterly appealing? Adrenaline spiked her blood, and urgent desire ruined her panties.

She fell into his arms. If he wanted her to make a declaration to her male and female admirers, she was more than happy to do so. "I need you." She sang his song. She knew the lyrics he needed to hear.

He guided her off of the dance floor. "What do you need, cowgirl? Tell me." His breaths were quick and his tone like gravel.

She turned back and grinned at the people applauding her dancing before she stared him down. "You inside me. Now."

"Done."

He took her hand and half guided and half dragged her toward the bar. She thought maybe they were going outside, but he took a hard left and led her up a darkened staircase. At the top, he pushed a door open and guided her out into the cool night air. Trying to get her bearings, she stepped out onto the brick flooring and was surrounded by wrought iron tables with closed umbrellas and stacks of matching chairs. "What is this?" she asked.

"They open the rooftop in the summer, but tonight it's just for us." Her heartbeat broke out into a fierce gallop.

"Have you ever...done this before?" She wasn't certain why she required that information, but it was suddenly very important.

He spun back to stare at her. "Been up here? Yes. Had sex up here? Never." Keeping a firm hold of her hand, he led her to a corner created by the tall brick fireplace along the north wall.

His lips crashed down on hers in a messy, almost clumsy kiss born from desperation. He ran his hands under her dress and trailed his kisses down her neck, allowing her breath.

"Jack," she panted. "What are we doing?"

"If you want me to stop, say so now," he demanded.

His urgency amped the electricity surging between them. "I never want you to stop. Not here. Not back in Oklahoma. Never."

He lifted his head and stared her down. "What does that mean, honey?"

"I don't want us to end."

"Thank god." He dove back in for another kiss. Their tongues tangled, and his deep groan spilled into her mouth. She wanted to feel every single one of his sounds. "I don't know how I'd ever let you go," he admitted before he nipped her bottom lip.

"Thank god." She laughed in relief.

He drank her laughter like a smooth shot of whiskey. Her hands made quick work of his belt and jeans. She needed to feel him, hot and heavy.

His hands moved up her thighs, clasped her panties, and yanked them downwards.

The elastic straps of the G-string tangled on her heels. He held her steady and untangled her. The panties went deep into the pocket of his jeans. She suspected she'd never get them back. That worked just fine for her.

His expert fingers were tracing over the wet auburn curls covering her mound. The cool night air taunted, and the warmth of his hand soothed. The effect was dizzying and delicious.

"You're drenched, princess," he whispered.

CHAPTER THIRTY-FOUR

Meridian's fingers wrapped mercifully around his cock as she managed to open his jeans enough to fully reveal him. Rewarding her efforts, he pressed his fingers between her swollen lips, teasing at her entrance. A choked moan shook from her.

"So fucking wet," he growled out again. "Is it being up here, baby? Do you like knowing someone could walk up here and see what you let me do to you?" Her responding gasp of his name spoke volumes. "Or did you like thinking about me fucking you filthy while you were dancing for me?"

"Yes," hissed from her. "Please, Jack. I need...."

"I know. I know what you need. Let me fuck that needy little ache away."

"It doesn't," she whimpered and pressed his cock to her pussy lips. "It never goes away." Precum leaked from his head as she dragged him back and forth against her clit. It mixed so readily with her juices. He shuddered from the delectable sight. "I always want more."

Thrilled at that admission, her broken pleas still shattered him. She was playing with fire, and he suspected she knew. "Baby, let me get a condom on." The last vestiges of the man he'd fought so hard to become urged him to never do her wrong. He reached back in his loosened jeans and managed to retrieve his wallet. He tossed it on a nearby table as soon as he'd located the condom.

He allowed her one more stroke along her slit. "I'm gonna come all over your hand if you keep that up."

A delighted though devious grin formed on her kiss-swollen lips. "Hurry," she urged.

"I love when you get impatient for me." He rolled the condom on in a fluid movement, then lifted her right leg and hooked her heel around his thigh. Aligning his cock at her entrance, he made his demand, "Take it." He thrust hard parting her and pressing deeper. The answer to his every prayer was deep inside of her, and he wouldn't survive without her absolution. "Take it all."

The thin night air filled with the scent of her arousal. Her hands dug into his hair as she held on. The brick and iron surrounding them juxtaposed with her soft heat and tender curves. Filtered sounds from the bar below mixed with a hint of the music pulsing under them. A few drunk patrons out on the street had no hopes of seeing them, but served to remind them that every hard, fast thrust was a formal declaration to all of Louisville. He was not the man he'd been born to be, nor was he who he'd fought to become. He was nothing more and nothing less than hers. His lost, confused identity was locked into the indentation he'd made in her.

All of the years of desperate silence and ultimate patience about how badly he wanted her found their worth on that rooftop in his hometown. His entire world reduced to the place where he filled her full. From there, he would reshape, reform, rebuild himself into whatever she needed him to be.

His thrusts grew faster and harder, more frantic and less rhythmic. The heated air between them filled with her breathy mewls of pleasure and his low groans of urgency. Her body tensed around him. Her head dropped to his shoulder and her lips swept over his neck and punished his skin. The pain only amplified his pleasure.

The divine agony overtook him as she cinched tight around him. He buried himself in her and wrapped her up protectively in his arms as he filled the condom with four years' worth of equal parts hunger and satisfaction.

He brushed tender kisses on her shoulders and eased away from her when they'd caught their breath. Eventually, they found their way to one of the loungers. He stretched out and guided her into his arms, her back to his chest. "That was incredible," he informed her.

She grinned up at him. "We are very good at that."

"I think we're very good at us."

"Yeah, I think you're right. Are you mad I was too stubborn to tell you that I liked you a long time ago?"

Jack shook his head and stroked his fingers over her cheek. "No, honey. I wasn't ready, and I will never be angry at you for being who you are. I love your stubborn side."

"Should we go back downstairs?" She didn't sound any more thrilled about that than he felt.

"Eventually."

"I like it up here better." Her confession held tender vulnerability.

"I like it anywhere you are." He wouldn't allow her to exist in that vulnerability alone.

She turned and buried her face against his shirt. "Me too." She let him nurture her and kiss her soft skin everywhere he could get his lips for several long minutes. "Do we keep us a secret back home?"

"If that's what you want," he whispered.

"I don't know what I want outside of you."

"Then why don't we figure it out when we get back home."

She nodded against him. "Okay. I hate that we figured this out because of a bunch of lies we told. That seems like a bad way to start a relationship."

Loving this insight into her mind, he tipped her chin up so he could stare into those whiskey-laden eyes. "Other than our exaggeration about being engaged, I'm not certain we've really lied."

He laid it all out on the line. Were they really in love? He wasn't certain, but if this wasn't love he couldn't fathom what that must be like.

She nodded and tucked back under his chin. He refused to press it further. Patience had gotten him right where he wanted to be, so he'd keep playing the cards that were winning.

They stayed on that lounger another half hour, and then he helped her up and they tried to put themselves back together in a way that wouldn't let everyone in Watershed know what they'd been up to. It proved largely impossible without mirrors, or perhaps it was that something inside each of them had taken root and they could no longer hide it externally.

He guided her back down the darkened staircase, and they found the rest of the Bastards close to where they'd left them. Sloan laughed at Jack outright. "I don't even need to ask what you two were doing."

Greer looked concerned to the point of admonishment, but he kept his mouth shut, a smart move on his part.

Drew rejoined their party after he walked Farrah to her Mercedes.

"How did that go?" Jack asked him.

"She's a Fitzgerald. At some point attractive turns into vapid."

Finn's eyes narrowed. "Yeah, but you wouldn't have been chatting her up for hours if she only had the emotional depth of her big sister."

Drew waved him off. "Whatever, man. She's in a rough place. Her parents are getting divorced, and you know all of Bourbon Country is going to feel that fallout."

"Indeed." Jack sighed. "Are you going to see her again?" He smirked. "You know...to help her through the rough patch."

Drew's chuckle sounded remarkably like all of the Denton brothers. "So what if I am?"

"I just think it's...an interesting choice."

"Getting laid is not an interesting choice, big brother. It's just fun." He gestured to Jack. "As you well know."

Meridian's cheeks flushed the color of her hair. Jack shared a conspiratorial grin with her, and laughter eventually erupted from them both.

Sloan shook his head at them. "Part of me wants to know where the hell you two were, but then I think I'd rather just not know."

"You'd rather not know," Sophie assured him. Lila nodded her agreement.

Jack smirked at his cousin. "I don't kiss and tell."

"Oh, really?" Sloan jerked the collar of his shirt to the side.

"What?" Jack couldn't see his own neck.

Meridian whispered in his ear, "So, there might be a very slight hickey on your neck."

He yanked the collar of his shirt back and refused to answer any of them. He loved wearing her mark. He was fairly certain if someone could remove a portion of his skin, they'd see the Holder brand firmly burned into his soul.

Greer was the first to head out that night, followed soon after by Drew, Lila, Sloan, and Sophie. Jack and Meridian settled back into the booth with Finn.

"Do you need anything?" Jack quietly asked his brother.

Finn shook his head. "Believe it or not, I do have a well-paying job, a great apartment, and I even remember to feed myself," he harassed. "You don't have to worry about me so much anymore."

"That's easier said than done," Jack admitted as he pressed the corners of a cocktail napkin against the table to avoid looking directly at his brother. Deep emotion wasn't generally the way of Denton men.

"Let's talk about you two instead then." Finn turned the tables rather suddenly. "When exactly did you figure out you were in love with her?"

Jack and Meridian both stared at him with their mouths agape. "What?" Jack finally stammered.

Finn looked like he was having way too much fun at Jack's expense. "For years now, every time I call you, all you talk about is Meridian does this and Meridian thinks that. I figured you'd either fuck her or marry her eventually. So, when did that happen? I feel left out."

Never wanting his brother to feel left out of anything after what his family had already put him through, Jack was at a loss as to how to answer.

Meridian saved him again. "I think we're still in the process of figuring that out."

"So, you aren't really engaged then," Finn summed.

"We're not sure about that either," Jack informed him.

His brother leaned on his forearms across the table. "Then let me give you some advice this time instead of the other way around, which is how it used to always go. Figure out what you are sure of and go from there. Make the foundation the truth no matter how long it takes you to build whatever it is you're going to have."

Meridian nodded. "That's really good advice."

Finn winked at her. "I have a really good big brother."

"Yeah, you definitely do," she agreed.

More than ready to duck out of the spotlight, Jack changed the subject. "I wish I knew what Greer's long game was. Why the hell did he show up here tonight?"

Finn nodded. "That's the fifty-million-dollar bourbon money question, now isn't it."

"Do you think it's possible he really is trying to apologize for his silence?" Meridian asked.

"Maybe," Finn shrugged. "But we'll never really know the answer. That's the thing with people who decide that it's easier to just keep the peace and never stand up for what's right. His existence is never on the line. There's no personal cost to him, so he has the luxury of playing nice. It's not like mine, or Drew's, or even Jack's now that he's thrown it all back in Dad's face. There's nothing louder than their silence. That's why we're sitting here debating his motives instead of believing what he said."

CHAPTER THIRTY-FIVE

Jack kept an eye on the road as Meridian happily drove them back to River Chase in the Cheyenne.

"I'm sorry about the hickey," she offered with a delighted grin.

"No, you're not." He laughed.

Her giggle broadened his grin. "I'm a little bit sorry."

"You are lying through your pouty lips, princess."

That elicited more laughter. "Okay, how about if I let you give me one?"

"Now that kind of negotiation will get you a whole lot further."

"I still don't think I'm a princess," she informed him a few minutes later.

"Not even my princess?"

Her entire face transformed as her smile reached her eyes. "Maybe that."

"Definitely that. Take the next right and follow the river for the next few miles. You'll see the entrance gates. We want the third entrance."

"Who is the first gate for?"

"The staff."

"And the second?"

"My parents' private garage."

"Fancy." She rolled her eyes.

"Ridiculous," Jack countered.

They parked the truck, took a few minutes to indulge in each other a little more, and then headed into the house. Jack's hopes that his parents might have already gone to bed were dashed as soon as they entered.

His mother's long-suffering sigh, the background music of most of his childhood, greeted them quickly. "Did you two enjoy yourselves?" It was clear from her question that if they did enjoy themselves they should be ashamed.

"Very much so," Jack informed her.

"I'm sure you'll be pleased to know that Tiffany has cancelled the bridal tea."

Jack stared at the woman who'd given him birth and wondered for the thousandth time how they were so different. "Why would I be pleased with that?"

His mother took a quick sip of water. "You seem to enjoy disrupting our lives. I assumed this would fit into your plans."

"What plans, Mother?"

"I let Tiffany know that you and,"—she waved her hand dismissively toward Meridian—"*she* would be happy to attend dinner tomorrow evening at Bellemenson."

Jack's head throbbed with everything wrong with her statement. "You did what?"

"Greer assured me that you'd be fine with that," she threw in his face.

Rage ignited in Jack's blood. "And since when do you and Greer keep my social calendar?"

"You are in my home, and even though you always brush off your responsibilities to this family and our obligations, it is your fault that this has happened."

Meridian gripped his arm rather hard. "Jack." She shook her head, but he wasn't going to be held back.

"I brush off responsibility? Me?" he shouted. "You can tell Tiff that

I'll be happy to dine with her when you can remember my fiancée's name. Otherwise, you can all take a yacht straight to hell."

Fury pulsed in his vision all the way down the lengthy hallway to his room. He almost ran over his brother as he burned a path forward. "What the hell are you thinking committing me to dinner with Tiffany? Who are you really playing for, Greer?" Jack seethed.

"I'm not playing for anyone. When I got back, Mom asked me if I thought you'd mind having dinner with Tiff and Brent. It didn't seem like that big of a deal. You were engaged to her."

Jack managed a few nods. "Did it ever occur to you to tell her to ask me if I minded having dinner over there?"

"No. What are you so pissed about? They have a great chef."

"Un-fucking-believable."

Unable to remain still even when they reached his childhood bedroom, Jack continued to pace. Meridian sat quietly on the bed watching him. She seemed to understand that motion was how he clung to sanity.

"How do they always manage to make me feel like I'm the one who's lost my mind?" he finally asked her.

Understanding weighted the nod she gave him. "People always think of themselves as the exception to the rule. If they're the most important thing in their own lives, then they must be the most important in yours. People can't see outside of their own heads. The favor they ask is just one favor, so to them it's no big deal. No one ever gets that there have been years of favors and just this or just that. Everyone has a breaking point. Everybody gets to a place where what's being asked of them is more than they can give because they've already sacrificed so much to keep the peace."

He stared at her and allowed himself to fully grasp the amazement that she allowed him to hold her in his hands. "How'd you get to be so goddamn smart?"

She grinned. "I come from a long line of people who always try to bend over backwards so they can fulfill all of the favors everyone asks for. Sometimes we can't. So, through the years, I've watched my family get dragged because we have to reinforce boundaries or flat out tell people no because what they're asking for only serves themselves and not the community."

"We're not going," he assured her.

"I don't mind going as much as I mind the fact that Greer prefers to make excuses for your parents' lies because that makes his life easier than acknowledging the truth."

Her words sparked a thought in Jack's mind. "Greer and Brent are pretty good friends."

She grinned. "So, if we do have dinner with them, maybe we could get a little insight into just what your brother is up to."

"Maybe, but I'm not dragging you out to Bellemenson. You hate it here. I can't imagine what you'd think of their estate. If they want to eat with us, we'll do it on neutral ground."

She stood up off of his bed and wrapped her arms around him. Her touch soothed his weary body and anger-riddled mind. "You know, I don't hate it here because of the monuments to stupid amounts of money your mother decorates with or because all of the staff are still curtsying to me. Although, I do hate that," she added quickly. "I hate it here because they can't see what an amazing man you are."

"I wouldn't go that far," Jack scoffed.

"Trust me. I know what I'm talking about. You know pool. I know you."

Another round of guilt turned to concrete in Jack's gut. "Speaking of me knowing pool, I owe you an apology."

"For what?"

"For tonight. My brothers made some lewd comments, and I didn't do a very good job of keeping what we shared to myself."

The grin that he was falling so hard for—equal parts mischief and delight—formed on her features. "You have met my brothers, right?" She laughed.

Chuckling at that, he nodded. "I have." It was distinctly odd to be laughing after everything that had happened in the last ten minutes.

"That's dinner conversation every night with Maddox and Jericho. Just remember, I'm way more cowgirl than princess. I sure as hell don't want to be treated like some corncob-up-her-ass southern-fried debutante. I loved tonight. All of it."

Jack took her hands in his own. "Good. I loved it too. But...if I ever do something you don't like, you'll tell me, right? I want the chance to fix it before you call this off."

"Cowgirls ride. Come hell or high water or blistering heat or knee-high snow. No matter what. When I decide I'm going to do something, I don't give up, and I won't give up on you or us."

He wished he could believe that, but it seemed entirely too good to be true. Nothing good ever lasted in his life because his life had been built on lies, just like this relationship had been. He'd brushed off her pointing that out at Watershed, but now the question ate him alive.

CHAPTER THIRTY-SIX

"It's just odd," Meridian commented as Jack drove them toward the agreed-upon restaurant the following evening.

"I'm going to need you to be a little more specific, sweetheart." Jack winked at her.

"We're going to dinner with your ex-fiancée, and you care so little about her it would be ridiculous for me to even be jealous a little bit. But for most couples, I think jealousy over this would be profoundly normal."

Jack squeezed her thigh. "I would have to have felt something for her when we were actually engaged for me to have any feelings other than annoyance about this evening."

"I can't imagine agreeing to marry someone that you have no feelings for. Maybe that's the weird part."

He offered her an apologetic glance. "Have you ever heard the folktale about the frog in boiling water?"

"Yeah. If you put a frog in boiling water it will jump out, but if you put it in pleasantly warm water and slowly raise the temperature, it will stay in there and cook?"

"Right. The lesson in that tale is true. What you live day in and day out becomes your normal. Nothing about it seems odd from inside that scalding pot. I had to propel myself out of it to even really grasp just how insane it all was. Up until the moment I was staring down grossly fraudulent tax claims that I was expected to make appear legal and watching them slowly erase Finn's existence, it all seemed normal to me."

Meridian considered that. "But surely you recognized that things weren't exactly above board before they sent Finn away."

"They raised the temperature on the water so slowly I was able to make excuses for each individual thermostat adjustment until I had to get out or be burned alive. When you want to believe what you're being told, it's harder to step back from it all and take a hard look in the mirror."

Meridian shook her head. "I still think it's amazing you were able to get out. Greer isn't as strong as you are."

"Don't make excuses for him. There's always a way. Although, I will admit I'm not sure I would've landed on my feet if it weren't for Thad's help."

"Who is Thad?" Meridian felt like she was missing key portions of Jack's story.

"Senator McCoy's son. He was a frat brother of mine at Duke. I told you about him."

"Yeah, you just didn't use his name, I don't think, but don't give him all the credit. You would've gotten out somehow."

Jack's phone rang before he could respond to that. "Would you mind answering that? It's difficult to talk on the phone while driving a stick."

"Sure." Meridian picked up Jack's cell from the old pull-out ashtray in the Cheyenne. She stared at the screen. "It's Tiffany."

"Good luck."

Pleased that he hadn't tried to figure out a way to keep her from answering the call, Meridian went on with it. This was going to be fun. "This is Meridian."

"Oh, um, hey," Tiffany sang. "Listen, can you tell Jack that Brent didn't get off the golf course in time, so let's just eat at Hearst Stone tonight. We already have a table."

"Hang on one second," Meridian said as she tried to make sense of what Tiffany was asking. Blocking the speakers on the phone with her thigh, she hoped Jack could make sense of the message. "Tiff says that Brent couldn't get his ass off the golf course in time for the dinner they arranged, and now they have us a table at Hearst Stone, whatever the hell that is."

Jack shook his head in what seemed like disbelief. "Turn it on speaker." Meridian followed his order. "No," was the first and only word Jack spoke as soon as Tiffany could hear him. Meridian bit back laughter.

"Oh, you are such a stick, Jackson. It'll be fun. We'll see you soon. Our table's at The Hunt. You remember. See you soon." She made a few kissing noises before the call ended.

Dear god. She was just too much. "I'm going to need you to translate all of that into middle-class," Meridian informed Jack.

———

———

———

Jack had absolutely no idea what to say. It took him a few seconds to register that Meridian needed him to do something. "Uh," he tried to sort through the barrage of fury that bombarded his mind. "Hearst Stone is the bourbon families' preferred country club. The Hunt Grille is one of the four dining rooms in the club. It's the elite dining room, and of course the Fitzgeralds have a standing table there."

"But don't you have to be a member of country clubs to be allowed inside? You're not still a member, are you?"

Disgusted at the thought, Jack scowled. "No, but my middle name is Hearst. As in Hearst Stone, and I was named that because Hearst is my mother's maiden name."

Her mouth dropped open for a split second before she gasped, "Your mother's family established the elite bourbon family country club?"

"And they most certainly would let me in if I wanted to go, which I do not."

"So, I take it this isn't even close to neutral ground."

"It would be neutral in the same way it would've been if FDR's son had agreed to dine with Mussolini's daughter in Berlin."

"No offense, but I think your dad is a far cry from Roosevelt."

"Agreed. I got lost in my own metaphor. Forgive me."

"No problem. Did she call you a stick?"

"In the mud would be the reference."

Meridian rolled her eyes. "You are so not a stick in the mud. She should've seen us last night." Her obvious thrill with their activities in the bar the night before soothed a little of Jack's sour mood.

"We are not going to Hearst Stone. Would you like to go back to Watershed? Or hell, anywhere else in this godforsaken town?"

"I kind of like Louisville outside of the whiskey river estate sector, and are you sure you don't want to go tonight? I think we need to go see what we can figure out about Greer and what the hell is going on with Tiffany and Brent. It's all very strange."

"Elaborate on that," Jack urged. He wasn't certain which parts she found most odd.

"They were supposed to meet her little sister at Watershed last night and didn't show, and now they've basically trapped us into going to this country club that's basically your mother's. Greer signed us on for this."

"Right. We're walking into an obvious setup."

"Yes, but not a very good one. This would be obvious from the International Space Station. I want to know what they're after."

Jack would've been lying to himself if he'd pretended that he wasn't curious to know that as well.

"My father's goal is always to bring me back to Louisville, back to the business. He wants me under his enormous thumb. My mother's goal since my birth has been for me to provide my parents with a strategic marriage that expands their empire."

"They're after control." She grew quiet for a minute, and Jack watched her think. It was one of his favorite things to watch her do. She was whip-smart brilliant, and the way she pursed her lips and furrowed her brow that created a little groove at the top of her nose was sexy as hell. Suddenly her eyes widened. "What if you own more of that real estate between the lines than you think you do?"

"How would that be possible?" Their conversation about his parents wanting to own the space between the lines replayed in his mind. It had only been the day before coming to Kentucky, but it seemed like an entire lifetime ago. Perhaps that was because in the span of just a few days, he'd seen what his life could be if he managed to play all of his newly shuffled deck of cards correctly for once in his life.

"Maybe your parents *think* you know about something you don't actually know about. Maybe that's why they're acting so awful about me. Maybe there was more to your and Tiffany's potential marriage than you saw. I don't know. There are a million possibilities. If their goal is to maintain control of you, what lengths would they go to before they feel like they have you safely back in the fold?"

"Are you saying that they're looking for something to hold over my head?"

"I'm saying it's a possibility."

Jack shook his head. "They already have that. They know that I can't ever report their bad business practices to the IRS because I signed off on some of it."

"Yeah, but maybe they realize they're losing ground the longer you stay out of Denton Distilleries."

"There's no statute of limitations on tax fraud. You know that."

"Of course I know that, but that isn't what I'm talking about. They're all up to something. They have to be. I want to know what it is. What if Tiffany's parents' divorce has some big effect on your family's business or something?"

Her point brought a thought that had been on the periphery of his mind since the dinner at River Chase to the forefront. "I would love to know why they're divorcing. You don't split a marriage like that for something minor."

"I don't know, but every single thing about this is just weird."

"So, you think we should walk directly into the lion's den and find out what is going on?" The thought of being around the Hearst Stone crowd again made Jack want to vomit.

"In this case, I think we're smarter than the lions. We are one kickass legal team, after all."

"I can't fathom what my parents believe that I know that they think I would confess to Tiffany." Concern and panic suddenly flared in Meridian's eyes. Jack's heart stopped momentarily. "What's wrong?"

"Me," she whispered.

"What?"

"Your mom told your dad that she didn't believe we were a real couple. She's been awful to me, and your dad hasn't exactly been kind. They want to see what we'll tell Tiffany about us."

Jack considered her points. His family had been extraordinarily horrible toward Meridian. They'd gone long past the point of annoyed disdain and had crossed over into egregiously rude. Perhaps she was right. "I don't care if they think this relationship is fake. We define what we mean to each other. No one else even matters."

"Family always matters, and I want to prove our relationship to your family."

He slowed the truck to make a U-turn back toward the country club. "This is more than I should ever have asked you to do."

"You didn't ask me. I'm asking you if we can go into this club and prove that we may've gotten a slow start but we're on fire now. I don't like people doubting us. That bothers me."

"Why?"

"I like firm foundations for everything important in my life."

He nodded. "Then I'll build you one, even if I have to gather materials from the lions." He went on with the warning that was brewing and bubbling angrily in his gut. "We have to be on constant alert. No one at this club owes me any favors. Their very existence is a monument to my mother."

Meridian narrowed her eyes in determination. "Maybe it's time for the monument to become an effigy."

CHAPTER THIRTY-SEVEN

Meridian's nerves continued to weave themselves into complicated knots as they passed through massive stacked stone pillars that marked the entrance to Hearst Stone Country Club. Jack's pallor tinged a little green, and Meridian wondered if asking him to bring her here was a huge mistake.

She gnawed her lip to keep from speaking that thought aloud and focused instead on what they were going to face that evening. It's always better to know what weapons your opponent has at their disposal both in the courtroom and outside of it. Her law professors had hammered that lesson home repeatedly. Never put yourself in a position to be caught off guard.

Jack interrupted her internal strategizing. "The only part of this I'm going to enjoy is parking this truck right in front of the club and telling the valets not to move it."

"We don't have to do this if you think it's a bad idea," finally poured from Meridian's mouth. She wasn't accustomed to doubting herself, but she was entire atmospheres outside of her league. "We'll do whatever you think is best. I trust you." She'd wanted to say those three words to him since last night, and now was definitely the time to say it.

"Thank you for that. I think you're right. We need to know what's going on, but I need you to follow my lead. No matter what I say."

"Okay." Meridian found it oddly reassuring to be able to vow that to him. Trusting anyone outside of her family was so far beyond her comfort zone, but it was also not nearly as frightening as she'd always believed it would be.

There was a massive ode to some kind of gothic cathedral in the distance, but Jack stopped the truck at a long row of golf carts. "This is new."

"What's new?"

"There used to be a circular parking area in front of the club. This has all been redone since I was last here."

"Maybe they knew someday you'd pull up in a kickass Chevy Cheyenne that would totally ruin their weird-ass haunted house, so they put in this golf cart raceway to foil your plans."

Chuckling at her explanation, he beamed at her. "You're still so incredibly dangerous, and I can't seem to care," he informed her, though his tone was more smitten than concerned.

"How am I dangerous? I've never even been to a country club. I have no idea what I'm doing."

He laced their fingers together. "You are dangerous because of how fast I'm falling for you."

Thrilled with that, a grin spread the width of her features. "Well, you're pretty irresistible yourself, District Attorney."

"I thought you wanted that job?"

"I'm rethinking that. See, that proves how dangerous you are."

He gestured to the castle atop the hill glaring down at them. "Let's go be dangerous together. They deserve it."

"Should I pretend to be Mata Hari?" Meridian laughed.

"As long as you'll continue to pretend that back at River Chase. Preferably, the part about her being an exotic dancer to get men to talk." Jack's smirk made her believe this entire night was going to be worth it.

She waggled her eyebrows for him. "And will you pretend to be a foreign spy I'm seducing for information?"

"I keep trying to tell you, I'll be anything you want, honey."

"Wait. When did we start dating?" Meridian spoke through her teeth as they climbed out of the truck. They needed to get their stories straight.

Jack didn't get a chance to answer. Some guy coming off the golf course handed his club back to a caddy and began pulling off his glove. Disbelief hung in his forced smile as he approached. "Jackson? Is that really you? Welcome back to the real world. I heard you'd broken down out in cattle country. Hey, if you're looking for a place, my father has some recent real estate investments you could discuss with him."

Jack did a decent job of turning his grimace into something akin to a polite smile. "We're just meeting someone here. I'm not moving back. How are you, Deke?" They exchanged a handshake. "This is my fiancée, Meridian Holder." He settled his hand on the small of her back. The reassurance in the warmth and familiarity boosted her waning self-confidence that she'd be able to handle this.

"Yeah, I heard about you." Deke shook Meridian's hand next.

She gave him a polite chuckle. "Probably shouldn't believe everything you hear."

Deke gave no response to that at all. "I can give you a ride up to the club." He gestured to his cart.

"Thanks." Jack sounded like he'd prefer to be trampled by wild horses. They climbed in the back seat of the golf cart. Meridian tried to act like she rode in golf carts all the time despite the fact that she'd never been on one in her life. She missed her horse.

"How are your parents? They were up here last night, but I didn't get a chance to talk to them."

Jack and Meridian shared a quick glance. So, his parents had been at the club and not out at Bellemenson. "They're...as good as they'll ever be." The truth in that statement held staggering weight, and yet Deke smiled and nodded his approval. How different the world must appear when people weren't willing to pull back the polished exterior and look below the surface.

"That's great, man."

"When did they change the drive-up?" Jack gestured to the monolithic fountain and landscaping that blocked anything larger than a golf cart from the club.

Deke's brow furrowed. "Your parents' landscaping company did this a couple of years ago for the Christmas Gala." His tone indicated that Jack should've known that. "It was so great of them. Your dad donated the whole thing."

Jack's features morphed to a statue of bitter gall. Meridian had a pretty good idea why, but she'd have to ask later.

Deke parked the cart right in front of the gothic disaster. "Hey, tell Greer we're on for next week."

Jack helped Meridian out of the cart before responding, "I'll let you pass on your own messages since I am not my brother's personal assistant. Thanks for the ride."

Pride welled through Meridian. That assuredness and his take-no-prisoners approach made her want to find them another hidden-away rooftop. "These people wouldn't know the real world if it slapped their ass and told them to call it daddy," she assured him. "And let me guess, your father doesn't have a landscaping company."

"Oh, I'm sure he did for as long as it took him to funnel money through the shell company to avoid paying taxes while also writing off the donation of tools, equipment, and labor. I'd bet my next three paychecks that he had the River Chase gardeners actually do the work while letting the tax documents show that they're separate employees of two different companies."

"Damn, that's...shady as fuck," Meridian whispered.

The castle-sized doors opened at their approach. "Welcome to the world of extreme wealth," Jack agreed. "Are you ready?"

"As I'll ever be."

They were greeted by four people all wearing Hearst Stone uniforms. An older gentleman looked as if Jack's arrival was the second coming. "Jackson, I cannot tell you how thrilled we are you're here and for the unveiling too. You always did have impeccable timing."

"The unveiling?" Jack sounded thoroughly nonplussed.

"Your parents' portrait will be unveiled in the Riviera Room at eight."

"Were the four already in there not enough?"

Meridian bit her lips together to keep from laughing.

Shock shadowed the man's hazel eyes. "Well, you know, we wouldn't be able to do what we do here without them, so we're always happy to show our appreciation."

Jack ground his teeth. "Are my parents attending this unveiling?"

"Not to my knowledge."

"Good."

Jack wrapped his arm around Meridian and guided her away from the man. She tried not to appear impressed with the grand entry hall, far more posh than anything at River Chase and yet every bit as money-drenched. The Hearst Stone fixtures operated under the belief that weight denoted wealth. Heavy stone, iron, and dense black hickory bedecked every surface. Her heels sank deep into the Persian rug, like quicksand under her feet.

Her heartbeat echoed her quick footsteps as they headed down an expansive hallway with low-slung leather sofas and marble tables.

"So, what's up with the portrait thing?" she whispered for lack of anything else to say.

Jack stopped and eased her to an offset corridor. He looked concerned.

Meridian shook her head. "Sorry. I'll stop asking so many questions. You can tell me later."

"No, honey. It's fine. I just have to be careful. All of the major whiskey barons have portraits painted and then the club purchases the portraits at a prearranged price at an auction. Then they write it off as a business expense since they're using them to decorate their establishment. Only they buy them at a massively inflated price of which they only pay a small percentage of. Everyone who attends this auction knows how it works."

"So, your father not only cheats on his own taxes, but he shows other companies how to as well?"

"It's all a part of the whiskey web. We just have to make certain we don't get trapped by the spiders. So, no more questions until after we escape, okay?"

"Sure."

He brushed a tender kiss on her lips. "I won't let them hurt you."

"I'm fine. I promise."

CHAPTER THIRTY-EIGHT

Jack had a plan. He was going to prove that the only way to get through hell was to keep walking and to tell the truth.

They entered the largest dining room in Hearst Stone. The golf course view glimmered from the ten-foot windows surrounding three sides of the restaurant.

Tiffany waved to them from their table, and Jack's stomach turned ominously. God, how had he ended up back here? After this trip, he was going to have to figure out how to get the staff what they needed without having to go to River Chase. It was all too much.

One of the waiters pulled out his and Meridian's chairs. He waited on her to sit and then followed suit. Whatever Tiff and Brent were up to, he was here to play, and he was going to win.

"Can I get you something to drink, Mr. Denton?" A beverage attendant approached the table. Jack was oddly pleased that he didn't know most of the staff by name anymore.

He turned to Meridian. "They only serve Denton whiskeys here." Looking up at the attendant he stated, "I'll have a club soda," loudly enough for the room to hear.

"I'll have the same," Meridian said. "With a twist of lime."

"Yes, ma'am."

Jack smiled to himself as he watched Meridian use one of her best lawyer tricks. She initiated conversation stitched together with concern. "So, how are you two after everything that happened Saturday evening? It's a lot to deal with."

Tiffany, who loved attention almost as much as she loved money, preened. "You are so right. It is a lot to deal with." She seemed to have made a quick recovery from her thoughtful introspection at River Chase.

Jack wasn't going to make it through this dinner without vomiting. He downed a quick sip of the club soda as soon as it landed on the table.

Meridian gave her a sympathetic nod. Jack was certain he was the only person at the table who noted the placating in her movement. He took another sip to cover his smirk.

"I'm sure. Have you made any decisions on the wedding?" Meridian was a decent actress, but patience would never be her virtue.

Brent cut in, "That's part of why we wanted to talk to you two."

Now they were getting somewhere. Jack braced his arm on the back of Meridian's chair. "What is it that we can help with?"

Tiff waved Brent off. "We can at least wait until we have food," she admonished. Jack knew that was her way of informing the table that she had not received enough attention to be ready for someone else to step into the spotlight. Meridian seemed to sense this as well.

They exchanged a quick, knowing glance. "We ran into Farrah last night," Jack informed her. If she wanted attention, he was happy to let her have it.

Tiffany bristled, and Jack narrowed his eyes. She really ought to learn to be careful what she wished for. "Yeah, we were supposed to meet her at that bar,"—she waved her manicured hand as if Watershed and her sister were a fly that needed to be batted away—"but I was just...too upset to come." She even choked up some fake tears to decorate her false declaration.

Brent handed her his handkerchief. "My parents are making certain everything is handled so there's nothing for you to worry over, but I know it's just a devastating situation. I think we should go on with the wedding. A month in Ibiza will be good for us. We can take our minds off of all of this and let someone else deal with the divorce. It's too much for you." They really did deserve each other.

The waiter came to the table and went on for five full minutes about how pleased he was to see Jack. "I appreciate your enthusiasm," Jack drawled, "but I assure you I won't be back for at least as long as I've been gone."

That finally shut him up long enough for him to let them know which dishes were available that evening at The Hunt. Meridian shot a concerned glance his way. Jack leaned in and brushed a kiss on her cheek. Then he whispered, "If you like seafood, the scallops are great, but the oysters aren't worth the hassle. If not, go for the smoked tortellini."

She gave him an adoring grin as he eased away. "I love you too," she informed him. Jack's heart threatened to pound out of his rib cage. She was just copying his move from the dinner party. Surely, that was it. But god, it sounded so good, and then there was the fervency that lit in her eyes as she stared at him.

It was dangerous to believe her. He'd never get over her. Never. And yet, he let himself have the moment as if it were true.

"I'll try the scallops," she told him, not the waiter. He'd had a few business-related dinners with her over the years, and he knew that Meridian was not a woman who allowed anyone to order on her behalf. She didn't allow anyone to do *anything* on her behalf. She'd just handed him a holy grail. She trusted him enough to take care of her, and he would never let her down.

He managed to make the order and even add his own, which given the state of his heart and mind was nothing short of a miracle.

Tiffany made a pouting face that Jack recognized, and he bet Brent and the waiter did as well. "I was really hoping y'all would have the sea bass." She went as far as poking out her bottom lip. Jack made no effort to hide his eye roll.

"I'll see if we have any in the back, Miss Fitzgerald," the waiter assured her.

She immediately perked up and told him he was her favorite.

The waiter seemed pleased with her assessment. "Can I bring you the appetizer tray this evening?"

"Definitely," Tiffany urged without asking anyone else at the table their preference.

Fully aware every eye in the room was poised on their table, Jack eased Meridian closer. A Denton son and a Fitzgerald daughter at this bizarre summit meeting would fuel whiskey gossip chains for the next decade. God, he missed Oklahoma.

No longer caring that he was being somewhat rude, he turned to whisper in Meridian's ear again, "I can't wait to go home."

She lit up like a firecracker on the Fourth of July. "Me either."

The arrival of the appetizers did nothing to soothe Jack's homesickness. It both pleased him and struck him as odd that the place that had raised him would never fill him the way the wide open plains and Oklahoma sunsets made him whole. Indulging himself in another glance at Meridian, who was dipping a piece of bread in infused oil, he understood. It wasn't the sunsets or the wide open spaces. It was her. Her against the backdrop of a technicolor sky, wild and free. That was his home.

Tiffany shook her head. "I just don't know how you eat like that and stay thin-ish." There was heavy emphasis on the *ish,* and Jack seriously considered cramming Tiffany's mouth full of the bread she was avoiding.

Meridian laughed in her face. "I'm not really the kind of woman who feels the need to fit into some societal preconceived, misogynistic idea of what a woman should look like. Plus," she leaned in for the kill, "Jack hasn't complained."

Lifting his eyebrow in lustful appreciation, he chuckled and then went on with his plan. "I love everything about her. I'm pretty sure I have since the day I first saw her. She was in one of the barbecue joints out where we live devouring a pork sandwich. It's the first time in my life I've been jealous of a food."

Shock betrayed the glare Meridian had fixed on Tiffany. "You remember that?"

"Of course. I stood there and stared at you while you ate for ten minutes before I finally came over to introduce myself. Remember?"

She laughed. "Yeah, but you said you didn't want to interrupt my lunch."

"That was the only somewhat acceptable excuse I could come up with. You'd scrambled my mind."

The whiskey in her eyes smoked with her delight. "You're the only man I've ever let stare at me like that without putting my boot up their ass. I definitely didn't mind the attention."

"You always have my attention, sweetheart. Always."

Tiffany and Brent both stared at them in shock, like they'd just realized that they'd bet their life savings on a crowbait pony. Brent stammered, "So, that's how you met, at a barbecue joint in the middle of nowhere?"

Jack turned his focused glare on Brent. "First of all, the middle of nowhere is the middle of our entire world, and yes, that's where we first met. I was to report for my first day of work at the courthouse at eleven o'clock that day. So, I show up and I was quickly informed that the way to survive in Holder County law was to nod and smile to the current district attorney, Clayton Barns, who was well in his eighties but held ideas that dated back to the eighteen-eighties, and to impress Meridian Holder. That instruction was vastly preferable to the nodding and smiling, so I went to find her."

"You impress the hell out of me on a regular basis," Meridian vowed, thrilling him.

"After I stumbled through that introduction, we went back to the office. I was setting up my files and bookshelves when I heard her informing the DA that he was more ornery than a fried toad and that he needed to remember that she was the one holding the skillet," Jack laughed. "I'm pretty sure that's when I fell in love with her."

Meridian's grin had expanded the full width of her face. Her eyes glimmered with delight. "Clayton was the most frustrating man-child I have ever encountered. I couldn't believe he kept getting elected."

Jack shook his head and took another quick sip of his soda. "Of course he kept getting elected. He always threatened to prosecute the two-dozen plus ranches in the county that were late with payments. He scared his way into keeping the seat every single election."

Tiffany looked thoroughly confused. "I thought you were the DA?"

"He is now," Meridian explained. "Clayton finally died and took his antiquated ideas to the grave with him."

"In the bed of his mistress, nonetheless. Mind you, he ran on a solid family-values platform every single time," Jack concluded.

Since this was not the kind of conversation that took place around tables in The Hunt, Brent and Tiff were stunned to the point of silence. This was the most fun Jack had ever had in the club.

Their food arrived a few minutes later, and Jack waited on Brent's next questions. He knew they were coming. He just had to be patient.

CHAPTER THIRTY-NINE

Brent wiped his mouth with the designer napkin and then folded it back in his lap. "When did you know you wanted to marry her?"

Jack grinned at Meridian and considered the question. "I think when I realized that any kind of life without her in it wasn't one I was interested in having. That's the thing—it's when you begin to understand that you can withstand almost anything but losing the person you're in a relationship with."

Brent and Tiff glanced uncomfortably at one another like they'd never even considered that. "Yeah, but everyone eventually gets divorced. Just look at my parents," Tiffany argued.

"Not everyone gets divorced," Meridian contradicted her. "I come from a long line of people all in happy marriages. You can't just marry someone for the moment, for the show, for the honeymoon," she pitched back in Brent's face. "You marry them because they're the person you want to fight with for the next fifty years." She grinned up at Jack. "Whether it's fighting beside them or with them to ultimately make the marriage even better and then the world a better place too. You don't marry someone because it's a good strategic move. You marry someone because they make you a better person." Her fervency was crystal clear. A boulder of emotion clogged Jack's throat. This wasn't at all how he would've planned to tell her these things, but maybe for him this was how it had to be.

Tiffany huffed, "Well, my daddy has paid a lot of money for our wedding. I'm sure that's not something you would understand."

Meridian nodded. "You're right. I don't understand how the wedding is more important than the lifetime. I don't want to."

"I fall more and more in love with her every single day," Jack interjected. "That's another way I know."

That was when he stepped over the trip line. He knew he was getting nearer with every word, but suddenly Tiffany triggered. "You know, Jack, it's all great and wonderful that you've found some hillbilly cowgirl who's somehow even more self-righteous than you are, but that's not how life really works."

Since Meridian didn't seem at all offended by the name-calling, Jack pressed, "Why don't you tell us how life works then?"

"Well," Tiffany stammered, "just look at everything we *do* for people. I mean, take this club. Without our families, everyone who works here would be out of a job. You just up and left. A lot of people were really upset. We didn't know what to think. You can't just leave."

That wasn't exactly what Jack had been expecting to hear, but that didn't make it any less arrogant and privileged. "How very noble of you for staying and working through the confusion," he sneered. But something about her declaration began to gnaw at him. There was an echo of it, and he was fairly certain the reverberations were in his own voice.

A half hour later, they finally escaped the dinner from hell. Jack clung to Meridian as they walked back down to the truck.

"You were amazing tonight," she whispered.

"I doubt that," he corrected her, "but there is something I need you to know."

"What?" She smiled up at him.

Swallowing down the terror that climbed readily up his chest, he went on with the culmination of his plan. "I did not tell one single lie tonight. Not one."

She trembled beside him. They stopped walking in order to hold the weight of truth between them. She finally managed a nod. "I know. I didn't either. And, just so you know, I fell in love with you that very next day after we met. Remember? It was when you told Clayton that I could handle the Midwest Meats case for fixing cattle prices because I was the most capable lawyer you'd ever met." She let her bottom lip scrape through her teeth. "And then you told him that if he could ever get over the fact that the best lawyer in the building was a woman, then Holder County would never lose another case."

Jack remembered the day well. He'd been absolutely certain he was about to lose his newly acquired job for his remark, but that hadn't been enough for him to keep his mouth shut. "I don't guess I've ever been too good at the whole nodding and smiling thing."

"That's one of the things I love most about you. You speak up even if there are personal consequences."

Still unable to fully process that, he shook his head. "I can't believe there's anything about me you love."

"Yeah, well, I feel the same way. I'm always too much for men, and I have no interest in changing."

Jack shook his head. "I never want you to change. You might be too much for weak men, honey, but you are never too much for me."

The rising moon sparkled in her eyes. "Want to go back to River Chase and celebrate that we finally told each other how we feel even if we actually told the prom king and queen back there first?"

"More than I want my next breath, but I have one more question, and I need you to tell me the truth about it as well."

They started back toward the truck. "Okay."

"What Tiff said about everything she *does* for people, and about everyone who would be out of work if it weren't for our families..." he paused, desperate to keep his fear from materializing in his words.

"Yeah," Meridian prompted. "What about it?"

"Isn't that along the same lines as what I'm doing?"

"What?! No. That's not at all what you're doing."

"Isn't it though?" The terror gripped his throat. "I come in here every so often and hand out checks to try to make up for what my parents are taking from the world, but what if I'm just allowing their world to go on without them ever facing repercussions? What if I'm not really speaking up because of the personal consequences?"

He opened the passenger-side door and helped her step in before he made his way around the Cheyenne. Meridian's face was thoughtful. They were at the entrance before she finally answered. "It's difficult to answer that question because we both know that in all likelihood your parents will never face any kind of repercussions. If you don't do what you've been doing, it all goes on the way it always has with no one to even try to level the playing field. My daddy always says that the road to hell might be paved with good intentions, but if you're actually doing the work of trying to help then that's worth its weight in gold. But if you want to alter your approach, I could help you figure out a way to help differently. I actually have an idea."

Thankfulness flooded his bloodstream. "Tell me your idea."

"I've been thinking about Maggie. She said her boyfriend worked in graphic design, right, but that he'd been fired from his job and got hired but only as a contractor. If we can get him a better job with benefits that's full-time, that solves a lot of the future problems. Then we can work on the current hospital bills."

"Finn," Jack gasped. "I feel incredibly stupid. Why didn't I think of that?"

"Well, I did have you pretty distracted the day she came to talk to you." Meridian laughed.

"That is true. Hang on one second." He made quick work of phoning his brother, putting it on speaker, and explaining the situation. It was the first time since Jack had asked to sleep on Finn's couch that he'd asked his little brother for a favor. Finn seemed thrilled to help.

"I have another question," Meridian said as soon as they ended the call.

"Anything." Jack assumed this was about their newly admitted dedication to each other, but he was wrong.

"I don't get why your dad would go to such lengths to help a country club cheat on their taxes, but he won't lift a finger to help his own staff."

"Some of it is a lens issue, the rest is that my father only extends his hand for it to be shaken. He always wants something in return."

"A lens issue?"

"If you view the entire country through a lens skewed in your favor, it becomes easy to be callous to the problems on your doorstep. My father would tell you that Maggie wouldn't be in this situation if she'd gotten an education and had gotten married and that she should have waited to have a child so that she could afford the baby. He refuses to grasp how expensive an education is and that most people don't have access to bank accounts with even a fraction of the money they have."

"How would her being married change anything about this?"

"It wouldn't. It's just an excuse he chooses to believe because it allows him to sleep at night without having to be bothered by issues that he could change but won't. The people in power are quick to constantly offer each other excuses to hold onto their money and their way of life."

"To not be bothered with the issues the rest of the world faces."

Jack nodded. "If it hasn't directly impacted them, then it must not really be affecting anyone that matters, so why should he waste his time or money on it?"

They walked toward the house hand in hand, taking their time, in no rush to be interrogated by his parents which he was sure would happen.

"Are we actually seriously engaged?" Meridian asked suddenly. "We...that...seems kind of crazy. Not that I'm necessarily opposed."

"No," Jack assured her. "Not that I don't want to be, but because you deserve a ring, and a date, and for me to beg your father, and a romantic tale to tell our grandkids. I owe your family that. I want to do everything right by you."

"My dad will say yes."

"Are you so sure about that, princess?" Jack certainly wasn't. He knew Gentry Holder wanted his one and only daughter to marry a cowboy.

"Our grandkids, huh?" She continued to process his statement.

"Maybe."

"I can't quite go there tonight," she admitted.

"You don't have to. I've been thinking about how much I'd love to have that with you for years."

Meridian sighed. "I'm pretty sure I've spent years wishing that I didn't want that with you so badly. Stubborn to the end."

Jack paused and brushed a kiss on her lips. "I keep hoping that if you and I try to make this work as hard as we tried to stay away from each other that there's no way it could ever fall apart."

"I like thinking about it that way."

"Are you ready to go face the firing squad?"

"Do I have a choice?"

"We could always sneak back into the guesthouse," he offered.

"Tempting," she laughed. "But I'm a little gun-shy after running into your dad in the kitchen."

"Then let's get this over with."

CHAPTER FORTY

They entered the house quietly, as if their peace might calm the incoming storm. The entryway was empty, the staff all likely either in their own rooms or in their own homes. Perhaps they could sneak up to his room without encountering his parents. Jack hoped against hope.

With each step they climbed, his hopefulness ascended. He had no idea where his parents were, but not near him was always his preference. His hope died a brutal death as they approached his father's office, however. Light spilled from the open door. They weren't going to sneak past without notice.

Then a shadow stepped into the hall and blocked the light altogether. Jack's father had timed his exit perfectly, of course. "For all of your nonsense about the way I do business, I hear you went to the club on my dime this evening."

"You heard incorrectly," Jack huffed. "I paid for our dinner, but it's good to know my whereabouts are still reported to you constantly. I guess some things never change."

"You don't eat at The Hunt without my influence, Jackson. You know that."

"And I'll never eat there again. I didn't want to eat there tonight. I was ordered there by Tiffany, and since you seemed to want us to dine with them, we went. You can't have it both ways. You can either be pissed that I went to The Hunt or happy that I did as you asked. Either way, we're going to bed."

"Not yet, you're not. We need to talk." He opened the door to his office wider while blocking them from moving deeper into the hall with his body.

Feeling childish for wanting to run away, Jack refused to give in to the notion. If his father wanted to fight, then they would bring the war.

The Tiffany lamps in the office cast odd rainbow glows on the rug, and the overhead light gave Jack the impression they were in for an interrogation. They settled in the chairs opposite the partner's desk his father had installed before Jack's birth. Palmer folded his hands and narrowed his eyes. Jack rolled his. Intimidation was no match for fury.

"I've made a few phone calls, and I'd like an explanation as to what is going on between you two. The truth."

Meridian plastered on a condescending smile, but Jack saw the warning flare fire in her eyes. "Who exactly did you call asking about us?"

"That's an excellent question and I have a follow-up," Jack tagged in. "Why would you assume anyone knows more about our relationship than we do?"

Palmer wasn't amused. "Since my son prefers to keep me out of his life as much as possible, I have always had other means of getting information that I need. It seems no one in Holder County is aware of your engagement. Why is that?"

"We haven't announced it yet," Jack stated factually.

"According to the people I spoke with, you two haven't even been dating."

"How would anyone else know that?" Jack restated.

Palmer turned his full focus on Meridian, and Jack longed to throw himself over her in an effort to keep her from his father's iniquities. "Are you in trouble, dear?"

Meridian's scowl reminded Jack that she did not need to be protected. She was extremely capable of scorching the earth when the need arose. "If you're asking if Jack and I are having a baby, I'm going to need you to never refer to our children as trouble ever again. I can assure you that no amount of whiskey money will do you a bit of good when you gall a cowgirl. But no, I am not pregnant, not that it's any of your business."

"Then why are you with her?" he asked Jack as if the answer wasn't seated before his very eyes.

"Because I'm desperately in love with her. That is how most people in this country go about getting married. Just because that's not a requirement for nuptials here in Bourbon Country doesn't mean it's how the rest of the country works. Perhaps you should get out more."

"Perhaps you should remember all of the money and sacrifice that went into your education and into your raising," his father countered. "You seem to prefer to forget that there are consequences for your actions."

Jack narrowed his eyes. "I keep in regular contact with Anna Rosa, and I've thanked her many times for all she's done for me, but if you'd like me to pay your hourly wage for the single phone call you placed to Duke, I'd be happy to."

"Generations of our ancestors poured blood, sweat, and tears into this business that you're so quick to throw away. It took years to build the connections we have. We also have standards."

More than done with this conversation, Jack stood. "Rome burned in a day. Never forget that, *Dad*."

———

———

Riding the wave of tension and offense mixed with confusion made Meridian a little woozy as they escaped to Jack's bedroom. He slammed the door, making her jump.

"I'm sorry," he offered. "And not just for slamming the door, but for everything you've endured since we arrived here."

She gave him a slight smile. "I think I'd be way more offended if they actually liked me, so no need to apologize."

At that, Jack turned the lock and shook his head. "He's the only person on the planet that makes me lose my temper like that."

That made her laugh. "That probably works well for us because literally any dumbass anywhere can make me lose my temper." She shrugged. "I'll try to work on that...maybe."

He shook his head. "If someone is dumbass enough to take you on, honey, they deserve what they get."

Slipping out of her heels, thankful to be done with them, she made her way to him and wrapped her arms around his waist. "I'm sorry your family sucks so bad, but my family is awesome and they already like you."

He cradled her in his arms. "That's because they aren't yet aware that I've broken down the castle walls and made off with the princess."

She nuzzled her head against his chest. "I was helpless against the lure of your broadsword."

Jack growled deliciously in her ear. "Just how I prefer you to be."

Try though she did, her nervousness made her shift on her feet.

"What's wrong, honey?" He lifted his head to meet her gaze.

"I know if he'd called my parents, they would've called me. I don't know. Your dad having spies is weird."

"I grew up knowing that my every move was being watched, but this time I don't believe him. He didn't phone anyone in Oklahoma. He was hoping to call our bluff."

"He knew we'd gone to Hearst Stone," she pointed out.

"One call to either Brent or Tiffany or any of the staff at the club would've confirmed that for him. Money and control are the only two things that make my father feel like he's accomplished something, so he seeks both constantly."

"But if all your dad had to do was call people to check up on you, how did you learn to trust anyone?"

Jack's head lowered a notch as he considered her question. "I'm... not sure that I did. Not until I went to college and was able to get out of this bubble ever so slightly. I learned to stay away from people who owed my father things, because knowledge about his kids was a valuable commodity."

Meridian hugged him tighter. "I can't believe you grew up thinking that you're a commodity."

"I can't believe I'm standing here with you in my arms, with a chance to make this work."

"That's why you wanted me to trust you so much." The realization breathed from her soul.

He planted a kiss on top of her head. "I know how important that is. Without trust, relationships are doomed."

"I know. It's just I'd made it a policy never to trust anyone outside of my family. It's dangerous for me to do that. In law school, men who thought I was taking something away from them by being there would constantly throw blockades in my way, hoping I'd stumble. My success was somehow their failure. And now, people need my family's help and we want to be able to help cattle ranchers everywhere, but we get held up by people like Marsden. So, I decided it was safer to push everyone else away, I guess."

"I know," he assured her. He took her hand and guided her to the bed before he continued. "I know what it must've been like for you, especially at Northwestern, and the way that I know is because my family would've been the men throwing the blockades and setting you up to fail because..." He sagged under the weight of whatever was coming next. But he looked up at her and smiled. "Because it's easier for them to call you a threat than for them to man up and own the fact that you scare the hell out of them because you're better than they are. They'd never admit even to themselves that if they're going to compete with you, they're going to have to get off their asses and work for it."

Grinning at that, she lifted her eyebrow. "You called me dangerous just a few hours ago."

"Yeah, well, I told you I come from a long line of idiots who thought that way. Old habits die hard, maybe."

She shook her head. "No, that's not it. You've never been afraid to work hard or to challenge me or to tell people that I knew what I was talking about."

He gave her an almost boyish grin that sped her heart and tied her breath in her lungs. "I think maybe we're not all that different. I have a very select handful of people that I trust. The Bastards, Senator

McCoy's family, and that's it. So, for me to bring you here and show you this disaster of greed meant that I had to trust you. I knew that as soon as I really let myself do that, as soon as you proved that you could handle this, I'd willingly hand over my heart. That's...why you're dangerous."

Meridian scooted closer to him on the bed. "I'll take good care of it. I promise. Just...trust me."

"I do."

CHAPTER FORTY-ONE

God, she was beautiful sitting there on the bed of his youth asking him to trust her instead of the other way around. How could he not trust her? His ego was the obvious ugly truth. That and the consuming confusion that came with accepting something good in his life that didn't come bound to terms and conditions.

Just then, all he wanted, all he needed was to lose himself in her. His ego and his hope, his terror and his solace, all of the good and all of the bad that made up the two distinct halves of his past and his present.

He had no idea how she could love either, but he vowed to himself that he would somehow become a sentinel guard over her heart. He would never let anything hurt her. He would destroy every barricade people threw in her path. And...perhaps even more importantly, he would let her protect him.

She wore her intelligence like custom lingerie, her capability a diamond crown on her long auburn locks—his princess indeed.

"What are you thinking about?" she whispered.

He'd gone quiet for too long it seemed. "How beautiful you are. How I don't deserve you."

"I have a better idea of how you could spend your time," she whispered.

Pleased with that, he grinned. "How?"

"Making love to me."

"And brilliant as well." He sank his lips to hers, tasting her quick gasp of breath, absorbing it.

A rush of memories of the past few days flooded his mind. He'd studied her for years, but now he knew the sounds she made and the way her breath caught when he moved his fingers just the way she needed. He knew how her kisses were a cipher to her needs. Slow and thoughtful when she wanted a protector for her vulnerability, hard and frantic when she needed his force. The way her nipples hardened just before she came. The way she'd gasp for a breath before she let him take her over the edge. The way she liked to be teased and tended. When she longed for him savage and when she needed him sane.

He was slowly constructing the puzzle he'd made in his mind of her, but he knew it would never be complete. She'd grow and change. They both would. Perhaps they could do that together.

He brushed kisses along her jaw while he worked through the buttons on her blouse. She reached and yanked his polo out of his khakis so she could splay her hands over his abdomen.

She trusted him and she was all fucking his. He'd never felt such a blinding desperation to protect and own her, even though those desires were with him constantly. One almost always in opposition to the other. Perhaps he'd gotten that wrong. Maybe what she needed was both sides of himself. He'd spend his life proving that he'd learned something from the mistakes of his past and proving to her that he would be better.

"Tell me what you need tonight, princess." He hummed against her neck as he shoved her blouse off of her shoulders and made quick work of her bra. "Tell me what you imagine when I fuck you." Her bottom lip slipped between her teeth nervously. "Trust me with that," he urged.

"I..."—she glanced away momentarily—"liked when you watched me dance." Her eyes closed and her body swayed with the truth. "I like...that you like to think of people watching us."

Jack grinned at that. "Maybe you like the thought that people might see the way you let me touch you." She nodded against the pillow as he went on. "I love the idea of people seeing the way I get to own you." She was his rebellion and his truth tied together in the most beautiful package.

Her eyes blinked open. "I imagine weaker men seeing how powerful you are and that you want me." She choked on the edges of her confession.

Jack slipped to his knees beside the bed, unzipped her skirt and eased it off, leaving her in nothing but a wet pair of panties. "I think we both need to feel seen, to be recognized for who we really are. There's nothing wrong with wanting that, with enjoying that." He hooked his fingers in her panties and removed them. That was precisely why she'd had the photographs made. She wanted to be seen for who she was, not for what everyone else wanted her to be, and that was precisely what he would give her. "Let me enjoy you, princess. I'll know when you want me to be gentle, and I'll know when you need me to make you ache. I know you. I love you. Let them all watch me take what's mine."

"Yes," hissed from her. "Please, Jack."

He growled against her inner thigh. Her arousal was perfumed with rebellion—a tailor-made scent all for him. He pressed his mouth between her legs, indulging in the fragrance and the need.

Her sounds that evening were quieter, as if she was focused solely on the way he made her feel. They held notes of her ache and the antidote she knew he would provide. He kissed at the top of her slit, spinning his tongue there gently, then eased away to watch the shiver he'd elicited.

"I know it's sensitive, baby. I'll be gentle." He guided her legs farther apart. "Let me take care of you." He teased at her still-hidden clit with his tongue, tempting it, coaxing her. He longed for her body to trust him as well. Her pussy pulsed against his fingertips as he slid them along her opening. "That's it," he soothed. "God, I love the way you respond to my touch. All for me." He rewarded her neediness and dipped his fingers in slightly just to feel her body begging for more of his.

Returning his tongue to her mound, he focused only on her pleasure. She lifted her head and watched him move his fingers rhythmically inside her as he kissed and teased and devoured. "You taste so fucking good," he groaned against her folds. "I'll never get enough."

She gave him those little, desperate gasps that assured him his fingers were right where she needed them, and slowly he earned his reward. Her body bloomed. He hadn't been patient enough the other times he'd held her this way. He hadn't allowed her to give herself to him, or perhaps he hadn't yet earned her trust.

Tenderly, he rewarded her clit with openmouthed kisses and soft suckles.

"Oh fuck, *fuck*," she whimpered. He managed to keep up the motions despite his grin.

"Say my name, honey. Tell them who makes it feel good."

"Jack, oh god, mmm," spilled from her lips as she writhed in the bed. Her hips pressed hard against his mattress. Her back arched and her fingers wove through his hair, holding him right where she wanted him now.

But as she began to fall, she eased her hands away and clasped her breasts instead. She lifted her head and watched. Those whiskey eyes locked on his as he tended and suckled. Her lips parted as her breath washed away. She fell apart for him while never looking away, crying out for him as the need shattered and he freed her.

He shed his clothes and climbed over her. Her hands drifted down his chest as he climbed until she wrapped her hand around his dick, so stiff and swollen he burned hot against her fingers.

"Where do you want that, princess?" he urged. "Show me where it hurts. I know my greedy girl needs more."

She pressed his dick to her folds and bucked against him. He watched intently as she slid him back and forth, soaking him with her cream. Leaning over her, he kissed his way from her breasts to her lips. "Taste yourself on my tongue," he demanded. She sucked her dew from his lips, and his tongue, and his jaw.

She finally turned her head and begged in earnest. "I need you. Please, I...want to watch you watch me."

He throbbed against her at that request. "Oh, you're going to watch me fuck you, princess. Watch me take what's mine. Watch that tender little pussy spread around my dick. Watch me fill you full."

"Please," whimpered from her again.

He grabbed a condom from the bedside table and rolled it on in record time. He propped pillows behind her so she had no choice but to stare as he thrust deep. "That's it. Fuck," he groaned. "You feel so damn good."

He held her knees over his arms, awarding himself a front-row view of his dick bathed in her juices, of her lips parting over him, of her clit as he pressed inside her slow and deliberate.

"More," she demanded. "I need more. I need faster."

"I know, honey. I'll take good care of you, but this is for me."

He sank himself slowly inside of her, watching with each pass, until her restless hips were frantic for more and her pussy clenched tight with every thrust trying to lock him deep inside.

There was nowhere else he ever wanted to be, but his princess needed his friction and his force. He knew.

Giving in to her body's demands, he eased her legs back to the mattress and lay out over her. "Hold onto the headboard, cowgirl." She immediately complied. "That's it. Now, take it for me."

He pounded into her without relent, rewarding her patience with his force. Her eyes closed as she met him thrust for merciless thrust. She was utter perfection, and he was so far gone, he would never recover. He never wanted to.

He threw himself into her tides and rode hard and fast. Her entire body tensed. The headboard creaked as she clung to it. Her mouth parted on a frantic plea of his name. She cried out for him as she collapsed weakly to his mattress.

The intense pulls of her pussy against him spiraled him over the knife's edge he'd clung to. She continued to shudder against him as hot spurts of cum filled the condom and his breath was torn from his lungs.

Eventually, he cradled her close in the bed that had seen him turn from boy to man to hers in whatever form she needed him to be.

CHAPTER FORTY-TWO

Jack kept his eyes closed the next morning as the autumn sun warmed River Chase. He could hear the kitchen staff preparing breakfast, and the knot of tension in his gut tightened.

Focusing instead on Meridian, he timed his own breaths to the whispers of hers over his chest. What would it be like to wake up like this every day for the rest of his life? Surely, no mortal man deserved such an extravagant pleasure. He may not deserve it, but he'd be damned if he wouldn't fight for it and fight against anyone who wanted to take his place.

His mind tumbled to the interactions with his parents. They were never warm, certainly never allowed him to believe that they heard him or even liked him, but this trip had been particularly gruesome. Their attacks normally had a notion of brutal politeness. This trip, they were just brutal.

Another bolt of tension twisted in his gut. Meridian was the obvious answer as to why his parents were behaving deplorably, but it made no sense to Jack. She wasn't a threat to them, only to the things they'd planned for his life. Surely, his abrupt departure years before had given them a pallet load of indication that his life wasn't theirs to direct anymore. But there were none so blind, he supposed.

Meridian shifted against his chest, and an automatic grin spread the width of his features. "Good morning, princess."

She made several whimpered huffs of frustration. Chuckling, he brushed a kiss in her hair. "Do you want to go back to sleep? We can lie here as long as you like."

"No," she fussed. "Maybe," she countered her own argument.

"I'm glad to know you even argue with yourself, my obstinate little cowgirl."

"I'm little but I get shit done...after I'm finished sleeping."

"No argument there. It smells like biscuits, and I'm sure there's coffee," he tempted.

She grinned against his chest. "I like those things. I like you more." She wiggled until her left leg was threaded between both of his. His morning wood throbbed almost painfully.

Before he could suggest they indulge in each other before breakfast, his bedroom door opened.

"Oh my god," Meridian gasped and yanked the covers up to her neck to cover the fact that she had nothing on.

Shocked to the point of speechless, Jack glared at his mother like she'd lost what was left of her mind. "Is there a problem?" he finally managed.

"Tiffany has called off the wedding!"

Taking care to keep Meridian completely covered, Jack ran his hand over his face trying to urge himself awake. "Why would we need to know that at"—he checked his phone—"seven thirty in the morning?"

"You are the only person who can convince her to go on with the wedding as planned," his mother urged.

"What is it, Mom? What is it about Tiffany and Brent getting married that means so much to you? I both cannot and will not convince either of them to do anything. I don't think they should get married. They like the idea of the wedding far more than the idea of a lifetime commitment."

His mother drew herself up to full height and then glared down at Jack and Meridian. "It is in the best interest of Denton Distilleries that this wedding goes off. I learned long ago that you can't see outside of your own selfish interests enough to help out your own family, but you do seem to care about the staff. So...do it for them," she fumed.

The fact that they were both naked made this argument far more difficult to navigate. His mother was likely bluffing, but he needed to consider this from every angle, and he needed Meridian's help. His next thought repelled him. He might even need Tiffany's help. "If you'll let us get dressed, we'll be happy to discuss this further outside of my bedroom."

"Your bedroom in my estate. You do seem to forget that."

"How could I forget? You and Dad remind me every single time you order me home that I'm walking on your land. If you don't want me here, stop inviting me."

With another Beverly Denton glower leveled his way, his mother finally made her sweeping exit.

"What the actual fuck?" Meridian gasped. "I thought you locked the door."

"I did. She picked it."

"Your family is insane."

"No, they're not insane. They're devious, and it takes quite a bit of brainpower to be as devious as they are. I need to figure out what's going on."

"That was quite a statement about you caring about the staff. Do you think she knows what the Bastards do?"

"If she knew, we'd all already be in handcuffs. The first thing I want to know is why Tiff and Brent's wedding matters to our family."

"Okay." Meridian sat up and scrubbed her hands over her face. "Let's start at the beginning. Tiffany's parents are splitting up, and theoretically that means they'll be dividing Fitzgerald Whitney Distributions, right? Would that be bad for Denton?"

"They bottle all of our whiskey lines, but I can't imagine how that would change, and if it did we could bottle our own or go with a smaller distributor. It certainly wouldn't pose a threat to Denton, as far as I know."

"It might slow down production. There would be a cost to bringing it in house. Would Sloan know?"

Jack phoned both Sloan and Tiffany, but they both seemed baffled as to why his mother would care about the wedding. Tiffany didn't fully understand her own parents' company so Jack wasn't terribly surprised.

"Let's go home," he announced as he tossed his phone on the bed after a wearing conversation with Tiff, who was incapable of focusing on anything but herself for any length of time.

"What?" Meridian climbed out of bed and began getting dressed, much to Jack's chagrin. "We can do that?"

"She called off the wedding. We were here for the wedding. I need to give Maggie another check and visit the garden staff. Other than that, we don't need to be here. I need to get out of here. I do my best thinking in my office at the courthouse. My parents are hiding something, but they're not going to play whatever cards they're holding in their hands until we leave. Sloan will let me know what it is they're planning and"—he lifted his eyes to hers wanting her to see his sincerity—"I want to be with you there, in Holder County."

She gave him that tender grin that he coveted more than any other. "Me too. I need this all not to feel like some kind of bizarre heavenly dream mixed in with a hellacious nightmare."

Shrugging into a dress shirt, he went on with his promise. "If you aren't ready to tell your family or anyone at home, I'll understand."

She shook her head. "I'm ready...I think."

"Still arguing it out in your head?" He knew.

"A little."

"Can I get in your deliberations at some point?"

She nodded. "If you must."

"I must."

They deliberated some while they ate breakfast alone and while Jack handed out bonuses to the garden staff. He gave another check to Maggie and then took Meridian to the offsite Denton offices at their original distillery location.

Sloan was at his desk poring over a spreadsheet. He glanced up as they entered. "I've checked all I can check on our contracts and distribution chains. We're Fitzgerald Whitney's largest supplier. I had legal pull the divorce filings. It's a generic irreconcilable differences. Even if one of them walked away from the business entirely, I can't see why they'd want to sever business ties with us. It would hurt them far more than Denton. Are you sure Aunt Bev isn't trying to scare you into talking to Tiffany? I got the impression that she'd convinced herself she could get you two back together before you arrived."

That would explain their hatred of Meridian, but it was as outlandish as it was ridiculous. "She's delusional," Jack retorted.

Sloan grinned. "That was before we met the lovely Meridian,"—he gestured to her—"so maybe Aunt Bev is just determined."

"Whatever she is, we're heading back to Oklahoma." He handed the Denton checkbook back to his cousin. "I signed the check on top but left it blank just in case, so keep an eye on that."

"I always do." Sloan slipped the checkbook into his desk drawer. "I hate to see you leave early though. I'm going to have to come out to Oklahoma and see what it has that Kentucky doesn't."

"Her." Jack put his arm around Meridian.

She grinned. "It was nice to meet you, Sloan."

"Likewise. I better get invited to the wedding."

"Of course," Jack scoffed.

They drove back to River Chase while Jack tried to determine the best way to bid farewell to his parents while also needing to secure the Denton jet. It was two hours from Holder County to the Tulsa airport, and asking one of the Holders to pick them up when Jack's truck was at the airfield seemed ridiculous.

If he knew his mother, and he was fairly certain he still did, she'd want them within Denton spy earshot as long as possible, so if the cards fell in his favor, she'd insist that Beckett fly them home.

CHAPTER FORTY-THREE

As Meridian walked with Jack toward the Denton jet, she let herself really take in their surroundings. The fog that had been there when they arrived was gone, leaving crystal blue skies in its wake. The noonday sun glimmered over the fat maple leaves, glinting them with brush strokes of rich tangerine and notes of envious green.

She understood why people flocked to Bourbon Country. It was stunning even if the rolling green hills cloaked far more than they uplifted. "That was pretty crafty of you," she finally commented.

"Getting her to let us use the plane, you mean? If her goal is to break us up and get me back together with Tiffany, then spying for her is a means to that end. The fact that the end is never coming is knowledge I can work to my advantage that she'll eventually figure out."

Meridian nodded and continued to try not to think of how much of her had changed over the last few days. She still looked the same even though she'd never felt more different. She wondered if her mama would be able to see the changes in her. Leigh Holder was the best mama in the world, so Meridian assumed she'd notice. She also hoped her mama could explain it all to her.

They boarded the plane, and Meridian settled in. Everything was different, but it was also better. She'd wanted Jack for years, and she'd gotten him. The accomplishment assuaged a little of her worry that she was giving up her ultimate career goals for a man.

"You're awfully quiet, cowgirl." He eased his arm around her, and she laid her head on his chest. "I thought you'd be excited to get back to the ranch."

"I am," she assured him. "I can't wait to get back. It's just...different."

"Different isn't bad, right?"

"No, just...different. The first thing I want to do is go check those pictures."

"I'd nearly forgotten about that. I'm sorry. We'll head to the office first thing."

He didn't have to apologize. She'd nearly forgotten it as well. Good Lord, how many crazy things had to have happened for that to have slipped her mind? She decided then and there that she was delighted to be going home. Everything made sense in Holder County. For the most part, people played nicely and took care of one another. She'd figure out exactly what she wanted to do with the rest of her life sitting on her front porch staring out at her family's land. Jack might've done his best thinking from the office, but she did hers on the ranch.

The late afternoon sun bathed the interior of the plane in a hot rusty glow as they made their descent. Between the sun and Jack's kisses on her head, Meridian awoke from her nap.

"We're almost there, sleepyhead," he whispered. She couldn't help but grin. She'd always thought affectionate names between lovers were ridiculous, but she loved when he called her both princess and cowgirl and honey and every other name he used that was laced with strings of adoration and love.

She sat up and noticed him yawning as well. He must've napped too. "Why are we so sleepy?"

He grinned at her. "We've stayed out rather late every night and just being there is exhausting." He leaned closer. "Plus, all of the amazing sex. I clearly wore you out."

Laughing at that, she stretched a few kinks out of her neck and thought of a few of his kinks she'd love to stretch as well. It didn't occur to her until she heard the landing gear locking into place that, "No one knows we're coming home."

"You didn't let your parents know?" he asked as he shook his head when Muriel offered them some coffee to go.

"No. Everything happened so fast I didn't think to."

"We'll go to the office, and you can call and surprise them."

———

———

———

Taking care to thank Muriel and Beckett for the flight, a wave of abject relief flooded through Jack as soon as his shoes touched Oklahoma soil. It wasn't quite as soft and lush as the bluegrass hills of Louisville, but it was home and he was thrilled to be back.

Now, he just had to make sure Meridian was as ready to announce their relationship to the town as he was. "Are you ready?" he asked as he set their luggage in the back of his truck.

"That's a loaded question," she teased.

"I suppose it is, but I'd still like an answer."

"I think so," she stated thoughtfully. "It actually feels really weird that I'm as prepared for this as I am."

"Why?"

"You wouldn't understand even if I explained it."

"Try me." It bothered him that she believed that, even if it was somehow true.

"Men don't have to give up things. Our entire society is set up that way. How many times have you heard reporters ask highly successful men how they balance work and home life? It never happens because everyone still thinks of home life as being the responsibility of the woman."

"Not everyone thinks that way. I certainly don't."

She grinned. "If you did, I wouldn't have fallen for you."

"I still don't like this idea that by being in a relationship with me, you're giving up something you want."

"I'm not sure that I am," she admitted. "But what I always thought I wanted is changing so...maybe I'm just giving up what I thought of as something I was owed. I shouldn't have ever thought that way, but changing the way you've always thought takes time."

Jack squeezed her hand. "It also takes an incredibly empathetic and intelligent person to step outside of their tribe and view it from other perspectives. It takes an even stronger person to try to change it."

"You would certainly know," she reminded him as he pulled onto the main drag that would lead them past her ranch and all the way to Holder Square.

He nodded. "I do know, so I also understand if it's hard and you struggle. I'm okay with all of that. I want to be there when you get frustrated, or angry, or any of the emotions that come with major life shifts."

"I definitely do not deserve you," she choked.

"That goes both ways." They drove on in silence. The sweeping flatlands dotted with cattle and rolls of hay set against the endless technicolor sky were a meditation unto themselves.

By the time he was parking in his spot at the courthouse, she seemed settled. She leaned across the console and brushed a kiss on his cheek. "You know, I do think I'm ready."

"If that changes at any point, talk to me. You aren't going to scare me off."

She was already climbing out of his truck, ready to take on whatever was coming next. "Whatcha want to bet Mitch is in there with his feet up on his desk?"

Jack chuckled. "He works hard. We can't complain too much."

"I can still complain," she assured him. "Because I had to work ten times as hard to get to where both of you started."

"You know what? You're right. Let's go give him hell."

She seemed pleased with his agreement as they walked into the red brick revival Holder County Courthouse.

Jack took care not to touch Meridian in any kind of intimate way, even though he desperately wanted to hold her hand or place his arm around her. He wasn't going to force them out until he was certain she was ready for that.

True to her word, as the elevator opened on the third floor and they stepped into their office suite, Mitch's boots were up on his desk and three of the other clerks were staring down at their phones and laughing.

Jack cleared his throat rather loudly, and everyone snapped to attention. Meridian shook her head at them.

Mitch somehow managed to go from a reclined position to standing all in one fluid movement. "You're back!" He nervously shuffled some papers on his desk into neater piles. "Why are you back?"

"Nice to see you too," Jack harassed. "We took care of everything we needed to do in Kentucky. Now, it's time to get back to work...all of you."

The clerks and assistants quickly busied themselves with work they should've been doing. All except Mitch who followed Jack and Meridian into her office.

Exchanging an annoyed glance with her, Jack tried to think of a way to get rid of their tagalong while Meridian nonchalantly went to her legal cabinets.

"How was the trip?" Mitch chirped.

"Fine," Jack assured him while never taking his eyes off of the love of his life. It took him a moment to wrap his head around finally acknowledging that she was indeed the person he wanted to spend the rest of his life with, in this messed up insane world.

She pulled the keys from her purse, turned the lock, and opened the top drawer.

Jack's heart leapt to his throat and pounded out a war drum cry. She flipped through the files and discreetly checked one in the back.

When her shoulders slumped in relief, so did Jack's. His frantic heartbeat settled. Clearly they were where she'd hidden them.

Mitch was still hanging on like a barnacle to a ship. "Did you get out to the tracks or do the bourbon trail tour?"

Jack ground his teeth. "Yes, to the tracks; no to the tour." He tried to remember what he would've asked if he'd been out for several days prior to his life taking this turn he'd never deserve but would also never refuse. "Did anything happen while we were gone that we should know about?"

Mitch considered for several beats while Meridian relocked the filing cabinet. "Two drunk drivings third offense brought in early Monday morning. They've been arraigned, but Judge Dickson wants to see you to discuss. From the early filings, it appears there's going to be a new case against adding additional wind farms that the mayor wants to bring in. I have the paperwork on my desk."

Mitch finally said something Jack could use. "Great. Can you bring me that now? I'm ready to get back to work."

"Oh,"—he looked put out—"sure." When he made his exit, Jack sealed the door behind him.

"They're all there?"

"Yep. Right where I left them. Maybe we should see if we can get some of the courthouse improvement fund money to replace the locks on these doors."

"That's a good idea. I should've done that when I found the cat on my desk."

"We were trying not to take any of the money. We wanted the courtrooms and exterior to get the updates," Meridian reminded him.

"Yes, well, forgive me for being selfish, but keeping anyone else from ever seeing what I prefer to think of as mine and mine alone has now moved into my top priority spot."

She walked over to him with that sexy, sly grin pinned on her lips. "That is very misogynistic of you." She didn't look like she minded.

"Forgive me, princess. You bring out all of the best and a few of the worst parts of me."

"Are the worst parts the ones that make you hold me down and make me wet?"

His dick swelled to the point he was convinced the damn thing was going to figure out how to work the zipper on his slacks. "Those are the ones."

"Then those are some of my favorite parts." She slipped her hand over the fierce swell behind his zipper, forcing him to choke back a groan.

"Very, very naughty, princess."

Her smirk coiled the need in his balls and made him burn. "Indeed," she whispered. "What are you going to do about it?"

He threaded his fingers through her hair and jerked her lips to his own. His other hand gripped her ass and ground her against the problem she'd created.

And that...was precisely what they were doing when Mitch walked back in without knocking.

CHAPTER FORTY-FOUR

Meridian fought the deep desire to screech at Mitch. Their kissing seemed to send out some kind of homing beacon to interlopers, and she was tired of being interrupted. But then she remembered where she was and *who* she was. She straightened her skirt and stepped away from Jack. She hated every inch of space between them. The only time any of this made any sense was when she was in his arms.

"I see the trip went *very* well," Mitch drawled.

Jack's jaw tensed before he spoke, "Listen—"

But Meridian shook her head. "It's fine," she assured him. "We're dating. There is nothing in the county bylaws that says we can't. However, if you think this will be an issue with either yourself or any of the DDAs, please let them know that my door is open for discussion."

"As is mine," Jack stated firmly.

"Problem?" Mitch laughed. "There is no problem. Are you kidding me? We're all thrilled. We've been hoping for this for years. Ever since they took *All My Children* off the air, you two were all we had. We had a pool going on when you'd finally figure your shit out. I think Sarah Beth from the tag office is going to end up being closest. Dammit."

"Wait," Meridian huffed, "it wasn't just a pool for people in legal? It's for the entire courthouse?"

Mitch gave her a sorrowful nod. "There isn't that much to do out here."

Jack lowered his head, and Meridian knew he was trying to conceal his laughter. The shake of his shoulders betrayed his efforts. She rolled her eyes. "Okay, well, let Sarah Beth know that we figured our shit out."

"I will, and we're all really glad you did," Mitch vowed kindly.

"Thank you for that." Jack's grin elicited one from Meridian as well.

"Of course." Mitch handed over a stack of file folders and two thumb drives. "The windmill filings." He shook his head. "I've never seen people so determined to prevent progress."

Jack nodded his agreement. "People tend to get very determined when they believe the progress is going to stand in the way of their gains. I'll take care of this."

"Congrats, you two. Let me know if you need anything." Mitch made a quick exit and they were alone again, only they could hear Jack's phone ringing from Meridian's office.

"I guess if we're going to successfully pull off this working relationship, I have to work instead of kissing you all day, huh?" he said.

Beaming at him, she nodded. "It seems so, but you could come over to my house for dinner tonight."

"Only if I get to stay and make you breakfast tomorrow before work."

"I like my eggs over easy."

"Your wish is my command as always, princess." The phone started ringing again. "I guess I better get that."

Meridian settled at her desk and tried to sort through life now that she was in a serious relationship...with her boss. Okay, so it was a little unorthodox. Nothing wrong with that. She could have her cake and eat it too. Nothing would stand in her way.

She would be the most kickass assistant district attorney, and a kickass girlfriend, and a kickass cowgirl. No problem.

It was only one more role to add to her playbill, and she'd spent the last decade juggling the other roles. The key was to play each role at the right time, and right now she was supposed to be working, even if technically she was still on vacation. She flipped open the Marsden file and started back through it with the knowledge that he had a brother in the Bureau of Land Management.

Her cell phone buzzed on her desk. Grinning at the caller ID she answered quickly. "Hey, Mama."

"Don't hey mama me," Leigh huffed, and Meridian cringed. "Sarah Beth McGillicuddy just called to tell me my own daughter is dating Jack Denton and that you're back in town when you told me you weren't coming back until this weekend. You shoulda heard her gloating when I didn't know what she was talking about."

"Sorry. I was going to tell you. It's been crazy. His family is awful, and the wedding we were supposed to go to got called off, and yes, we're dating officially but I never meant to leave you out. I'm so sorry."

Meridian had gotten a fair amount of her spitfire spite from her mother, so she knew she'd likely have to apologize several more times before she gained forgiveness. Unless.... It was a gamble, but she doubted Jack would mind. "Actually," she forced, "Jack and I were wondering if we could come over for dinner tonight so we could tell you all about it. He wants to impress you and Daddy. He's so worried you won't like him." She could almost hear her mother melting from twenty miles away.

"Well, isn't that just the sweetest," Leigh drawled. Meridian bit her lips together to keep from laughing. "Of course you can come over, and you tell Jack that we already knew he was a good, upstanding man so he has nothing to worry about. Of course, your daddy doesn't really think anyone is good enough for you, but I'll work on him between now and then. What kinds of things does Jack like to eat?"

"He's not picky. Why don't you make your famous meatloaf and mashed potatoes?" She knew it was her mother's favorite meal to prepare and that she loved the gushing praise her potatoes always garnered.

"I can do that. How about a peach cobbler for dessert?"

"Perfect." So far, Meridian was pleased with how the day was turning out, even if she was certain over half the county now knew she and Jack were dating.

"By the way, I know you're only doing this so I'll stop being angry at you," her mother warned.

"I really am sorry. Wait until I tell you everything that happened in Kentucky. You won't believe even half of it."

"Right now, I want to know how Jack finally asked you to be his girlfriend, and I want all the parts including the ones you aren't gonna tell your daddy."

Wrinkling her nose, Meridian tried to solidify the past four days into some kind of tellable tale. "Uh, well, I think it kind of all started when I demanded that he kiss me on his family's swanky private jet when we were landing on their estate."

"Meridian," her mother huffed. "My word. I don't even know where to start with that statement."

"Hey, you know when I set my heart on something, I don't take no for an answer."

"Fine. So, their family has a jet that lands on their estate?" She blew a low whistle between her teeth. "Goodness, I thought only the Kennedys had such a thing."

"It was completely overwhelming, and his parents hate him."

Her mother went quiet. Meridian checked her phone to make certain she hadn't lost the cell signal. "I don't see how a mama could possibly hate her child," Leigh finally decreed.

"Well, he has a brother that's gay, and they kicked him out of the house."

"Where does his brother live? Can he come to dinner with you? You know, we always have extra plates. I'll peel some extra potatoes, and I bet your Aunt Susannah's got some extra beans we put up last fall. I'll call her."

Reveling in the moment that her parents were truly the salt of the earth, she let the deep dusty air of the county that had raised her fill her lungs. God, it was good to be home. "He still lives in Louisville, but maybe he'll come over when he comes out to visit Jack sometime."

"Does he need a ticket, because I just saw a commercial about flights being cheaper, so we could get him a few?"

"He's doing okay for himself now, but I promise you Jack's family is really awful."

"Why is that?"

That question took Meridian aback. "What do you mean why? They just are, I guess."

"No, honey. People don't behave like that for no reason."

"Then I guess greed."

"Mm, the love of money has hurt a lot of people, not that we weren't warned. Sounds to me like there's a whole lot of hurt going on out there in Louisville. I have to say I suspected as such. Jack always walks around looking over his shoulder like he expects to be smacked at any moment. Breaks my heart."

Meridian considered that. Jack did occasionally look like he expected the sky to fall at any moment. "I figured the Holders could show him how families are supposed to be."

That pleased her mother as well. "We will do our best. What time will you be here?"

"We'll come straight after work."

"You'd better."

Meridian told her mother how much she'd missed her and how much she loved her, but then that call was interrupted by a call from Harper. Good grief. The rumor mills were now in full-tilt. She'd be lucky to get off the phone in time to persuade Jack to have dinner at her parents'.

She fielded calls from three other cousins, Sarah Beth McGillicuddy, her Aunt Sara, her Aunt Susannah, and Erma who ran the BBQ joint on the square.

It was almost four thirty before she escaped, sans cell phone, to Jack's office. She closed the door and let her head fall back against it, hoping for a little peace and quiet.

Jack's brow furrowed, but he was also on the phone. Meridian refused to go back anywhere near the vicinity of her cell phone, so Jack was just going to have to be okay with her being in his office.

"Are you okay?" he mouthed. She nodded and sank into one of the chairs in front of his desk. "Yes, Mayor, I'm listening," he ground out with an accompanying eye roll. "I really don't think it's going to be a problem. The accusations that windmills cause any kind of damage to either the earth or to anyone's health are absolutely preposterous. This case will be another slice of the same pie as the mineral case, and that appeal was struck down."

Of course. Mayor Jennings would want to make sure that Jack was on the windmill case, and he'd also want a minimum of an hour of Jack blowing smoke up his ass.

"I'm sorry," Jack mouthed this time.

Meridian waved him off. She just wanted to escape to his vicinity, and wasn't that telling. She smiled at the thought.

"You know, I am supposed to still be on vacation," Jack reminded the mayor rather tersely. Meridian choked back laughter.

He continued on with his uh-huhs for the next five minutes. An idea suddenly struck Meridian—a delicious, decidedly naughty, and a helluva lot of fun idea.

She tiptoed to the door and turned the interior lock, then spun back around and gave him a wicked grin.

CHAPTER FORTY-FIVE

Keeping her eyes locked on Jack, she sank slowly back down in the chair with her legs open. His chest lifted with a few rapid breaths. His eyes darkened as they moved up her body.

Meridian slowly dragged her fingers under the hem of her skirt, sliding the fabric up her thighs. His mouth opened like he might encourage her if he'd been able. Heat bloomed between her legs. Her heart beat against the cage of her ribs, as if it were seeking his hands. She craved him.

Her fingertips trailed up the front of her thighs until she reached the lacy elastic edge of her panties.

Jack managed to turn a greedy moan into something of a cough. She closed her eyes and imagined his long, nimble fingers stroking her slit over the satin.

"I...uh," he stumbled over whatever he was trying to tell Mayor Jennings, "I don't think...that's necessary."

She let her eyes drift open and found his gaze locked between her thighs. He pierced her with a desperate, needy look. No one had ever made her feel so exquisitely sexy. She imagined his hands gripping her hips as he pounded into her.

With her own fingers, she traced along her slit and bit her bottom lip to quell her own moan. She moved her fingers faster until the satin was soaked and she needed more.

Jack worked the buckle of his belt and opened his slacks with one hand.

Easing the crotch of her panties aside, she spread the wet warmth up to her clit, and Jack growled out, "I'll have to call you back." He ended the call and dropped the receiver. "It looks like you need something, princess. Come here to me. Let me make it feel better."

Her body pulsed to the sound of his order. She was so close, and yet this wasn't for her. This was for him. She wiped the dew of her need between her legs and made her way to his desk. He reached for her, but she was quicker. She dropped to her knees and licked her lips.

"Fuck, yes." His head fell back as she revealed his dick, already dripping for her. She wrapped her hand around his thick shaft and spun her tongue over his head, tasting him. Releasing her hand for a split second, she licked down the throbbing veins and then back up for another taste of his salty, earthy flavors.

"Suck me, cowgirl," he growled. "Suck me hard."

She obeyed readily, the only man she'd ever take orders from because he was the man who loved every side of her. She pulled him deep into her mouth and moved in rhythm with her hand.

He gripped her hair, guiding her. With her free hand, Meridian traced over his sac as it drew tight.

"Jesus," choked from him. "Don't make me come, honey. Not yet. Not until I'm deep in that naughty little pussy."

A breathy moan escaped her mouth, breaking the suction she had on him. He used the moment to pull her head away. "On your feet," he ordered. "Put that ass up in the air for me."

Having a pretty good idea where this was going, she climbed to her feet. He stood, turned her, and leaned her over his desk in one fluid movement. He yanked her panties down and used them to keep her from fully spreading her legs.

"Did you really think you could come in my office and tempt me like that and you wouldn't be punished?" He spun two fingers deep in her channel. "My tight, naughty little princess." She saw him toss the condom wrapper in the trash can, and the next moment he gripped her hips and thrust deep and hard, tearing the air from her lungs.

A feral growl filled her ear as he leaned over her. "You look so fucking beautiful rubbing your cream all over yourself. What else was I supposed to do but give you what you need?" He thrust harder, driving her against his desk. Her fingernails dug into the leather inlay as she tried to cling to any available anchor. Another moan pressed from her lungs. "Be quiet, honey. Or everyone in this office will know what a bad girl you are for me."

That was precisely what he wanted. She knew.

"Tomorrow when you're sore, I want you to remember what you did to earn this. You need to remember who this pussy belongs to."

And that was precisely what she craved.

"Yes," washed from her lungs as she tensed around him. He trailed biting nips and kisses along her shoulders and then stood to pound harder. "Oh shit," she finally whimpered. "Don't stop." One more stroke, maybe two. Frantic need pulsed up her spine. The leather pressed against her heated skin. His rock-hard body pinned her in place. She had nowhere to go but over the cliff of ecstasy he pushed her constantly toward.

"Beg me," he demanded. "Or I will stop. I'll pull out, put you back on your knees, and come down your throat instead."

"Please, please," she begged readily, far too desperate to feel any shame.

"That's a good girl." He gave her another deep, ragged thrust. His balls slapped at her inner thighs. The leather pressed constantly against her clit. Her mind spun. And he filled her past full. She spiraled over with a husky cry of his name. The spasms of her pussy had him tensing and cursing a few seconds later.

Several minutes later, he was cradling her in his lap and brushing kisses on her temple. "I love you," he whispered.

A sizzle of pure bliss cascaded outward from her chest. "I love you too. I'm glad we got our shit together."

Laughing, he nodded against her. "Me too."

"We're about ten minutes late for dinner with my parents."

"What?" He sat up, almost dumping her on the floor, but he managed to keep her in his arms.

"Sorry. Mama was upset that Sarah Beth knew about us before she did. I was trying to make it up to her by promising we'd come eat with them and tell them all about us."

She felt Jack's jaw tense against her head. "I almost wish you'd mentioned this before you started masturbating in front of me...almost."

"It's fine. We'll just tell them the mayor wouldn't shut up."

"I'd prefer not to be late when I'm going to beg your father to let me date you."

Meridian climbed out of his lap and tried to smooth the wrinkles out of her skirt. "My father does not get to decide who I date."

"Still." He quickly tucked in his shirt and re-buckled his belt. "Should I...get them a gift? I probably have some Denton Small Batch at my house somewhere."

It was sweet that he was so worried, but it was also completely unnecessary. "It's fine. They already like you."

"I hold that they like me as the DA, not necessarily as the man sleeping with their one and only daughter."

"Let's maybe not refer to you as the guy sleeping with their daughter." She ran her fingers through her hair and wondered just how sexed she might look.

"What should we call me? Is boyfriend okay with you?"

"I told you last night that I wanted to be engaged to you, so yeah, boyfriend isn't an overstep."

"I'm sorry. I just...don't want to mess this up."

Meridian brushed a tender kiss on his jaw. "You're not going to. If Daddy makes some huffy remark about you not being a cowboy, just let me take care of it."

"We could go by Prairie Outfitters and I could pick up a hat if that would help."

Shaking her head at him, she was overwhelmed with how much it meant to her that he wanted to impress her parents this much. "You do not need a cowboy hat. That would be disingenuous. Besides, you don't just go buy a hat. It's a process and not a fast one."

"All right. Then let's go so we don't make them wait any longer." He paced after her while she raced back to her office to gather her bags.

"Jack," Meridian stopped him by the door. "They already like you. That isn't going to change. The whole world isn't like your family. You're not a commodity to the Holders. You're a person."

CHAPTER FORTY-SIX

Jack's mouth was dry enough for tumbleweeds to take root as he stepped inside Leigh Holder's small but warm kitchen. She grinned at him. "Well, hey there, Jack. Y'all come on in."

Meridian brushed a kiss on her mother's cheek. "Sorry we're late. The mayor called Jack and wouldn't shut up."

"Ever since that man got elected he's been of the opinion that he's getting paid by the word." Leigh rolled her eyes. "I'm sorry you got stuck on the phone with him."

Guilt thudded in Jack's empty stomach. He hated to lie to her, but telling the Holders that they were late because he'd had their daughter bent over his desk begging was definitely not an option.

Jack stiffened when Gentry and Maddox walked into the kitchen.

"Hey, Daddy." Meridian threw her arms around her father, and Jack watched as he swayed his daughter back and forth, closing his eyes in reverence of the moment.

"Hey, pumpkin," he soothed.

Jack grinned. "Pumpkin?" he whispered when she came back to stand beside him.

She gave him a mocking glare as a fresh round of heat flooded her cheeks. "When I was born, my head was kind of oval-shaped and my hair was orange."

Chuckling at that, he put his arm around her. "I definitely need to see your newborn photos."

"You suggest that like I haven't spent the last twenty years hiding every last one of them."

"No hug for your big brother?" Maddox pretended to be offended.

"I don't know," Meridian came right back, "are you covered in shit?"

"You better not be," Leigh commented as she scraped mashed potatoes into a serving bowl.

Jack sprang into action. "Here, let me hold that for you." He took the pot, allowing Leigh to scrape more effectively.

"Thank you, sweetheart. I appreciate that."

"Of course."

They sat down to eat at a scrubbed wooden table covered in a stained checkered tablecloth. Jack knew his mother would've scoffed and ridiculed, but he loved every square inch of not only the tablecloth but the family that surrounded it.

Meridian laced her fingers through his as they said grace. A warmth and peace that Jack had never felt at River Chase soothed the rough patches and scrapes they'd endured the last few days.

This was the way life was meant to be lived. The food was simple and delicious. It filled him in a way he hadn't known he could be filled. This was how he wanted to live his life. This was all he'd ever really wanted.

Gentry cleared his throat. "Now, Jack, where would you say you see yourself in ten years?"

Meridian gave her father a dramatic eye roll. "Daddy, is this really necessary?"

"It's a fair question," Gentry insisted.

"He has two college degrees from Duke and is the youngest district attorney Holder County has ever had. I'd say he's been more than successful."

Jack patted her leg. "May I?" Gentry Holder was not the kind of man impressed with degrees and accolades. He was impressed with heart, and Jack knew that.

"Fine," she begrudged.

"I've been enamored with Meridian for years now, sir, and I don't think any amount of time into the future is going to change that. If anything, I would say I'll only grow more fond of her. I come from a family that's able to buy and sell the world, and they're miserable. All of them. If I learned anything from their misery, it's that I don't want to buy or sell the world. I only want to hold a very small part of it, and I want to share it with her. I want to use what we have to make the world better."

Leigh was dabbing her eyes with her napkin. "That is just the sweetest thing I've ever heard."

"Wow," Meridian whispered in his ear.

He took a chance and kissed her cheek. Her father didn't seem to mind so Jack took that as a good sign.

Gentry also didn't seem to have a rebuttal.

After supper, Jack helped Meridian's mother serve bowls of peach cobbler and Blue Bell ice cream. He sat down beside Meridian on the front porch to enjoy their dessert. She stared out at the lands that had raised her and the five generations of Holders that had come before her.

There were dozens upon dozens of acres between them and the high gates of the ranch. Nothing could touch them as they shared bites of cobbler and watched the indigo of night seep into the orange sunset, until the sun ceded its power.

"I love it out here," she whispered as Jack wrapped his jacket over her shoulders.

"I love watching you out here."

It would've been the perfect moment had the chug of an approaching truck motor not broken the peaceful spell of the lowing cows and the stillness of night.

Meridian sighed and then hollered toward the screen door, "Daddy, Uncle Barrett's here."

Thoroughly enjoying the whole of the evening, Jack even delighted in how the Holders frequently showed up at each other's houses without invitation. It was so informal. He found it utterly charming, but the warmth of the evening took on a hardened chill when Jack saw the look on Barrett Holder's face as he approached the porch lights. Phil Cloats, a prominent realtor in Holder County, walked beside him.

Meridian stood. "What's wrong?" launched from her mouth before Jack could get to his feet. "Is it the mustangs? Is one of them in labor?"

"Simmer down, sweetheart. The mustangs were fine when Wes checked them before supper. Where's your daddy?" He lifted his hat to Jack, but it wasn't in Barrett's typical friendly way. Something was definitely wrong.

The third helping of potatoes Jack had indulged in solidified in his stomach. Gentry and Leigh made their way out onto the porch.

"Phil just brought this over. I wanted to talk to you about it. I didn't know you had company."

Jack had seen enough real estate offer contracts to recognize them even in the shaded light of the porch. Dread clawed under his skin with jagged nails. He pled with any deity willing to listen for this not to have anything to do with his family. He somehow knew he wasn't that lucky.

Gentry scowled. "Guess you weren't lying about your family thinking they can buy and sell the world."

"What?!" Meridian jerked the offer from her father's grasp. She spun and pierced Jack with a furious glare. "Your father is trying to buy our ranch," she seethed.

Making certain he wasn't going to vomit if he spoke, he managed, "I'm so sorry. I'll take care of this. I had no idea."

Barrett spoke with heavy-handed authority. "You can let your father know that we don't sell Holder land to anyone, and we never will. If this is your idea of some grand gesture to get Meridian's hand, I am not impressed."

"No, I swear." Jack could barely breathe. "I had no idea he was planning this. I would never." This wasn't working. He had to do something. Yanking his phone from his pocket he called his father's cell. He got his voice mail three times. Asshole. "Give me your phone," he demanded of Phil.

"Do it," Barrett ordered. That did it. Phil handed over his phone.

His father answered on the second ring. "What the hell do you think you are doing?" Jack's fury echoed over the fields. "This ranch is not for sale. Are you incapable of letting me have anything good ever? What? I walked away from your corrupt business so you're just going to punish me for the rest of my goddamn life."

All of the Holders took a step back and did at least look impressed.

"Everything is for sale," Palmer scoffed. "The offer is at least one and a half times what it's worth."

"No, Dad. Not everything is for sale. This land, these people's lives, my life, those things are not on the block for the highest bidder. Did you really think that you flashing cash in front of them would have them selling land that has been in their family since before Oklahoma was a state? Surely even you are not that stupid."

"Fine, I'll double my offer."

"Can you for one minute actually listen to me? This land is not just land, it is their hard work and blood and sweat and tears. It is every cow that has been born here and then raised and marketed. It's every horse that's ever galloped here, every barn that's been built to endure winters. Every field that's been burned and risen back green. This is their life, Dad. My god, it's their souls. It is not for sale for any price!"

"That girl is a loose cannon, Jackson. I can't have that. She's a threat to our company and our way of life. She made that more than apparent. You can find some other cowgirl to fuck if that's what you think suits you. But either they sell me that ranch so that I have some control over what she can say and do, or you end your relationship with her."

It had been a very long time since his father managed to shock him, and yet he did. Jack shook his head in abject disbelief. "The fact that you still can't get it through your thick skull that you have no say over me has clearly driven you insane if you believe you can threaten me. You can take your offer and shove it so far up your ass you spit dollar bills when you whistle for all the fucks I give. The Holders will never sell to you, and if you ever so much as think of them again I'll have you arrested for criminal harassment." He ended the call and handed Phil back his phone.

Adrenaline continued to surge through him. He could no longer remain still so he started walking.

"Jack?" Meridian tried but he couldn't even face her. *My god. How could he ever face them again?*

"Meridian, honey, go after him. No one should have to work through something like this alone," he heard her father urge.

She took off and had caught up to him by the end of the front yard. He didn't even know how to discuss this yet, but she walked steadfastly by him until he finally found words.

"Why would he do this? He doesn't know anything about ranching. He's never even been past the Mississippi." Jack already knew the answer, but it helped to hear himself ask it out loud.

"You said he wants control. Maybe he thought this would somehow lure you back to Denton Distilleries." They made it another hundred paces before she spoke again. "You were amazing back there. Dad'll probably want to book the church for this Saturday." She was trying so hard, but Jack was too angry and too hurt to respond.

So they walked on, never reaching a gate or even a barn. Eventually he understood that she'd guided him to her house. She led him inside to her couch where she curled up beside him.

"My first year in law school I was nominated by two of my professors to compete in the National Appellate Advocacy Competition. I was the only woman on the team. But we were a team, or at least that's what I told myself even when I wasn't told about practices or when I was given the wrong moot cases to review. I refused to believe what was right in front of my eyes because we were a team. I thought that meant something. When we arrived at the competition, I walked up on the stage and"—her voice cracked and Jack wrapped his arms around her in an effort to soothe the fractures—"uh, I gave the opening statement for the case I'd been told we were appealing. It wasn't the actual case. They lied to me. That's how badly they wanted me out of their law program. I had better grades, better elocution scores, and I was a helluva lot smarter than any of them, and those were the reasons that they needed me gone. They were willing to throw the entire competition to get me to leave. I know it's a million times worse when it's your family that sets you up. I can't imagine what that must feel like, but I need you to know that I get what it feels like to know that the people who are supposed to be on your team are the ones trying to erase you. You are allowed to take up space anywhere that you want to exist. The Holders will be your family. You don't need them."

As touched as he was by her vow, Jack shook his head. "If I ever meet any of the assholes that did that to you, I plan to let them know exactly what I think of men like that. But there's more to this than my family trying to erase me. My father doesn't take no for an answer. Ever. I have no idea what he'll come up with next, but it terrifies me."

"No one can make us sell our land, and I never take no for an answer either. If he wants to take on the Holders, he's going to find himself in a match he can't win."

CHAPTER FORTY-SEVEN

The next morning, Meridian drove Jack out to see the mustangs before she took him back to her parents' to get his truck. "It should be any day now," she explained.

"Now that your uncle has reported them to the Bureau, I don't see how Marsden's case has a leg to stand on."

"You know, it wasn't supposed to work this way."

Intrigued at that declaration, Jack scanned the herds. "What wasn't supposed to work what way?"

"When the program was passed in the state senate, it was set up to help the rye farmers keep the wild mustangs off of their crops because they were destroying them. The idea was that the Bureau would round up the horses and let them come live on ranches that had adequate land and were willing to care for them. We don't make that much money off of this program. Between food, land, medicines, minerals, all of the things we do for them, we just do a little better than break even. But there were tons of people in the senate who wanted the horses destroyed." She shook her head. "So, they had people in the Bureau round up way more than the state even knew existed. Instead of allowing the ranches that have them to break them and donate them to farms and ranches that need horses but can't afford to buy them, they defunded the program. Now, all of these beautiful creatures are here, and they're happy and healthy but..." She shrugged.

"You're always afraid that the political tides could turn, and the horses will be on the losing end of man's greed."

"Isn't that almost always how it works out? One party puts together a viable, workable plan and the other sets out to destroy it by not allocating funds so they can prove that their opposition failed."

It broke Jack's heart to finally understand the scope of her worry over the beautiful creatures before them. "You would've won that competition if your teammates hadn't been damned and determined that you weren't going to," he assured her. "Which means that you are the ideal lawyer to take an appeal all the way to the Supreme Court if need be, and I will fight right there beside you until we win."

"Jack, look!" She pointed ahead and eased her foot off the brake as they drove along the fence line.

There in the distance one of the mustangs was lying on the ground. The dirt under her was wet. "Is there something we can do to help her?" Jack had never seen a horse give birth, but he was certain Meridian would be able to tell him what to do.

"Not unless she needs help. Can you take my truck back to my parents' house and tell someone to bring the foaling kit out here? Then tell them to call Doc Halverson and tell him to be ready. I'll stay here in case she needs help."

"Sure."

Jack drove as quickly as he was able across the slick morning grass. He prayed all went well with the birth and that it was a full-blooded mustang. He pulled up in front of Gentry and Leigh's home to find Meridian's father on the porch with the paper.

Leaping out of the truck, he raced to Gentry. "One of the mustangs is in labor. Meridian needs the foaling kit, and she wants someone to call Doc Halverson.

Gentry was on his feet in record time. "Has the water broken?"

"Yes, sir."

"Maddox," he called into the house, "get a foaling kit out to your sister. One of the mustangs is in labor."

"I'll call Doc Halverson," Leigh answered from somewhere inside.

Maddox and Deacon both raced out of the house. "Where is she?" Maddox asked.

"About a mile due east of Wyn's barn," Jack explained.

"We're on it, Dad." Deacon climbed into Maddox's truck and they drove the opposite direction. Jack's brow furrowed.

"Foaling kits are in the barn," Gentry explained.

"Sorry. I don't know much about ranching, I guess."

Gentry chuckled. "Well, I don't know much about lawyering so I'd say that's okay. I wanted to tell you I'm sorry if Barrett upset you last night. We all get a little protective of Holder land. He let his temper get the best of him."

"He had every right to be upset with me. I'm the one who owes all of you an apology. I have no idea why my father is the way he is. I don't understand what end he's working for here. Why betray me? What is that going to get him?"

Gentry gave him a kind fatherly nod. "The thing about betrayal is that it can't ever come from an enemy. Then it's not a betrayal. It don't hurt like it either."

"My father only ever works for his bottom line. I just can't figure out what this ranch would do to bolster his economic standing."

"I 'spect you'll figure that out in time. All that matters to me is that you decided to rise above your raising. That takes a lot of strength and a lot of smarts. And I appreciate what you said to your old man last night. You came out swinging on our behalf. I couldn't ask for more than that."

Jack considered what had finally triggered him to run the night before. "He said something about needing to control Meridian. I don't think I've ever been so furious with him, and he's done a profound number of horrible things."

Gentry's grin expanded the width of his sun-worn face. "I think you might just be in love with her, and I think we both know that the chances of anybody controlling my little girl are between slim and none. I can assure you that slim left town the night she was born."

"I do love her, very much," Jack vowed.

"Then I'd say we need to teach you to do a little ranching. You ever seen a foal birthed?"

"No, sir."

"Hop in my truck. We'll get you set to rights. I'll tell you this, too, there ain't nothing that leaves its mark worse than your family betraying you, but if anybody's got enough love and fire in her to get rid of that bruise, it's my girl."

Over an hour later, Jack was unable to stop smiling. Meridian was delighted with the new foal that was, without a doubt, full mustang. "She's so cute," Meridian stated for the fourth time on their way into the office.

"She is that."

"And she's full mustang which means Marsden has exactly zero legs to stand on. Other than me wanting to brand your father for what he did to you last night, it's the perfect day."

"We do still have to go through with the case."

"I know. The inspector is coming out to check the horses today."

"Good. Hopefully we can get Marsden to drop it before we take up the judge's time."

They stepped into the elevator, and Jack knew they'd figure out how to work together effectively and be a couple. This wasn't even going to be difficult.

"You are forty-five minutes late for our meeting," Mayor Jennings raged as soon as they stepped into the legal suite.

Shit. Jack ground his teeth. "What meeting?"

"The meeting you agreed to yesterday. We're to discuss the wind energy suit at nine this morning."

Meridian cringed and spoke between her teeth. "I am so sorry."

Jack straightened his tie. "I'm sorry, sir. We were helping birth a foal out on Holder Ranch this morning. Time got away from me. Please," he unlocked his office door, "come on in."

CHAPTER FORTY-EIGHT

To avoid another incident like the one with the mayor, they'd negotiated a few changes to how their relationship would work at least while they were *at* work. Sex at the office could only occur if neither one of them was on the phone when the foreplay began, and Jack would go in at his normal time while Meridian did her ranch chores in the mornings.

The stability and routine they'd quickly fostered made Jack genuinely happy. The November winds darted through his dress shirt as he unlocked the courthouse early one Friday morning. Another great thing about being in love with a cowgirl was that even with her chores she was still willing and ready to allow him to indulge her in morning sex before they got their days started.

Grinning as he recalled that morning's session, Jack had managed to push his father's asinine offer on the ranch to the furthest recesses of his mind. Meridian had been right. No one took on the Holders and won, and Jack would fight beside them to make certain that was always the way it worked.

He settled at his desk and allowed himself a few minutes to recall Meridian's small curves pressed to the leather inlay. He swallowed down the onslaught of lust that filled his mouth.

Shaking himself, he reviewed the monthly court docket that had been slipped under his door. That failed to hold his attention. He missed Meridian. He hadn't spent a night in his own home since they'd returned from Kentucky, so he debated going by his house and packing more clothes to kill some time before she arrived at the office.

Telling himself he was behaving like a lovesick school boy, he ordered himself to get some work done. He tried and failed to read a contract from the Bureau of Land Management to Holder County involving a potential geothermal resource bid that the mayor wanted his legal input on. That proved about as thrilling as watching grass grow, so he moved on to the drunk and disorderly arrest from the night before.

That, at least, was somewhat humorous. He heard the rest of the staff arriving, with Mitch's teasing laughter and the slide of office chairs from the rest of the prosecutors. The glug of the water cooler and flip of the coffee maker switch made him smile. The sounds of the courthouse waking up always got his blood going.

His cell phone lit with Meridian's name. Grinning, he answered immediately. "Hey there."

"Hey,"—she sounded excited—"the last mustang foaled and I have afterbirth all over me. I'll be there as soon as I can, but I need a shower."

Jack cringed. "No problem. Take your time. I don't think we have any appointments until after lunch."

"Actually, there's a warrant request on my desk that needs to go back over to the police station. I need more information on the prior criminal. Can you seal it up for me and get Mitch to take it back to the station now? I want it back today."

"Sure."

"My request envelopes are in my filing cabinet."

"No problem. I'll take care of it. Is the foal okay?"

"Yeah, but it's a colt, so we'll have to move him to another ranch in a few years."

That was part of how the state kept the mustang population somewhat under control. "I'm sure he'll be fine."

"Yeah, I know. It just makes me sad when we have to separate them. You should see me when we wean calves. I'm a disaster. I cry every single time." She paused for a split second. "Never tell anyone I said that out loud."

Jack grinned at that. "For what it's worth, I think the fact that you love every animal on that ranch is what makes you such a kickass cowgirl."

"Thanks." He could hear the smile in her tone. "I promise I'll be in as soon as I get cleaned up."

"No rush. Hey, cowgirl..."

"Yeah?"

"I love you."

He loved her delighted laugh almost as much as he loved her. "I love you too," she vowed. "See you soon."

He made his way to her office and located the warrant request quickly. Glancing at her denial, he agreed with her assessment. They needed more information.

Before he could unlock her filing cabinet, his phone buzzed in his pocket. He fished it out and stared down at the text from her.

A stunning image of her about to step into the shower while blowing him a kiss. Even the shower cap was sexy as hell. He could only see the mischievous smirk on her face and the top of her cleavage.

He responded, *Move that camera a little lower, honey.* She was going to kill him, and he wasn't even going to mind.

He wanted more, always more of her. He was insatiable, but she didn't seem to mind. Forcing himself to think of something besides her in the shower, he unlocked her cabinet and found her envelopes.

His eyes fell to the file in the very back. She had tempted him after all. He closed her office door and turned the lock before retrieving the pictures from the folder. Accepting the fact that he was torturing himself, since he would be hard up for the entire work day, he decided it was worth it. Maybe he could talk her into another tryst in his office when everyone else was at lunch.

Easing the photographs from the folder, he helped himself to her desk chair and began going through them one by one. This wasn't the first time he'd done this, but this time was without the wash of guilt that had threatened to drown him before. This time he could relish, appreciate, and worship. Now he knew how to care for her when she needed his hands to tend her delicate preferences and his dick to ravage her when that's what she required.

His mouth went dry and his member swelled its approval as he stared at a black and white shot of her by gauzy curtains at a window. She wore nothing but a white lace thong. He swallowed down the desperate, dangerous desire to bring himself relief.

He now knew every shadow, owned every hollow. Every sweet, tender curve held his mark. He felt the sharp cut of her eyes and was healed by the lush bow of her lips. God, how had he avoided falling in love with her for so long? Or perhaps he hadn't. Perhaps he'd just become a masterful liar to himself.

Flipping to the next picture, he shifted uncomfortably in her seat. Meridian in black lace trappings that he longed to free her from. He slowly appreciated each and every picture.

Until a lightning bolt of panic jerked him from his lusty stupor. He'd seen each picture years ago. He'd memorized them. Hell, they'd occupied every wet dream and every shower session with his hand. Where was the shot of her wearing nothing at all? She'd been on her knees on a bed. It had been his favorite. He'd thought of it daily.

Carefully going back through them in case some had stuck together, he began to vibrate with abject panic. The photograph wasn't there. He tried to tell himself perhaps she'd taken it home, but his brain refused that solution. Why would she take one photo home and leave the rest in the office? If they were intended for him, wouldn't she leave them where they most often saw each other?

He put the remaining photos in an old envelope he found in her desk drawer and secured them in his interior jacket pocket. The filing cabinet didn't appear to have been forced. Did someone make a copy of one of their keys? An expert lock pick maybe? A hundred gut-wrenching scenarios played out in his head. Every single person in the entire courthouse lined up on his suspect list.

He would protect her. He was not only a damn good attorney, he was a decent detective as well. Remembering his purpose for being in her office in the first place, he sealed the warrant denial in the correct yellow envelope and marched to Mitch's desk. "Deliver this to Chief Riggins. We need more information before we issue this warrant."

"Will do." Mitch eyed him cautiously. "Are you okay?"

"I'm fine," Jack lied while he sized up Mitch. He neither seemed willing nor capable of breaking into Meridian's filing cabinet, but in this case he was guilty until proven innocent. "Are you certain you didn't see anything odd in Meridian's office when you let me know about the door being open while we were gone?"

"There was nothing that I noticed. Why? Did you find something out of place?"

"No. I just wanted to make certain."

Mitch shrugged. "I figured our resident tomcat was on the prowl again. I'll get this down to the station. I might stop for some coffee on the way back. Can I get you anything?"

"No. Thanks, though."

"Oh, I almost forgot, there's some hoity-toity lawyer waiting on you in your office. Something about the Marsden case. I assumed he's here to let you know it's been dropped. Don't know why he couldn't have just phoned, but he seems like one of those people who likes to show up places just to irritate."

"I'll get to him in a minute."

Jack made a cursory glance of the office surrounding him. Some of the prosecutor's doors were closed but most were open. Some had been here since before Jack's arrival, but he'd personally hired the rest. They all seemed to love Meridian or, at the very least, respect the hell out of her.

None of this made any sense. He needed to think. The answer had to be right in front of him, and he was somehow missing it.

Dragging himself to his desk, he set to dispense with the lawyer in his office quickly. He needed to at least have a viable suspect before Meridian got to work.

"Can I help you?" he demanded rather tersely.

The man stood and lifted his hat to Jack. "I'm Steve Elsten, from Elsten, Elsten, and Nash outta Tulsa. I'm here representing Ralph Marsden against Holder Land and Cattle Corp." The implication that

Jack should roll out the red carpet for a founding partner in some big city law firm made him want to vomit.

"I am not that easy to impress," Jack assured him. "What do you need?"

"We received your demand that we drop the case for lack of evidence."

"And?" Fury continued to mount in Jack's chest.

"And it seemed to me that you must not have seen the latest report from the Bureau inspector."

"I did see the last report. That's why I sent the demand. Your client has no grounds to file the suit. There is no evidence that the mustangs housed on Holder Ranch aren't being cared for or that they have caused any damage to your client's property. If you press on, we'll pursue full charges for the frivolous lawsuit."

Elsten laughed. He genuinely laughed, and Jack longed to sink his fist into his face. When Steve pulled a file from his briefcase, Jack jerked it from his hands. He flipped it open, and all of the heated blood that had filled his head drained slowly to his feet.

"This isn't the copy of the report the Holders received from the Bureau of Land Management. One of them is obviously fake. Since your client is the one that stands to profit from this ridiculous claim, I'm going to assume your copy was falsified."

"That's the copy my client brought to me when he hired me. That's the one we're taking to court. I just wanted to come out here and see this ranch and the idiot who thinks he's going to court against me." He slapped Jack on the shoulder and pointed to the diplomas hung behind Jack's desk. "You made my day."

With that, he turned and waltzed out of the office. It took him approximately four seconds to look up Elsten, Elsten, and Nash in the legal database. Jack's mouth dropped open at their hourly rate. How the hell was Marsden affording a lawyer like that? And why would someone like that take on a case like this?

It took Jack two seconds too long to put the final piece of the puzzle into place. Someone else was obviously now paying Marsden's legal fees. Someone with more money than either sense or morals or both combined. The assessment on the mustangs at Holder Ranch could be redone. The falsified document wasn't Jack's primary concern. It was the knowledge that his father would stop at nothing to make the Holders' lives miserable until Jack finally walked away.

He scribbled a note to Meridian and booked himself on the next one-way flight from Tulsa to Louisville. This ended now. He'd play his final ace to save her.

CHAPTER FORTY-NINE

Meridian quickly grabbed her keys, phone, and lipstick, and then set about searching for her handbag to store all her items. She grabbed her leather jacket as she passed the recliner in the living room where she'd flung it the evening before. She hoped Jack didn't mind that she wasn't all that neat because she had no plans to change.

"I made coffee," her mother announced from the kitchen.

Meridian clutched her chest. "I didn't know you were here," she gasped.

When her breathing returned to something near normal, she gave her mother a sorrowful smile. "I wish I could stay, but I'm already late."

"Just one cup. I hear you're in good with your boss so he won't mind. I haven't seen you without Jack even once since you got home. I miss you."

That did it. Meridian set the jacket and her belongings back in the chair. "Okay, but just one cup, then I have to go."

Her mother made quick work of pouring two cups of coffee and loading them with cream and sugar. They settled on Meridian's sofa.

"Yum. Why is it always so much better when you make it for me?" Meridian asked her mother.

Leigh grinned. "Coffee that someone else made is always better, but I like to think it's just because I'm so sweet."

Laughing at that, Meridian shook her head. "I've missed you too, Mama. I'll do a better job about balancing my time."

Her mother waved her off. "It's fine. I understand what it's like to fall in love and do a little life rearranging."

"It's odd to me that I didn't mind the rearranging at all. That's weird, right?"

"Not at all," Leigh assured her. "That's how you know it's real." She moved a few strewn magazines, the TV remotes, and one of Jack's undershirts off of the coffee table to make room for her mug. Shaking her head, she sighed. "Is Jack as messy as you are?"

"We're not messy; we're busy," Meridian corrected.

"Um hmm, busy getting messy."

"Mama!"

Leigh laughed as she set to organizing all of the wayward things that had accumulated on the table in front of the couch. "What is all this?" She lifted the stack of papers Meridian had printed on the Dentons.

"Oh, that was me obsessing about what I was getting myself into before we left for Kentucky. Jack kept telling me how awful his family was. I didn't really believe him, so I set out to prove him wrong. I printed out everything I could find on them. Plus, I wanted to be prepared before I met them."

Leigh started sifting through the papers. She shook her head at each one. "Goodness at the people his family knows."

"Well, they're one of the wealthiest whiskey baron families around."

"I imagine it would be hard to know if all of these people want to be around you or around your money."

"His family is only interested in people for their money or for what they can do to help the Dentons get more of it. I'm sure their friends are the same."

"Then those aren't really friends. Look here,"—Leigh lifted one of the papers deep in the stack—"his mama and daddy at the Capitol with our illustrious senator and his wife."

Meridian almost dropped her mug. She set it shakily on the table. "What?"

Leigh handed her the photo, and Meridian was certain she was going to vomit. "Oh my god." There was more than one photo of them all standing together smiling. Leigh handed over another photograph. This one had a picture of Senator McCoy in the highly recognizable entryway of the Dentons' estate house.

"Honey, what is it?"

"Oh my god," was all Meridian was capable of saying.

"I need you to elaborate on that."

"Mama, this is...oh my god. Senator McCoy is who got Jack the job here."

"So?"

"He doesn't know. He trusts Senator McCoy's family. He thinks... oh my god."

"Meridian, you are scaring me," her mother fussed.

"I have to talk to Jack. Right now." She grabbed her things and raced out of her home, leaving her mother and the coffee.

Her truck tires skidded along the dry, gravel road. A cloud of dust chased her to the gates of the ranch. She debated exactly how to proceed. Did she just show Jack the pictures? That seemed awful. Should she do more research? That didn't seem like it would make this any easier for Jack to take. The very short list of people that he trusted continued to crush her chest. How many things could you take away from a man who'd already been so badly scarred by his own family? She had to think before she went to him. She refused to add more to his battered soul. She had to protect him.

Pulling herself together as she climbed out of her truck, she tried to think of some way to hide from Jack while she figured out exactly how deep this relationship went. He hadn't been lying when he'd explained that he paid close attention to her.

Most of the time she loved that, but right then, she needed him not to.

Praying he'd be in his office with the door closed, she stepped off the elevator and into a cluster of prosecutors, aides, and paralegals surrounding Mitch's desk whispering.

"What is going on?" Meridian demanded.

Mitch stepped away from the crowd. "We were hoping you could tell us that. Jack raced out of here an hour ago. He said he was going back to Louisville. That's all he said. Like that's...it."

"He didn't say why?"

"Not a word. We were hoping you had some idea. He left right after the new lawyer on the Marsden case showed up with the paperwork."

Baffled as to why Jack would willingly go back to Louisville, Meridian also didn't like the idea of appearing uninformed. "Okay, I will go figure out what is going on with Jack. Will you all please get back to work?"

She let herself into Jack's office and prayed that Finn's cell number would be listed as Jack's contact on his employment records. She needed some answers.

Adrenaline flooded her mind, making her much too thoughtless. Instead of searching the employee records, she called Jack. There was no way he would've made it to the airport yet. Maybe she could figure out what the hell was going on from him.

After four calls and no answer, she understood that she was being shut out. "Dammit, Jack. You're supposed to trust me," she huffed. But one look at the photographs of the senator and Jack's father reminded her how incredibly difficult it would be for Jack to trust her or anyone else.

Doubling down on her abject hatred of his family, she set to work. She found Finn's number in the file and then went to Jack's laptop, determined to see just how many pictures she could find of the Dentons and the McCoys.

But the file open on his desk snagged her attention immediately. "What the hell?" She read over the obviously fake report on the mustangs at Holder Ranch. It looked nothing like the one hand delivered to her uncle by Scotty at the Bureau.

She didn't have time to worry about Marsden just then, but the gall ate at her and wouldn't let her concentrate. The intent to proceed letter was on some fancy-ass letterhead. Where had that come from? Last week Marsden's lawyer had been Fred Gickel from out in Odell.

They'd been bunkmates when they were ranch hands or something like that. Who the hell were these people and who was paying for them?

"Oh god." She breathed out the words, uncertain if they were a prayer or a curse.

Terror gripped her throat. It had claws. It tore through her lungs and burned deep through her chest. She knew why Jack was on his way to Louisville. She could not let him go to jail to protect her. She refused.

If she was going to save him, she was going to have to do some damn good lawyering, and she was up for the job.

She started at the IRS website and then dug deeper, thought harder. Why was Jack's family so interested in the ranch? That was the part that made no sense. Unless....

Her fingers flew across the keyboard. She sent document after document to the printers. She marched out into the open space where the paralegals worked and made her announcement. "Listen, Jack is about to do something really, really stupid because he thinks he has to, but he doesn't have all of the information. I know you all love Jack. Please, I need all of you to help me before I take this to the Oklahoma Department of Justice. I don't have long." Everyone in the office readily volunteered as she handed out research assignments. This was bigger than Holder Ranch.

She was running out of time.

Jack would be boarding a plane any minute now. She called him three more times but got his voicemail each time. She pleaded with him there, but knew he was every bit as determined to throw himself on the sword to save her as she was to save him.

She had to work faster. Another hour passed.

Finally, she called her parents and her uncles to help her too. She phoned Finn, who confirmed that he was picking Jack up at the airport in forty-five minutes. "Stall him," Meridian ordered. "He's planning to march into the distillery and get himself arrested. Just stall him until I get there. Please."

"I'll do my best. He's not likely to listen if he thinks he's saving you though."

She got Sloan and Lila's numbers from Finn and went back to work.

If there was any truth to the information she was uncovering, they would all save Jack together.

"Meridian!" Deidre Scully, one of their top prosecutors, raced into Jack's office. "You have to see this. You're not going to believe what I found. Look, that's Clayton's signature."

"I do believe it actually." Meridian shook her head. "That's what this has been about the entire time. What I can't believe is that anyone would stoop so low for an extra buck." But it all made sense. Clayton Barns, the former DA of Holder County, was as dirty as the rest of them.

"I guess this is why Clayton always seemed to favor Jack no matter what he did or said," Deidre commented.

Meridian nodded. The onslaught of adrenaline mixed with the emotion in her chest. "If anyone else had ever defended me to Clayton the way Jack always did, they would've been fired." But Jack hadn't known that his father and Clayton were friends. Jack had defended her even if it could've cost him his job. He'd told Clayton she was the best attorney in the building because he believed that.

She forced herself to slow. She had to make certain she understood every intricate piece of this malignant web that had been created with the specific purpose of choking out her family. She would leave nothing to chance.

Finally, she phoned Sheriff Riggins. "It's Meridian," she leapt in as soon as he answered his phone. "I have evidence that we need to bring Ralph Marsden in for questioning on conspiracy. I'll send a paralegal down with the files, but I need a warrant back on my desk in fifteen minutes. I'm running out of time, and I need Marsden's confession."

When she struck the match, everything would burn.

When she was certain she had her case, she called the airlines and booked three one-way tickets to Louisville. Barrett and Maddox had insisted on coming with her, even though it was completely unnecessary. She could take care of herself.

Hopefully.

Meridian climbed into her uncle's truck. This was the most important case of her entire career, and she intended to win it.

"Go on with it," Barrett encouraged. "I'll get us to the airport as fast as I can."

Unable to fully grasp what she was about to do, she lifted her phone from her purse. Certain she was having some kind of out-of-body experience, her hands trembled as she dialed the number from the files in her lap. "Yes, this is Meridian Holder, ADA from Holder County ID 7925418. I need to speak with the Attorney General."

"Regarding what, ma'am?"

"I'm filing a formal ethics complaint against Senator McCoy."

"Hold, please."

CHAPTER FIFTY

"Meridian ordered me to stall you, so that's what I'm doing," Finn explained to Jack.

Jack didn't have time for this. "I appreciate her trying to stop me from doing this, but it has to be done. Dad will never stop unless I put an end to it."

"She sounded pretty certain that there was a bunch of stuff you don't know."

"Meridian is the best lawyer I've ever seen. She's stunningly brilliant. That is one of the many reasons why I fell in love with her. But she can talk her way into and out of most anything, so of course she sounded certain. I'm sure she is certain she doesn't want me to go to jail, which I appreciate, but this ends today."

Finn shook his head as he continued to drive in circles, refusing to take Jack to the distillery offices. "You know what your problem is?"

Jack rolled his eyes. "What?" He'd placate his brother just long enough to get him to go to the offices.

"Your God complex is even bigger than your ego. You're a good guy, but you're not Jesus H. Roosevelt Christ. You're not here to save all of us."

"What the hell is that supposed to mean?"

"Do you really think that me or Drew or Sloan or Meridian or anyone else is just going to stand by and let Dad figure out how to make sure you're the only one who goes down with the ship? That's a bunch of bullshit. Your job is not to throw yourself on the sword just because you feel guilty for not realizing sooner how fucked up our parents are."

Jack ground his teeth and refused the emotion that threatened to clog his throat. "I will never forgive them for what they did to you."

"You don't have to forgive them," Finn's voice fell several notches. "I don't need you to forgive them. I need my big brother to stay out of jail. You don't always have to do these massive dramatic dives off the high board, man. It's okay to just let yourself be happy."

"Don't you get it?" Jack raged. "I'd love to just be happy. I'd fucking love to marry her and move onto that ranch and forget River Chase and Hearst Stone and all of it even exists, but he won't let me. I don't have a choice. Now, take me to the offices."

"Not until she gets here."

Shock sizzled through Jack, igniting another round of fury deep in his gut. "Why is she coming here?"

Finn chuckled as he continued to drive them farther and farther away from where Jack needed them to be. "How can you be so goddamn smart and also a complete idiot?" Jack refused to respond to that so Finn continued. "She loves you. Really, really loves you. That's not a one-way street. It doesn't work the way Mom and Dad do it. It's not all about what you can do for her or how you can save her. She's not a bank account where you deposit all of your protection and love and she spends it. You both want to save and protect each other and that's love. She's not going to let you do this and neither am I. I'll take you to the offices when Sloan picks her up from the airport."

"There is nothing she can do to stop me. She doesn't know what she's getting into with Dad. I'm calling the auditors."

Finn still seemed amused. "I'll tell you this much, I sure as hell wouldn't bet against her. I have a feeling when your woman is done with Dad, he's gonna feel like the fucker that brought a pocketknife to a gun fight."

Jack shook his head. Finn had never been deep in the Denton businesses. He didn't know. "I can't let her do whatever it is she thinks she's going to do to save me. It won't work anyway."

"I'm pretty sure"—Finn glanced his way before returning his eyes to the highway—"you can't stop her."

————

————

Meridian sprinted up the corridor at the airport. "There he is." She pointed out Sloan in the crowd near the counters.

Sloan must've heard her shout because he headed their way. "Here," he handed over the final piece of evidence that she needed. "But I…"

"I know," Meridian assured him.

"A lot of people that I love are going to lose their jobs when you do this," Sloan went on with his warning.

"If I have any say at all, the only person who will be losing his job will be Senator McCoy."

"I don't see how you're going to pull that off, and even if you do, this is going to kill Jack."

"That's the part that makes me not want to do any of this, but I can't let him go to jail. We all have a much better chance of making him understand that he can trust us if he's not in prison."

"She's the best lawyer on either side of the Mississippi," Barrett informed him.

Sloan forced a polite nod. "I take it you're the uncle."

"Barrett Holder. This is Maddox, Meridian's brother."

"Pleasure," Maddox drawled. "Can we get on with this? I'm not real keen on my little sister taking on some kind of whiskey millionaires who are in bed with dirty senators. Political crimes tend to get a whole lot of people, with a whole lot of money and the state police in their back pocket, real, real twitchy."

"Understood." Sloan led them out to his car. "I have no idea how you're going to pull this off, but you know the Bastards have your back. Drew's sitting outside the gates, and Lila's already at the office ready to claw Uncle Palmer's eyes out. Finn's pissing Jack off by refusing to take him over there until we get closer."

"Thank you. Really. I can't thank you enough."

"Just make sure neither of you end up in prison."

Maddox brought his buzzing phone to his ear. "Good. Let me know if anything changes," was the extent of the conversation.

"Who was that?" Meridian demanded.

"T-Byrd. Federal DOJ just issued the inquiry. FBI's on the way to McCoy's house in Virginia." As much as she hated to admit it, Meridian deeply appreciated that her brother was skilled enough to work for one of the country's best government contracting firms.

Her pulse pounded frantically, jarring her skin and shaking her bones. They were doing this. She made a silent prayer that somehow Jack would recover from one more brutal blow.

CHAPTER FIFTY-ONE

Meridian was unable to keep her legs still. Her heartbeat wasn't anywhere near even-paced. She just needed to see Jack, to make sure he was okay. Then she could go on with what she had to do.

They could get through this together. She hoped.

They pulled up to the gates of Denton Distilleries and Brews. The guard waved Sloan's car through.

"That's Finn's car." Sloan pointed to the blue Camry in the lot. "They're already here. Uncle Palmer hasn't seen Finn in years. This is gonna be one hell of a blow-up."

"Good," Meridian's voice quaked. "He deserves the fallout of that."

"Are you ready?" Sloan parked his car beside Finn's.

"No, but I don't get that choice, so let's do this."

Prepared for war, Meridian marched beside her brother through the lobby. Sloan waved off the receptionist and put his key in the elevator.

As they exited on the top floor, Sloan pointed to the left. As Meridian raced that direction, she could hear Jack's threats to his father. "I've already spoken to an auditor from the IRS. They'll be here any moment to start seizing financials."

"What?" Palmer's seething voice propelled Meridian to a sprint.

"You are aware that you signed off on most of the things they'll be seizing."

"Then they can put us in handcuffs together. Isn't that what you really wanted? Me back under your thumb. Maybe we can share a cell and work out our familial tension."

The hatred in Jack's tone wounded her. She ran faster.

"There is one thing I'd love to know before the IRS shows up," Jack huffed. "What the hell do you want with her ranch?"

"You'll pay for this," Palmer shouted.

"No, he won't." Meridian rounded the corner into the office. "He won't pay for anything, but you will. Do you want to tell him why our ranch is so important to you, or should I?"

"Thank god," Finn grumbled from the corner. His entire body sank in relief.

"Meridian, honey, what are you doing here?" Jack pled.

"You are not going to jail, because tax fraud won't be what the charges are for."

"What?"

A harsh swallow contracted Palmer's throat as he glared at Meridian.

She turned to Sloan. "Do you have copies of the shipment receipts?"

"Several," Sloan assured her.

"Okay, just please know how sorry I am to have to show you all of this," she vowed to Jack.

"Show me what?" he demanded.

She handed the copies of her evidence to both Jack and his father and took a deep breath that did nothing to help steady her. "There is a great deal of evidence that suggests that the year both of us were seniors in high school, your parents struck up a friendship with Senator McCoy and his family."

"What?!" Jack's wounded gasp crushed Meridian, but she pressed on. God, why did saving someone you love have to hurt them?

She managed a haggard nod. "The pictures are in the first file there. Five years prior to that, Holder Ranch signed a contract with the state of Oklahoma to take on and house wild mustangs in the state's Wild Horse and Burro Program. That is also the year that Senator McCoy began campaigning for the seat. His predecessor, Senator Cambridge, had fought against the plan, stating that it would cost the state entirely too much money. He believed that the animals should be killed. Backlash to his cruel plan is what we all believed got McCoy elected, but we were wrong. McCoy and Cambridge had been working together. Cambridge set it up so that he dropped out of the race five weeks prior to the election, creating a situation where McCoy ran unopposed with what I suspect was a backdoor dealing that ultimately he would end the Wild Horse program.

"McCoy's brother, Jude, owns one of the largest rye farms in Oklahoma, spanning over four hundred thousand acres along the Texas line. Back in the nineties, some of his crops had been destroyed by the wild horses. He would've been able to write the loss off, of course, but common sense tells us that it likely pissed him off. It was about that same time that Elbon Rye became a hot commodity for making whiskey, and two years after you met Thad McCoy and began your friendship at Duke, Denton Distilleries launched four highly profitable rye labels making use of Elbon Rye."

Meridian's eyes closed. She wasn't certain she could go on. Suddenly, Jack's arms were around her. "You're incredible, you know that?" he whispered in her ear.

"It gets so much worse." She trembled against his chest.

He stepped back. The pain and cynicism mixed with pride in his eyes. "Keep going then," he choked.

She glanced at her Uncle Barrett, and he gave her that soothing smile that he'd given her all her life. "Want me to take over from here?"

"Sure," she managed.

"As the century turned, Holder Ranch ultimately came to care for more wild mustangs than any other ranch in the state. Although most of it is not profit for us, the state does pay us quite a tidy sum for caring for the animals. McCoy frequently gets called out by his political opponents for the amount of money the state writes to us. But for a few years there, his brother no longer had the problem of mustangs trampling the rye, so we mistakenly assumed their family would be pleased. Of course, that would also mean that his brother didn't have that loss to report on his income. But the Holders remained a major burr in McCoy's saddle in terms of the mustang money." Barrett shook his head. "Honest to goodness, this is all so convoluted and ridiculous I'm afraid I'm mixing my Herefords with my Holsteins."

Palmer's nostrils flared as he bared his teeth. Meridian squeezed Jack once more, prayed that wouldn't be the last time she felt his arms around her, and took back over. "The grievance between our family and Senator McCoy grew with each new delivery of horses we accepted and each check we were written. Only, we were largely unaware that McCoy hated us specifically. We knew he disliked the program, but we had no idea how resentful he really was. I also didn't know until today that Senator McCoy and Clayton Barns were very close friends."

Jack's eyes widened and then his head fell into his hands.

Tears pricked Meridian's eyes. "Jack, I'm so sorry, but it seems that it was around the same time that Clayton got his colon cancer diagnosis that you left Denton Distilleries and started looking for a job."

He lifted his head and stared down his father. "You set me up. You had me sent to Holder County. You and Senator McCoy put me there because you knew I'd run for DA. You even orchestrated who my roommate would be at Duke all for your bottom line."

Finn shook his head. "That's all we've ever been to Dad. I thought you knew that."

Palmer refused to speak, and Meridian's head weighted with a nod. "Clayton knew if they didn't get someone else in the office willing to run against me and win that my family would have another notch of power to keep the mustang program going."

"Oh my god, that's why you hate her so much!" Jack raged in his father's face. "If I'm in love with her, then I won't keep playing your puppet against her family!"

"It's actually even worse than that," Sloan stepped in. "For the past four years, since Jack's departure from the company, it would seem that Jude McCoy hit on another round of bad luck. Papers from Davidson to Randlett ran stories where Jude claimed thousands and thousands of acres of his rye had been destroyed by fire. No one thought too much of it because there had been fires in the area. Only, Denton accepted shipments of rye that are inordinately close to the amount of rye that Jude said had been destroyed."

Meridian forced herself to go on. "One of my cousins is a firefighter. He searched the database records for me. If there were fires on McCoy's farm, he never reported them to any rescue services."

"Un-fucking-believable!" Jack's fury spilled off of him in hot waves. "So, he was able to take a massive tax write-off, you got free rye, and let me guess—the way you paid for it was in campaign finance donations to the senator."

Meridian was certain that was the case as well. Sloan confirmed, "Denton issued checks—that you signed, Uncle Palmer—to Rye Freedom. I didn't think much of it at the time other than that McCoy must think himself quite the farmer to have a business by that name. But I started digging today and discovered that Rye Freedom is a Super PAC that helps keep McCoy in his seat."

Meridian gave her closing argument. "The police arrested Marsden for conspiracy before I left to come out here. He was the ideal person to bring charges against Holder Land and Cattle. His brother made certain that the Oklahoma Bureau of Land Management report failed to include that four of the mares were pregnant, and Marsden himself was already looking for a payout from my family. I suspected that your father was who was paying for Marsden's new legal team, but that wasn't quite right. It's Senator McCoy. If they can prove in court that we're not caring for the horses, from what we can tell, the Senator will use his sway with the governor and the state senate to destroy the program and the horses. Marsden and his brother are just their front men. His brother knew they'd sent us pregnant mares and timed the lawsuit to try and create evidence for their case, just like you suspected." She hoped that might help bolster Jack somewhat.

"The picture," Jack choked.

Meridian was afraid he was losing it. "What?"

"One of the pictures of you is missing. Does McCoy have it?" He narrowed his eyes to slits as thin as blades as he glared at his father. It took Meridian a second to understand which picture he was referring to.

Dread and shame threatened to claw through her chest, but she refused them. That's what men like this wanted her to feel, and she refused.

"The senator has a right to an insurance policy." Palmer latched onto what it appeared he thought was going to be his saving grace.

Meridian laughed in his face. "Oh, do tell me which of his websites and rags he plans to run it in to try to keep me quiet. I'll send them the rest." She shook her head. "Those pictures were for your son, but if you are that morally bankrupt, and you can't find it in yourself to think of anything but your bottom line, then go right ahead. I don't care what you do to me. I only care that you are so willing to hurt your own sons for a business deal. People are going to judge me no matter what I do, so I'm going to do what I know is right."

Jack shook his head. "I can't...I just...can't."

He stalked out of the room. Meridian turned to run after him, but Finn caught her shoulder. "Let me talk to him."

"I'm coming with you," she argued.

"Someone needs to stay here to make sure he's still sitting in that desk when the auditors show up."

Greer turned the corner into the office just then. Meridian had no idea how much he'd heard. "I'll make sure he's sitting there." He shook his head as well. "I can't believe this, Dad. I was the one that defended you to them and then you do something like this. I know you never really thought I was as good a businessman as Jack, but I'm going to try to negotiate your ass out of this with the IRS by making sure you pay back every single penny you owe. I will not let every single person who depends on Denton for a job be out of work. On one condition—you will raise every salary of every single person who works for us. You will give everyone enough hours for them to qualify for complete healthcare, and if they've been with us longer than ten years they get a chance to buy into the company. I should've spoken up a long, long time ago. I'm sorry I didn't. But I am now."

CHAPTER FIFTY-TWO

Jack had no patience for waiting on the elevator, so he flew down three flights of stairs until he was finally out of the hell that existed inside the building. Only now, he had no idea where to go or what to do.

Defeat filled his lungs, leaving no room for oxygen. The human mind clung to assurances, and he had none. The particles of his life drained through his hands, too small to hold. Everything he'd thought he'd earned had been handed to him. No matter how hard he'd fought to become the king, he'd always been his father's pawn.

"Jack, wait!" Meridian's plea was muffled through his agony. Even she hadn't been earned. He'd been put there to hurt her, to keep her from getting what was rightfully hers. If not now, someday surely she would resent that.

He continued to run toward the gates though he had no idea where to go from there. He was a man with no place to call his own because he'd earned nothing.

"Dammit, Jack, would you stop?" Finn urged. But Jack kept going.

Until Barrett Holder's voice reached him. "Son, I am too old to chase you all over Louisville. Now stop and listen to me."

Having no idea why that had done it, Jack slowed and turned back to face them.

Barrett shook his head at him. "I am so sorry for all that you've been put through."

Jack rolled his eyes. "I'm not some poor little rich boy, sir."

"I'm aware of that." He paused a minute to catch his breath. "I'm also aware that you have no idea who to trust because the people that you thought you could rely on have let you down time and time again. But here's what else I know—you can trust yourself. You can also trust the people who really do love you, not for what you can do for them, but for who you are. Meridian, your cousins, your brothers. I know that's mighty hard to do right now, so just trust you. Look at what you've managed to do. You were put in a position to hurt my family, and instead you earned our respect and ultimately the hand of Meridian. You were there to disrupt, and you've created one of the best groups of prosecutors our county has ever had. You should've seen them today all helping her fight to protect you because they admire the hell out of you and so do I."

Jack shook his head. "I took what was supposed to be hers. My ego overran my good judgment, and I played right into their hands. She should hate me."

"Well, I don't," Meridian defied. "I love you, and I don't care if you're the DA. I don't need or want that position." She held her hand out to the dynasty headquarters that stood behind them. "Look around you. A really well-thought-of man from a century or two ago said, 'Absolute power corrupts absolutely. Great men are almost always bad men.' He wasn't wrong. Greed is never satisfied. We studied it in law school, remember? My family doesn't need to hold every seat in our county. We need to serve the people that we can help and feed the people who need meat. That's our job. My job specifically is to help you put away men who are bad, men who want to control absolutely, and to protect the people that they hurt. I want to keep doing that with you. Please," her voice shattered right along with his heart, "don't walk away thinking that you don't deserve me, because that's what he wants."

She edged closer. "Remember? Sometimes you just have to do something really rebellious to remind them who you are. Please,"—she stepped close enough for him to reach her—"be a rebel with me. Let me show them who you are and that we won't be controlled."

Jack wasn't certain of anything but the fact that he wanted her to be right and that he was too weak to deny her. So, he took her hands and pulled her into his arms and clung to the only thing that would ever make any sense to him at all.

A small round of applause broke out, making her laugh. Jack lifted his head. Lila's whistle reached them long before she did. "The IRS is here. Uncle Palmer and Dad are pretty much set to maim, but they're both signing paperwork promising to make payments until everything is caught up. It doesn't come near to solving all of the ass-backward issues this distillery has, but it's a start. They're going to want to talk to you and Sloan, but I think as long as they make regular payments, no one will end up in federal prison."

"I can't believe you managed this." Jack was truly in awe of Meridian.

"We did this," she vowed. "You and me and a whole lot of people that love you. It wasn't just me. I didn't call the IRS. I didn't even know about the picture."

"Still,"—he brushed her hair behind her shoulders—"you were brilliant in there."

She beamed at him. "I'm brilliant everywhere." She laughed.

"And that is sexy as hell." He barely had strength enough to flirt with her, but he managed. She was the best lawyer he'd ever seen. He used what waning powers he had to make sure that she knew they'd figure this all out together.

"The most annoying part of all of this is that Senator McCoy will likely get by with just a slap on the wrist. Men like that almost never pay real consequences," she fussed.

Jack agreed. "There are a lot of people in jail that shouldn't be, and the ones that should will never darken the doors." He gestured to his father's office. "It's infuriating, but we can fight it."

"Maybe we can change it," she urged.

Her grin filled him. It gave him something small to cling to, a place to start, a known to hold in his hands.

CHAPTER FIFTY-THREE

A week later, Jack sat at his desk reading newspaper headlines about the ethics complaint against Senator McCoy. He shook his head, still largely unable to believe what Meridian had uncovered.

She opened his office door and slipped inside with a coy grin.

"Did you need something, Ms. Holder?" he drawled flirtatiously.

"I missed you."

Jack struggled to wrap his head around every lie he'd ever believed, but it was much easier when he stood in the presence of her truth. "I was in bed with you less than an hour ago," he teased her.

"I know." She came around his desk, and he gave himself a moment to draw a deep breath of her scent mixed with his cologne. "What are we looking at?" she asked.

"I think I figured out why my mother was so adamant that I try to talk Tiff and Brent into going on with their marriage."

He loved that look that formed on her features that said she was impressed with him. He'd happily live his entire life just trying to impress her. "Okay, why *was* your mother so into them being together?"

"One of my mother's key business skills is being able to see the writing on the wall before other people notice that it's there. The

Denton ties to Brenton Cox's family PR business are through the Fitzgeralds. My mother was terrified when I told her who I was bringing to Tiffany's wedding, but she managed to keep it mostly to her standard haughty remarks until the Fitzgeralds announced their divorce.

"She knew if you figured out about the Denton ties to Senator McCoy, they would need the skill set of Brenton's family to keep the Denton name out of the news. So far, not one paper or news source has mentioned my father at all. She got her wish even though Brent and Tiff still aren't going on with the wedding as of yet."

"Taking down a dynasty isn't a one-shot deal," she reminded him. "Did you ever figure out why the Fitzgeralds are divorcing?"

"He wants out of the bottling business," Jack informed her what Sloan had found out that morning.

"Why?"

"Sloan thinks he's been fraternizing with a woman at least half his age who apparently believes that corporate greed will be the downfall of humanity."

Meridian considered that for a few minutes. "I don't necessarily disagree, and that's a different take from the normal gold digger, I guess."

Jack shook his head. "They're not getting divorced because he's having an affair. They're getting divorced because he wants out of the business. Their whole world is so fucked up I still can't believe I was able to get out of it."

"I'm so proud of you," Meridian gushed.

Sometimes they both felt like their entire relationship had grown in spite of a million interruptions. So someone knocking on the door wasn't a surprise, but Jack was tired of it. "Go on a trip with me," he begged.

"What?"

"Anywhere you want. Just me and you. Please, I need to figure the rest of my life out, and I want to do that with you uninterrupted."

"Okay." She nodded. He loved watching her mind work. "We could go to the Grand Canyon, or, oh, I've always wanted to see the California coast but it's kind of cold right now. My family has a chalet in Telluride. We could go there."

"Anywhere, just not here. Come in," Jack finally answered the current interrupter.

If he'd known who was at his office door, he might've begged for her to go on a trip with him later. This took priority. Thad McCoy walked in his office, looked at Meridian, and blushed. Jack's fists clenched of their own accord.

"I brought you this." He handed Jack an envelope.

Maintaining his cool, Jack stood, took the envelope, and managed a nod. "Meridian, sweetheart, this is Thad McCoy, my college roommate and apparently the son of a federal felon." He knew her picture was inside that envelope. Thankfulness and fury went to war in his gut.

Meridian gave him a cool nod. "Lovely to meet you." No one in the room thought she was being sincere.

"Look," Thad launched into the speech Jack had assumed would come. "I didn't know any of that shit that our dads and my uncle were into. I broke into his office to get that back for you. I'm sorry about all of it, but I didn't do it. It wasn't me. It's just politics. Besides, we were frat brothers. You can't just walk away from that."

Jack rolled his eyes. "This," he held up the envelope, "is not politics. It's breaking and entering a government facility along with theft by taking. It's ten to twenty minimum. You, and your father, and your uncle, and my dad are not above the law. So, I will walk away from anything or anyone that proves that whatever team it is they're playing for is more important to them than standing up for the people who are being hurt by their tribalism. You delivering something to me that was stolen does not make us cool," he huffed. "It makes your father a thief and a liar and basically just completely morally bankrupt. So, get back to me when you're calling out his bullshit, and then we'll reminisce about our frat boy days."

That earned him another one of those Meridian smiles that said he'd just impressed the hell out of her again. Yeah, making her do that for the rest of their lives. That was a truth he could build on.

"I did tell my dad he'd gone way too far messing with you," Thad insisted. "I told him you'd figure out a way to have him arrested."

"Yeah, but listen to yourself. You protected me because we used to be friends, because you know me. Would you have done the same for all of the other people your father has inevitably hurt along the way? The ones you didn't room with at Duke?"

Thad looked utterly confused by the question. "I don't know. I never really think about Dad's job."

Meridian nodded. "Maybe you should think about it."

"Okay, I guess." Defeat sank slowly through Thad's tone. "For what it's worth, I'm happy if you're happy," he vowed to Jack.

"I am happy." Jack wondered for a moment if that was true. There was still so much wrong with the way the Dentons did business. Even if they did pay back all of their back taxes, they'd hurt people along the way. But in that moment, with Meridian by his side and the chance to right so many wrongs in their future, he decided he was happy.

"Good." Thad glanced from Jack to Meridian and then to the door. "I guess I'll see y'all around."

"Bye, Thad," Jack urged. "Close the door behind you on your way."

Once he was gone, Meridian clutched the envelope to her chest. "I know I talked a big game in your dad's office about not caring about this, but I'm really glad we have it back, and I'm going to need you to completely support me in my delusion that they didn't make a copy of this."

Jack wrapped his arms around her, keeping her and the photo safe by the might of his body. "I am so sorry that I got you into this, and I will completely support that delusion because it is all that is keeping me from going out to the parking lot and beating the shit out of him for looking at what's mine. I'm trying to be a really cool, laid-back, non-sexist, ally kind of man who knows that your body is your own, but I'm failing at the moment."

Meridian's laughter vibrated through his chest from their proximity. Sharing that with her was another truth he could build on. "I don't so much mind you being possessive."

"Good. Then I would also like to claw Senator McCoy's eyes out with a dull pickaxe."

"We have several of those in the barn."

"That saves me a trip to the hardware store."

She nuzzled her head against his chest, cooling his temper just a little. "Can we go back to talking about our trip?"

"Definitely. I'd prefer not to go to Telluride if it's okay with you. I was hoping to take you somewhere no one knows either of us."

"That sounds like heaven."

Jack thought about that. "Being anywhere with you is heaven, but I was thinking somewhere like Hawaii?"

She lifted her head and stared at him like he'd lost his. "Can we afford to go to Hawaii?"

Pleased with just how smooth this was going, Jack smirked. "We could if I didn't renew the lease on my house next month, and I get my deposit back."

The golden flecks in those whiskey eyes shimmered. "You know, I sometimes leave really gross boots on the front porch."

"As long as I can also leave dirty boots on the porch, I think I can live with this. But you know, sometimes I eat pizza straight from the box on the couch when I'm reviewing for a trial. There are even a few nights when I leave the empty pizza box out if I'm up really late."

She nodded thoughtfully. "I'll concede your pizza and the box, as long as beer bottles left on the table until the next morning can be negotiated."

"No negotiations required. I'll allow it. I will also promise never to leave a wet towel on our bed."

"Good, and I'll promise not to take up the entire bed at least three nights a week."

"How generous."

Meridian grinned. "I thought so."

Jack gestured to his package. "My client and I would like to negotiate that you wear nothing to bed on the other four nights then."

Smirking at that, she offered, "That...might could be arranged."

"Then my client and I will allow the lack of bed space. I will also offer to make you coffee every morning."

"With two big scoops of sugar and more cream than could possibly be healthy?"

"Is there any other way to make it?"

Her grin continued to expand. "Mama says that coffee someone else makes for you always tastes better."

"I want to make every day the best day it can be for you."

"I want to do that for you too, so that sounds like a pretty good relationship."

"I completely agree. I also love you and somehow love you more every single day I spend in your presence."

"I love you too," she vowed, "and I really like your client as well." She waggled her eyebrows.

Jack gripped her ass. "He can be very persuasive when he needs to be or when you need him to be."

"I need him to be."

"Go make sure that door is locked."

CHAPTER FIFTY-FOUR

A week before Christmas, Jack was propped up on his elbows in the warm Kauaian sand watching as Meridian emerged from Hanalei Bay. When she settled back beside him, he wrapped her up in a towel. Her sun-kissed skin now sported the beginnings of tan lines despite constant suntan lotion applications he personally saw to. They'd only been there for two days.

"This entire island is amazing," she gushed.

"I agree, but we haven't even seen all of it yet."

Meridian grinned at him, a calmer sweeter grin than he saw when they were at work, one she only gave him at home. "I am very excited to see the cattle ranches, which I know is such a weird thing to do on vacation. Thank you for indulging me."

"Indulging you is one of my favorite pastimes," he explained. "Before we go get ready for our cattle ranch tour, I'm hoping you'll indulge me in more shave ice."

"I will definitely indulge you in that. Too bad we can't take any home with us."

"We'll just have to come back sometime." The fruity ice confection was delicious and no matter how many times they stopped by the stands there was no way they were going to be able to try all the flavor combinations before they had to leave for home.

"You're still talking like you have the salary of a bourbon baron's son instead of the district attorney."

Jack chuckled at that. "I didn't say how soon we'd be able to come back, just that we would." He shrugged. "Maybe for our honeymoon."

Her only response was a smirk.

He was doing a terrible job of keeping his plans for the evening a secret, but the ring he'd hidden in their villa was burning a hole in his swim trunks.

Nerves constantly twisted in his gut. *What if she didn't say yes?* As soon as the thought took hold of his mind, she smiled up at him with one of those adoring grins he'd gotten pretty good at earning. She was going to say yes. His nerves were just getting the better of him. They'd been inseparable for months now. But what if it was too soon?

He needed a drink. He scanned the endless blue horizon and then his gaze fell back to her wet hair and sun-pinked cheeks. Or maybe, he just needed a hit of her.

Coaxing her face closer to his, he indulged himself in the flavors of her salty lips. When she offered up her neck for his affections, he almost asked her right then and there. He wrapped his arms around her and held tight. He'd worked hard on this plan, and he was going to execute it perfectly.

"Are you ready to head back to the villa?" he whispered against her slick shoulder.

"One second." She dug in her bag and pulled out her phone. "I want to remember every second of this." She held the phone up with one hand and laid her head on his shoulder. He couldn't help but grin. She was pleased with the created selfie even if they weren't the type to post pictures anywhere. "Okay, now we can go."

They packed up and walked the trail back to their beachside villa. They'd paid a small fortune for the private cottage, and it had been worth every penny. He turned on their outdoor shower and shed his swimsuit. With a wicked grin on his face, he took hold of one of the strings of her bikini top and arched his eyebrow. If she moved, the bikini top would come undone.

Her flirty giggle was everything as she shook her head at him. "The indoor shower is bigger and warmer," she reminded him.

"I know." He pulled the string and watched her top loosen. "Indulge me."

"In what exactly?" Her smirk betrayed her false innocence.

"Letting people hear *me* indulging *you*."

A heavy note of hunger stirred in her eyes. Her bottom lip slipped between her teeth, and she shot a nervous glance toward the next closest cottage, like she'd been given a script of his darker fantasies. And of course, she had. They'd talked even more than they'd fucked in the last few months, and that was how he knew she was going to say yes.

After their lengthy outdoor shower, Jack offered to go get them a glass of POG, a drink they'd fallen in love with on the plane, while she finished getting ready. Meridian seemed to know he was up to something, but she went along.

He made his way past a few other cottages, waved at bike riders, and tried to memorize the scent of hibiscus on the winds so he could cling to that wild freedom the next time he had to deal with his family.

He passed the hotel pool and finally arrived at the main house. Smiling at Kealia at the front desk, he slipped inside.

"Everything's ready, Mr. Denton," she assured him.

"Please, call me Jack," he insisted again.

"Okay," she shrugged. "The table is set up on the beach. Sunset is at 5:35. The boat leaves the Kukui'ula Harbor at 7:00. Just make sure you're there in time. Captain Keyes doesn't wait around."

"Thank you for your help. I couldn't have done any of this without you." He hesitated. "You're sure the hot dog and mai tai thing is the way to go for this?"

"You're just going to have to trust me." She grinned. "I've helped a lot of couples get engaged here. It's kind of our specialty." She gestured to the surrounding pavilions and villas.

Jack tried to believe her, but he was struggling. "If you were getting engaged tonight..." he started.

"It's exactly how I would want my boyfriend to ask me. If I had a boyfriend, that is." She wrinkled her nose. "Even a prospect would be nice."

Jack felt bad for asking. "I broke off an engagement and then spent years refusing to admit I was in love with Meridian, so never say never," he tried.

Kealia laughed. "My Tutu keeps trying to fix me up."

"I recommend against family involvement in every way."

"Clearly you are not from Kauai," she goaded.

He nodded his acceptance of that. "Maybe some things are more universal than they appear."

"Maybe." She shrugged. "Do you have your order ready? I'll call them and get the rest set up. You just head to Poipu and leave soon or you'll get stuck in traffic in Kapáa."

"Wish me luck." He wished his hands would stop shaking.

"You don't need luck. You have Kauai."

Jack gave her their hot dog order and supposed she was right. The entire island was magical. From the oceans to the winds to the sandy kisses they'd shared, this was the perfect escape they'd needed. Every uninterrupted conversation healed him.

They spent the afternoon touring two of the Kauaian cattle ranches. Just before they left for their dinner, a broad grin spread the width of Meridian's features. "Oh my gosh, you're Levi Wohlers."

A rather well-built Hawaiian man turned to smile at them. "Aloha," he offered. "Do I know you?"

"No, but I'm Meridian Holder. This is my boyfriend, Jack Denton. You competed at our Founder's Day Rodeo in Holder County last year. Jace is my cousin. You won for team roping, right?"

Levi nodded. "I took a year off of the circuit to help out around here, but tell Jace I miss him."

"I didn't know you lived here."

"This is home." Levi nodded. "For now, anyway."

Jack wondered if Levi planned on leaving soon or if something was happening to their ranch. He didn't want to be nosy.

Meridian also looked concerned. "I hope everything's okay," she offered.

Levi shrugged. "Yeah, me too."

They didn't press further. Jack offered him his hand. "We're heading down to Poipu tonight. If you ever get back to Holder County to compete, you should come out to Holder Ranch."

"I'll take you up on that. You two have fun tonight. If you ever want to get away from the rest of the tourists, give me a call. There's a lot more to this island than what's on Travelocity."

Jack and Meridian shared an excited glance. "We'd love that," Jack assured him as he handed over his phone.

Levi entered his number, and they waved as they headed back to their rental car.

Kealia had been right. The hot dogs with coconut and mango relish were amazing. The sunset picnic on Poipu Beach was perfect as well. And yet, for some reason, Jack couldn't bring himself to get down on one knee.

He called himself a coward, but that wasn't it. Something about all of his planning wasn't right. It wasn't real.

They went on their cruise and relished the mai tais and each other, but he still didn't ask. Something was clearly wrong with him. He lay awake next to her that night and mentally pummeled himself. What the hell was wrong with him?

It didn't occur to him until the sun was warming their lanai the next morning what had actually been wrong. It was what Levi had said. There was a whole island they were missing because they were only seeing the external cover splashed in brochures for tourists. Meridian was perfection because of her authenticity, and he wanted their engagement to be equally as authentic.

His cowgirl princess wasn't the kind of girl who wanted to get engaged at sunset on a tourist locale beach. Before she awoke, he snuck into the living room and phoned Levi.

After another day spent laughing, talking, eating, and having sex, Jack told her he had a surprise for her. She got suspicious the farther south they drove.

"Where are we going?" she asked.

"Just let me surprise you."

"I don't like surprises."

"You'll like this. I hope. Just trust me," he reminded her.

"I do."

He let those two words ring in his mind as he turned in the entrance of Hanchett Ranch. He could tell it was killing her not to demand to know why they were back there, but she seemed determined to prove that she trusted him. He fell even more in love with her.

After he parked the car, he guided her toward the small family market on the ranch where they sold locally crafted meats and goods. Levi met them outside with two saddled horses. Meridian all but started jumping up and down and applauding. "Are we going riding?!"

Thrilled with her reaction, Jack brushed a kiss on her cheek. "I thought you might be missing Kagan."

"You are the best," she gushed.

Smiling at that, Jack took the lead line from Levi. "Just stay on the trail. It'll take you all the way to the table. My sister'll meet you out there."

"Thanks so much for this," Jack urged.

"It might be us who owes you a mahalo. You two have fun."

They climbed into their saddles and stuck to the trail just like Levi had instructed. Meridian leaned low to hug her horse several times. Jack fought not to laugh at her outright. His cowgirl princess indeed.

This time, by sunset they were seated at a perfectly positioned table that overlooked a bluff. They were surrounded by blue skies, red dirt, and a God-made flower garden that would put anything at River Chase to shame.

They ate steak and drank Kauaian rum punch. Levi's sister's megawatt grin as she and her mother served them their meals only served to make the entire meal even better.

And as the sun gave off its last vestiges of light, Jack grinned at Meridian. "Hey cowgirl," he whispered.

She beamed at him. "Yeah?"

He got down on one knee, and her gasp delighted him. "I'm pretty sure I have been in love with you since I first laid eyes on you. I know it's fast, and I know everything going on with my family makes it harder sometimes, but I want to be married to you. I want to have everything with you. I never want to own the world, but I do want to own your heart...as cheesy as that is now that I've said it out loud." He cringed.

Meridian's laughter made the moment even better. "You haven't actually asked me," she teased.

"Meridian Skye Holder, I love you. I love you when you're stubborn, and when you're wild, and I love you just as much when you're tired of fighting with the world and want to be held. I want to be the one that's there for every single side of you, always. Will you do me the honor of marrying me?"

"Yes!" She leapt from her seat into his lap, and they both collapsed in a heap on the soft grass.

After several lengthy kisses, he managed to get the ring on her finger. She stared down at it. "I love this almost as much as my straw wrapper one." She laughed.

He knew that was true. She still had that straw wrapper ring tucked safely in a drawer back at their house. It wasn't the diamond that meant so much to her. It was them together.

Levi's sister, Lealani, rushed to the table as soon as they'd composed themselves. "Congratulations!" she gushed. "Also, if I managed to talk my grandparents, and my parents, and my stupid big brother into letting me set up our ranch as an engagement destination, would you leave us a Yelp review? This would be such a great way to diversify. We could save our ranch doing this."

Jack wasn't certain on the details of the troubles on Hanchett ranch, but Meridian assured her that they would love to do that and to help out with the new venture any other way they could.

As they walked back to the car in the moonlight, she gave him a coy smile. "You do know I'm not taking your name, right?"

Jack pulled her closer and painted another kiss on her cheek. "I was kind of hoping maybe I could take yours. Jackson Holder would really irritate all of those people back home that don't like the Holders holding too many county seats."

"You do love irritating pretentious people, don't you?"

"It's a bad habit."

She waggled her eyebrows at him. "I love all of your bad habits."

"I'm glad. Let's get back to the villas and I'll show you a few more of them, princess."

CHAPTER FIFTY-FIVE

The Next Spring

The shrill blare of the alarm shook Jack from his deep slumber. He grinned before opening his eyes, wanting to stay in the warm cocoon created by their covers and Meridian's body entwined with his. That day's planned activities filtered slowly through his mind, but he pushed them off. He didn't want to deal with them yet.

Meridian whimpered and then slapped at her phone until she'd successfully silenced the alarm, either turning it off completely or snoozing it. Jack didn't particularly care which, just so long as he could keep holding her close and feeling her burrow deeper and press closer to him. He'd never really known sleep until he'd officially moved onto Holder Ranch. He swore he didn't even dream here unless his dreams were just swift, soft flashes of her body, her warmth, her laughter, and her smiles from his memories.

The first notes of sunlight played at the window blinds. Meridian's eyes blinked open slowly.

"Good morning, cowgirl," he whispered.

She brushed a tender kiss on his neck. "We're getting married tomorrow," she said as if he might've somehow forgotten.

Chuckling, he eased her wild mane of hair behind her back and reveled in the pool of warm contentment they were cuddling in. "I'd heard something about that," he teased.

She sat up and rubbed her hands over her face. She was wearing nothing but a thin pair of panties and a sated expression. Jack swore he somehow managed to find something new to love about her each and every day.

"Are you nervous?" she asked.

"About today? Yes. About tomorrow? Definitely not." He forced himself to sit up as well. The coffee maker was all the way in the kitchen and that was going to be necessary for their day. Getting up was inevitable as much as he'd love to spend the day in bed with her.

Meridian gave him a sympathetic expression. "I can only imagine what Beverly Denton will have to say about Holder Ranch. It's going to be like that old show *Green Acres* only a million times worse."

"I wish I didn't regret inviting them," Jack admitted for the first time.

"No—" Meridian shook her head"—don't regret it. I know the relationship is rocky at best, but we want all of the Bastards to come. It's going to be fine. I promise."

Despite her reassurances, three hours later, Jack paced nervously back and forth near the elevator at the airport as they awaited the Bastards arrival. His parents were coming on the private jet a little later that afternoon.

When he'd left Kentucky to set out for a new life in Oklahoma, he'd been certain that the two entirely different worlds that he'd lived in, his past and his present, could never meet. That they couldn't exist together. He'd been wrong, and it was all because of the gorgeous redhead standing on her tiptoes trying to see up the elevator so she could welcome his past to their present.

Jack stopped pacing and joined her. "I love you," he whispered.

She beamed at him. "I love you, too."

"Thank you for loving them, too." He gestured to the top of the elevator as Finn and Sloan came into sight.

Meridian laced their fingers together and laid her head on his shoulder as they waited on their guests to descend. "I'm still trying to love your mama and your daddy, but I'm struggling," she confessed.

Jack nodded. "Me too."

Finn hopped over the elevator railing near the bottom to land right at Jack's feet. "I'm here. Let's get you two married."

Shaking his head, Jack hugged his brother. "Welcome to Oklahoma."

Finn glanced around the airport. "I feel lied to. I was told that there was nothing but cattle. I haven't seen any cows yet."

"Oh, just wait," Meridian assured him. "I can show you cows for days."

Finn gave her the signature Denton smirk. "Lead the way, Ms. Holder."

Jack hung back and waited on Sloan, Lila, and Drew. "I guess you decided not to bring Sophie," he broached hesitantly to Sloan.

He shook his head. "I'm ready to say fuck it and tell everyone. She's...not."

Visible tension was locked in Sloan's shoulders. Jack offered him a consoling grin. "It took me and Meridian four years to even admit we had the hots for each other. Give it time. She'll come around."

"Yeah, I know. I just don't like doing things without her."

Jack hated it for Sloan that Sophie was hesitant, but he certainly couldn't blame her. As they made their way to baggage claim, Drew and Lila caught Jack up on life in Louisville.

They stopped by the tux shop on the way back from Tulsa. All of the Bastards, including Lila, were going to be Jack's grooms-people, so she wanted a tux instead of the dresses Meridian had chosen for her bridesmaids.

The dreaded hour of Jack's parents' arrival loomed ever on the horizon, but he tried to enjoy the comradery he always felt when he was with the Bastards and in their ultimate acceptance of his life in Oklahoma.

An hour after they'd gotten the Bastards settled in at the ranch, Jack and Meridian drove back to the airstrip to pick up his parents and Beckett, who'd also been invited to the wedding.

Meridian wrinkled her nose. "I don't think Sloan and your brothers quite knew what to do when they found out they were going to have to stay in one of the bunkhouses."

Jack squeezed her leg reassuringly as he slowed his truck again in no real hurry to arrive at the airstrip. "It'll be good for them."

"I hope so."

She'd been gnawing on her bottom lip all afternoon. He knew she was nervous, and he hated that his parents were the cause. "I know it's difficult, and I know that because I still haven't mastered it, but try not to care what they think. They're miserable, and their misery makes them unable to be happy for anyone else."

She managed a quick nod. "I guess it's nice they decided to come even though we told them that we weren't doing this without Drew and Finn here."

"I think they're mostly relieved that we're having it here instead of in their world."

Despite his best efforts to slow their progression, they did arrive at the airstrip to find his parents, Greer, and Beckett waiting.

"It's like I've always said, punctuality was never your strong suit, Jackson," Beverly sneered.

"Be nice, Mom," Greer ground through his teeth.

"Hi, Mom." Jack ignored her. That was better than letting her get to him. He no longer felt the need to openly defy her. He'd finally earned the life he'd always wanted. He had Meridian. He didn't have to prove anything else, and that peace wasn't something he would ever trade just to go toe-to-toe with Beverly. The contentment he'd been seeking was standing right beside him in Wranglers and a cowgirl hat, trying to decide if she was going to respond to his mother's asinine comment.

"It's not worth it," Jack whispered in her ear.

"I know," Meridian agreed.

That evening the Holders hosted a massive potluck picnic on the ranch for most of the county as the rehearsal dinner. It was almost comical to watch his Kentucky relatives try to make sense of the lack of waitstaff and them trying to navigate eating outdoors on paper plates.

While Gentry and Meridian's three uncles, Barrett, Wyn, and Landon all manned four massive grills, since Holder Ranch was supplying the meat, Leigh Holder noticed that Beverly and Palmer had seated themselves at one of the folding tables but hadn't acquired any of the side dishes the guests had all provided.

"You all go get your plates," she encouraged.

Jack bit his lips together. He almost felt sorry for his parents' complete lack of understanding. He decided to step in and help. "Get a plate and one of the napkin rolls of silverware at the beginning of the line. Then you walk down the long tables and pick out whatever you'd like to eat, then stop at the grills for steak or a burger."

"This is a rehearsal dinner, Jackson," his mother gasped.

"Yes, and this is precisely how Meridian and I wanted it. Spending a ridiculous amount of money on a pre-wedding party isn't how we're doing this. I'm sorry. I know that's not something you're accustomed to."

His mother's lips drew to a pinched fury, but at least she kept them shut as they made their way over to the line. Eventually Jack and Meridian were seated at the table with his parents, Finn, Barrett and Sara Holder, and Meridian's parents. The tension was thicker than Sarah Beth McGillicuddy's seven-layer chili cornbread salad.

Ever the gracious hostess, Leigh Holder plastered on a kind smile. "It's so nice to finally meet some of Jack's family. We're all so pleased you could make it." She directed this to Finn and the Dentons.

Palmer wiped his mouth and the made a quick scowl at the paper napkin. "Yes, well I suppose...we're...happy to have been invited."

Jack narrowed his eyes. "Speaking of you being invited, I think you still owe the Holders an apology for what happened last fall when you decided to try to buy the ranch."

Barrett and Gentry both set down their forks. Palmer eyed both of his sons with outright disdain. "I'm sure you understand," he cleared his throat uncomfortably, "it was just business."

Barrett shook his head. "Seems to me it was a way to try to cover up a mess of lies you didn't want your son and my niece to find out about, so try again."

Jack and Finn shared a conspiratorial grin. This was too good. No one had ever forced an apology out of Palmer Denton.

"Yes, well," Palmer bristled, "I understand that no one believes me when I say this but everything I do, I do with the intention of protecting my sons."

Finn choked on a piece of brisket. Jack slapped him on the back and handed him a cup of water. When Finn finally cleared his throat, he stared at his father like he'd just announced his intentions to give up the whiskey business. "How do you figure that buying these people's ranch is a way to protect us?" he finally demanded.

"I'd love to know that as well," Jack challenged.

Palmer shook his head as if the obvious answer was sitting in front of them on the table and they'd somehow missed it. "I want to make certain that you're taken care of when I'm gone."

Barrett leapt before Jack could. "You ever think maybe all of your boys would appreciate you trying to take care of them while you're here instead of worrying about them having enough money after your gone?"

After a few minutes of awkward silence, Leigh tried to smooth things over again. "Finn, now, I know you and Jack are close, so you are welcome out here anytime. We'd love to have you."

Grinning at that, Finn squeezed Leigh's hand from across the table. "Thank you, Mrs. Holder. I stay pretty busy with work, but I should get out here more often just to harass to Jack."

They eventually made their way through the awkward dinner and the fireworks spectacle that all of Meridian's brothers and most of her cousins put on to celebrate.

Red and white glimmers of light sparkled in Meridian's eyes as they watched the show. Overcome with how magical he knew she was and filled with relief that after tomorrow they could get on with the marriage portion of their life together, Jack brushed his lips across hers.

She grinned against his lips and then deepened the kiss.

"Save that for tomorrow, you two," Gentry teased them. "She's still my little girl for one more night."

Meridian lifted her head and grinned at her father. "I'll always be your little girl, Daddy."

"I sure do like the sound of that." He winked at her. "But you two still leave room for Jesus between ya at least until I go to bed."

Jack couldn't help but laugh. He loved her. He loved her family, and he was thrilled to become a part of it. He hoped that his father had really heard Barrett's question about taking care of his sons and really took it to heart, but Jack no longer felt that he was responsible for saving his family. He would do what was right and the rest was up to them.

The next afternoon with the sun high in the sky and the low sounds of mooing cattle in the background, Jack stood beside his brothers and his cousins and beamed as Meridian appeared on horseback to make her way down the aisle.

When her horse, being led by her father, got to Jack, he held out his hands and let her slide off the saddle and into his arms. Then they turned and united their worlds, and their families, and their lives, forever.

ABOUT THE AUTHOR

Bestselling author Jillian Neal likes her coffee strong and sweet with a shot of sinful spice, the same way she likes her cowboys. In fact, her caffeine addiction is quite possibly considered illicit in several states as are a few of the things her characters do. When she's not writing or reading, you'll find her in the kitchen trying out new recipes or coming up with ~~excuses~~ reasons to purchase yet another handbag or make an additional trip to Sephora. Though she'll always be a Bama girl at heart, Jillian hangs up her hat and kicks up her boots outside of Atlanta with her hunk-of-a-husband and her teenage sons.

For more information...
jillianneal.com
jillian@jillianneal.com

ALSO BY JILLIAN NEAL

HOLDER COUNTY

Oklahoma Sky

Standing Outside the Fire

BROKEN H.A.L.O

H.A.L.O. Undone

H.A.L.O. Redeemed

Fractured H.A.L.O.

CAMDEN RANCH

Rodeo Summer

Forever Wild

Cowgirl Education

Un-hitched

Last Call

Wayward Son

BOHO BEACH TO CAMDEN RANCH

Boho Cowgirl

Coincidental Cowgirl

9 781940 174594